THE END HAS COME

THE APOCALYPSE TRIPTYCH

EDITED BY JOHN JOSEPH ADAMS AND HUGH HOWEY

STORIES BY

CHARLIE JANE ANDERS

MEGAN ARKENBERG

CHRIS AVELLONE

ELIZABETH BEAR

ANNIE BELLET

TANANARIVE DUE

JAMIE FORD

MIRA GRANT

HUGH HOWEY

JAKE KERR

NANCY KRESS

SARAH LANGAN

KEN LIU

JONATHAN MABERRY

SEANAN MCGUIRE

WILL MCINTOSH

LEIFE SHALLCROSS

SCOTT SIGLER

CARRIE VAUGHN

ROBIN WASSERMAN

DAVID WELLINGTON

BEN H. WINTERS

THE END HAS COME

The Apocalypse Triptych, Volume 3

Copyright © 2015 by John Joseph Adams & Hugh Howey
Page 307 constitutes an extension of this copyright page.

All rights reserved. No part of this book may be reproduced in any form by any electronic or mechanical means including photocopying, recording, or information storage and retrieval without permission in writing from the authors.

Edited by John Joseph Adams & Hugh Howey
Cover art by Julian Aguilar Faylona
Cover design by Jason Gurley
Interior design by Hugh Howey

ISBN-13: 978-149-748-440-5
ISBN-10: 149-748-440-5

For more about The Apocalypse Triptych:
www.johnjosephadams.com/apocalypse-triptych

First Edition

Printed in the U.S.A

For the future

TABLE OF CONTENTS

Introduction • John Joseph Adams 1

Bannerless • Carrie Vaughn 5

Like All Beautiful Places • Megan Arkenberg 23

Dancing With a Stranger in the Land of Nod • Will McIntosh 31

The Seventh Day of Deer Camp • Scott Sigler 43

Prototype • Sarah Langan 57

Acts of Creation • Chris Avellone 67

Resistance • Seanan McGuire 75

Wandering Star • Leife Shallcross 91

Heaven Come Down • Ben H. Winters 99

Agent Neutralized • David Wellington 111

Goodnight Earth • Annie Bellet 129

Carriers • Tananarive Due 139

In the Valley of the Shadow of the Promised Land • Robin
        Wasserman 153

The Uncertainty Machine • Jamie Ford 173

Margin of Survival • Elizabeth Bear 181

Jingo and the Hammerman • Jonathan Maberry 197

The Last Movie Ever Made • Charlie Jane Anders 211

The Gray Sunrise • Jake Kerr 225

The Gods Have Not Died in Vain • Ken Liu 239

The Happiest Place... • Mira Grant 259

In the Woods • Hugh Howey 273

Blessings • Nancy Kress 287

INTRODUCTION

John Joseph Adams

The world dies over and over again,
but the skeleton always gets up and walks.

—Henry Miller, "Uterine Hunger," from
The Wisdom of the Heart

The Apocalypse Triptych was conceived as a series of three anthologies, each one covering a different facet of the end of times. Volume one, *The End is Nigh*, contains stories that take place just before the apocalypse. Volume two, *The End is Now*, focuses on stories that take place during the apocalypse. And, naturally, this third volume, *The End Has Come*, features stories that explore life after the apocalypse.

But we were not content to merely assemble a triptych of anthologies; we also wanted *story triptychs* as well. So when we recruited authors for this project, we encouraged them to consider writing not just one story for us, but one story for each volume, and connecting them so that the reader gets a series of mini-triptychs. So several of the stories contained in this anthology—eighteen of the twenty-three tales—have related stories in *The End is Nigh* and *The End is Now*. They conclude with *The End Has Come*.

If you're one of the readers who read and enjoyed volumes one and two: Thank you! We're glad to see you returning for volume three. You made the first two volumes a resounding success, and we couldn't be more thrilled both with how well the books have done in the marketplace and with how well they've been received by readers and critics.

If you're a reader who has not read *The End is Nigh* or *The End is Now*: Welcome! And fear not: You needn't have read either of the previous volumes in order to enjoy the stories in this one. Although several of the stories in *The End Has Come* pick up where other volumes left off, we're confident that the authors have provided sufficient context that you can jump into their worlds without any prior knowledge.

• • •

Now for a confession: Although I'm fascinated by all the different modes of the apocalypse—as evidenced by volumes one and two of this Triptych—post-apocalyptic fiction is my first and dearest love.

My fascination with post-apocalypse narratives began with the 1988 video game *Wasteland* (and then was reinforced by its spiritual successor, *Fallout*). I have been hopelessly hooked ever since. Years later, when I started pursuing writing and editing, the first piece I ever sold was an article about post-apocalyptic fiction. Later, the first anthology I ever sold (*Wastelands: Stories of the Apocalypse*) was a reprint anthology with the same focus. So in some ways this final volume of The Apocalypse Triptych is like seeing my career come full circle.

Which seems appropriate, as coming "full circle" is what post-apocalyptic fiction is all about. From the dust we came, and to the dust we shall return. But once everything has turned to dust, what then will rise from the ashes?

THE END HAS COME

The Apocalypse Triptych, Volume 3

BANNERLESS

Carrie Vaughn

Enid and Bert walked the ten miles from the way station because the weather was good, a beautiful spring day. Enid had never worked with the young man before, but he turned out to be good company: chatty without being oppressively extroverted. Young, built like a redwood, he looked the part of an investigator. They talked about home and the weather and trivialities—but not the case. She didn't like to dwell on the cases she was assigned to before getting a firsthand look at them. She had expected Bert to ask questions about it, but he was taking her lead.

On this stretch of the Coast Road, halfway between the way station and Southtown, ruins were visible in the distance, to the east. An old sprawling city from before the big fall. In her travels in her younger days, she'd gone into it a few times, to shout into the echoing artificial canyons and study overgrown asphalt roads and cracked walls with fallen roofs. She rarely saw people, but often saw old cook fires and cobbled together shantytowns that couldn't support the lives struggling within them. Scavengers and scattered folk still came out from them sometimes, then faded back to the concrete enclaves, surviving however they survived.

Bert caught her looking.

"You've been there?" Bert said, nodding toward the haze marking the swath of ruined city. No paths or roads ran that way anymore. She'd had to go overland when she'd done it.

"Yes, a long time ago."

"What was it like?"

The answer could either be very long or very short. The stories of what had happened before and during the fall were terrifying and intriguing, but the ruins no longer held any hint of those tales. They were bones, in the process of disappearing. "It was sad," she said finally.

"I'm still working through the histories," he said. "For training, right? There's a lot of diaries. Can be hard, reading how it was at the fall."

"Yes."

In isolation, any of the disasters that had struck would not have overwhelmed the old world. The floods alone would not have destroyed the cities. The vicious influenza epidemic—a mutated strain with no available vaccine that incapacitated victims in a matter of hours—by itself would have been survivable, eventually. But the floods, the disease, the rising ocean levels, the monster storms piling one on top of the other, an environment off balance that chipped away at infrastructure and made each recovery more difficult than the one before it, all of it left too many people with too little to survive on. Wealth meant nothing when there was simply nothing left. So, the world died. But people survived, here and there. They came together and saved what they could. They learned lessons.

The road curved into the next valley and they approached Southtown, the unimaginative name given to this district's main farming settlement. Windmills appeared first, clean towers with vertical blades spiraling gently in an unfelt breeze. Then came cisterns set on scaffolds, then plowed fields and orchards in the distance. The town was home to some thousand people scattered throughout the valley and surrounding farmlands. There was a grid of drained roads and whitewashed houses, solar and battery operated carts, some goats, chickens pecking in yards. All was orderly, pleasant. This was what rose up after the ruins fell, the home that their grandparents fled to as children.

"Will you let the local committee know we're here?" Bert asked.

"Oh, no. We don't want anyone to have warning we're here. We go straight to the household. Give them a shock."

"Makes sense."

"This is your first case, isn't it? Your first investigation?"

"It is. And… I guess I'm worried I might have to stop someone." Bert had a staff like hers but he knew how to use his for more than walking. He had a stunner and a pack of tranquilizer needles on his belt. All in plain view. If she did her job well enough he wouldn't need to do anything but stand behind her and look alert. A useful tool. He seemed to understand his role.

"I doubt you will. Our reputation will proceed us. It's why we have the reputation in the first place. Don't worry."

"I just need to act as terrifying as the reputation says I do."

She smiled. "Exactly—you know just how this works, then."

They wore brown tunics and trousers with gray sashes. Somber colors, cold like winter, probably designed to inspire a chill. Bert stood a head taller than she did and looked like he could break tree trunks. How sinister, to see the pair of them approach.

"And you—this is your last case, isn't it?"

That was what she'd told the regional committee, that it was time for her to go home, settle down, take up basket weaving or such like. "I've been doing this almost twenty years," she said. "It's time for me to pass the torch."

"Would you miss the travel? That's what I've been looking forward to, getting to see some of the region, you know?"

"Maybe," she said. "But I wouldn't miss the bull. You'll see what I mean."

They approached the settlement. Enid put her gaze on a young woman carrying a basket of eggs along the main road. She wore a skirt, tunic, apron, and a straw hat to keep off the sun.

"Excuse me," Enid said. The woman's hands clenched as if she was afraid she might drop the basket from fright. As she'd told Bert, their reputation preceded them. They were inspectors, and inspectors only appeared for terrible reasons. The woman's expression held shock and denial. Why would inspectors ever come to Southtown?

"Yes, how can I help you?" she said quickly, nervously.

"Can you tell us where to find Apricot Hill?" The household they'd been sent to investigate.

The woman's anxiety fell away and a light of understanding dawned. Ah, then people knew. Everyone likely knew *something* was wrong, without knowing exactly what. The whole town would know investigators were here within the hour. Enid's last case, and it was going to be all about sorting out gossip.

"Yes—take that path there, past the pair of windmills. They're on the south side of the duck pond. You'll see the clotheslines out front."

"Thank you," Enid said. The woman hurried away, hugging her basket to her chest.

Enid turned to Bert. "Ready for this?"

"Now I'm curious. Let's go."

Apricot Hill was on a nice acreage overlooking a pretty pond and a series of orchards beyond that. There was one large house, two stories with lots of windows, and an outbuilding with a pair of chimneys, a production building—Apricot Hill was centered on food processing, taking in produce from outlying farms and drying, canning, and preserving it for winter stores for the community. The holding overall was well lived in, a bit run down, cluttered, but that could mean they were busy. It was spring—nothing ready for canning yet. This should have been the season for cleaning up and making repairs.

A girl with a bundle of sheets over her arm, probably collected from the clothesline the woman had mentioned, saw them first. She peered up the hill at their arrival for a moment before dropping the sheets and running to the house. She was wispy and energetic—not the one mentioned in the report, then. Susan, and not Aren. The heads of the household were Frain and Felice.

"We are announced," Enid said wryly. Bert hooked a finger in his belt.

A whole crowd, maybe even all ten members of the household, came out of the house. A rough looking bunch, all together. Old clothes, frowning faces. This was an adequate household, but not a happy one.

An older man, slim and weather-worn, came forward and looked as though he wished he had a weapon. This would be Frain. Enid went to him, holding her hand out for shaking.

"Hello, I'm Enid, the investigator sent by the regional committee. This is my partner, Bert. This is Apricot Hill, isn't it? You must be Frain?"

"Yes," he said cautiously, already hesitant to give away any scrap of information.

"May we step inside to talk?"

She would look like a matron to them, maybe even head of a household somewhere, if they weren't sure she didn't have a household. Investigators didn't have households; they traveled constantly, avenging angels, or so the rumors said. Her dull brown hair was rolled into a bun, her soft face had seen years and weather. They'd wonder if she'd ever had children of her own, if she'd ever earned a banner. Her spreading middle-aged hips wouldn't give a clue.

Bert stood behind her, a wall of authority. Their questions about him would be simple: How well could he use that staff he carried?

"What is this about?" Frain demanded. He was afraid. He knew what she was here for—the implications—and he was afraid.

"I think we should go inside and sit down before we talk," Enid said patiently, knowing full well she sounded condescending and unpleasant. The lines on Frain's face deepened. "Is everyone here? Gather everyone in the household to your common room."

With a curt word Frain herded the rest of his household inside.

The common room on the house's ground floor was, like the rest of the household, functional without being particularly pleasant. No vase of flowers on the long dining table. Not a spot of color on the wall except for a single faded banner: the square of red and green woven cloth that represented the baby they'd earned some sixteen years ago. That would be Susan—the one with the laundry outside. Adults had come into the household since then, but that was their last baby. Had they wanted another child badly enough that they didn't wait for their committee to award them a banner?

The house had ten members. Only nine sat around the table. Enid took her time studying them, looking into each face. Most of the gazes ducked away from her. Susan's didn't.

"We're missing someone, I think?" Enid said.

The silence was thick as oil. Bert stood easy and perfectly still behind her, hand on his belt. Oh, he was a natural at this. Enid waited a long time, until the people around the table squirmed.

"Aren," Felice said softly. "I'll go get her."

"No," Frain said. "She's sick. She can't come."

"Sick? Badly sick? Has a doctor seen her?" Enid said.

Again, the oily silence.

"Felice, if you could get her, thank you," Enid said.

A long stretch passed before Felice returned with the girl, and Enid was happy to watch while the group grew more and more uncomfortable. Susan was trembling; one of the men was hugging himself. This was as awful a gathering as she had ever seen, and her previous case had been a murder.

When Felice brought Aren into the room, Enid saw exactly what she expected to see: the older woman with her arm around a younger woman—age twenty or so—who wore a full skirt and a tunic three sizes too big that billowed in front of her. Aren moved slowly, and had to keep drawing her hands away from her belly.

She might have been able to hide the pregnancy for a time, but she was now six months along, and there was no hiding that swell and the ponderous hitch in her movement.

The anger and unhappiness in the room thickened even more, and it was no longer directed at Enid.

She waited while Felice guided the pregnant woman to a chair—by herself, apart from the others.

"This is what you're here for, isn't it?" Frain demanded, his teeth bared and fists clenched.

"It is," Enid agreed.

"Who told?" Frain hissed, looking around at them all. "Which one of you told?"

No one said anything. Aren cringed and ducked her head. Felice stared at her hands in her lap.

Frain turned to Enid. "Who sent the report? I've a right to know my accuser—the household's accuser."

"The report was anonymous, but credible." Part of her job here was to discover, if she could, who sent the tip of the bannerless pregnancy to the regional committee. Frain didn't need to know that. "I'll be asking all of you questions over the next couple of days. I expect honest answers. When I am satisfied that I know what happened here, I'm authorized to pass judgment. I will do so as quickly as possible, to spare you waiting. Frain, I'll start with you."

"It was an accident. An accident, I'm sure of it. The implant failed. Aren has a boy in town; they spend all their time together. We thought nothing of it because of the implant, but then it failed, and—we didn't say anything because we were scared. That's all. We should have told the committee as soon as we knew. I'm sorry—I know now that that was wrong. You'll take that into consideration?"

"When did you know? All of you, starting with Aren—when did you know of the pregnancy?"

The young woman's first words were halting, choked. Crying had thickened her throat. "Must... must have been... two months in, I think. I was sick. I just knew."

"Did you tell anyone?"

"No, no one. I was scared."

They were all terrified. That sounded true.

"And the rest of you?"

Murmurs answered. The men shook their heads, said they'd only known for a month or so, when she could no longer hide the new shape of her. They knew for sure the day that Frain ranted about it. "I didn't rant," the man said. "I was only surprised. I lost my temper, that was all."

Felice said, "I knew when she got sick. I've been pregnant—" Her gaze went to the banner on the wall. "I know the signs. I asked her, and she told."

"You didn't think to tell anyone?"

"Frain told me not to."

So Frain knew, at least as soon as she did. The man glared fire at Felice, who wouldn't lift her gaze.

"Aren, might I speak to you alone?"

The woman cringed, back curled, arms wrapped around her belly.

"I'll go you with you, dear," Felice whispered.

"Alone," Enid said. "Bert will wait here. We'll go outside. Just a short walk."

Trembling, Aren stood. Enid stood aside to let her walk out the door first. She caught Bert's gaze and nodded. He nodded back.

Enid guided her on the path away around the house, to the garden patch and pond behind. She went slowly, letting Aren set the pace.

The physical state of a household carried information: whether rakes and shovels were hung up neat in a shed or closet, or piled haphazardly by the wall of an unpainted barn. Whether the herb garden thrived, if there were flowers in window boxes. If neat little water-smoothed stones edged the paths leading from one building to another, or if there were just dirt tracks worn into the grass. She didn't judge a household by whether or not it put a good face to the world—but she did judge them by whether or not the folk in a household worked to put on a good face for themselves. They had to live with it, look at it every single day.

This household did not have a good face. The garden patch was only just sprouting, even this far into spring. There were no flowers. The grass along the path was overgrown. There was a lack of care here that made Enid angry.

But the pond was pretty. Ducks paddled around a stand of cattails, muttering to themselves.

Enid had done this before, knew the questions to ask and what possible answers she might get to those questions. Every moment reduced the possible explanations. Heavens, she was tired of this.

Enid said, "Stop here. Roll up your sleeve."

Aren's overlarge tunic had wide sleeves that fell past her wrists. They'd be no good at all for working. The young woman stood frozen. Her lips were tightly pursed, to keep from crying.

"May I roll the sleeve up, then?" Enid asked carefully, reaching.

"No, I'll do it," she said, and clumsily pushed the fabric up to her left shoulder.

She revealed an angry scar, puckered pink, mostly healed. Doing the math, maybe seven or eight months old. The implant had been cut out, the wound not well treated, which meant she'd probably done it herself.

"Did you get anyone to stitch that up for you?" Enid asked.

"I bound it up and kept it clean." At least she didn't try to deny it. Enid guessed she would have, if Frain were there.

"Where did you put the implant after you took it out?"

"Buried it in the latrine."

Enid hoped she wouldn't have to go after it for evidence. "You did it yourself. No one forced you to, or did it to you?" That happened sometimes, someone with a skewed view of the world and what was theirs deciding they needed someone to bear a baby for them.

"It's me, it's just me. Nobody else. Just me."

"Does the father know?"

"No, I don't think… He didn't know I'd taken out the implant. I don't know if he knows about the baby."

Rumors had gotten out, Enid was sure, especially if Aren hadn't been seen around town in some time. The anonymous tip about the pregnancy might have come from anywhere.

"Can you tell me the father's name, so I can speak to him?"

"Don't drag him into this; tell me you won't drag him into this. It's just me. Just take me away and be done with it." Aren stopped, her eyes closed, her face pinched. "What are you going to do to me?"

"I'm not sure yet."

She was done with crying. Her face was locked with anger, resignation. "You'll take me to the center of town and rip the baby out, cut its throat, leave us both to bleed to death as a warning. That's it, isn't it? Just tell me that's what you're going to do and get it over with—"

Goodness, the stories people told. "No, we're not going to do that. We don't rip babies from mother's wombs—not unless we need to save the mother's life, or the baby's. There's surgery for that. Your baby will be born; you have my promise."

Quiet tears slipped down the girl's cheeks. Enid watched for a moment, this time not using the silence to pressure Aren but trying to decide what to say.

"You thought that was what would happen if you were caught, and you still cut out your implant to have a baby? You must have known you'd be caught."

"I don't remember anymore what I was thinking."

"Let's get you back to the kitchen for a drink of water, hmm?"

By the time they got back to the common room, Aren had stopped crying, and she even stood a little straighter. At least until Frain looked at her, then at Enid.

"What did you tell her? What did she say to you?"

"Felice, I think Aren needs a glass of water, or maybe some tea. Frain, will you come speak with me?"

The man stomped out of the room ahead of her.

"What happened?" Enid said simply.

"The implant. It must have failed."

"Do you think she, or someone, might have cut it out? Did you ever notice her wearing a bandage on her arm?"

He did not seem at all surprised at this suggestion. "I never did. I never noticed." He was going to plead ignorance. That was fine. "Does the local committee know you're here?" he said, turning the questioning on her.

"Not yet," she said lightly. "They will."

"What are you going to do? What will happen to Aren?"

Putting the blame on Aren, because he knew the whole household was under investigation. "I haven't decided yet."

"I'm going to protest to the committee, about you questioning Aren alone. You shouldn't have done that, it's too hard on her—" He was furious that he didn't know what Aren had said. That he couldn't make their stories match up.

"Submit your protest," Enid said. "That's fine."

• • •

She spoke to every one of them alone. Half of them said the exact same thing, in exactly the same way.

"The implant failed. It must have failed."

"Aren's got that boy of hers. He's the father."

"It was an accident."

"An accident." Felice breathed this line, her head bowed and hands clasped together.

So that was the story they'd agreed upon. The story Frain had told them to tell.

One of the young men—baffled, he didn't seem to understand what was happening—was the one to slip. "She brought this down on us, why do the rest of us have to put up with the mess when it's all her?"

Enid narrowed her gaze. "So you know she cut out her implant?"

He wouldn't say another word after that. He bit his lips and puffed out his cheeks, but wouldn't speak, as if someone held a knife to his throat and told him not to.

Enid wasn't above pressing hard at the young one, Susan, until the girl snapped.

"Did you ever notice Aren with a bandage on her arm?"

Susan's face turned red. "It's not my fault, it's not! It's just that Frain said if we got a banner next season I could have it, not Aren, and she was jealous! That's what it was; she did this to punish us!"

Banners were supposed to make things better. Give people something to work for, make them prove they could support a child, *earn* a child. It wasn't supposed to be something to fight over, to cheat over.

But people did cheat.

"Susan—did you send the anonymous report about Aren?"

Susan's eyes turned round and shocked. "No, of course not, I wouldn't do such a thing! Tell Frain I'd never do such a thing!"

"Thank you, Susan, for your honesty," Enid said, and Susan burst into tears.

What a stinking mess this was turning in to. To think, she could have retired after the murder investigation and avoided all this.

She needed to talk to more people.

By the time they returned to the common room, Felice had gotten tea out for everyone. She politely offered a cup to Enid, who accepted, much to everyone's dismay. Enid stayed for a good twenty minutes, sipping, watching them watch her, making small talk.

"Thank you very much for all of your time and patience," she said eventually. "I'll be at the committee house in town if any of you would like to speak with me further. I'll deliver my decision in a day or two, so I won't keep you waiting. Your community thanks you."

• • •

A million things could happen, but these people were so locked into their drama she didn't expect much. She wasn't worried that the situation was going to change overnight. If Aren was going to grab her boy and run she would have done it already. That wasn't what was happening here. This was a household imploding.

Time to check with the local committee.

"Did they talk while I was gone?" Enid asked.

"Not a word," Bert said. "I hate to say it but that was almost fun. What are they so scared of?"

"Us. The stories of what we'll do. Aren was sure we'd drag her in the street and cut out her baby."

Bert wrinkled his face and said softly, "That's awful."

"I hadn't heard that one before, I admit. Usually it's all locked cells and stealing the baby away as soon as it's born. I wonder if Frain told the story to her, said it was why they had to keep it secret."

"Frain knew?"

"I'm sure they all did. They're trying to save the household by convincing me it was an accident. Or that it was just Aren's fault and no one else's. When really, a household like that, if they're that unhappy they should all put in for transfers, no matter how many ration credits that'd cost. Frain's scared them out of it, I'm betting."

"So what will happen?"

"Technology fails sometimes. If it had been an accident, I'm authorized to award a banner retroactively if the household can handle it. But that's not what happened here. If the household colluded to bring on a bannerless baby, we'd have to break up the house. But if it was just Aren all on her own—punishment would fall on her."

"But this isn't any of those, is it?"

"You've got a good eye for this, Bert."

"Not sure that's a compliment. I like to expect the best from people, not the worst."

Enid chuckled.

"At least *you'll* be able to put this all behind you soon," he said. "Retire to some pleasant household somewhere. Not here."

A middle aged man, balding and flush, rushed toward them on the path as they returned to the town. His gray tunic identified him as a committee member, and he wore the same stark panic on his face that everyone did when they saw an investigator.

"You must be Trevor?" Enid asked him, when he was still a few paces away, too far to shake hands.

"We didn't know you were coming, you should have sent word. Why didn't you send word?"

"We didn't have time. We got an anonymous report and had to act quickly. It happens sometimes, I'm sure you understand."

"Report, on what? If it's serious, I'm sure I would have been told—"

"A bannerless pregnancy at the Apricot Hill household."

He took a moment to process, staring, uncertain. The look turned hard. This didn't just reflect on Aren or the household—it reflected on the entire settlement. On the committee that ran the settlement. They could all be dragged into this.

"Aren," the man breathed.

Enid wasn't surprised the man knew. She was starting to wonder how her office hadn't heard about the situation much sooner.

"What can you tell me about the household? How do they get along, how are they doing?"

"Is this an official interview?"

"Why not? Saves time."

"They get their work done. But they're a household, not a family. If you understand the difference."

"I do." A collection of people gathered for production, not one that bonded over love. It wasn't always a bad thing—a collection of people working toward shared purpose could be powerful. But love could make it a home.

"How close were they to earning a banner?" *Were.* Telling word, there.

"I can't say they were close. They have three healthy young women, but people came in and out of that house so often we couldn't call it 'stable.' They fell short on quotas. I know that's usually better than going over, but not with food processing—falling short there means food potentially wasted, if it goes bad before it gets stored. Frain—Frain is not the easiest man to get along with."

"Yes, I know."

"You've already been out there—I wish you would have talked to me; you should have come to see us before starting your investigation." Trevor was wringing his hands.

"So you could tell me how things really are?" Enid raised a brow and smiled. He glanced briefly at Bert and frowned. "Aren had a romantic partner in the settlement, I'm told. Do you know who this might be?"

"She wouldn't tell you—she trying to protect him?"

"He's not in any trouble."

"Jess. It's Jess. He works in the machine shop, with the Ironcroft house-hold." He pointed the way.

"Thank you. We've had a long day of travel, can the committee house put us up for a night or two? We've got the credits to trade for it, we won't be a burden."

"Yes, of course, we have guest rooms in back, this way."

Trevor led them on to a comfortable stone house, committee offices and official guest rooms all together. People had gathered, drifting out of houses and stopping along the road to look, to bend heads and gossip. Everyone had that stare of trepidation.

"You don't make a lot of friends, working in investigations," Bert murmured to her.

"Not really, no."

· · ·

A young man, an assistant to the committee, delivered a good meal of lentil stew and fresh bread, along with cider. It tasted like warmth embodied, a great comfort after the day she'd had.

"My household hang their banners on the common room wall like that," Bert said between mouthfuls. "They stitch the names of the babies into them. It's a whole history of the house laid out there."

"Many households do. It's a lovely tradition," Enid said.

"I've never met anyone born without a banner. It's odd, thinking Aren's baby won't have its name written anywhere."

"It's not the baby's fault, remember. But it does make it hard. They grow up thinking they have to work twice as hard to earn their place in the world. But it usually makes people very careful not to pass on that burden."

"Usually but not always."

She sighed, her solid inspector demeanor slipping. "We're getting better. The goal is making sure that every baby born will be provided for, will have a place, and won't overburden what we have. But babies are powerful things. We'll never be perfect."

· · ·

The young assistant knocked on the door to the guest rooms early the next day.

"Ma'am, Enid? Someone's out front asking for the investigator."

"Is there a conference room where we can meet?"

"Yes, I'll show him in."

She and Bert quickly made themselves presentable—and put on their reputation—before meeting.

The potential informant was a lanky young man with calloused hands, a flop of brown hair and no beard. A worried expression. He kneaded a straw hat in his hands and stood from the table when Enid and Bert entered.

"You're Jess?"

He squeezed the hat harder. Ah, the appearance of omniscience was so very useful.

"Please, sit down," Enid said, and sat across from him by example. Bert stood by the wall.

"This is about Aren," the young man said. "You're here about Aren."

"Yes." He slumped, sighed—did he seemed relieved? "What do you need to tell me, Jess?"

"I haven't seen her in weeks; I haven't even gotten a message to her. No one will tell me what's wrong, and I know what everyone's been saying, but it can't be true—"

"That she's pregnant. She's bannerless."

He blinked. "But she's alive? She's safe?"

"She is. I saw her yesterday."

"Good, that's good."

Unlike everyone else she had talked to here, he seemed genuinely reassured. As if he had expected her to be dead or injured. The vectors of anxiety in the case pointed in so many different directions. "Did she tell you anything? Did you have any idea that something was wrong?"

"No… I mean, yes, but not that. It's complicated. What's going to happen to her?"

"That's what I'm here to decide. I promise you, she and the baby won't come to any harm. But I need to understand what's happened. Did you know she'd cut out her implant?"

He stared at the tabletop. "No, I didn't know that." If he had known, he could be implicated, so it behooved him to say that. But Enid believed him.

"Jess, I want to understand why she did what she did. Her household is being difficult. They tell me she spent all her spare time with you." Enid couldn't tell if he was resistant to talking to her, or if he simply couldn't find the words. She prompted. "How long have you been together? How long have you been intimate?" A gentle way of putting it. He wasn't blushing; on the contrary, he'd gone even more pale.

"Not long," he said. "Not even a year. I think… I think I know what happened now, looking back."

"Can you tell me?"

"I think… I think she needed someone and she picked me. I'm almost glad she picked me. I love her, but… I didn't know."

She wanted a baby. She found a boy she liked, cut out her implant, and made sure she had a baby. It wasn't unheard of. Enid had looked into a couple of cases like it in the past. But then, the household reported it when the others found out, or she left the household. To go through that and then stay, with everyone also covering it up…

"Did she ever talk about earning a banner and having a baby with you? Was that a goal of hers?"

"She never did at all. We… it was just us. I just liked spending time with her. We'd go for walks."

"What else?"

"She—wouldn't let me touch her arm. The first time we… were intimate, she kept her shirt on. She'd hurt her arm, she said, and didn't want to get dirt on it—we were out by the mill creek that feeds into the pond. It's so beautiful there, with the noise of the water and all. I… I didn't think of it. I mean, she always seemed to be hurt somewhere. Bruises and things. She said it was just from working around the house. I was always a bit careful touching her, though, because of it. I had to be careful with her." Miserable now, he put the pieces together in his mind as Enid watched. "She didn't like to go back. I told myself—I fooled myself—that it was because she loved me. But it's more that she didn't want to go back."

"And she loves you. As you said, she picked you. But she had to go back."

"If she'd asked, she could have gone somewhere else."

But it would have cost credits she may not have had, the committee would have asked why, and it would have been a black mark on Frain's leadership, or worse. Frain had them cowed into staying. So Aren wanted to get out of there and decided a baby would help her.

Enid asked, "Did you send the tip to Investigations?"

"No. No, I didn't know. That is, I didn't want to believe. I would never do anything to get her in trouble. I… I'm not in trouble, am I?"

"No, Jess. Do you know who might have sent in the tip?"

"Someone on the local committee, maybe. They're the ones who'd start an investigation, aren't they?"

"Usually, but they didn't seem happy to see me. The message went directly to regional."

"The local committee doesn't want to think anything's wrong. Nobody wants to think anything's wrong."

"Yes, that seems to be the attitude. Thank you for your help, Jess."

"What will happen to Aren?" He was choking, struggling not to cry. Even Bert, standing at the wall, seemed discomfited.

"That's for me to worry about, Jess. Thank you for your time."

At the dismissal, he slipped out of the room.

She leaned back and sighed, wanting to get back to her own household—despite the rumors, investigators did belong to households—with its own orchards and common room full of love and safety.

Yes, maybe she should have retired before all this. Or maybe she wasn't meant to.

"Enid?" Bert asked softly.

"Let's go. Let's get this over with."

• • •

Back at Apricot Hill's common room, the household gathered, and Enid didn't have to ask for Aren this time. She had started to worry, especially after talking to Jess. But they'd all waited this long, and her arrival didn't change anything except it had given them all the confirmation that they'd finally been caught. That they would always be caught. Good for the reputation, there.

Aren kept her face bowed, her hair over her cheek. Enid moved up to her, reached a hand to her, and the girl flinched. "Aren?" she said, and she still didn't look up until Enid touched her chin and made her lift her face. An irregular red bruise marked her cheek.

"Aren, did you send word about a bannerless pregnancy to the regional committee?"

Someone, Felice probably, gasped. A few of them shifted. Frain simmered. But Aren didn't deny it. She kept her face low.

"Aren?" Enid prompted, and the young woman nodded, ever so slightly.

"I hid. I waited for the weekly courier and slipped the letter in her bag, she didn't see me; no one saw. I didn't know if anyone would believe it, with no name on it, but I had to try. I wanted to get caught, but no one was noticing it; everyone was ignoring it." Her voice cracked to silence.

Enid put a gentle hand on Aren's shoulder. Then she went to Bert, and whispered, "Watch carefully."

She didn't know what would happen, what Frain in particular would do. She drew herself up, drew strength from the uniform she wore, and declaimed.

"I am the villain here," Enid said. "Understand that. I am happy to be the villain in your world. It's what I'm here for. Whatever happens, blame me.

"I will take custody of Aren and her child. When the rest of my business is done, I'll leave with her and she'll be cared for responsibly. Frain, I question your stewardship of this household and will submit a recommendation that Apricot Hill be dissolved entirely, its resources and credits distributed among its members as warranted, and its members transferred elsewhere throughout the region. I'll submit my recommendation to the regional committee, which will assist the local committee in carrying out my sentence."

"No," Felice hissed. "You can't do this, you can't force us out."

She had expected that line from Frain. She wondered at the deeper dynamic here, but not enough to try to suss it out.

"I can," she said, with a backward glance at Bert. "But I won't have to, because you're all secretly relieved. The household didn't work, and that's fine—it happens sometimes—but none of you had the guts to start over, the guts to give up your credits to request a transfer somewhere else. To pay for the change you wanted. To protect your own housemates from each other. But now it's done, and by someone else, so you can complain all you want and rail to the skies about your new poverty as you work your way out of the holes you've dug for yourselves. I'm the villain you can blame. But deep down you'll know the truth. And that's fine too, because I don't really care. Not about you lot."

No one argued. No one said a word.

"Aren," Enid said, and the woman flinched again. She might never stop flinching. "You can come with me now, or would you like time to say goodbye?"

She looked around the room, and Enid wasn't imagining it: The woman's hands were shaking, though she tried to hide it by pressing them under the roundness of her belly. Enid's breath caught, because even now it might go either way. Aren had been scared before; she might be too scared to leave. Enid schooled her expression to be still no matter what the answer was.

But Aren stood from the table and said, "I'll go with you now."

"Bert will go help you get your things—"

"I don't have any things. I want to go now."

"All right. Bert, will you escort Aren outside?"

The door closed behind them, and Enid took one last look around the room.

"That's it, then," Frain said.

"Oh no, that's not it at all," Enid said. "That's just it for now. The rest of you should get word of the disposition of the household in a couple of days." She walked out.

Aren stood outside, hugging herself. Bert was a polite few paces away, being non-threatening, staring at clouds. Enid urged them on, and they walked the path back toward town. Aren seemed to get a bit lighter as they went.

They probably had another day in Southtown before they could leave. Enid would keep Aren close, in the guest rooms, until then. She might have to requisition a solar car. In her condition, Aren probably shouldn't walk the ten miles to the next way station. And she might want to say goodbye to Jess. Or she might not, and Jess would have his heart broken even more. Poor thing.

· · ·

Enid requisitioned a solar car from the local committee and was able to take to the Coast Road the next day. The bureaucratic machinery was in motion on all the rest of it. Committeeman Trevor revealed that a couple of the young men from Apricot Hill had preemptively put in household transfer requests. Too little, too late. She'd done her job; it was all in committee hands now.

Bert drove, and Enid sat in the back with Aren, who was bundled in a wool cloak and kept her hands around her belly. They opened windows to the spring sunshine, and the car bumped and swayed over the gravel road. Walking would have been more pleasant, but Aren needed the car. The tension in her shoulders had finally gone away. She looked up, around, and if she didn't smile, she also didn't frown. She talked, now, in a voice clear and free of tears.

"I came into the household when I was sixteen, to work prep in the canning house and to help with the garden and grounds and such. They needed the help, and I needed to get started on my life, you know? Frain—he expected more out of me. He expected me to be his."

She spoke as if being interrogated. Enid hadn't asked for her story, but listened carefully to the confession. It spilled out like a flood, like the young woman had been waiting.

"How far did it go, Aren?" Enid asked carefully. In the driver's seat, Bert frowned, like maybe he wanted to go back and have a word with the man.

"He never did more than hit me."

So straightforward. Enid made a note. The car rocked on for a ways.

"What will happen to her, without a banner?" Aren asked, glancing at her belly. She'd evidently decided the baby was a girl. She probably had a name picked out. Her baby, her savior.

"There are households who need babies to raise who'll be happy to take her."

"Her, but not me?"

"It's a complicated situation," Enid said. She didn't want to make Aren any promises until they could line up exactly which households they'd be going to.

Aren was smart. Scared, but smart. She must have thought things through, once she realized she wasn't going to die. "Will it go better, if I agree to give her up? The baby, I mean."

Enid said, "It would depend on how you define 'better.'"

"Better for the baby."

"There's a stigma on bannerless babies. Worse some places than others. And somehow people know, however you try to hide it. People will always know what you did and hold it against you. But the baby can get a fresh start on her own."

"All right. All right, then."

"You don't have to decide right now."

Eventually, they came to the place in the road where the ruins were visible, like a distant mirage, but unmistakable. A haunted place, with as many rumors about it as there were about investigators and what they did.

"Is that it?" Aren said, staring. "The old city? I've never seen it before."

Bert slowed the car, and they stared out for a moment.

"The stories about what it was like are so terrible. I know it's supposed to be better now, but…" The young woman dropped her gaze.

"Better for whom, you're wondering?" Enid said. "When they built our world, our great-grandparents saved what they could, what they thought was important, what they'd most need. They wanted a world that would let them survive not just longer but better. They aimed for utopia knowing they'd fall short. And for all their work, for all our work, we still find pregnant girls with bruises on their faces who don't know where to go for help."

"I don't regret it," Aren said. "At least, I don't think I do."

"You saved what you could," Enid said. It was all any of them could do.

The car started again, rolling on. Some miles later on, Aren fell asleep curled in the back seat, her head lolling. Bert gave her a sympathetic glance.

"Heartbreaking all around, isn't it? Quite the last case for you, though. Memorable."

"Or not," Enid said.

Going back to the way station, late afternoon, the sun was in Enid's face. She leaned back, closed her eyes, and let it warm her.

"What, not memorable?" Bert said.

"Or not the last," she said. "I may have a few more left in me."

LIKE ALL BEAUTIFUL PLACES

Megan Arkenberg

One

The damned thing is, I still don't like San Francisco.

The present tense sounds wrong. It catches on the way out, like a ballpoint pen running dry and dragging an invisible indentation in the shape of a letter. But after everything, after the end of everything, it's the truth.

I still don't like the city, its steepness, its damp chill, the feeling that something is lying in wait behind the crest of every hill. All those crowded sidewalks, slabs of concrete unevenly pieced together like a half-hearted mosaic, the cracks gathering cigarette butts and blackened chewing gum. People everywhere at all hours, and that sour smell that hangs in the air of seaside cities, unless you're close enough to the ocean that the salt is burning your sinuses instead. I never was a city girl: Mama was right about that, in the end. Right about me, and right about *him*.

Felix. Fucking Felix-from-fucking-San-Francisco, Mama always said. *He has nothing to give you but heartbreak, Grecia. What are you thinking?*

You can hate someone who's dead, can't you? And some place—it's the same thing. You even feel the same guilt, saying it.

There's nothing left now. The rain has stopped, and a bare skeleton of a city remains. I borrow Mahesh's binoculars, stand in the prow and look out across the bay, and every time the sight turns my stomach. There's a few cement pylons clinging to the hills, tangles of steel, and slabs and slabs of white concrete broken and pocked like a sponge. Just north of us, the frame of the Bridge still arcs out toward Yerba Buena, but then it disappears. Down into the black water, its eerie stillness turned iridescent by the sun, like a puddle of oil. There's life returning to Oakland, or at least scavengers; late at night, you can see the lights bobbing through the ruins south of the port. But San Francisco is still and quiet.

And here, on a container ship grounded in the Oakland Outer Harbor, I have this recurring dream.

I'm stepping out into the courtyard behind the tiny theatre in the Mission where Felix rigs the lighting. Or I'm standing on the fire escape outside our kitchen window, at the top of a Victorian row house that no one bothered to paint properly—the layers of trim lost in a uniform pastel pink, like the chalk they give you to cure an upset stomach. Or I'm cresting one of the hills— Potrero, walking home from the theatre, my arms laden with groceries or costumes that need repair—and I half-expect to meet a monster on the other side. I half-expect to find the end of the world, the whole city sliding down a sheer cliff into nothingness, just ocean as far as the eye can see.

And in the dream, I'm right. There's nothing on the other side of the threshold. No downhill street, no rows of homogenous-hued Victorians marching like lemmings toward the freeway and the sea. No murals of goddesses and butterflies or undulating koi fish over the overflowing dumpsters behind a Chinese café. Just gray static, like the analog television in our bedroom that collected stacks of unpaid bills. There's a faint ringing in my ears, a buzzing sound like fat garbage flies.

Does it count as a recurring dream when it's the only one you have? I think I ask myself this question every time, just before I wake up.

Two

"Again," Lena says. "Please."

Coming out of the immersion is excruciating, like all my senses are being slowly dragged across sandpaper. My eyes water as I peel away the visor, and for a moment the inside of the shipping container vanishes, and I'm caught again in the gray world of the immersion—scentless, colorless, the only sound the faint static prickle in my earphones. The coolness along my left side tells me the container's sliding door is open, letting in light and the clear, dry air that smells like absolutely nothing. I blink the tears away, and Lena looks up from her computer screen.

"Let's do it again, please."

On the table in the other end of the container, she has her own set of pieces laid out. Compression gloves, the hood with its broad blue-tinged visor, and yards of rubber-coated wires to link the suit and a miscellaneous suite of suction cups back to her computer. Her dark hair, damp with sweat, is flopping out of her barrette. I see the traces of gritty saline paste at her temples, which means she's been trying to record again. Which means the flicker of memory I felt inside the immersion, the lapping rhythm that may have been waves and the roughness of *something* against my palm—steel? concrete?—belonged to her.

"Give me a second." I sit up slowly, feeling the blood rush to my head. My legs feel asleep below the knee. "I felt something, right toward the end. Rough and solid. What was it supposed to be?"

Lena sighs, leaning against the corrugated wall. She slowly drags her fingers through the loose strands of hair.

At the university where she used to work, back in D.C., Lena says they had an almost perfect immersion. A fairground, somewhere in Nebraska, programmed and rebuilt piece by neural piece. They'd spent years, first, assembling the brain scans and the sensations—the feeling of dusty gravel underfoot, the sound of blowing grass, all the smells and motions and minute variations of light. She has them all copied, here, in the dozens of drives scattered throughout her makeshift containership laboratory. She also has me, and Mahesh and the half-dozen other survivors on board, and all our memories of overpriced coffee, uneven sidewalks, poorly painted Victorians, and the soft crunch of cigarette butts on our doorsteps.

Enough, she thinks, to remake San Francisco. A ghost of it, at least. As much as you'd ever find in a museum, or as much as you'd ever remember at a funeral. An outline with a few spots of high relief, as sharp as the day you first felt them—that's what she's hoping for.

What we've gotten, so far, is gray.

A lot of fog again. Guess that's why you picked San Francisco. I make the same joke every time, and Lena always smiles. But it isn't the truth.

She picked San Francisco because she loves San Francisco. Because it was home for her, years and years ago, long before the quakes and eruptions and atmospheric decomposition, and long before the rain swept away everything that was left. If you're going to raise a ghost, it should be one that you loved.

"That was supposed to be the bridge," Lena says. Her fingers have reached the end of her ponytail, and she flips it back over her shoulder. "The Golden Gate, I mean. Walking across it, going north. Nice and iconic."

"I never did that," I say. "Too touristy."

"You're kidding."

"About the touristy part, sure." I wink at her, and she smiles, just a brief flash of teeth. "But I really never walked across the Golden Gate. Didn't have that kind of... leisure time."

"Fair enough." She knows I'm teasing her now. She stands up a bit straighter, stepping away from the wall and rolling her shoulders. "I only remember it because we didn't do it often. My sister and I, we made that walk maybe five, six times in all the years we lived there."

I know better than to ask what happened to her sister.

I think there's a paradox here, and it's starting to frustrate Lena, whether she'll ever admit it or not. When a city is wiped out as completely as San Francisco was, the people who really knew it are gone. Gone in all kinds of horrible ways, burned or suffocated or sunk to the bottom of the sea. The only people who remember it are the ones who went away. People like Lena, who had to leave—or people like me, who ran.

The city has millions of stories that I don't know. Never did and never will.

"Okay," I say. I flip the visor back over my eyes, and the container flickers away behind a wall of blue. "Let's do it again. Same thing. I think I almost got it."

For Lena's sake, I always try again. As many times as she asks. No matter how I feel about this city, I can admit—you deserve to be remembered by someone who loves you.

Three

I wonder if anyone alive remembers Felix.

What a disaster that *turned out to be.* I hear this in Mama's voice, although of course I never heard her say it. She had a bad feeling about Felix, and now it colors everything in retrospect. I close my eyes and see him approaching me like a harbinger of doom, all honey-colored beard and blue eyes like the heat death of the universe. Tight black turtleneck sweater, showing off a trim waist and hiding a beautiful map of ink, sleeving both arms and tracing his sides from hip to collarbone. I can't remember half the images, only the brightness of the colors.

He came up to my register with a bill for a turkey sandwich and small coffee, and handed me his phone number with his credit card. "Felix," I asked, "is that 'happy' or 'lucky'?" I don't think he understood the question, but I called him anyway.

I did love him, at least at first. Enough to follow him north and west to what felt like the edge of the world, a finger reaching up into the Pacific, reaching or pointing for something unimaginable. Not that I saw the ocean side with any frequency. Our home overlooked the bay, if you stood on tiptoe and squinted through the gap in the houses, over the distant slice of 280. On warm nights, we stood on the fire escape as long as we could bear it, sipping wine from CVS out of plastic cups and pretending it was romantic.

He got me a job at the theatre, coming in after each performance to clean up the lobby and the seats. I swept up water bottles, abandoned programs, the ends of joints, and sometimes unspeakable or unidentifiable things more suited to Hazmat than the lighting guy's girlfriend. I hated the job, but for his sake I tried to love the city. And sometimes I even succeeded. There was a corner shop with reasonably priced cigarettes that smelled like incense and played Lebanese pop on an ancient boom-box behind the counter. The *panederia* across the street sold delicious spiral-shaped cookies rolled in pink sugar. But mostly, I failed. And the more I hated where I was, the more I hated who I was with.

Oblivious. That's the kind word for it. *Self-absorbed.* But it was worse than that, stupider, and maybe more tragic. A snake chewing on the tail of its own failing ambitions. A house building itself on a foundation of mud and quicksand. A city straddling a fault.

Then the earthquake came, like a miracle. And I ran.

The last time I saw Felix, he didn't even look sad. He was on the phone with the electric company, running down his battery for no Earthly reason other than that scolding other people made him feel like he was accomplishing something. He waved me out the door, the phone still raised to his beautiful pink lips. Didn't even hand me my suitcase.

But the damned thing was, I couldn't stay away.

I didn't even make it back to Mama. Got stuck a little south of Stockton, out of cash and out of breath. I thought I was going to die there, in that motel room with its hundred staring eyes of knotty pine.

But the rain came, and I didn't die.

And when the rain turned out to be toxic, chewing through stone and metal like battery acid, I found a job with the relief efforts. They gave us truckloads of filters and pH balancing tablets to distribute, and we drove back to San Francisco. I looked for him, first thing, as soon as I could get away from the desperate lines on Mission. But by then he was gone—the apartment empty, the theatre boarded up. Everyone was looking for everyone and no one knew where to start.

The rain kept coming, and soon everything else was gone, too. Pounded into powder and washed out to sea.

Lena and I found each other because of the ship. Before he died, one of my co-workers had told me where the filter shipment was coming in. "It is, without exaggeration, the most important thing in the world," he said. "Do you understand me? If something happens to me, you get to that ship." Hours later, the house we were staying at in Oakland collapsed into a sinkhole, and whatever was left of him wasn't strong enough to climb out. I went to the harbor, and saw the massive container ship grounded on the shifting floor of the bay.

Lena and Mahesh were already there. They had come here for precisely this purpose, all of Lena's equipment loaded into two trucks, looking for a city to save. I found them hooking up generators and solar panels, labeling each container by its contents. Food, water, filters and medical supplies—keep. Plastic crap—toss, pallet by pallet. They mapped paths onto the exposed roofs of the lower-level containers, little squares of tape placed end to end like dominoes: green for east, yellow for west. So you know where you're going, if you're going anywhere.

Not knowing what else to do, I stayed.

So the question now is fairly simple. If you put aside Lena's project, put aside the questions of its value and its feasibility, if you bracket the question of what I'll find on shore. The rain has stopped, and life is returning to the hills, so shore must be survivable. And knowing that, the question is easy to ask: Do I leave, or do I stay? Go out into a world whose shape I no longer recognize, without even the thought of a person who might be looking for me? Or stay on the edge of the corpse of a city that I still don't like, with the people who are trying to raise its ghost?

If Felix has taught me one thing, it's that I have never been good at making choices.

When you have a hard decision, Mama said, *close your eyes and count to five. Then say the word out loud. Your heart knows what it wants, if you stop ignoring it. You just have to listen.*

Four

Once, only once, I tried to go back.

I had a reason, maybe, but not one I could articulate. We were six weeks into Lena's project at that point, and hadn't exchanged so much as a breeze, a whisper of leaves in the gutter, the faintest whiff of coffee. I didn't think I was going to find anything, exactly. Maybe I was trying to convince myself that there was nothing to find.

We didn't have gasoline for the container ship's lifeboat, but there was a small canoe-like contraption that Mahesh had put together early on, when they were shuttling equipment from Oakland to the ship. It would hardly have been seaworthy a year ago. But now, the bay lying flat as a mirror, it was exactly what I needed.

I set off early in the morning with a few water filtration packets and a bag of chips for company. Left a note tucked in my sleeping bag for Lena, if she came looking for me, just to tell her I wasn't gone for good. But I didn't tell her where I was going, either.

And then I rowed. And rowed. And rowed.

Each splash of the oars echoed. I remember how vivid that sound seemed, out there on the flat water, under the flat unbroken sky. I had thought about going straight across the bay, along the east span of the bridge and then across the empty water where the west span used to be, landing over what had been the twenty-something piers. But the clearness was tempting, and I found myself wondering. Wondering and turning the boat north.

Under the bridge, around Treasure Island, and I turned west again. And there, between the tips of the peninsulas—on my left, traces of steel and concrete, and on the right, leafless trees toppled like a giant's stack of driftwood—there was nothing but sky. A sky that seemed too big for itself, too solid blue for too many miles, almost threatening to collapse. The towers were gone, the cables and the six-lane span of road vanished without a trace. Even the concrete that had anchored it to the shore. All of it underwater, being steadily rusted away.

I waited just long enough to rest my aching arms, and then I turned back.

I rowed west of Treasure Island and Yerba Buena this time. Closer to the city's shore line, which even now was losing sheets of rock and mud to the silent and steadily encroaching water. There was a scraping sound as the bottom of my boat connected with an object beneath the surface, and I looked over the side to see the outline of something vast and rust-black. Huge, and magnified by the water, and my brain ran to sea-serpents and dragons, the monsters you find off the edge of a map.

It was so close to the surface. I wasn't thinking, not quite. I pushed my sleeve up past my elbow, balanced the oars across each other in front of me on the prow, and then I reached for the fragment of bridge.

The water felt intensely cold, like dry ice, or putting a bare ice cube on a sunburn. My fingertips found the rough steel and I spread my fingers, pressed the flat of my palm against the metal. Rough as an emery board, pocked with holes as large as coins.

The water lapped above my elbow, wetting the sleeve of my sweater, and the scratch of wet wool brought me back to myself. I drew my arm out with a gasp. The thinnest imaginable layer of skin was starting to lift away from my forearm, the skin beneath it showing pink and freezing cold.

I thought I was going to shudder, or groan, or begin to cry. And I knew if I started doing any of those things that I wouldn't be able to stop. I bit my lip and squeezed my eyes shut until the cold ebbed away and the ache of overtaxed muscles returned, spiked now and then with electric sparks of pain though the damaged skin.

When I opened my eyes, I had drifted away from the ruin. I took up the oars again and started back toward home.

Five

"Again," Lena says, and I'm in.

The suit flexes around me, channeling warmth. The press of the sleeping bag against my back vanishes and twin needles of sensation run up my legs. Standing. Now walking. And there—the flicker of something against my right palm.

Stronger now. My hand against a rail, curling around a rail. It feels rough and warm, and I remember that file-rough sheet of metal, the ruin of a different bridge beneath the water. Faintly, through the earphones, there comes the sound of traffic nearby, the sound of waves across a vast distance.

And I've reached five.

"I got it this time, Lena. I definitely got it." I hear myself babbling through the sandpaper-scrape of the immersion peeling away. I pop out the earphones and pull off the visor, and Lena is watching me like a woman afraid to believe what she's hearing.

"Are you certain?" She leans away from her computer, putting some distance between herself and the data, almost as if she's afraid to breathe on it. "It was definitely a bridge? You could tell it was a bridge?"

"Yeah," I tell her. "Everything but the visuals, Lena. You've got it."

"Good." She clears her throat. "I mean, really good. Thank you."

She helps me out of the rest of the suit, helps me to my feet, and now I'm facing the open door of the shipping container. There's a warmth to the air from outside. It might even be spring.

If you really listen, you can hear the faintest lapping of the waves.

"We'll do it again, later," I tell Lena. It's supposed to be said out loud, after all.

"Oh, yes," Lena says. She's looking out the door, too. The sun hangs just above the horizon, and the roofs of the containers on the level below us are stripped with gold. The sunset magnifies each ripple in the water, weaving a pattern of light and shadow. "And there's a whole city after that."

I still don't like San Francisco. Although I'm wondering, now, if this place will ever become someplace else. Take a new name, a new geography, given enough time. I wonder if I might learn to like whatever comes in its place.

I've gone so many times, stayed so many times without a reason. What would it be like to give myself a reason, for once?

I look from Lena to the water, and from the water to the shadow on the horizon. In the sunset, the ruins look almost beautiful.

DANCING WITH A STRANGER IN THE LAND OF NOD

Will McIntosh

As the closing music to *The Lion King* rose from the back speakers, Teale fumbled for the next DVD in the stack, keeping her eyes on the empty, snow-covered highway. She lifted the DVD into her field of vision. It was *Frozen*.

She lowered her window halfway and tossed it out.

"How about some music?" She glanced in the rear-view mirror, at Elijah to the right, Chantilly to the left. The only thing to indicate they were alive was the occasional blink, the gentle rise and fall of their chests. "It's Elijah's turn, isn't it? How about Rich Homie Quan?"

She dug out the CD, popped it into the Mercedes R-350 minivan's CD player. Before the nodding virus, Teale had despised hip-hop, but now Elijah's music was a comforting link to the days when Elijah could jump, run, and dance. In the rear view, Elijah's eyes darted around as if he was frantically looking for something. His eyes—and only his—did that from time to time. She had no idea why.

Teale reached across to the passenger seat and patted Wilson's knee. "Don't worry, the grown-ups get a turn next. Maybe some..." The thought vanished as she noticed the temperature gauge on the dashboard.

The needle was higher than she was used to seeing—almost in the red. Had it been like that the whole time she'd been driving? She'd taken the minivan straight from a dealership for the trip, so she wasn't familiar with its settings. The one thing she couldn't afford was to break down in the middle of Colorado, in winter. That's why she'd picked a brand new Mercedes. What could be more reliable than a brand new fucking Mercedes?

The needle crept higher. Closer to the red. What would she do if the car broke down? It was twenty degrees outside.

She watched for exit signs.

"Come on."

A hint of smoke whipped out from under the hood.

"Come *on*."

It grew thicker, blacker.

Teale tried to remember when she'd last passed an exit, or spotted a town through the thick foliage. Twenty miles, at least. If the car broke down, she'd have to head forward and hope the next exit was closer than that. How long could her family survive inside the van with no heat? She had no idea.

The van bucked, sputtered. Teale pressed the accelerator, but the van didn't respond.

"Shit. *Shit.*" She slapped the steering wheel, her heart racing as they rolled to a stop on the shoulder. There was nothing in sight—no buildings, no side roads, nothing. Wilson's face was slack, as always, but there was bright, wet alarm in his eyes. Their eyes were the only part of them that seemed alive, as if their entire selves had retreated inside them.

She turned, faced the kids. "There's nothing to worry about. I'm going to get us another car. I'll be back soon."

Opening and closing her door as quickly as possible to keep the heat in, Teale raced around to the back, opened the hatch and pulled out the suitcase holding their winter gear. She put coats, gloves, and hats on the kids, trying hard to seem calm as the kids watched, terrified. She wrapped them in the comforter, gave them each a drink from their thermoses, startled as always by how animated their faces became when the straw touched their lips and they sucked on it reflexively. After dressing Wilson, she pulled on her own gloves, scarf, and hat, then leaned over and retrieved the handgun from the glove compartment and stuck it in her backpack.

"Okay, be strong and keep the faith. I'll be back before you know it."

A gust of biting wind hit her as she left the warmth of the van. She locked the door, then took off at a sprint, aware that her family was watching and that she had to look fast and strong, had to look like she could sprint the whole way to the next town like it was no big thing.

When the minivan was out of sight, she slowed. Her lungs were burning, her legs rubbery. She was not a runner; she was an indoor woman carrying an extra thirty pounds who felt at home behind a desk in a climate-controlled room. The opposite of Elijah, whose ADHD had kept him in perpetual motion before the nodding virus took his body away from him.

Teale spotted a sign a half-mile ahead. She tried to pick up her pace; the green sign crept closer, but she still couldn't make it out. She slowed to a walk to steady her jarring vision, squinted at the sign, gasping for breath.

Gunnison 13

Teale stifled a sob. Thirteen miles? That would take hours. She pictured her family in the van, probably freezing cold already. She eyed the dark woods hugging the highway. Cut through the forest? But what if it was a thousand acres of wilderness?

There were no good options. Trying not to panic, she went back to jogging along the shoulder of the highway.

Within ten minutes she was feeling nauseous and had to slow to a walk again. Pressing her hand against the stitch in her side, she pressed on, images of her family sitting in that van, silent, plumes of white mist coming from their cold mouths. She imagined returning to find them frozen, dead, and—

Teale stopped walking. For the briefest instant she'd felt the most horrible emotion as she imagined returning to find her family dead.

Relief.

Relief that she wouldn't have to change their diapers any more, or feed them, or carry them to bed. Relief that they would be free of bodies that had become prisons. And relief that she wouldn't have to witness their deaths, yet hadn't abandoned them like so many others had abandoned their loved ones.

A humming caught her attention. It took her a moment to identify the soft rumble of an engine rising in the distance. She stopped, spun.

An SUV appeared, barreling toward her.

Teale stepped into the road, waved her arms. "Hey. Hey, *help!*"

The SUV slowed, stopped on the shoulder a hundred yards short of her.

Teale headed toward it.

When no one stepped out, she paused. Why weren't they coming out? Were they waiting to make sure she was alone and unarmed?

She swung her pack off her shoulder, deliberately retrieved the handgun so whoever was in the vehicle could see it, then stuck it in the waistband of her jeans. Hopefully the signal was clear: *I can defend myself, but I mean you no harm.*

As she approached the SUV, she prayed it was filled with women, or old people. Not men with thick beards and automatic rifles.

The driver's door opened. A white guy in combat boots stepped out, slung a rifle over his shoulder.

Teale's stomach lurched. She stopped walking, put her hand on the pistol grip. "Are you alone?"

"No." Head down, the guy stepped toward her.

Teale backpedaled a few steps, drew her pistol. "Hang on. I don't want you any closer."

The guy stopped, spread his arms, palms up. "You waved me down. Do you need help, or not?"

"I do. I broke down a few miles back. My family's still back there."

He gestured toward his SUV. "Get in. We'll pick them up. I can take you to the next town."

Teale eyed the SUV. From this distance, with the truck's tinted windows, she couldn't see inside. "Who's with you?"

"My wife and daughter."

He opened the back door as she got close, then stepped away. Teale tensed as she leaned in, half-expecting someone to grab her.

There was a girl about Elijah's age sitting frozen in the back, a woman motionless in the passenger seat.

"Climb in."

She eyed the back of the SUV, packed tight with supplies. "How is my family going to fit? There are three of them."

"I'll leave some of this stuff behind." He shrugged. "It's not like there's a shortage of food and supplies. At least not yet."

Teale climbed into the seat beside the preteen girl. That was true. You could go into most any house—if you could stand the smell—and help yourself to canned food, tools, bedding, guns. Not to mention jewelry, home furnishings, DVDs, toilet paper. The whole house if you wanted it, and were willing to move the bodies.

"Where are you headed?" the man asked. "I'm Gill, by the way. This is Season," he gestured at the woman in the passenger seat, "and our daughter Arial."

Teale smiled and nodded at Arial. "Teale. We're looking for a town to settle in for a while. We're coming from Denver."

"Too many bodies in Denver?"

"You got it. Maybe I could deal with it once they're just bones, but right now it's too much."

"Plus there's disease to think about. Same story with us." He had a gravelly voice; his sleeves were pulled up to the elbow, revealing tattoos of eyes shedding teardrops.

They exchanged snippets of information they'd picked up on the radio, or from other survivors they'd met in the months since the fall. The President still made radio addresses, but nearly everyone was convinced it was an impersonator. The voice just wasn't quite right.

"You think the world will ever look anything like it did before?" Teale asked.

Gill slowed as Teale's minivan appeared around a curve. "Sure. Sooner or later things will get back to normal."

It seemed a wildly optimistic assessment. Teale wondered if Gill had said it because his family was listening. That's what Teale would have done if her family was in the car.

It felt strange, leaving food on the side of the road to rot. Then again, there was food spoiling everywhere. All the fresh food rotted in the weeks after the outbreak. Now all the boxes of cereal and bags of chips were going stale. In a few years there'd only be canned food left. There would be plenty of that, though. They had time to get their act together and learn how to plant crops, to corral all the livestock running free.

Teale reached over and patted Chantilly's knee. She touched her family a lot now, much more than before.

"So what did you used to do, Teale?"

"I was a lobbyist for the Marijuana Policy Project. It was a group working to legalize marijuana nationwide."

Gill burst out laughing. "Well, it looks like you succeeded. People are free to smoke as much weed as they want."

It had seemed important work back when things were normal. She'd believed in it. Now it seemed meaningless, like so many other aspects of pre-plague life. When ninety-seven percent of the population was dead or in a catatonic state, a lot of things that had once been important became meaningless.

"How about you? What did you do?"

"Most recently I was a stay-at-home dad. Before that I was a high school substitute teacher and girl's tennis coach, and before that I worked for a cable company. I've had a lot of jobs."

The sign welcoming them to Gunnison, Colorado proclaimed it the home of Western State College, which must have been a tiny college given the size of the town. As they cruised down Main Street, which would have been quaint if not for all the broken windows and the nodding virus victims in white body bags stacked along the curb, Teale stopped scanning for a replacement vehicle, and instead studied the town itself. It was the epitome of small-town USA. Maybe this was far enough from Denver.

An old woman in a blue tracksuit walking along the sidewalk paused to watch them pass. Teale waved; the woman raised her hand before turning to continue.

She spotted a Holiday Inn up ahead, on the left. "You know what, Gill? Why don't you drop us at that Holiday Inn? I can find a new car later." Gill, who'd been cruising slowly while taking in the town, put on his turn signal.

"You letting the squirrels know you're turning left?" Teale asked.

Gill chuckled. "Habit." He pulled up to the front doors of the hotel and twisted to look at Teale. "I'm wondering if you're thinking the same thing as me, that this would be a good place to settle down for a while."

"Great minds think alike, I guess."

"Cool. It would be nice to know at least one of my neighbors."

"One of your four neighbors, probably," Teale joked as she climbed out of the SUV.

The door into the lobby was unlocked. Teale looked around in the dark lobby until she spotted a luggage cart.

"You going to find a place and move in right away?" Teale asked as Gill helped her load Wilson onto the luggage cart. She would have to wheel her family to a room one at a time.

"We'll probably do the same as you: crash somewhere for the night, and scout for a permanent location tomorrow."

"Why don't you stay here, then?"

"You sure?" Gill said. "If you guys want some space, there are plenty of other hotels." He gestured down the street.

"I'm guessing my family likes seeing new faces for a change." And so did Teale. Especially a face that could talk back to her. Sometimes her family's silence left her feeling more lonely than if she'd actually been alone.

• • •

Teale held the cup steady while Wilson drained the heavily-spiked eggnog in a half-dozen pulls on his straw, as Nat King Cole crooned *White Christmas* on the stereo.

Her throat was one big knot. Her glands hurt from holding back tears. The flood of memories from past Christmases kept tumbling out, leaving her raw.

Had it been just last year that Chantilly and Elijah tried to stay up all night on Christmas Eve, only to fall asleep at four or five and sleep until noon on Christmas Day? And five years ago today, Wilson donned a Santa outfit and ran across the snowy backyard, into the woods, while the kids watched from the upstairs window, shrieking with excitement at glimpsing Santa Claus?

The song ended. "Whose turn is it to pick the music?" Teale asked in a strained-cheery voice.

"Arial's, I think." Gill sprung up, exuding good cheer and energy, his smile terribly stiff. He put on some boy-band's Christmas CD. As he stood facing the stereo for much too long, Teale noticed his shoulders bobbing slightly, and realized he was crying.

He slipped into the kitchen without turning around.

"You want some more eggnog, hon?" Teale lifted the empty cup from the coffee table and headed into the kitchen.

She found Gill on the floor, clutching his stomach, sobbing silently. When she put a comforting hand on his shoulder he looked up, his face wet, eyelids ringed red.

"I miss them. I grieve for them, but I feel *guilty* for grieving, because they're still here."

"I know. I know." She sank down beside him, her back braced against the cabinets.

Gill pulled on a towel draped over the handle of the stove, wiped his cheeks and eyes, his breath still ragged. "Sometimes I wonder if I'm doing the right thing. I'm terrified that if Season could speak to me one last time, she'd say, 'I'm in hell, let me go.'"

Teale didn't answer. She'd wondered the same thing many times, but she didn't want to think about it.

"I can't, though," Gill said. "How could I, without knowing it's what they want?"

The tears she'd been holding back for the past three hours started to flow. "Have I told you Elijah has ADHD?"

Gill shook his head.

"Before the virus he couldn't sit still for a minute. It must be absolute torture for him, to be like this." The pain of knowing her kids might never move again hit her, fresh and new. "I can't stand seeing them like this. It hurts so much."

"But you don't want them to see you hurting," Gill said.

"That's right." She was having trouble taking a breath; it felt as if there was an anvil sitting on her chest. She wanted that damned boy-band to stop singing. "I also don't want them to see how much I hate them sometimes."

Teale's own words startled her. She covered her mouth with one hand, turned and pressed her forehead into Gill's collar, sobbing.

He rested a hand on her head, whispered, "Yeah. That too."

It had been lurking down in the darker places of her mind, the resentment, the revulsion she felt at their helplessness. It wasn't fair that she felt it—it wasn't their fault—but she felt it, and hated herself for feeling it.

"I wish we'd ignored Christmas and pretended this was just another day," Teale said into Gill's neck.

"I'm sorry. If I hadn't kept track of the days, we wouldn't have known."

"It was my idea to celebrate Christmas. We could have ignored it."

Teale raised her head, intending to sit up. When Gill's face brushed close to hers, she leaned in and kissed him.

She felt a rush of warmth, of comfort, as she kissed this near-stranger. It was the first time in forever she'd felt something other than pain and fear.

When their lips parted, Teale rested her head on his chest. They stayed that way as *Ding Dong Merrily on High* gave way to *Jingle Bell Rock*.

"We'd better get back in there." Gill's voice was tight.

"Okay."

Gill hung back a moment, as if not wanting the others to see them go in together.

• • •

After she'd put the food away and put everyone to bed, Teale went for a walk to clear her head, to think about what had happened in the kitchen. She felt sick about it, guilty as hell, but also alive in a way she hadn't felt in a long time. Kissing Gill had been the last thing on her mind until the moment she'd done it; it had been like lunging for a life preserver as she was going down for the final time.

Were you depressed if you felt hopeless and sad but had good reason to feel that way? Teale didn't know. It probably didn't matter what she called how she felt. Call it "depressed," or "sad," or "the new normal."

"Hey." Gill was leaning on his SUV, one foot on the bumper. A thrill went through Teale. She tried to tamp it down, wondering if Gill had come outside hoping she would, too, or whether it was just coincidence.

She joined him by the SUV.

"You want to talk about, you know, the kitchen? Or just forget it happened, or—" Gill trailed off.

"Or? Is there a third option besides talking about it or not talking about it?"

He smiled. He was nervous, not meeting her gaze. "Help me out here— I'm kind of lost."

Teale gave a dry, bitter laugh. "You think I'm not?"

That wasn't fair, though—she'd kissed him, not the other way around. She truly was lost, though. In the other world, before, she'd never kissed another man, even when she was drunk. Even after she learned about Wilson's affair with Beth Edwards.

"I can't touch Season. In a sexual way, I mean. I tried once. It felt like I was molesting her, not making love." Gill pressed a hand over his eyes. "I don't know why I'm telling you this."

"I haven't had the courage to try with Wilson. I know it's not Wilson's fault, but it's hard to get in the mood when your partner is wearing an adult diaper. Once in a while I, you know, *relieve* him. With my hand."

With everything else that had been happening in the aftermath of the virus, Teale hadn't realized how much the silence, the isolation, had worn her down. What a simple pleasure, to say something, anything, and have another human being respond to it.

Smiling, Gill said, "You're a good wife."

"I *thought* I was." Teale realized the problem wasn't so much that she'd kissed Gill, it was that she wanted to kiss him again.

There was an orange glow in the distance, over the rooftop of the muffler shop. Someone must have built a bonfire in their backyard.

"I should probably go in," Teale said.

This time it was Gill who kissed her.

• • •

Someone whispered Teale's name, jolting her awake. "Wilson? Is that you?"

Wilson lay beside her, his eyes closed, arms at his sides, just as she'd positioned him.

"Please say it was you." She watched his face, looking perfectly normal in sleep, as if he might open his eyes at any moment and give her a big, warm Wilson smile.

Did he know? Did he suspect? And if he did, did he understand, or was he inside there, screaming in jealousy and anguish? Teale never had to lie, because Wilson couldn't ask.

"Teale." An urgent whisper from outside. Teale went to the window.

Gill was standing in the darkness, hands buried in his pockets.

Teale padded out of the room, checked on Chantilly and Elijah before pulling on a coat and heading outside.

She melted into Gill's arms. "How're you?"

"Good, now."

"You making any progress on the grand City Council project?"

"I don't know about progress." Gill kissed her neck. "I finished the census, at least. There are officially sixty-nine residents of Gunnison, Colorado."

"Interesting number."

"I thought you'd like that." Gill let her go, took her hands. "Listen, I have something I want to ask." He licked his lips. He looked nervous.

"O-kay."

Letting go of one of her hands, he drew a little white box out of his coat pocket, flicked it open with his thumb.

A diamond ring sat nestled in the box. Marquis style, the diamond three carats, at least. "I want to ask you to marry me."

Teale reached down, touched the ring already on her finger, with its half-carat diamond. She twisted it, struggling to make sense of what was happening.

"I love you," Gill said. "I don't want to hide it any more. I *can't.* I can't sneak around behind Season's back. I know it bothers you, too."

Yes, it bothered her. She'd walked around for the last month with a perpetual knot in her stomach. Sometimes she felt sure Wilson knew where Teale was going when she said she was going for a walk.

"But what's the alternative? *Tell* them?" Teale tried to imagine telling Wilson she was marrying Gill. He wouldn't react, of course. Neither would Chantilly and Elijah. How would they *feel*, though, when Mommy explained that she loved Gill? "Imagine having to sit, frozen, day after day, while your wife kisses some other man. I'd rather be dead."

Gill looked at the ground. "For all we know, they'd rather be dead anyway."

Teale flashed back to those terrible days when the nodding virus was raging, the hushed conversations about painless ways to release loved ones from their suffering. How much Oxycodone or Valium you needed to mix into their water. Teale had been there, a scarf pressed over her nose and mouth, when their friend and neighbor Mark Melancon gave his son Valium-laced grape juice. She could still see the tears rolling down Mark's cheeks as Jeremy drank. A few days later, Vanessa Melancon held the cup while Mark drank.

"If I was in their situation, I'd be grateful if Season slipped a dozen Oxycodone tablets into my juice," Gill said. "If I didn't *know* I was about to die? If I just drifted off gently? That would be the kindest thing she could do for me."

"Then why don't you?" Teale asked softly. She never asked survivors what had happened to their families, why most of them were alone, with no diapers to change. They'd made a different decision than Teale. She wouldn't judge.

Gill stared at the ground between them. "I know it would be a kindness. I'm not sure I can do it, though."

I'm not sure *I can do it.* A month ago he'd said he *couldn't* do it.

"I'm not sure I could, either," Teale said.

Out in the street, something hurried past—a groundhog, or a raccoon. Gill turned around to see what she was looking at.

"Are we saying—" Gill's voice hitched. He cleared his throat. "Are we saying we should do this?"

"I don't know what we're saying." Teale looked up at the window where her children were sleeping. Her lips were numb, her chest aching. She didn't want to have this conversation; she wanted to go to bed, and stay there for days.

"Maybe this is the push we needed, to finally do the right thing," Gill said. "Maybe we've been selfish, keeping them this way with no hope of recovering."

It was a bizarre thought, but in a brain-twisting way it made sense: they'd needed some selfish motive to goad them into doing the right thing for the wrong reason. The reason wasn't what mattered; what mattered was to do what was best for her kids.

And there—another illusion had just fallen away. It was all about Elijah and Chantilly, wasn't it? If not for the kids, Teale would have put Wilson out of his misery long ago.

Yes. That felt true. Fuck Wilson. Were Elijah and Chantilly better off alive or dead? That's what it boiled down to. Teale closed her eyes, tried to forget Gill, Wilson, everything, and just listen to her heart.

Finally, she opened her eyes. Between hitching breaths, she managed to get the words out.

"I think we have to let them go."

· · ·

Teale put earbuds in Elijah's ears, turned on Iggy Azalea. While he listened, she brushed his teeth, then combed his hair. His hair was getting long again. She'd have to cut it again soon—

The thought formed in an instant of forgetfulness that was followed by a plunging despair as she remembered. It was time to let them go. Today. Today she and Gill would be strong, would let their families go, out of love for them.

Elijah's eyes were darting around again—his pupils bouncing like twin superballs on concrete. Just as they'd done when she put on Rich Homie Quan in the minivan, and a dozen times before that. Teale caressed his cheek, which was sprouting adolescent peach fuzz. She smiled wide, determined not to give the slightest hint that this day was different from any other. It was crucial they not suspect anything. Teale wanted them to drift off, nice and easy. No pain, no fear.

Elijah's eyes went on dancing as Teale got Chantilly ready for the day, choosing her white pants and an Olaf the snowman sweatshirt—

She froze, one of Chantilly's arms in the sweatshirt, the other out.

Dancing.

That's what Elijah was doing. He was dancing, with his eyes.

How many times had Teale tried to get them to use their eyes to communicate? Look left for yes, right for no. But they couldn't; they couldn't move their eyes voluntarily. Their eyes tracked reflexively toward movement, the same way their lips wrapped around a straw.

But Elijah's eyes could dance. For him dancing was as reflexive as drinking. And reflex or not, he was enjoying the music. Her son was feeling pleasure.

Maybe this wasn't all hell for them, after all.

· · ·

Sunlight peeked through the distant Rockies as Teale slid the note under Gill's hotel room door and headed outside.

She climbed into the Honda Odyssey, which was already running, her family loaded up. Choking back tears, she put on her fake cheery tone. "Here we go. Just a few hours' driving, then we'll find another hotel."

Thankfully, Gill was nowhere in sight. If he came running outside now she knew she'd break down, and if Wilson didn't already know, he'd know then.

"Who gets to pick the first CD?"

As she pulled out onto the street, she grabbed a jewel case at random. Rich Homie Quan.

"In the spring we're going to see the country. Starting with the Grand Canyon, then the redwoods, the Pacific Ocean, up the coast. On from there."

In the rear view mirror, she watched the town fade, and she could see Elijah's eyes dancing.

THE SEVENTH DAY OF DEER CAMP

Scott Sigler

"Have you been harmed in any way?"

They asked it every time, during the thrice-daily videoconferences. George had a dozen different ways to answer that question. Had they physically hurt him? No, they had not. Had they emotionally hurt him? Yes: a year gone by without seeing his boys in person, without touching his wife, without satisfying the simple yet overpowering need of spending time with his family. But that was the trade-off—those in control wanted him gone, and preventing his family from seeing him was one of the many tools they used to try and get their way. If George really wanted to see his wife and sons, all he had to do was leave.

"No," George said. "They haven't hurt me."

"And are the children still alive? Are they unharmed?"

The children. That phrase used to mean a lot of different things to a lot of different people, but since that first moment George had stood in front of a news camera, it had taken on one specific definition.

"The children are fine," he said. "Unharmed, so far."

George wished he could drop the *so far* bit, but he could not. The world was watching him. As far as he knew, he was the only thing standing between the children and knives, microscopes, autopsy tables, and secret facilities of the United States government.

"Good," the mask said. This one sounded French. Maybe French-Canadian, George wasn't sure. The voice changed every day, but the mask was always the same: Guy Fawkes. The symbol of the Anonymous movement, a movement that had grown to a hundred times its original size following the alien attack that had shattered cities, killed millions. A movement that had grown because of *the children,* because of a rampant distrust of governments, of militaries and the police, because of the world's need to know something positive could come out of that tragedy.

Three times a day, he reported in. If he missed an appointment, shit hit the fan: Hackers from America, China, Russia and more would go to work, sabotaging targets that had been pre-selected and pre-qualified. There was no mistaking the correlation between George not appearing for an update and the instant retaliation against multiple targets from multiple sources.

And if there were no online targets, pre-programmed physical demonstrations happened within minutes: flash mobs that blocked the entrance to the Lincoln Tunnel; a thousand people climbing the White House fence for a calm stroll across the lawn; bomb threats at airports; instant sit-ins at police stations with hundreds of individuals willing to be arrested, willing to go to jail, willing to take a nightstick to the head in order to send a message. That message? George was not to be touched, not to be harmed, not to be delayed from talking to the world in any way for any reason.

"Good," the mask said. "Is there anything else you need to tell us?"

George shook his head. "Nothing else. There's no reason I shouldn't be back online for the next update in four hours."

"Very well. Keep up the good work. We are watching."

That last bit wasn't meant for him: It was meant for his hosts. Maybe *captors* was a better word for them.

The screen went blank.

A strong hand on his arm.

"Mister Pelton, we will now escort you back to your quarters."

George nodded absently. He stood. "Thank you," he said, because he was a Midwestern boy and being polite was so ingrained in him he said such things automatically, even to a soldier who would put a bullet in his head if so ordered.

He wondered, as he always did after the check-ins, how many more days could he spend here? He wondered if he had made the right choice, if he should've just gone home to his family after saving those kids.

Instead, he had made a phone call. A simple call that had changed the course of human history.

• • •

In the wilds of Michigan's Upper Peninsula, George's cell phone reception had always been shitty. One bar, if any at all, courtesy of AT&T's weak network. But on that day at the end of the world, sealed into a room on a crashed starship with little aliens standing around him—*little aliens,* for God's sake—George got *two* bars.

He had to do something. He had to find help. But who could he call?

The invasion had come without warning. At least, no warning that George and his childhood friends knew of. Ships from outer freakin' space attacking major cities worldwide. One of those ships must've got sidetracked, or malfunctioned or something, because it crashed in the deep woods close to the tip of Michigan's Keweenaw Peninsula.

The hunting cabin where George and his friends had spent two weeks every November for the last thirty years had been close to the crash site, so close that a war machine or mech—or whatever you called an alien piloting a suit of powered armor—had attacked the cabin, blown it to pieces. Luckily, George, Toivo, Jaco, Bernie, and Arnold had been outside when that happened. They returned fire against the attacker, killing the alien inside the machine. From there, a hike through the deep snow and the frigid woods, following colored lights, to the crashed ship—an actual flying saucer, or at least it used to be before a high-speed impact and tumble through the woods turned it into a dented, cracked, smashed thing that had more in common with a T-bone-totaled station wagon than an interstellar vessel.

Inside that ship, bodies. Non-human bodies. Pieces and parts all over, living beings torn to shreds by a crash that gouged a fifty-foot-wide trench through snow-covered ground, pines, and the birches. So many bodies, so many dead. But not *all* dead, as George found out when he opened a sealed door. Inside, a room clearly designed to withstand such crashes: the evidence for that being a dozen alien children, alive and well.

It started out as a dozen, but that number dropped to eleven when George's friend Toivo shot one in the head. Toivo wanted to kill the rest of them—as did Bernie and Jaco—but George put himself between the children and the barrel of Toivo's hunting rifle.

George still wasn't sure why he'd protected the alien kids. Maybe it was the fact that they were helpless. Maybe somewhere in his head he knew this was a history-changing event, and that the sane thing to do was preserve these eleven alien lives even though the aliens' kin had probably killed millions of people.

Or, maybe, it was the crash seats.

He stood in a room with the eleven alien children. The same room with the crash seats, or *chambers* or whatever they were, that had kept those children alive during the crash. The grownup aliens had seen to the kids first, safely strapping them in—just as George would have done for his own children.

His friends were elsewhere in the ship. He knew Bernie was probably tending to Mister Ekola, keeping the old man warm as winter slowly and surely stole the heat from the ruined hull. George didn't know what Jaco was doing. Rooting through the ship, probably, because it was an *alien ship*, and would he ever get a chance like this again? The one that worried George, though, was Toivo.

Toivo, who had already killed one of the alien children in cold blood.

Toivo, who clearly wanted to kill the rest of them as well.

Toivo, who had never left the area, who still spoke with the Yooper accent George had shed years ago. *Da* instead of *the*, ending every other sentence with the rhetorical *eh?* If George hadn't moved away, would he still have that accent? Would he have wanted to shoot the children? So hard to know if his urge to save them was something he was born with, or something cultivated from living somewhere other than this remote, homogenous culture.

A silly time to worry about nature vs. nurture.

The phone buzzed in George's hand. One bar... it had reconnected to the network.

He could dial 9-1-1. But would anyone answer? Had the attacks hit Milwaukee? Detroit? And if he did get through, what would he say? *I've got an actual ship here, with survivors.* Who would respond to that? Who would be dispatched?

George looked at the eleven alien children.

Paralyzed with indecision, he imagined how things might play out. If he called 9-1-1, the local police station, or any government office—and he got through—word would quickly go up the ladder. George knew where that ladder ended: the Army.

The military would come. These children would be taken away. Hidden. Studied. Interrogated.

What if someone did that to *his* children?

George looked at the phone. A sense of panic crept over him, lodged in his chest, burrowed in his heart. What if he did the wrong thing? A call could get the children killed. *Not* calling could mean they might die, because what the hell did he know about goddamn alien children? What did they eat? What needs did they have?

He was a fucking insurance salesman, for Christ's sake.

Then, the phone's single bar blinked out.

Zero bars.

No connection.

George started to shake. He'd missed his chance. How long until the cold pushed its way inside this shattered ship, started to freeze the very children he wanted to protect? Not just them: his friends would freeze as well, the boys he'd grown up with. And the one man who had helped them all understand what it meant to actually *be* a man? Mister Ekola was hurt; he needed help.

One bar re-appeared.

Maybe a chance to make only a single call before that bar blinked off again.

His thumbs worked the smartphone, bringing up a web browser. He had to get a number and get it fast.

One call… maybe he could save Mister Ekola and the children both with one call…

• • •

The guard escorted George to his room. Maybe ten minutes to himself, tops, then George had to get to the ship and check on the children. He *always* had to check on the children.

The children.

The *goddamn children*.

They had become his entire life, at the expense of the life that had been his before all of this started. Yes, a year ago he had been a simple insurance salesman. Now the face that looked at him from the mirror happened to be the most-recognized face on the planet.

What was it now… four billion YouTube views and counting? The interview had been downloaded and re-uploaded so many times no one really knew for sure just how many total views there were. A million views the very first day, he was told. Within two weeks, the interview had passed by that Korean guy with the funny glasses—and that one pop-singer girl who wore crazy outfits—to become the most-viewed video in the history of mankind.

The guard stopped at the door to George's small room. Seemed like a nice enough kid, but he didn't say much. None of the guards did. They were ordered not to, probably. Loneliness, lack of communication with other people—just more tools for the government to isolate the thorn in its side.

George entered. The guard stayed at the door.

Twelve feet by twelve feet. A twin bed. A small desk with a computer that let him send and receive screened email. Email, and nothing else. The irony was hard to process: the Internet's most popular person wasn't allowed to use the Internet.

He checked email. Like clockwork, the daily missive from his wife, Mary. This one started the way all of her emails started. First line, two words: *Come home.*

Then, a picture of the boys. Dressed in spandex singlets this time. Youth wrestling must be starting up. God, but they were so beautiful.

Michael and Luke had grown so much. When George had left for his two-week hunting trip, Michael had been six, Luke, eight. Now they were seven and nine. George had missed an entire year of their life. A year and counting that he would never get back.

Luke had stopped smiling for pictures. George wasn't sure when. A year ago, the boy had been all giggles and squeals. Now every shot of him showed a scowl, a frown. Was that normal for a growing boy, or was it because his father was gone? Mary said it was a phase, but George knew the meaning behind her words—the phase wouldn't have happened if George had been around.

After *come home* and the picture, the usual update. The boys' grades were slipping. Luke had gotten into a fight at school. Both of them were being more and more disrespectful at home.

How much of that was boys growing up, and how much of it was Mary, unintentionally easing up on the reins, letting the boys run wild because it would carve at George, make him want to give up this fool's quest and come home? He hoped he was wrong about that, but he had been with Mary most of his adult life; deep down inside, in the places he tried to ignore, he knew of his wife's expertise at subtle manipulation.

He closed the email without replying. As the weeks rolled on, there was less and less to say. In his head he knew he was doing the right thing, that he was standing up for the faceless masses who didn't trust their governments, their police, their military. He was preserving a cultural touchstone that wouldn't come again in his lifetime, in his children's lifetime... perhaps in all the human lifetimes to follow. It was *important*. In his head he knew that, but in his heart, he was just a man who desperately missed his family.

And if he left this place to see them, he would never be allowed to return.

George rubbed at his face.

It was time to check on the children.

He left his room. The guard turned sharply on one heel, knowing where George was going and leading the way without being told. George followed, amazed as always that this had all begun with one simple phone call.

● ● ●

George finished his call. Or, rather, the call finished for him when the signal dropped. The bars vanished and didn't return. He was pretty sure he'd given good directions before he'd been cut off. If so, he would find out soon enough.

Through the hull's cracks, the wind eased from a howl to a moan. The storm died down, like all storms do.

He heard Toivo arguing with Bernie. George couldn't make out the words. Toivo sounded pissed. Maybe he was campaigning for the others to join him, to murder the children.

Exactly how far was George willing to go to stop that from happening?

"Don't know what to do," he said.

The children didn't answer.

"You guys are a big help."

The words turned to white as they left his mouth.

Temperature dropping. Winter's fist was slowly squeezing tight around the wreck, snatching away what heat remained.

The children... they were shivering.

From the cold? Maybe. Or, maybe, from fear.

He terrified them.

Which was fine, because they terrified him.

A human shape that could never be mistaken as actually *human*. Two arms and two legs, but thin, *so* thin, tree branches come to life with fluid motion. Black eyes—three, not two—set in heads too big for the death-camp-skinny bodies. And those mouths... George did all he could not to look at their mouths.

An hour passed.

A banging on the door. The sound reverberated through the room, bounced off the twelve crash chambers, or shock seats, or whatever the capsules were that had kept these children alive while their parents had been turned into paste. The children flinched at the sound, huddled to-gether, made noises that sounded frightened and pathetic.

George unslung his rifle. He held it nervously in both hands. He thought of slinging it again—was he going to *threaten* his lifelong friends or some-thing? The pounding came again. George decided to hold onto the weapon.

He pushed the door open.

There stood Toivo and Jaco. Toivo, who had already executed one of the children, and Jaco, *little Jaco*, who had shown more bravery than George and the others combined.

"Give me your phone," Toivo said.

George didn't move.

Jaco stared past George, at the children. He hadn't seen them yet. The man seemed oddly calm in light of the situation. George wondered if Jaco wanted to kill them, just like Toivo did.

"The phone," Toivo said, holding out a hand palm-up. "Bernie's phone ain't got shit for signal. Mister Ekola isn't doing great, we need to try and get help."

George nodded absently. "Already called someone," he said.

That caught Jaco's attention. "Who?"

"Ambulance," George said. "That's part of the deal."

"What deal?" Toivo said.

George was suddenly unsure if he'd given enough info before the call cut off. Did they know where to go?

"I had a signal but it's gone," George said. "I made a call. Help is coming."

Toivo's eyes hardened. "For the last time, Georgie—give me your phone."

Any pretense of friendship had evaporated. Three decades they had known each other, come here every year to reconnect, shared all the experiences life had to offer. It was all gone. If George had raised his rifle as Toivo had, if, together, they had slaughtered these helpless beings, that friendship would have been strengthened beyond any measure—but George had chosen otherwise.

He pulled the phone out of his pocket and handed it over. Jaco and Toivo huddled over it as if it had a secret warmth that might chase away the encroaching winter.

"No bars," Toivo said. He looked at Jaco. "And it's almost out of power, eh? What are we gonna do? How do we get Mister Ekola to da hospital?"

Jaco stared at the phone for a moment, perhaps hoping for a connection to suddenly appear. He shrugged.

"I dunno, eh? Maybe we can see if da snowmobile made it through da explosion?"

The three men—and the eleven alien children—fell silent. In that void, the sound of the wind, dying even further, from a moan to a whisper. And through that whisper, another noise. The faint, growing whine of a distant siren.

Jaco and Toivo looked at George.

"You called an ambulance?" Toivo said.

George nodded.

Jaco shook his head. "There's a fucking alien invasion, and you got an ambulance to come out to da middle of nowhere? How? And da roads are snowed shut—how did you pull this off, Georgie?"

George shouldered his rifle. He felt nervous without it in his hands, naked, as if his friends might suddenly aim and fire, taking more innocent lives. He glanced at his friends' weapons, at them, until they got the hint. The attitude of both men had changed: Somehow, George had got help for the man who had raised them all.

They both slung their rifles.

"Let's get outside," George said. "It will take us at least thirty minutes to hike back to the cabin. We need to be there when they come, or they might drive on by."

• • •

George would later learn that the alien attack had failed within the first twelve hours. Ships had appeared out of nowhere over the skies of the biggest cities in the most-advanced nations: Beijing, New York, London, Paris, Moscow, Mumbai, Berlin and more.

Trouble was, the most-advanced nations had the most-advanced militaries. Air-to-air missiles blew flying saucers out of the sky, turned them into flaming wrecks that plummeted into the cities below. Some US pilots said it was like shooting down a space shuttle—a target that couldn't dodge, that exploded easily and spectacularly. Others used more colloquial terms: It was like shooting flaming arrows at hydrogen-filled fish swimming in a barrel of jet fuel.

Maybe the plan had been to take out the strongest first, in hopes that the weakest would then surrender. Whatever the reason, it turned out that the great military minds of the attacking aliens weren't that great. Some guessed they weren't military at all. Sociologists theorized that the invasion was more religious than military in nature, that it was more the covered wagons of armed civilians crossing the great plains than it was the landing craft of D-Day.

One thing seemed certain: The ships that attacked were not built for battle. Now it was assumed that the aliens had gone to war with what they had, because they had no place else to go. The children were proof that their species could breathe just fine on Earth. After some trial and error, they were able to safely eat many kinds of food. The aliens, so the theory went, had to abandon their own planet, and Earth was the only place they could reach.

They could have tried to communicate, but instead they declared war, and they paid dearly.

The conflict had been so fast, so decisive, that the only alien ship left intact was one that hadn't fought at all—the one that crashed not far from George's hunting cabin. Some assumed it was destined for Chicago before the malfunction that brought it down. Every other vessel had been engulfed in flame, then hit the ground like a bomb. End result: very little material remained intact. Very little material, and no survivors—save for George's eleven charges.

Through the thrice-daily interviews, George had learned there were no known alien survivors except for "the children." That made them beyond important, an immeasurable resource. If there were other survivors, they were locked up tight in some secret government location. People speculated that was true. George was one of those people.

The invasion changed the world, but not in the way scifi authors or great intellectuals might have predicted. Governments didn't come together. If anything, they were more divided than ever. What changed was the people. *The people* came together, ignoring racial and cultural divides. They came together with one common interest: absolute distrust of authority. Among the countless conspiracy theories was the top dog of them all: that governments knew what had been coming and hadn't warned their people. Theories like that weren't new. They'd been part of the populace since governments had formed. What *was* new was a technology that no government could completely control. The Internet. Cell phones. Local networks. People organizing, encrypting, working together as one against anything that smacked of authority. In the years before the invasion, people had come to fear their governments. Now, the governments feared the people—and with good reason.

• • •

George, Toivo, and Jaco stood by the ruins of a hunting cabin that had been the centerpiece of their friendship for three decades, the centerpiece of Mister Ekola's relationship with his own childhood friends for the two decades before that. Over half a century of tradition, now nothing more than shattered timber and scattered camping supplies.

The wind's ebb hadn't lasted long. Whitened treetops swayed slightly. The woods were here before people. The woods would be here after people were gone. The woods just didn't give a shit about any of this. Those trees bracketed a long stretch of white: the road, thick with snowdrifts three feet high, motionless waves in a snapshot of a frozen ocean.

And coming down that road, a moving spray of snow rising up in grand arcs, crashing to the sides in puffing clouds of white that caught the morning sun. Through those clouds, a pulsating orange light.

"Ambulance lights are red," Toivo said.

"Not an ambulance," Jaco said. "It's a goddamn snowplow. Let me guess, Georgie—an ambulance is right behind it?"

George nodded. "I sure hope so."

The flashing orange light came closer. As it did, the three men could make out the cabin of the snowplow itself, highway-maintenance orange seeming to surf on a flowing, crashing wave of snow.

Toivo turned to George. "How'd you get a snowplow to come out here, eh?"

Jaco laughed, the first time that sound had been heard since the alien ship had torn open the night sky with a boom so loud it shook the ground.

"Because it ain't just da plow and da ambulance," he said.

• • •

George hadn't called the police. He hadn't called the military (not that he would even know *how* to call the military, or if such a thing was even possible). And, he hadn't called an ambulance—not directly anyway.

He'd called Channel 10.

The attack had hit major cities. As far as George knew, Houghton and Hancock—the closest cities of any size at all—hadn't been hit. The hospitals wouldn't be flooded, the ambulances wouldn't be swamped. He hoped that if he acted fast enough, he could put someone to work getting the resources needed to help Mister Ekola.

Not knowing how long his connection would last, George had talked fast, not caring who answered the phone, hoping that whoever it was could remember all the info.

He'd been so nervous he'd been shaking. He'd known, somehow, that he was committing himself to something big, something long-term. The words had rushed out of him. He'd heard his own voice as if there were two of him, one speaking on the phone, the other listening to every syllable.

I don't have long, so take notes. My name is George Pelton. I grew up around here. An alien ship crashed near my deer camp. It came down during the storm. No one saw it, but you don't have much time before the major networks and the military come. I can show you the ship. I have alien survivors—I can put them on camera. If you want this story, you need to get here as fast as you can. The roads are snowed-in—find a way to get here. You have to bring an ambulance, and no police. If there isn't an ambulance, I won't show you. If there are police, I won't show you. One reporter, one cameraman. I'm giving you three hours to get an ambulance here, or I'm calling Fox News.

George had given the cabin's address, then the signal had dropped. Even if he'd had a full cellular connection, how many calls would he have had to make to try and get an ambulance *and* a snowplow out here? Would anyone have even listened to him? Maybe, maybe not, but a reporter, a *motivated* reporter, would do anything in his or her power to make it happen. That'd been George's guess, and from the way things turned out, he'd guessed right.

• • •

Paramedics worked on Mister Ekola. George was still in the room with the children, but had caught a few snippets of conversation, enough to know that Mister Ekola would be all right. George's friends clustered around the old man and the paramedics. Other than a smile from Bernie, knowing nods from Toivo and Jaco—the three friends' way of saying *thanks* to George—they didn't give a damn about the reporter, the cameraman, or the alien children.

George stood in front of the children, who clustered together, cowering. Maybe they didn't know the difference between a rifle and a camera. How could they? The last time a human had pointed something at them, one of their friends had died.

Surprisingly, George recognized the reporter—a woman named Nancy Oostergard. Even though he didn't live up here anymore, he'd seen her faces on billboards in the area. That was because she wasn't a "reporter" at all—she was the nightly news anchor. Maybe the anchor of a small-town station didn't have a lot of pull on the national scene, but she had enough to be the one that drove out on the freshly plowed road to do this shoot.

"Mister Pelton, are you ready?" Nancy asked.

George nodded.

Nancy stood by him, her left shoulder almost touching his right, a microphone in her hand.

The cameraman re-settled the camera on his shoulder, then switched on the lights mounted atop the rig. The small room lit up. The children squealed in fear, clutched at each other even tighter.

"Four... three... two..." the cameraman said.

Nancy took a slow, deep breath through her nose, let it out even slower through her mouth.

"This is Nancy Oostergard, reporting live from near Eagle Harbor. I am inside a crashed UFO, the same kind that has laid waste to cities all across the planet. This ship has actual alien survivors, the first we've heard of through the sporadic reports coming from across the planet."

George watched the cameraman step to the side, trying to get a shot of the children. The children saw this—as a huddled, mewling pack, they moved to keep George between them and the camera.

"Yes, these are actual aliens," Nancy said.

The camera swung back sharply, locked on Nancy and George.

"They were discovered by this man, George Pelton," she said. "He was here on a hunting trip with his friends. Mister Pelton, could you describe what you saw the night this ship crashed?"

The camera's small light burned brightly, nearly blinding George. How did reporters stare into that night after night? Was he on local TV? Or was this signal carried across America? Across the world? He shouldn't be doing this. He should be in the other room with his friends helping get Mister Ekola through the deep woods and to the ambulance waiting by the cabin.

"Mister Pelton?" Nancy said. "This is a live signal. I'm told we're being watched all over the globe. Can you describe what you saw?"

George took one look behind him, at the children. Cowering, terrified. He looked at the walls, at the crash seats the children's parents had used to keep their beloved little ones alive. And in that moment, something deep inside of George awakened.

Awakened and took over.

He looked dead into the camera.

"These kids haven't done anything to anyone," he said. "They're helpless. They're innocent. Everyone watching this, we can't let the government get them, cut them up, study them. What if they were your kids? Would you want your babies butchered?"

The cameraman moved again, tried to get an angle. The children were too many to fully hide behind George, but they tried anyway.

George took one step toward the camera, leaned toward the lens.

"They're just *kids,*" he said. "I'll stay with them, try to keep them safe, report to the world however I can, till we know they won't be killed for some experiment. I'll stay with them. The government lies—I don't."

• • •

If only he had known the way the world would interpret his words. If he had, would he have said them?

"Mister Pelton, ready to go in?"

George stared at the airlock door, at the guard standing next to it. Behind that door lay the ruined ship. In a matter of days, the Army had built a huge pole barn around the wrecked vessel; within a week, they'd built a second building inside the first, one that covered the alien vessel like a shell. That was where George was headed now.

The dead bodies had been removed, the debris cleared away, and the wreck had been scanned for radiation, poisons, gasses, anything that might harm a physiology humans knew very little about. Nothing dangerous had been discovered. Not knowing what might hurt the aliens, the government scientists had decided to leave them in their own ship.

"Mister Pelton?"

"Yes," George said automatically. "Thank you, I'm ready."

Thank you… ever the Midwestern boy.

The guard nodded. He wouldn't be coming. Another guard would be waiting inside, this one in a hazmat suit. Everyone entering the wreck wore one. Everyone except George. The children had been exposed to him, after all, and he'd been exposed to them.

George knew that if he left to see his own children, he wouldn't be allowed back in because of potential pathogens he might bring with him. New bacteria. Contaminants. The government would have a reason to cut him out of the picture, to tell the world that he was now a potential danger to the children instead of their protector.

If not that reason, they would find another. If he left this place, it was over.

George often wondered why he'd said the things he'd said when that camera light flicked on. He'd never been very political, never believed in any conspiracy theories. At least not before this had started. He'd never been involved in local government. He hadn't even watched the news. Yet that diatribe had flown out of him almost as if he'd written it in advance. It had made him a global sensation: the brave, selfless protector of alien children.

It also made him very much alone.

The airlock door opened. As expected, inside awaited a hazmat-suited guard.

George knew the children would be happy to see him. They would cling to him as they always did, ask him questions in a language he didn't understand. The few words he'd learned weren't enough to convey thoughts of any complexity. But he didn't need to be fluent to understand what they wanted—they wanted to know when they could go home.

Trouble was, they *were* home. They were never going to leave.

If George stayed true to his word, neither was he.

He stepped forward. The airlock door closed behind him.

PROTOTYPE

Sarah Langan

My transfer orders arrive nine months early, and I'm not happy about it. *Can I have more time?* I request.

Radio silence.

So Rex and I pack my best prototypes, break down my lab, and wait. He licks too much, but otherwise he's a good dog. The second-best I've ever had.

A few hours later, a sand ship's masthead pokes up from the desert horizon. I pull Rex close. He's been showing his age lately, shitting in odd corners, eating just half his food, needing his name called more than once. I've overlooked it until now, just like I've overlooked the bald patches on his scalp, poor guy.

The rig floats closer. Its sail, about eighty feet tall and Mylar coated, is embroidered with a Kanizsa Triangle, the emblem of the Pacific Colony. A Class C driver waves from the deck. He wears a modern sand suit with liquid stitching; much better than I'd expect for his low rank. The colony must be thriving.

I bend down next to Rex and take his jaw between my thumb and third finger. Turn his head to one side. I cleaned his breathing apparatus just yesterday, so it doesn't make those bark-sounding exhales that dogs are known for.

"They have no respect for the past in the city. No one there knows what they come from. They're not like us, Rex. We don't belong there."

Rex laps my thumb. I lean into his wet nose. "You think we'll be okay?"

Rex nods. People think I'm crazy, but I know he understands me.

The ship pulls astride my laboratory's dock. Rex and I walk along the clear, sand-proof gangway, and board. The hull's enclosed in porous, wind-resistant plastic, with holes about ten microns wide. It's great for short trips, useless for long-term survival.

Pretty vehicle for Nevada, I say.

My driver shrugs. Class Cs are literal half-wits. They follow orders and that's about it.

He drives. What he lacks in social graces he makes up for in creepiness. Most of us add a little personality to our suits. His is shining black with just a single C-Class insignia across his left breast. He looks like a six-foot tall, man-shaped oil slick.

We head up a wide dune, pumping the wind-powered engine as we crest, then letting momentum ferry us down. Sand spits from the spiked wheels like fountain water. Its grit drifts, little by little, inside the ship.

"'S okay, boy," I say. But we both know it's not.

A mile out, we pass a giant crater that used to be Lake Mead. It was man-made, its edges smoothed, its color indigo-dyed blue. I've seen pictures and every time I pass, I imagine how it used to be. Did people marvel, or did they take for granted man's dominion over nature?

This whole area used to belong to the American Air Force. Nukes were tested to the north and east. The Underground's still radioactive. I picked this abandoned military base for my lab because it's as far away from the city as my superiors would allow me to go. Some of the hangars survive, still stocked with planes. Rex and I like to sit in this one B-2 together, looking out over its needle nose. We imagine flight.

I spend my days testing lighter and more graceful Above Ground suits in my lab. It's the kind of engineering that requires A-Class creativity. If I wasn't so good, I'd have been decommissioned long ago. I'm past retirement. I'm probably the oldest person in the entire colony.

My suits have to be sand-proof, yet porous enough for respiration. Remember that sand gets as small as one micrometer—just 20% larger than an oxygen atom. Not a lot of room for error. If my designs fail, we get brain sickness. I'm the best in Pacific Colony, which is why they let me live like a hermit. Every few years, I get transferred back to the city to oversee mass production. But other people make me anxious. The roughness of this world has hardened them in ways I never want to be hardened. Take Rex: Animals disgust them. But what's the point of living if we can't protect the things in this world that are weaker than ourselves?

Now, Rex licks my Driver's sand-proof Mylar boot. It's a way of letting the guy know he's not a threat—he respects the chain of command. He hunches his forearms and play-barks, forcing extra air through his breathing apparatus.

Keep your animal to yourself, my driver warns. *Why isn't he wearing a suit?*

What do they fill C brains with these days? Dogs can't wear suits. Their skin's too porous. They'd suffocate, I answer. And then: *So, what do I call you?*

Nothing, he tells me.

I'll call you Linda, I say.

I'm male.

Great. Progress. *Then I'll call you Linus, after Linus Pauling. He liked Vitamin C, so I'll keep an eye out for lemon concentrates for you.*

Linus sneers. I can see the hint of it through his skin-tight sand suit.

I laugh, and decide I'll spend the rest of the trip needling him. At least one of us will be entertained.

Sand blows against the hull. The boat speeds. My smile fades. I can smell electricity in the air: a storm's coming. Trouble. I should have stayed home and ignored my orders. Screw these guys.

But maybe we'll get lucky. Maybe it'll pass us over.

• • •

We're not lucky. By nightfall, the wind hits fifty knots. Hurricane. I finger a heap of sand from Rex's ears, then cover his orifices with tightly woven gauze. He's trusting enough to hold still for me. "Don't bite at it, Dog. It's medicine," I say. And then, "Good, good, dog."

It's dark except for the bow's navigation lights. With all the airborne sand, I can't see what we're driving through. Lightning keeps flashing, but not for long enough. And then, suddenly, the whole sky goes ablaze with a loud crackle. A dozen sand devils whirl across the flat plains. They're three-foot-wide, six-foot tall cyclones.

One of them scissors straight for our bow. I push Rex down and cover him with my body.

Slam!

Sand breaks through the plastic like a giant wave. Rex tries to jump out. I noose him to the seat with a rope. He struggles, rope tightening against his neck. The barking starts: *Aaaackp! Aaaackp!*

We need shelter, I say.

Linus ramps the engine to full power. We don't speed up; instead we just groan and rattle. We push ahead like that for another half-mile, tacking hard to avoid the brunt of the sand-devils. We're not sailing anymore, but boring like worms. Rex's heart beats twice as fast as it should. At the bottom of his bark comes this mechanical *grinding* of interconnected metal gears that have lost synchronicity.

Stop the ship, I say.

Linus ignores me. He's got orders, and Cs can't think in abstractions.

There's a way-station at Red Rock. Looks... due one hundred meters East. If you don't stop I'm jumping out.

The dog is not essential, Linus answers.

I untie Rex and stand, trying to figure out how to jump with him in my arms, neither of us getting hurt, when Linus jerks the wheel and drops anchor.

Fine! He says as he seals-up the sails, secures my prototypes, and jumps off.

Rex and I follow.

We trudge through a skyscraper canyon. The wind's worse here, focused. We walk with our backs bent eighty degrees. Sand pelts so hard that my joints feel like gristle. I hold whimpering Rex tighter, my lips humming against his warm, knotted hair. All around us are thousand-foot tall buildings with empty windows and smashed neon signs that used to read *Gambling! Live Ladies! Las Vegas!*

I've seen pictures. There was even a rollercoaster.

The manhole radiates a signal. It's marked by triple orange triangles arranged in a circle like a cut-up pumpkin pie. Linus and I work together to lift its cover. He goes down first. I follow, carrying Rex. With my hands full, I can't pull the cover back over us. I consider asking Linus for help, but the bastard's already two flights down.

"Come on, Boy. 'S okay."

Rex barks air: *"Clk! Clk! Aaap!"* The new clicking means his left lung has locked. The sound echoes, lodging into my spine.

"Stay with me boy. We'll get through this."

He looks at me with a wise and weary expression, then snuggles against my chest as if to say, *Okay, big guy. Whatever you say. Just, please, make this better.*

Fairy lights in plastic, wind-powered packets glow as I pass down the first, second, and third flights, where Linus waits. We're deep down enough that our signals don't connect.

Old tunnels like this cover most of the globe. People hid inside them when the asteroid Aporia first hit. Their design was pretty uniform—narrow openings that headed down a few hundred or thousand feet, then a flat base with tunnels spiraling out like plant roots. The roots kept fallout to a minimum. People expected Above air to clear up after a decade. To be safe, they took enough supplies to last twenty years. But the air never did clear up. Not even a hundred years later.

The things they did to survive. It's good no one took pictures.

We descend to the wide bottom base. Rusted, illegible signs point into the mouths of eleven darkened tunnels. Nine of them are caved in. The other two need clearing. This shelter is shallower than I'd expected—just two hundred feet. There must be a granite bedrock.

Graffiti's scrawled all along the walls:

Down the with cyborgs!
Mike loves Dori
Fuck All Who Enter Here, Literally.
Chitin is for pleibs!
I see you walking around tunnels
With the man I love and I'm like
Haiku.

Linus and I take off our suits and shake the sand out, then reapply. The fabric is sturdy and sheer, sticking like liquid paint once it's on. I'm wishing Rex's body would take to it as I bend over and pet his grumbling belly. He's too tired to stand. But his color's still pink, so at least he's getting oxygen.

"Do you know when they cleared this place of survivors?" I ask Linus. Our ports aren't connecting, so I actually have to use words.

"They didn't clear it," he answers. His voice is sand-clogged. "Not worth the effort. The specimens down here all had radiation poisoning. Genetic abnormalities. F-Class brains. Let 'em rot."

So there might still be a few hanging around.

I look to the ceiling. There's a crude old drawing up there of a town with a main street and stick figure people waving outside old-fashioned ranch houses. I remember the designer: Frank Lloyd Wright. A tempura yellow-white sun shines bright. It used to be such a wonderful world.

I remember the musician: Louie Armstrong. He sang happy songs, even when he didn't have much to be happy about.

I clear the sand from Rex's ears. I don't dare touch his nose: He's bleeding at the fusion sites where his metal respiratory tract and his organic tissue meet.

A gust of wind rushes down from the manhole. It ushers a sand devil with it. The whirling monster bears down. I'm knocked to the ground.

Stunned, eyes closed, I count to three. I dig at the mound I've found myself buried inside until I'm out. I keep digging, frantic, until I feel him. Rex!

"Help me, Linus!" I cry.

"No, it's just a dog."

"Fuck you." I climb back up by myself.

Sand has collected on the steps. I crawl to get to the top. Then I grab the edges of the iron cover with joint-achy hands and use the soft part of my head to balance it closed.

Click! The wind's shriek hushes to a whisper.

I go back down to find Rex laboring on a bed of sand at the bottom, but Linus is gone.

"Good boy. Hold on."

I pull one of the metal rebars peeling down from a caved-in tunnel and gong it against the graffiti wall. The sound echoes all through. Linus, that jackass, doesn't come back. Maybe he got scared. Maybe the sand got into his brain somehow and he went crazy.

I hate Class Cs.

Yellow goop has glued Rex's eyes closed. His nose is clotted. I need two things: a medical kit, and water. I've got two tunnels that I can check for old supplies. I pick the left one, because I figure warriors always go right, artists left.

"I'm going to find medicine," I tell him. Then I scratch under his chin, the only place where it looks like he's not hurting. "I love you."

Rex nods, and I swear to God, it's because he wants me to know he loves me, too.

The tunnel's too caved to walk through, so I crawl. Granite rocks fall around me, heavy enough to break my back. I know it's stupid to do this for a dog. Rationally, I belong in the city with a modern lab and assistants. I ought to get over this disdain I harbor for my own kind and make real friends. If I did that, I wouldn't feel so alone. I wouldn't talk to myself and imagine that my dog understands me. Except, he does understand me. And they don't.

I keep crawling.

Rocks fall behind me, blocking my way back. It gets dark so I shine a light. I go another few feet before a boulder stops me entirely. I'm strong. Under ordinary circumstances, I could lift it. But not here, without leverage.

I hear a scraping from the other side of the rock. Something digs. A mole? A mouse? A survivor?

God, please help me, I say as I try to roll the rock. I manage to push it a millimeter. It rolls back into place. I punch it. I punch the wall. I punch myself. It's so dark in here. I've gone mad. What the hell do I care about a dog?

I try one more time. Use my legs as I push. The rock shifts. I keep pushing, groaning. I'm clear. There's nine inches. Maybe I can squeeze.

A face appears on the other side. It's got albino red eyes. "Ugh!" it grunts as it jabs an arrowhead through the crack, right into my shoulder.

The staff it's using is made from a human tibia. I yank the tibia, get hold of the things' skinny arm, and tear it off.

By the time I get back out, Linus has returned and is bent over Rex. "Leave him alone!"

Linus stands back. Rex's eyes are bandaged. He's breathing better now, but coughing sand.

"Found a medicine kit," Linus tells me. "He's blind and deaf but he might live if we get him to the city and replace his respiratory tract."

I drop the gristly arm I've found in front of Rex's mouth. He tries to chew just to please me, but he's too sick to swallow. I get on the ground and hug him so he knows he's not alone.

"I thought you ran off," I tell Linus.

"Class As are so neurotic," he answers. Charming.

We wait out the storm down there, and don't head up again until first light. I cuddle Rex for most of that time. His company calms me.

Up above, I pretend that the cave ceiling is a perfect blue sky. There are birds cawing. I'm playing catch with my shiny-pelted Collie while my wife and family watch from the windows of our beautiful ranch house in a town just like the drawing.

Wonderful World plays and I hum along.

The woman's name is Lorraine, I decide, and she smells like tea. The child is a little girl. I imagine their warmth, the feel of them, and remind myself that this is love.

I remember.

• • •

I use my shoulder to shove the manhole aside. Then we're out. The sand has shifted, obscuring the entire west side of the skyscraper canyon. Old balconies with rusted terraces peek out as if etched from stone. A sulfur red sun beats down. I check for a signal. It's weak, but back.

Ship's buried over there, I say.

Linus hurls himself like a burrowing crab into the great sand mountain where I've pointed.

It'll take a day, at least, for him to find and repair our vehicle. By then, Rex will be dead.

I pick him up. It's a few hundred miles to the city. On foot, we'll make ten. But we can't be the only people on this strip of road. I should be able to flag someone down. I start walking.

We've gone less than a mile in the hot sun, Rex slack in my arms and worrisomely heavy, when the droning starts. It comes slow from the direction of Las Vegas. As it gets closer, I recognize the Kanizsa Triangle.

I stop, more tired than I'd realized.

Linus pulls up. Sand weighs the ship low to the ground. He kicks down a rope ladder and I carry Rex with one arm and hold the ladder with the other, my stabbed shoulder screaming. Has it been hurting all this time, only I haven't noticed until now?

Sand's gotten inside my suit because of the hole. Linus looks us both up and down. *I should change into my prototype,* I say.

Yes.

I change. We sail.

• • •

It takes less than a day to get to the city, where the Pacific Ocean ushers a welcome rain. Sand's less of a problem here than ultrafine particulate matter. Animal lungs turn to soup up here in just a few hours.

The city of the Pacific Colony is built in a semi circle around one of the last survivor tunnels on the West Coast. The genetic pool down there is fantastically diverse. Class As have been manipulating DNA for ages and have developed all variety of neural matter.

Linus docks our ship. The signal is strong with exactly the kind of chatter I despise, only more nonsensical than usual. They've found an old song they all like. They keep replaying it to different beats and instruments. Someone resurrected old photos of the first Above shelter and we're supposed to have a moment of celebration at mid-day. Lastly, there's been a survivor revolt in the Atlantic Colony.

The first thing we do, at my insistence, is head to the medical center. A pair of Cs carry Rex to a gurney. I hold his forearm as comfort as they inject the morphine-oxygen IV, then pull out his sand-crusted respiratory tract. They keep this morphine-oxygen IV handy, just for me.

Have I mentioned that this is not my first dog? Nor even my hundredth? *Will he be okay?* I ask.

None of the Cs answer, because they're not smart enough to draw conclusions.

• • •

Once I'm out, I'm met by the team of Class As that run the Above Survival Apparatus division. They ask for my latest prototype and I point at my own body. I explain: *It's better than the previous, because it allows for more sensation of physical touch. For instance, I can feel Rex's warmth, and that signal carries through my nervous system. I can also feel cold, though I find that less pleasant.*

They nod with excitement.

In addition, I'm looking into gonadal sensitivity. Wouldn't that be wonderful?

The head A smiles, to be polite. Plastic stretches across his metal teeth in a phony way. I'm reminded why I hate it here: They think I'm crazy.

You'll make the appropriate modifications for mass production?

I always do, don't I?

• • •

I spend a week in the city. It's a terrible, loveless place. The houses are sleep chambers. No one touches. The only people who feel this lack are the As, and none of them will admit it. Instead they conduct more experiments.

They keep trying to find the right combination—the thing that sparks our evolution. But it never happens. We don't change. We can't. It's our nature. We are always the same.

The revolt in the Atlantic Colony is quelled. I find myself sorry to hear it. In what dreams I still have, I imagine them rising up. I'll find them when that happens. I'll help them.

• • •

On the last day, I collect Rex from the medical center. One look and I know it's not my dog. *You cloned him,* I say. *He won't know me. Now he's just a sick, old dog.*

The C walks away.

Show me his body.

Incinerated, Linus tells me. He's wearing a shining new suit. It's agile. Slightly more human in appearance. In a way, I envy Cs, and even Bs. They never kill themselves. They're not smart enough to juggle oppositional perspectives.

My last stop is the survival tunnel over which the city stands. We spray it at night so they don't wake up when we experiment. It would be kinder to clone them from parts, but we want the variety that environmental stress provides.

I was one of the first to discover this particular tunnel a thousand years ago. I came down with another A class, and there they were. These blinking, beautiful creatures who'd turned pale and waiflike in the dark. They hadn't interbred or poisoned their cells with prions like so many others. They'd stayed strong.

As I'd looked at them, I'd thought that we could live together. Or maybe we ought to act as the cyborgs they'd created us to be, and serve them.

They fired the first shot. In return, we slaughtered all who resisted, and took the best brains for our pool. A thousand years later, they're sickly things who've lost the use of language. Their mutations, which we've stimulated, are at turns sublime and grotesque.

I go down to the lowest part of the tunnel. I pick a C class human. She's pulled from the stocks for above ground respiratory tract insertion as my new dog. I always pick children, so they grow to love me.

I head out the next day. The forecast is clear. I've got a Class D driver this time. It speaks in binary code. The dog whimpers at my side. I pat its head. "'S okay, Rex. I'll keep you safe. I'll tell you so many stories," I say. "Did you know? I had a house, once. I had a family. I had a dog I trained to fetch. This was before the asteroid. This was when the world was wonderful... I used to be human once, too."

ACTS OF CREATION

Chris Avellone

A gnes waited as the ID number above the cell changed to green, and the steel wall dissolved into a transparent gel. Taking a breath, she stepped through the viscous barrier, suppressing a shudder as the gel clung to her body. Agnes had never become accustomed to the feel against her skin. Once she cleared it, she relaxed as the wall hardened behind her.

The cell was empty.

Agnes reassured herself Reeves was still corporeal; the cell's air filters were Sensitive to changes in the oxygen count that would indicate transformation. Usually, the signs were evident hours or even days prior to the change—the subject could then be terminated before it occurred. Usually.

"Hell(----)o, Doc(--)tor."

Agnes looked up and saw the spindly, naked prisoner crawling on the ceiling, smiling toothlessly at her.

"Come down," Agnes said sharply.

Reeves' smile widened, displaying blackened gums. The staff had been forced to remove his teeth soon after his imprisonment; in a moment of desperation, he had started biting himself to draw blood to paint with. Since that time, teeth, hair, fingernails—anything that could be used to render an artistic form—had been surgically removed from Reeves and all other Sensitive inmates; blood clots and contraceptive blocks had been formed in their bladders and genitals, preventing excrement or semen from being used as a medium for their creative talents. In questionable compensation, intestinal and gland implants recycled their waste and saliva with 70% efficiency. The Sensitives needed only a few grams of protein every month to sustain themselves.

"The(----)se wall[-]s are *wonderful!*" Reeves' forearms and legs bulged with the effort of holding himself suspended from the softcell ceiling. "I can put [---] my hands in [--] it, but I [---] can't make them s(-)tick [---]. And [---] when I release my [--] hands, it goes right [--] back to its origin(--)al shape [-] as if I had never [---] touch(---)ed it at all." His smile widened, the skin on his neck stretching, outlining his throat.

She ran a safety diagnostic. The ECCO box stuttered Reeves' speech, turning his syllables arrhythmic. It was regulation for all Sensitive patients after the MONO tone implants had proven ineffective—two months ago, 84J had recited a poorly-structured haiku and vaporized the Central Corridor, killing himself, the interviewer, and several other Sensitives. After this incident, many of the frontline neurotechs had suggested removing the vocal cords of the inmates entirely, but this motion had been struck down by Agnes and others in Executive Main: research clearly showed that voiceless Sensitives gained telepathy faster than those who could still speak. Telepathy, in turn, accelerated the transformation and worse, allowed them to transmit destructive thoughts without a vocal medium.

"Get down, Reeves." His name felt dirty on her lips. Agnes would have preferred his numerical designation, but Sensitives were psychologically incapable of comprehending their designations—they had to be referred to by the names they had possessed before creation. "This is your last warning."

Reeves detached his legs from the ceiling and swung back and forth, ignoring her.

"Reeves, the walls of this cell are alive and hungry. Release them or they will devour you."

Reeves gave a startled yelp and dropped, his naked body tumbling to the floor in a tangle of limbs. Whimpering, he scrambled to his feet, hopping on one leg, then another, trying to keep as much of his flesh away from the floor as possible.

"S-s-so(--)rry. I jus(----)t want(--)ed to b(--)rachiate." His voice was apologetic and frightened.

"The floor will not eat you if you sit over there," Agnes said firmly, pointing to a corner of the cell. Reeves, desperate for safety, leapt over and squatted down, drawing his knees up to his chest. As he crouched, Agnes scanned him for any external damage or open wounds.

He was thin, even by Sensitive standards. Ribs protruded from his sunken chest. His hairlessness and his dead-white skin marked him for what he was—the former by institute regulation, the latter by quarantine. Agnes frowned. Reeves had been losing weight steadily. She logged a mental note to have the engineers check the status of his implants and linked the note to a visual of Reeves with a few blinks.

"Chair," she said crisply.

The floor near Agnes liquefied and a softcell platform slowly ascended to knee-height. In moments, it had solidified into a foamy chair, and Agnes sat down on it, holding in a sigh of relief. She had been making rounds all day, and despite frequent shots, she found herself growing more tired by the end of each shift.

Reeves' eyes were fixed on the chair, his fear of the floor forgotten. "Can [---] you [--] make [-----] any(--)thing else?" Entranced, he crawled over to the seat and tentatively prodded its surface with his finger. He yanked his finger back as the foam indented at his touch, then, wide-eyed, watched the imprint he had made fill itself in.

Agnes accessed her auditory system and edited the ECCO scrambler from his speech—it enabled her to decipher his words without turning off the ECCO box. "Reeves, say something."

"Did you bring a pen?" he asked immediately. He had lost all interest in the chair and was looking at her hopefully.

Agnes shook her head, faintly irritated. "All information, case history, record sessions, and commentary—" Agnes called up Procedures onto her eyelids, and her voice became a monotone as words were fed into her mouth, "—is imprinted in tailored neurons within the brain of the interviewer. At no time is an interviewer to use or permit subjects access to instruments of creation—" She stopped as Reeves crawled back to his corner and curled up into a ball, burying his face in his arms.

"—no writing instruments are required." Agnes lowered her voice. "You knew that, yet you continue to ask me. You know all our procedures here. Recovery would be much easier if you would simply absorb what I tell you. Our tests show you're capable of it—"

Reeves raised his head; folding his arms and mimicking Agnes' stern expression, he stuck out his tongue. Agnes restrained herself from making a comment. It would just encourage him.

She tried a different track. "Reeves, I came to ask you about the transformation."

Reeves shrugged. "I know." He turned away from Agnes and started to press his palms into the softcell floor.

Agnes frowned. "Oh?"

Reeves lifted his palms and watched the floor flow back to its original shape. "It's what you *always* come to ask me about." He rubbed his nose with his finger and glared sullenly at the floor. "You don't care about me at all."

Agnes bristled. "That's not true, Reeves. I care about you and the rest of the Sensitives here at the station. That's why I need you to tell me about the transformation. Can you do that for me?"

"It's against the rules." His eyes darted worriedly at the ceiling. "They kill tattlers here."

"Reeves, there is no social interaction among the inmates. Your life is governed only by the rules we administer. Now tell me about the transformation and how to stop it."

Reeves shook his head.

"Why not?"

"Because," he said flatly, "you're mean to me."

"How am I mean to you?"

Reeves shrugged. "You don't love me. You won't let me call you anything but 'Doctor' and that's not a name at all and you call me by my name *all the time*. You don't give me any clothes, you won't let me leave, and you won't let me touch you." Reeves raised his voice. "You're just *using* me. You don't care about me at all." He tucked his head into the shelter of his arms. "I can see it when I look at you."

Agnes froze. "What do you mean by that?" She felt her heart race as she called up the cell's oxygen count. It had decreased twenty parts per million. "What do you mean, *'when you look at me'?*" Reeves continued to sulk, and Agnes braced herself. "Reeves, look at me."

He peeked out from behind his arms.

"What do you see now?"

Reeves slowly uncurled himself and crawled over to her, stopping in front of her chair. Raising himself to his knees, their eyes met—

an old woman radiant silver gray hair spilling around a face despondency worn with age tracery of lines and wrinkles gathering at the corner of her mouth voice a forgotten song buried

—and Agnes tore herself away, severing the connection. "Oh, no." Her mind began to race, slipping from her, falling away to fear. "Oh, Reeves."

Reeves' mouth was open slightly, showing scarred gums.

"Oh, Reeves. It's started."

Frustration tore at Agnes as she ran projections on Reeves' deterioration. It wouldn't be long—only a few hours, a day at most. There was no way to stop it, not now. Reeves would make the 35th patient this month, an escalation of—

From the corner of her eye she saw him reach out to touch her. With a swift burst of anger, she slapped his hand away.

"Don't *touch* me!" she hissed. "Don't you *ever* touch me."

Reeves' eyes widened. "Your face fell apart," he whispered, as if in wonder. Without another word, he crawled back to his corner, staring at her.

The mechanism of the transformation had long eluded the staff. Hundreds of theories had been proposed: neurological decay, suspension of disbelief in the Sensitives themselves, an undiagnosed virus… The only thing the theories had in common was a lack of supporting evidence. Agnes felt that the transformation was somehow activated by the Sensitives themselves, perhaps through the sharing of a thought, a memory, a rhythm…

But she had no basis for her theory, only intuition. And intuition was not enough to stop it. Thirty-four Sensitives had perished in the last month, manifesting bursts of telepathic communication before they disintegrated. Not a single treatment had proven effective, it was as if without any other means to communicate, their thoughts strengthened, their minds adapted to their new cells to allow… expression.

"It's not your fault," Reeves said quietly.

Agnes glanced at him.

"I *want* to go. It's time, anyway. I don't want to hurt anyone anymore." He paused. "I don't want to hurt you."

"Reeves, don't you know what this means? You won't *exist*—"

Reeves fingers twitched nervously. "I d-d-don't *want* to exist. I h-h-hurt, Doctor." Reeves struggled for words. "I h-h-hurt all the time. I can't understand what you w-want from me. I don't like being here… y-*you* don't like being here with me—"

"I am here for *your* benefit," Agnes interrupted. "What I want is irrelevant. The danger you, all of you, represent to yourselves and to the societal construct is… incalculable." Her voice gave over to the words, sterile, familiar, even though she had written them long ago. "It is our responsibility to disarm you and allow you to rejoin society. If you are not cured, the loss of life you inflicted during the war could happen again…"

Reeves was staring at her.

"Are you *listening* to m—"

Without meaning to, she met his eyes and—

a symphony joined planet laid waste surface mosaic swirling ash, compressed sculpture bodies, drifting shades of incandescent flame, wreckage of fleets drifting alone in dead cold of space, ruptured husks, metal beasts burning in blackness herds of flickering afterimages static thoughts incomprehensible silhouette skeletons scattered across the barren planet surface in the wake of creation

—and Agnes shut her eyes and severed the connection. Her mind burned, a film of sweat forming on her brow and running into her eyes. Reeves' thoughts had been more structured, more dangerous this time. She took a deep breath, checked her neural paths and winced at how raw they had become from recording Reeves' telepathic transmission. If he had infected her, if he…

The burning sensation rose in her mind, and she acted quickly.

"Reeves, your eyelids are heavy," she gasped as a new wave of pain hit her. "…too heavy for you to open them." Working carefully, quickly, she isolated the sections of Reeves' memories she had absorbed, and severed them from the rest of her mind, stemming further neural path spread. Her thoughts were tinged with adrenaline, and behind it, she could hear her own voice, cold, calm, dictating treatments: cauterize the thoughts, inject a mental block, sensory deprivation… a hundred other useless options that had never worked with any patient… she steadied herself. Took a breath.

Reeves was floundering helplessly on the floor, his eyes shut tight.

"Reeves." She kept her voice level. "You are not to make eye contact with me or any other interviewer from now on." Reeves stopped flailing as she spoke, and his head turned as he sought the direction of her voice. Agnes doubted the command would last, but she couldn't allow him to transmit any more thoughts—if he had been able to vocalize the images they both would have died. Only the immaturity of his telepathy had saved her.

"D-D-Doctor, I can't open my eyes." His voice trembled, and she swept away a spike of pity. His face was contorted, and his hands slowly moved around him, shaking fingers grasping the floor of the cell.

"Reeves, you can open your eyes now. Do not look at me."

Reeves blinked. He huddled against the floor, facing away from her. "I didn't want to hurt you," he said quietly. "It's just I can't talk to you because my words come out funny—" his hands clawed at his throat "—and I want to tell you because I don't think you understand." Reeves paused. "I don't want to be here anymore. *You* don't want me to be here. You're sorry you ever made us—" Reeves' hands began to twitch again. He was either nervous or angry.

"Reeves, that's not tr—"

"YES, IT IS!" Reeves screamed, and his fists thrashed against the floor. "YOU WISH I HAD NEVER BEEN MADE AND YOU HAD FOUND SOME OTHER WAY TO KILL PEOPLE AND YOU TELL ME THINGS THAT AREN'T TRUE TO *HURT* ME AND I *HATE* YOU!" Reeves pummeled the foamy floor uselessly with his fists, his screams the only sound in the small confines of the cell. "I *HATE YOU I HATE YOU I HATE YOU!*"

He began to sob, and his fists unclenched. "W-w-why did you *make* us if you didn't *want* us? W-w-why did you make *me?*"

Agnes paused, structuring her response.

"You were… required, Reeves. Because of you, we won the war. We made a mistake. I made a mistake. Now, we are trying to cure you."

"I don't *want* to come back. I can't live here."

"Why not?"

"Everything's… *wrong.*" Reeves' mouth opened and closed in confusion as he searched for words. After a moment, he gave up. "It *hurts*. Your voice hurts when you ask me questions or tell me things. You use words in place of what you see in your head…" His voice became ragged, as if forcing an idea out through his lips. *"Cure,* when you mean a shadow… *d-d-disarm…"* The word was like the yowling of a cat, and Agnes felt a spike of fear. "You say *m-m-mistake,* I see a c-c-cloak over geometries of planets, c-c-covered with husks and molds that once held people…" Reeves paused. "Your *thoughts* hurt, locked inside words your lips spill, wanting to get out… I don't like it here. None of us do—" Reeves stopped in mid-sentence and looked uncomfortable.

"Who's *us,* Reeves?"

Reeves fidgeted and Agnes pressed the initiative.

"You are isolated in this cell. You are permitted to speak to no one else but me. " She leaned forward. "Who is *us?"*

"I don't know."

"Answer me."

"I don't know."

She tightened her fists.

"Reeves, there is an itch in the middle of your back. It is just out of reach and growing more unbearable by the second. If you answer my questions, the itch will fade." Agnes leaned back in the chair. "Who do you communicate with?"

Reeves strained and groped at his back, fingers without nails pulling at the skin uselessly, trying to scratch but unable to. Agnes was impressed: Reeves writhed on the floor in discomfort for almost a minute before he answered.

"Th-th-them. The others here." Reeves still looked uncomfortable. After a few seconds, he rolled over and began to rub his back against the floor. "Make it stop."

"I don't believe you."

Reeves' expression became pained. "It's t-t-true."

Agnes frowned. "How, then? How do you communicate?"

If his tear ducts had not been removed, Agnes was certain Reeves would have been crying. "L-l-like we were just now. No words. They say I don't *need* words anymore." His eyelids began to flicker. "Please *stop* it."

Agnes did not hear him.

The patients had been communicating telepathically.

"How long?" Agnes asked frantically. "How long, Reeves?"

"N-n-not long… short time only," Reeves started rubbing his back again, but the softcell floor provided no friction. He whimpered. "Th-th-they talk to everyone now. They say we should leave. We don't belong here."

"How did you plan to leave, Reeves?"

"Please make it stop."

"How did you plan to *leave?*"

Reeves thrashed on the floor, his whimpering changing to moans as he bent his arms behind him, trying to reach the illusory itchy spot.

"I am *not* going to ask you again."

Agnes waited—Reeves continued to struggle on the floor, until he suddenly stopped, exhausted. Sighing faintly, he closed his eyes.

And his body *flickered.*

Rising to her feet, she plugged into the security net: As she made contact, her mind was filled with a low buzz, the sound of hundreds of transmissions—the entire facility was alive and broadcasting signals. Her eyes were filled with the static of warnings and flashes streaming past. All the same message as the one she had prepared to send. The facility was losing its patients. All of them.

Reeves lay on the floor, his stark face turned toward her. As she watched, his outline flickered again and the skin blurred. She blinked several times but could not focus on him.

"H-h-had to try." His voice was a whisper. "Had to try and make you see, make you come with me. I'm sorry…"

Reeves' words died as his body became a silhouette and faded from view.

The indentation where he had lain on the floor slowly flowed back to its normal shape.

The cell around her felt suddenly, impossibly small. The thought was not hers.

In her mind, Reeves' memories burned, calling to her to follow.

RESISTANCE

Seanan McGuire

January 2029

The gray world moved around me, and I moved in the gray world, untouched and unforgiven. I wasn't alone there. No one was ever alone in the gray, which lived, in its own strange, soft way. But there were flickers of motion through the layered film of fungal strings—fast, hot animal motion, signaling the presence of cats and squirrels that had yet to succumb. Maybe some of them never would. Resistance had to exist in all branches of the animal kingdom for it to have any meaning at all. Maybe some of them would shrug off the searching spores over and over again, shaking their coats clean before resuming the endless, futile search for food that was not soft, was not slow, and was not of the gray.

I had seen a dog a week or so before, a big beast of a creature rendered thin and weak by starvation. Strains of gray had been clinging to its muzzle, places where it had fought the fungus for the remains of bigger, bulkier things. Dogs weren't made to digest fungus, were they? I had never cared enough about dogs to know. I vaguely remembered that cats were obligate carnivores, needing meat in their bellies if they wanted to survive, but were dogs?

Judging by the big black dog that had greeted me as I walked through the gray, if they weren't purely carnivorous, they weren't well-suited to an all-fungus diet, either. I didn't know if any mammals would be. Cows were herbivores, not fungivores. Maybe they could eat until they burst, and still starve.

The dog had been frail and slow, hampered by fungus growing in its fur, even if the gray hadn't seeped into its bones. It had shown me its teeth. I had shown it the crowbar I carried, and that night I had slept beneath a veil of gray with my belly full of dogmeat. It had been red and raw and hot, so hot, so much hotter than the world around me.

In a kinder world, we might have been friends, that dog and I. We might have been bosom companions, the two of us standing against all obstacles, my hand resting on its proud canine head, my daughter standing nearby, ready to roll her eyes and complain about the state of her wardrobe. Together, the three of us could have faced anything.

But the gray had taken Nikki to punish me for my hubris, in thinking that I could save her, and the gray had given the dog to me to keep me strong, because my punishment was not over, my punishment would never be over, and the gray wouldn't let me die. That would have been too merciful, too kind, and while the gray might be soft and all-covering as a child's favorite blanket, it was not merciful. Mercy had no business here, in the slow softness.

Neither did I, but still I moved through the gray world, and still the gray world moved around me. I had been walking for a very long time. I realized, with the dull surprise that was all that I could manage anymore, that I was tired. There was no reason to look for shelter—what could threaten me, the woman who moved through the gray and was not touched by it? There was no need to look for comfort, either. I stopped where I stood, dropping to the ground and stretching out in the spores and puffed filaments that covered whatever surface I had been walking on. Concrete or flowerbed, it didn't matter: the softness was everywhere.

I sank down deep into a mattress of mold, the dry, dusty scent of it filling my nostrils, and closed my eyes. Sleep came like a welcome friend, wrapping its arms around me and pulling me down into a better world, one where I was not alone, was not living my worst nightmare one aching, itching moment at a time—and where I didn't deserve exactly what I was living through. I would have slept forever, if I could have.

I slept so deeply that I never felt the tranquilizer dart, or heard the running feet. I didn't feel them lift me into the back of their truck, or notice when the gray world slipped away.

I just slept on.

• • •

The smell of antiseptic cleaning fluid and bleach tickled my nostrils like a long-lost friend, comforting and reassuring me. I sighed through the haze of wakefulness that was settling in all around me. Dreams of cleanliness were so rare these days, when it seemed like I would never be clean again, like the world would never be clean again. I didn't want to wake up. I didn't want to let this go.

"I think she's waking up."

The voice was male, unfamiliar and fast, so fast, more like the black dog (*so delicious, it had been so delicious, even as I hated myself for killing it*) than the soft gray world that had become my entire universe. I snapped the rest of the way awake, although I didn't open my eyes. I needed to know what was going on around me. I needed to know how much danger I was in.

One small, treacherous part of my mind relaxed its guard, uncurling and sending a wave of sudden peace washing over me, diluting my protective panic. If there were voices, if there were *people,* then the smells of bleach and cleaning fluid might be real, not just olfactory hallucinations. Bleach couldn't exist anymore, not since the gray had taken the stores and cleaning services. Sometimes I smelled it all the same, as my overtaxed mind attempted to create sense out of a world that had gone quietly, conclusively mad.

My body was waking up, whether I wanted it to or not. It began sending reports to my brain, things like "you need to use the bathroom" and "there is a pain at the crook of your left arm." The pain was almost encouraging. That sort of pain, in that sort of place, could mean an IV drip. I was dehydrated, I knew that: all the sources of standing water had been long since covered by the gray, and it hadn't rained in months. Drought conditions again. It had been a warm, dry winter, thanks to the changes humanity had made to the weather with our cheerful denial of global warming, before the gray had come along and made rising sea levels a moot point. Almost anywhere else in the country, I would have frozen. The gray would have frozen. But here, where the dry desert land met the unforgiving Pacific, thirst had been my greatest enemy.

There was a sort of clean, clear beauty in that. Thirst was the only thing that reliably killed the gray, the only thing that consistently cut it down and left it withered on the pavement. Fire would burn it clean, but the spores could survive. Desiccation, on the other hand, was the scourge from which even the gray could not recover, and desiccation was the death I had deserved.

Until this space, this clean-smelling space, and this needle in my arm. Someone was saving me. Someone was saving *me,* and I didn't know why, and I didn't deserve it.

"Has she said anything?" The new voice was female, older and slower than the first, filled with the weight of so many horrible things. It was a voice that had seen things it could not unsee, done things it could not undo *(the dog, the black dog in the gray world),* and it was closer to me than any human voice had been since Nikki had died.

The gray had taken her from me. The gray took everything, in time.

"Not yet." The first voice again. "She was pretty severely dehydrated, and she's malnourished enough that it's a miracle she was still alive."

"It's a miracle that any of us are still alive, Cadet." The female voice moved closer still as it spoke, until it was originating only inches from my face. "Since you are among the living, Dr. Riley, I suggest you open your eyes and start acting like it. Your future depends on it."

"I don't have a future." My voice was... rusty, almost, like the gray had eaten pits in its surface. How long had it been since I'd spoken? How many days, weeks, months since Nikki left me for the soft world, and I had no more cause to open my mouth for anything but eating and screaming? "I buried my future in the gray."

"Megan Riley. Civilian. Last known survivor of Project Eden. Two degrees, the first in molecular biology, the second in molecular genetics. Widowed early in the outbreak, when your spouse, Rachel Riley, succumbed to a *R. nigricans* infection. Am I ringing any bells, Dr. Riley, or shall I begin reading your daughter's school records? Where is Nicole?"

"Please stop." I did my best to shout. My voice was barely a whisper, soft and gray and featureless, like the great gray world outside.

"I would be glad to stop, Dr. Riley. Only open your eyes, and confirm that you are uninfected."

Opening my eyes would mean facing the fact that the clean white room I had constructed in my head was not a reality. It would mean going back to the gray, to the impossible ubiquity of the soft, broken world. I didn't know if I could bear that. But I knew I *couldn't* bear her saying my daughter's name one more time.

I opened my eyes. My pupils constricted in the glare from the lights overhead, an involuntary tear squeezing out of either eye. I didn't blink. I didn't dare.

The white room was real.

The walls were blank, featureless, devoid of any stains or rotten patches. I hadn't seen anything so beautiful since I'd pulled Nikki's smooth-polished skull out of the soft rot that had been her body. A mirror dominated one wall, reflecting back the scene in front of it: a skeletal mannequin of a woman in a white-sheeted bed, an IV connected to her arm, the bones of her own skull showing through the tight canvas of her skin like a palimpsest of the person she had been, before the gray world came and took it all away. I recognized and rejected myself in the same moment. I was irrelevant.

The woman standing next to my bed had short-cropped brown hair and wore Army green. Her face was hard but not cruel, the face of a woman who had taken a stand against the wolves of the world, and while she might not have won, she had at least acquitted herself admirably. There was a man on the other side of the cot, younger and thinner than the woman, occupying himself with the dials on the machine that controlled my IV drip. I couldn't really see his face, because of the way he was standing. His cheekbone looked melted somehow, like wax.

I looked away.

The smell of bleach and cleaning fluid was real; either that or my over-taxed mind had finally decided to reject the world as it was in favor of the world as I wished that it had been. I turned my head toward the woman in green, who had been waiting patiently while I got my wits about me.

"Dr. Megan Riley?" she asked again.

I nodded minutely.

"I am Colonel Handleman of the Army of the Commonwealth of North America," she said. "Do you confirm that you are Dr. Megan Riley, last surviving member of the Project Eden research team?"

So they were all dead, then: all those foolish men and women who had decided I didn't need to know about the contamination in their superfruit. They'd been trying to develop hardier, easier-to-grow produce that could thrive in the world's changing climate, produce that would shrug off things like droughts and flooding and early frost. Maybe they would have succeeded, if they hadn't accidentally engineered a flesh-eating strain of hyper-virulent bread mold first. Science was not a toy, and it objected to being treated like one.

"I was Megan Riley," I said carefully. "I'm not really sure anymore." Can a thing still be itself when it's removed from all context? Maybe I had died out there in the gray, and this was the afterlife. That would explain the clean white walls and the sweet smell of bleach. I was dead, and this was paradise.

"Your identity is enough, Dr. Riley," said Colonel Handleman. "I'm glad we found you. It is my duty to inform you that you are under arrest for treason against the former United States of America, the former nation of Canada, and the former United Mexican States."

Ah. I knew this had been too good to be true.

• • •

There were some questions after that—where had I been, what had I been doing, how much of Project Eden had I been aware of—but I could barely keep my eyes open long enough to answer them. I was exhausted, I was broken, and I was *done*. If they wanted to arrest me, let them. If they wanted to put me on trial for what my people had done, let them do that too. It was no less than I deserved. Maybe mine hadn't been the hand that held the test tube, but I had been the one who approved each procedure and test. The team had falsified data, and they had died for their crimes. I had believed their lies. Who was to say that my crime wasn't just as bad as theirs?

I don't know how long I was asleep. When I woke up, I was still in the white room, with the smell of bleach hanging in my nostrils. There was another smell underneath it, a deep, earthy smell. I wrinkled my nose automatically, rejecting it. This was the safe place. This was the *clean* place. There was no room here for smells like that one, which made me feel like spiders were running across the soft folds of my mind, looking for places to spin their webs.

"Ah, good, you're awake." Commander Handleman sounded almost cheerful. Maybe having someone to try for treason had improved her day. "Open your eyes, Dr. Riley. See what I've got for you."

I didn't want to. But she had been willing to talk about Nicole before, willing to remind me *(of the gray, the gray eating away at her, my little girl, her skull clean and polished and smooth in my hands)* what had happened to her. She didn't know the details. She didn't need to know the details. Anyone who had access to my files would be able to figure out that my wife and daughter were the most important things in my world. Rachel had died early. If Nicole wasn't with me, then she was dead too, and it was my fault, because I had been the lab manager for Project Eden. This was all my fault.

I opened my eyes.

Commander Handleman was dripping with mud. It was splattered liberally all up and down her uniform, but was thickest around her feet, where it was packed on so thick that the fabric was no longer visible. Tracks led back to the door, marking her progress across the room. She smiled when she saw me looking at her. Then she lifted her right foot and calmly, casually, stomped it on the floor. Mud splattered off of her in thick sheets, dark and terrible.

A high, keening noise sliced through the room, like a teapot announcing its contents were boiling. I realized belatedly that it was coming from my own throat. That didn't mean I could stop myself from making it.

"I've read all your files, Dr. Riley," she said, still smiling as she stomped her other foot and sent more mud cascading to the floor. "You always did an admirable job of managing your OCD. One of your colleagues—Henry Tsoumbakos, I assume you remember him—left a full confession before he succumbed to the *R. nigricans* infection. He attempted to absolve you of blame, said you hadn't been told about the contamination because of your disorder. He said you would have shut down the project over hygiene concerns. Wasn't that kind of him? He wanted to clear your name, even as the monster he created was stripping the flesh from his bones one cell at a time."

"Please stop," I whispered.

"So we looked a little deeper. This has been your personal hell, hasn't it, Dr. Riley? Did the death of your wife upset you as much as the sudden untidiness of the world? Mold everywhere, and nothing that was capable of killing it. Nothing but fire, anyway, and since there have been no reports of uncontrolled burns from the area you were known to be in, it's clear that you didn't take that route." Colonel Handleman abandoned her smile for a look of exaggerated, insincere sympathy. "Couldn't you find any matches?"

I didn't say anything. Asking her to stop wasn't doing any good, and if I opened my mouth again, the taste of mud would clot my tongue and stop my breath. It would kill me, I knew it would kill me, and I also knew that it would do no such thing, and *that didn't matter.* My pills had been gone for months. Nothing to put a fine pharmacological veil between me and the mud that was falling, in splats and blobs, to the floor.

"It's interesting. Most people with your sort of disorder fear germs, or obsess on little rituals. You got hung up on cleanliness. Everything had to be just so around your lab, every protocol had to be followed, every rule had to be observed. It's no wonder your people decided to stop telling you anything. Working under you must have been like following a preschool teacher to the ends of the world."

"There's no one true way to have OCD," I whispered. It was an old argument, one I'd been having over and over again since I was in high school, usually when some teacher wanted to say that the concessions I required were just me being a prissy little princess, and not a genuine function of my mental health. I didn't count. I didn't have a lot of really obvious rituals. Most of mine involved thinking of the right sequence of numbers when I dropped something, or always eating my food in a clockwise direction, no matter what sort of terrible food combinations that entailed. It was about separation, cleanliness, *order*, because when I failed to be perfect, that was when the walls would crumble, and the monsters would come.

I had known that simple fact all the way down to my bones for what felt like my entire life, even though I hadn't been formally diagnosed until I was eleven: if I slipped, even for a moment, if I allowed one speck of disorder to enter my life, then everything would fall apart. People had been telling me I was crazy for what felt like just as long. Well, guess what? I had slipped. I had allowed disorder to enter the world, and everything I loved had been burned away and buried in the gray. I wasn't crazy.

I was the only person in the world who was genuinely, unforgivingly sane.

"Maybe there's not one true way to have OCD, but you're the one whose mental issues were indirectly responsible for the creation and release of a bioengineered super weapon." She stomped her foot again. Another fat clot of mud detached from the leg of her uniform and fell to the floor with a sickening plop. I groaned.

"Anyone else, I would think you were afraid the mess would breed *R. nigricans* in a formerly safe environment. This mud has been thoroughly sterilized down to the molecular level—but you don't care about that, do you? All you care about is the mess. The nasty, awful mess."

"Why are you doing this?" I couldn't stop my voice from coming out broken and small, like the voice of a child. I wanted to scramble away from her, ripping the IV out of my arm and retreating to a place where the smell of bleach could still overwhelm the smell of wet, terrible earth. I didn't move. I was weak and she was strong; she would follow me, and she would grab me with those muddy arms, and she would hold me where I stood. I would die if she touched me. I would die.

"Because you seem to have given up, Dr. Riley, and I'm afraid that simply isn't an option. Less than two percent of the population had the right combination of cytokines and enzyme expression to resist the fungus. Immunity is very, very rare, and I suppose it's only poetic justice that saw it running through your veins. There are a great many people I would have saved in your place."

I didn't say anything.

"Then again, I suppose that's true for you too, isn't it? You would have saved your wife if you could have. You would definitely have saved your daughter."

"Don't talk about her." I glared from the safety of my bed, resisting the urge to shrink even further away from the mud that was covering the floor. "She's not for you. You don't talk about her."

"No? How about I talk about my three sons, instead? The eldest was about to graduate from college. He was going to be a high school teacher. I told him not to, told him that he'd never pay off his student loans on a teacher's salary, but he was determined. He wanted to help people. Isn't that nice? Wanting to help people? He tried to help a little girl who'd fallen on her way into the shelter. The scrapes on her hands spread your science project all over his skin. He died screaming, and he took his baby brother with him. Randal never could stay away from David when he thought his brother was in trouble."

Colonel Handleman took another step toward me. Her eyes were cold and hard. "My middle son, now, he was a special case. That combination of cytokines and specific enzyme expression that makes you so unappealing to the fungus is found almost entirely in the female population. Two percent of those exposed turn out to be immune, and ninety percent of those with immunity are female. But we didn't know that at first. Walter was exposed, and he was fine, and we thought he had won the same lottery that you had... that I had."

"A maternal parent with immunity can pass resistance to their offspring." My voice was a broken whisper, dry and desiccated and empty. "I'm so sorry."

"He stopped being careful. He thought he was safe—*I* thought he was safe—and so he stopped being careful, and he cut his finger. When the mold appeared, I thought he would fight it off." Colonel Handleman took another step forward. "It took a full week for *R. nigricans* to steal my boy from me. He died in his sleep. He couldn't even cry. There was no moisture left in him."

"I'm sorry," I whispered.

"Sorry doesn't bring my boys back, Dr. Riley. It doesn't bring your girl back either. You knew about the resistance, didn't you? You watched her die."

Images of Nikki, shrouded and swaddled in mold, danced across my mind. I tried not to focus on them. If I looked, if I showed them how much I cared, they would never go away. *(The black dog in the gray world, and Nikki, mermaid Nikki, with her tail of growing gray, beckoning from the shadows of the U-Haul that had been her tomb...)*

I swallowed. My mouth was dry as dust. "Yes," I admitted. "She got... she got sick, and I thought she was finding... finding equilibrium with the mold. I thought she was fighting. It was just eating her slower." So much slower. So slowly that I had had the time to remember what hope was, how it tasted on the tongue.

It tasted like ashes and failure and regret. Hope was the cruelest thing in the world.

"I won't say I'm glad that you had to live through that. From one mother to another, no one should have to watch their child die. Certainly not like *that.* A slow, cruel, inhumane death that I wouldn't wish on a dog." Colonel Handleman took another step. She reached out her hand and, before I could fully register what she was about to do, ran her fingers down my cheek, leaving cool wetness behind. She stepped back again.

"We're all dirty here, Dr. Riley." She smiled as I whimpered, and her eyes were cold, and there was no forgiveness there. Maybe there never could have been. "You made this mess. *You made it.* Every speck, every smear, every fruiting fungal body, it's all yours. It belongs to you. Now what are you going to do about it?"

She turned before I had a chance to remember what words were, walking calmly back to the door. She let herself out. The bolt clicked a moment later, and I was alone with the mess she had made, here in the ruins of the world I had destroyed.

The mud was drying on my cheek. I couldn't move. All I could do was sink lower into the bed, and close my eyes, and wait for the end to finally arrive.

• • •

This is the thing about OCD: everyone remembers the "compulsive" part. They remember the cleaning, the counting, the tapping, the little rituals that construct a scaffolding for a life that never seems stable enough to be real. When I first started dating Rachel, she seized on the way I always sorted my cafeteria fruit salad onto separate quadrants of a paper plate—grapes here, watermelon chunks there, strawberries somewhere else altogether, and pineapple in the remaining quarter. The sad bits of cantaloupe and honeydew had remained at the bottom of the bowl, slouching together like naughty children.

Rachel had stabbed her fork at them and asked, "Why?"

"Why what?" Even then, I had been helpless before her, a mere mortal stunned by the presence of a goddess. We'd met at a mixer for the school's LGBTQ association. She had spoken passionately about the need for more asexual and genderqueer representation, before asking me if I wanted to have pancakes. I had basically fallen in love before the syrup hit our plates.

"Why aren't you eating the melon?"

"Oh." That was the moment where all of my previous attempts at relationships had fallen apart: over something as small as a few chunks of melon in the bottom of a bowl. "They're too superficially similar to separate, but too different to eat together."

Rachel had blinked slowly, taking this in, before she'd asked, "So you don't eat them?"

"I don't eat them," I had said, and paused, waiting for her to tell me that I was too strange, that I was being unreasonable, that I was wasting food. I had tried countering all those arguments in the past. I had pointed out that everyone had food preferences, and that it wasn't my fault that the only fruit salad came with chunks of interchangeable melon. I had explained that I was afraid of developing an allergic reaction to one and identifying it as the other, which would make it impossible to keep my medical history straight. I had done all those things at one time or another, and all of them had failed.

Rachel had thought about this for a moment longer before she said, "I guess I'll be eating double melon." Then she had dipped her fork into my bowl, and I had seen the future unspooling in front of me like a beautiful dream. It had taken another three years before I could convince her to marry me. It had been worth every single day of trying.

Rachel had understood that for me, the compulsions were always second to the obsessions. I knew, in the place where most people know that gravity works and the atmosphere is unlikely to be sucked off into space, that if I made a mistake—just one—it would be the end of everything. I had known it since I was a child, when I had accidentally skinned my knees on the playground and ruined my new jeans, and my parents had told me they were getting a divorce that same night. I wasn't the most important person in the world. I wasn't special. I was just the one whose mistakes mattered more than anyone else's.

And here was the proof: the all-consuming softness, which had spread from the lab I managed, consuming *my* wife before it went on to satiate its hungers on everything else. The mistake had been mine: I had believed that my people would trust me, that they would tell me if something was going wrong in Project Eden. But like so many others before them, they had seen only the compulsions, only the cleanliness and order. They had seen me as the end of their grand experiments, and they had stayed silent.

If I had reviewed their work more closely, I might have been able to spot the holes where they hadn't fully documented their research. If I hadn't trusted them to trust me, my wife and daughter might still have been alive. All my life, the whispers in my head had said "you will destroy everything you love." And they had been right. They had been right all along.

My tears dampened the mud, but they couldn't wash it away. That was only fair. In a world that had sunk into a mess of my own making, I never deserved to be clean again.

● ● ●

Time was an inconsequential thing in this well-lit, semi-sterile room, with mud on the floor and the machines quietly, contentedly whirring along behind me. As long as I didn't open my eyes it could have been an hour, or it could have been a lifetime. The IV was keeping me hydrated, which would stave off death by dehydration. As my veins began to re-inflate and remember what it was to be whole, the rest of my body began sending signals that I would have been happier to ignore. Starvation had been my constant companion since Nikki left me, held back only by *(the black dog, running, gray strands on its fur, so trusting, so condemned)* what little I could scavenge out of the gray world. I had eaten more out of penance than out of hunger. I didn't deserve to die before the soft could claim me. If I waited long enough, if it ate enough of the world, it would find a way to swallow me as well.

All I'd needed to do was wait. But now here I was, and the gray was far away from me, and my penance was denied.

The IV fluids had restored enough of my bodily equilibrium that all the tears I hadn't been able to shed for the past few months were leaking out at once. They kept the mud on my cheek from drying completely, turning it wet and terrible as they fell. Every time they stopped I could feel it harden and crack, and then the tears would start again, until it started to seem like the IV was a useless affectation: I was pumping moisture out faster than I could possibly have been taking it in. Everything was white and bright and terrible. I had grown unaccustomed to hard lines and clean edges, spending my days walking through the soft gray world. I didn't know how to handle them anymore.

(*"I'll be eating double melon," Rachel had said, and she'd dipped her fork into the bowl, and I had been so consumed with loving her—so eaten alive by my own desires—that I hadn't stopped her, not then and not ever, even though I knew the melon was cursed. I had allowed her to cross so many lines, to break so many rules that I knew would lead to ruin. It had all begun with double melon. It had ended with the death of everything I'd ever loved.*

I should have seen this coming. I should have known there would be consequences.)

I had no way of knowing how long I lay there, crying but failing to wash the mud from my face, so overcome with hopelessness that the very idea of movement seemed like a cruel joke. At least if I had died outside I would eventually have gone into the gray and been reunited with my family. But I had allowed Rachel to eat the melon; I hadn't stopped her, even though I'd known there would be consequences. There were always consequences. My first and greatest mistake had been believing I could somehow avoid them forever.

The door hissed softly as it was opened. They probably had some sort of airlock system to keep the mold out; positive pressure combined with sufficiently thorough sterilization would do it. The anti-fungal drugs that had been in use at the beginning of the gray world hadn't worked, but if people had continued to search for better options—working even as their flesh dissolved into softness—they would have been able to find something. Human ingenuity always found a way, even if the cure was sometimes worse than the disease.

That led to a new, cruel thought, chilling as a hypodermic needle sliding under my skin: if I hadn't run, I could have been one of those researchers. I could have steered their work along the lines that had already been pioneered by Project Eden, and whatever advances they had made would have been immediately available to Nikki. Nikki, who had been uninfected when I pulled her out of the hospital and into the short, bitter life of a fugitive. I had done what I thought was best for her at the time, but how much of that had been my fear speaking? Fungus was messy. It was inherently unclean. I hadn't been prepared to live with a world where I could never be clean again, and so I had run, and I had damned my daughter in the process.

"Have you moved at all?" Colonel Handleman sounded more curious than anything else, like this was somehow a surprise. She had my files. She knew what she was doing with the mud on the floor—the mud on my *face*—and yet she was still surprised when she realized she had incapacitated me. "Don't you have to go to the bathroom?"

"Yes," I said, without opening my eyes.

"But you haven't moved."

"There's mud on my face," I said, like that explained everything—and it did, to me. If Rachel had been here, she could have translated for me. She could have pulled Colonel Handleman aside and said that this was not the way to make me answer questions or follow rules. But Rachel wasn't here. Rachel was part of the gray world, and the gray world was beyond me now.

"I see." There was a clank, and a sloshing sound. The smell of bleach became suddenly overpowering, washing everything else away. Something wet and warm hit my chest. I stiffened, terrified to find out what it was. After the mud, I wouldn't put anything past these people.

Colonel Handleman sighed. "Open your eyes, Dr. Riley. I promise it's something you'll like this time."

I opened my eyes.

The sponge was bright orange in the way of very artificial things, things that had been born in sterile rooms, crafted from synthetic polymers and steamed in a hundred cleansing vats before they were released into the messy, complicated world. It was covered in small, delicate soap bubbles, which popped even as I stared at them. The smell of bleach wafted off of it, and the smell was good.

"It's not a trick," said Colonel Handleman. "It's a mixture of bleach and Simple Green. Probably not great for your skin, and you shouldn't drink it, but it gets the job done surprisingly well. The adult fungus doesn't like Simple Green. The spores don't like the bleach."

"Bleach won't kill them," I said, forcing my hands to stay flat by my sides. I itched to grab that sponge, to scrub my face clean before starting on the rest of the room. I didn't trust her not to snatch it away as soon as I gave in. "I bleached the bowl that held the fruit that killed my wife, and the fungus just grew back." It sounded like a line from a children's song, misshapen and ugly in my mouth.

"Bleach won't kill them *all*," corrected Colonel Handleman gently. "It kills some. It kills enough to be useful."

There were two kinds of spore, reproductive and resting. Reproductive spores would be smaller, weaker, and more plentiful. Resting spores—chlamydospores—would be bigger, stronger, designed to survive in even the cruelest of conditions. They would be so much harder to kill. The structure of the fungus was a mixture of manmade and natural; it was as much a cousin to the plastic sponge on my chest as it was to the mushrooms that grew on the lawn after a stiff rain. It ate them too, those mushrooms; I had seen shelf fungus and toadstools decaying under a thick layer of soft grayness. Project Eden's accidental creation was as opportunistic as they came.

"Have you found a way to kill the chlamydospores?" I asked, despite myself. I looked toward her as I spoke. She had changed her uniform; the mud was gone, although I could still see it coating the floor, staining and profaning this clean place.

Colonel Handleman smiled, and while there was no joy in her expression, there was a certain cold triumph. "Not yet," she said. "Get yourself cleaned up. I'll be back in a little while."

She turned and walked out of the room. I glanced down automatically, to see what had made the sloshing noise when she first arrived.

The bucket of bleach and soapy water was the most beautiful thing I had seen since Nikki died. I was crying again. This time, I didn't care.

Getting out of bed was hard. My body was weak, worn down by months of wandering through the gray and waiting for it to take me. In the end, the only way to rise was to fall, pulling the IV out of my arm before tumbling gracelessly into a heap of skeletal limbs and bruised flesh beside the bed. I crawled to the bucket, the sponge in one hand, and I washed the mud from my face, and I began to wash the mud from the world.

I should have worn gloves. I should have worn thick jeans to protect my knees and legs from the chemical cleaners. All I had was a thin hospital gown and my bare skin, which had been dirty for so long. All I wanted was to be clean. So I knelt on the stained linoleum, bare skin to cold floor, and I scrubbed until my fingers were cracked and bleeding, until all traces of the mud had been long since obliterated; until I was washing the floor for the third time, and what little water remained in my bucket was as dark and muddy as day-old coffee. I cried the whole time. I was undoing the IV drip's good work, and that was fine, that was fine, because I was *clean*.

When I could scrub no more I dropped the sponge and collapsed where I was, face against the floor, surrounded by the good clean smell of bleach. For the first time since I had held my daughter's frail, fungus-ravaged skull in my hands, I did not dream.

I did not dream at all.

• • •

Colonel Handleman woke me with a toe to my ribs, prodding hard enough to hurt, but not hard enough to leave a bruise. "How're you feeling there, Dr. Riley? A little better? A little more like being a reasonable human being? Or shall we leave you to wallow in your own regrets for a few more days? I warn you, my superiors won't like it."

"Your superiors sent you to find me and arrest me for treason." I rolled over onto my back, staring at the ceiling, the blessedly clean, blissfully sterile ceiling. There wasn't so much as a spider's web to break the lines of the walls. Paradise. "I'm not sure what they could tell you to do to me." Even as I spoke the words I knew that I was wrong, and felt the weight of my mistake press down on me like a mountain.

They could lock me in a room filled with sewage. They could talk about the six billion dead, the end of civilization, and when that didn't hurt enough, they could find every picture of Nikki and Rachel that had been preserved on computers and in school records. They could play me an endless slideshow of what I had lost. They could sit down and explain, in slow, cruel detail, how all of this was my fault, and I would believe them, because they would be telling the truth. There was so, so *much* that they could do to me, and I would deserve every agonizing bit of it. I always had.

"They could tell me to release you," said Colonel Handleman calmly. "You would always know that there was a safe haven somewhere in the world, a place where things were still—what's the word? Ah, yes. Clean. You would know that you had been rejected, and when we inevitably fell to the rot, you would know that it was your fault. The world would collapse, and if you lived long enough to see it, you would be fully aware that every person who succumbed did it with your name on their lips."

I stared at her. "You wouldn't."

There was no mercy in her eyes; no forgiveness. There was only the same bleak look that had graced the black dog before I brought the crowbar down on its skull; the emptiness that had lurked in Nikki's face as the softness leeched her life away. "Try me."

I sat up, hands slipping on the still-damp floor. "What do you *want?* You say I should start acting like a reasonable human being, but you haven't given me anything to be reasonable *about.*"

"Oh, I'm sorry, Dr. Riley; I assumed that you would have figured it out by now, a smart lady like you." She leaned closer. "You made this mess. We want you to clean it up."

I blinked at her slowly. "What?"

"We want you to fix it. Whatever you require will be provided, and at the end, you'll walk away a free woman. No charges, no consequences, just your own conscience. We'll even keep your role in the original outbreak quiet. It's easier now, with most of the media destroyed. You could be a hero, if that was what you wanted."

It wasn't what I wanted. What I wanted was a little house with an art studio in the spare bedroom, and a laughing, dark-eyed woman eating the melon I couldn't bring myself to touch. What I wanted was a teenage girl curling her lip at the sight of her mothers dancing around the living room like goons. What I wanted was dead and gone and buried, and it was never coming back.

But there was a mess to be seen to. There was a mess, and there was a secret somewhere that would give me the right combination of chemicals, the right sequence of enzymes, to clean it up and beat it back. I sat up.

"You said that two percent of the population had the right combination of cytokines and specific enzyme expression."

"Yes."

"What degree of the population has one of the two, and what percentage of them showed resistant traits before succumbing?"

"I don't know, but I could get you the figures."

"How many people are left?" This was the big question: this was the one without which nothing else mattered. Too few, and we might as well be like Nikki, like Rachel, like the black dog—we might as well go into the gray, and let the softness have dominion over all.

Colonel Handleman smiled slowly. "Enough."

This wouldn't make amends. This wouldn't bring back what had been lost. I had allowed Rachel to eat the melon, I had allowed Nikki to steal the juice; I had done this to the world. It was only fair and just that I should have to set it right.

I picked myself up from the bleach-covered floor, watching Colonel Handleman all the while. "I'm going to need some clothes," I said.

"That can be arranged," she replied. "Welcome to the cleanup crew, Dr. Riley."

"Thank you," I said.

There was work to do.

WANDERING STAR

Leife Shallcross

*xhibit 42: "Jessie's quilt." An extremely rare early 21st Century Australian me-
mento quilt. Artist unknown. Various fabrics.*

*This textile work is unusual firstly because it has survived such a tumultuous
period in history, but also because it appears to have been primarily assembled from fabric
cut from children's clothes, rather than from the purpose-produced craft fabric widely
available in Australia in the early 21st Century. Due to the variety of fabrics used, the
age of the quilt and the item's likely early history, it is extremely fragile.*

*It has been assembled by a combination of hand- and machine-piecing and is hand-
quilted. An embroidered inscription on the back reads "For Jessie, love Mum, 2017."*

• • •

I realize I've been sitting in my car, in my driveway, staring into space
for at least ten minutes. It's a perfect day. The sun is shining. The garden is
flourishing. There's the possum box in the tree by the gate, with the possum
asleep inside it. I can just see her ears from where I'm sitting. Her baby will
be curled up at the back.

I hear jubilant shouts from the back garden, and Jessie stumbles into
view, laughing. She's soaked to the skin. She turns and hurls a water bomb
at her little brother.

I look down at the bags of shopping on the seat beside me. I spent the
last bit of money in my account on cans of baked beans and packets of
pasta. There weren't any matches. Gavin has been stocking up on petrol. At
the checkout, I caught myself assuming I'll have the opportunity to shop
again when I get paid next week. Then it dawned on me: This is it.

• • •

Twelve blocks make up the quilt, each constructed using three distinct fabrics in a traditional nine-patch pattern known as Wandering Star. The three fabrics in the first block are: A cotton flannelette printed with a pattern of pink rabbits; a pink and white striped cotton terry cloth; and a cotton/polyester fabric in lilac that has been machine smocked and machine embroidered with small, pink roses. All three are typical of early 21st Century infants' clothing.

• • •

I can't send them. I can't let them go. When I think about it, I can't breathe. These little people I've raised and loved. I've patted them to sleep until my hand is numb. I've worried about how long to breastfeed them, spent hours pushing organic vegetables through a sieve. I've read to them or sung them songs every night of their lives. I've attended their soccer games and harangued them to do their music practice and their homework. I've found lost library books and made emergency dashes to school with forgotten lunch bags.

I have spent the last eleven years looking after every aspect of their lives. And they trust me to do just that. To keep doing that.

How can I send them away? Who else is ever going to do even half of what I've done for them?

• • •

Block three comprises three cotton fabrics: a fine, blue denim, with remnants of decorative patches applied to it; a white cotton poplin with red polka-dots; and a pink cotton knit fabric that appears to be stained with colored paint.

• • •

I lug the bags inside. Gavin is sitting on the couch watching the TV, but not in a relaxed way. He looks alert, as though he's about to hear something critical. Some news anchor is interviewing a scientist again. My fingers itch to turn it off. There's not going to be anything new.

Ever since the news broke a week ago, there's been endless rehashing of what will happen. Fireballs and blast waves. Megatsunamis. Global quakes. Rains of fire and clouds of ash hiding the sun for years. This guy is usually the one with the fun facts. Now he just looks gray. His is the face of the bearer of unbearable knowledge. He's got kids.

Gavin turns to watch me come in the door. His face is serious.

"They've announced ground zero," he says. "It's going to come down forty K north of Bathurst."

So close.

"The Government is telling us not to panic," says the TV interviewer earnestly.

"Panic is futile," says the scientist. "It won't stop the impact."

• • •

Block four is something of an enigma. Many of the other blocks in the quilt are made of fabrics that have a generally feminine quality to them. Block four is comprised of three fabrics with an overall masculine theme. The first is a soft, pale blue polyester/cotton velour. The others are: a black cotton flannelette with a pattern of skulls-and-crossbones in bright colors; and a cotton drill in a blue-toned camouflage print.

• • •

The next news item is about the Government's negotiations with key allies to take the children. They announced that last night.

That's how bad it will be. Until I heard about that, I had fantasies of survival. A comforting triptych of flight, resurgence, and ultimate triumph playing out in my head.

I make tea for me and coffee for Gavin, wondering how long fresh milk will continue to be part of our lives. I take the drinks over to join him on our much-beloved leather couch, worn to scuffed softness from its years of service to uncareful children. I'll endure the horror of the news for one more chance to sit quietly next to my husband drinking hot tea while the kids yell happily in the background. I lean into the solid warmth of his shoulder, his thigh against mine, and stare at the talking heads on the screen.

How can the outlook be that grim?

"Is it really going to be any better anywhere else?" I ask. Gav shrugs. The TV flashes up hotlines for parents who want to arrange billeting for their kids in the U.K., Canada or the U.S. Just the kids, though. The world is only prepared to take the children. They won't let the rest of us off this doomed continent.

Gav shakes his head.

"Once it hits, the whole world is going to turn to hell," he says.

What are my two kids, not even teenagers, going to do on their own? Who knows if they'll even be together?

All I can think about is the footage they play of those tiny, forlorn human beings from the 1940s, rendered in black and white, leaving the ships clutching their cardboard suitcases and staring about with big, frightened eyes. The stories they tell of brothers and sisters who never saw each other again, children who were never reunited with their parents. I remember watching the official Government apology, so many years later, to the abandoned, the abused and the forgotten. The children who languished in cold institutions, or were delivered into the hands of the unscrupulous. Why should it be different this time? There are so many reasons to think it will be worse.

Nate runs past the window carrying a giant, pump-action water gun. His seven-year-old grin is gap-toothed, and his hair stands up in wet spikes.

I can't send them.

I don't even have anyone overseas. No relatives outside Australia. No one to take them in and love them even a fraction as much as I do. No one who will fight to feed them once the skies have darkened and the fields and orchards are burning.

• • •

Block six is strikingly rendered in red, black and white. These fabrics appear to have been cut from a school uniform; the name of the school is partially visible on the pieces of red cotton knit. The other fabrics are a polyester/cotton gingham in red and white, and a black cotton drill. This block has been ornamented with a red, satin hair-ribbon stitched across the star.

• • •

"Jess said her teacher wasn't there today," I tell Gav while I make dinner. "Nate's teacher was, but he said another year three teacher didn't turn up and half the kids weren't there anyway."

"Yeah, they said they'll close all the schools by the end of next week," says Gav. "I want to leave before then, though."

"Should we send them to school tomorrow?" I ask. I don't know whether to try and act normal for them, or just keep them home with me and… and what? Hug them all day?

"Yeah, send them," says Gav. "It'll give us a chance to pack. Sort through some stuff."

For a moment I want to protest. He's so fucking practical. You'd almost think he wasn't fazed by this whole End of the World thing. When they announced it, he just went straight into operational mode, focusing on getting us ready to go. But I know he's right about tomorrow. And it might be the last chance for them to hang out with their friends.

"Tina is sending her kids overseas," I say.

I don't know why I've mentioned it. I can't stand to think about it.

"I saw her at school today. She got them both tattooed."

"What?" He gives me an incredulous look.

"Their names and birthdays," I explain, "with the other one's name and Tina's and her husband's names underneath."

"Jesus," says Gav.

I thought she was crazy at first, but now I wish I'd done it too. When I drove past, the tattoo parlor was closed.

Gav puts his arm around me, and I realize I'm staring into space again, my eyes full.

"We're not sending them anywhere, baby," Gav assures me. "They're staying with us."

But what can we do to keep our kids safe anywhere? What if we don't send them with the rest and something happens to us?

God, I want them to know how completely they are loved, how much I wanted a different life for them.

• • •

The backing fabric is a cotton sheeting fabric in a floral print. It has been identified as a Laura Ashley duvet cover from a children's range produced in 2008.

• • •

Once the kids are in bed, Gav starts getting out the camping gear and piling it in the hall. If I ignore what's on television, I can almost imagine we're just planning a weekend down the coast. But we're not. In a few weeks, there won't be a coast anymore.

The reality is, no place on Earth will be unaffected. There are places—New Zealand, Papua New Guinea, Hawaii, any Pacific island you care to name—that will be obliterated almost as surely as the east coast of Australia. Everywhere else is going to burn and starve.

So very few got away. Eleanor went to her sister in London before they closed the borders. She left straight away, took almost nothing. Their beautiful house stands empty. Renovated just last year, filled with antiques and electronics... all useless now. I suppose it will all just burn, unless it's looted first. I doubt I'll ever see her again. My daughter will never play with Isabelle again—the best friend she's known since preschool. They'll never again sit in the tree house together, with bare feet and icy poles, singing along to pop music playing on Jessie's iPod.

• • •

Block seven is known as the "Green Block." A logo of a tree or clouds, surrounded by the words "Green Team," has been screen-printed on two of the fabrics: an apple-green cotton knit and a basic undyed calico. The third fabric is a lightweight blue denim showing ingrained grass stains.

• • •

There was supposed to be a P&C meeting at the school tonight, to plan the Sustainability Fete next month. I remember it when I go to put out the recycling and the rubbish. I have no idea if anyone will come to collect the bins tomorrow. I stand out on the street in the dark, wondering what it was all for. All those efforts to save the environment. The Great Barrier Reef, the Murray-Darling River Basin. What a joke.

• • •

The fabrics used to construct block eight are: a plain, light blue polyester/cotton, a bright blue synthetic knit that appears to have come from a uniform for a football club, and a white coarse-weave cotton printed with a design based on the artwork of young children. Names are visible in two of the white pieces: Jessie, age 5, and Isabelle, age 4¾. This block is ornamented with a number of Australian Girl Guides achievement badges.

• • •

I harangue the kids into getting ready for school the next morning. We ride down on our bikes. There's only half as many kids in the main quadrangle as usual—playing handball, climbing on the monkey bars. I catch snatches of conversation from other parents. Most people seem to be waiting for the authorities to tell them what to do. I remember the newscast from last night. "Don't panic" is manifestly inadequate. There are so many questions and so little information. How far west do we have to go? Will there be evacuation centers? Will there be any point?

When I get back home, Gav has the TV on again. And, once again, instead of anything actually useful, the news is filled with a bunch of rhetoric on the Great Australian Spirit. *Pulling Together In A Crisis. Helping Out Our Mates.* The fact is, we're going to need international aid. Us. Australia. It's laughable.

I go into Jessie's room to get some clothes together. She's put her blue Girl Guides uniform on the bed. *Shit,* I think, *it's Wednesday.* She has Girl Guides on Wednesday. I don't know whether to laugh or cry. This is the first time she's ever remembered to put it out on her own.

Jesus, Jess. Now?

• • •

Block ten has suffered the most distortion over time, due to the differing fabrics used in its construction. The pale yellow polyester/cotton knit has a printed design that suggests it was taken from a souvenir T-shirt from New Zealand. The rayon fabric is a traditional block-printed sarong pattern from Fiji. The third is a black cotton base, heavily embroidered with rayon thread and decorative beads, most likely from Bali, Indonesia.

• • •

Later in the morning, the news gives us stories of protests in China and India over the prospect of an influx of Australian refugees. We burned those bridges long ago, it seems. Our more traditional allies are a little more sympathetic. But it's clear they have their own set of problems to deal with, and are as baffled as we are about what to do.

What will we be to a world where resources are grown scarce and whole countries are no longer habitable? Where an entire continent of twenty-three million (give or take the few million who will perish in the impact) are suddenly displaced and looking for new homes? Not to mention all those from any of the other countries that will be destroyed by the repercussions. Japan's population is close to one hundred and thirty million, for God's sake.

How can we expect compassion and generosity when everyone else will be scraping for survival?

• • •

Block twelve is remarkable. The three fabrics are all distinctly older than the other textiles used to construct the quilt. The oldest fabric is a white linen, dated to the early 20th century, showing signs of severe yellowing from age. It is decorated with pin-tucks and hand embroidery characteristic of christening gowns from that period. The cotton floral print has been dated to the 1970s. The third fabric is a synthetic knit with a nautical motif that suggests it came from an item of boy's clothing from the 1960s or early 1970s.

• • •

The phone rings as Gav and I are finishing lunch. We're drinking one of the few bottles of wine we have stashed in the cupboard. No point keeping it now.

It's Mum.

"Hi sweetie," she says, all super-charged sunshine like she gets when she wants to rope me into something.

Mum, I mouth at Gav and roll my eyes.

"I thought we'd better talk about what we're going to do."

For a moment, I don't understand.

"What are we going to do when?" I ask.

"Where we're going to go, when we'll leave," she says. The undertone of anxiety in her voice suddenly registers.

"Oh." I glance at Gav. He's looking at me with a frown on his face. "Well, Gav and I are thinking about leaving tomorrow. Beat the weekend rush. Maybe make it as far as Adelaide by Friday."

Silence.

"You're going on your own?"

Shit.

"No, Mum," I lie.

It's too late. There's a breathy gasp.

"You were going to go…" Her voice cracks. "Did you even think of helping me get your Dad out of here? What about your brother?"

"Calm down, Mum," I tell her. "Of course I was going to call." *Lie.* "I've just been so flat out." *Truth.* "Can you give me a few minutes? I'm in the middle of something." *Lie.* "I'll call you back. Calm down. I love you." *Truth.*

I hang up. For a moment, the guilt is intolerable, and then it is obliterated by an unexpected burst of fury. How could *she* think that *I* could think about anything other than how to keep my children safe and alive? *Look after yourself!* I want to cry at her.

My resentment burns up as quickly as it engulfed me. I stare at the phone in my hand.

How could I forget about my own mother? How could I be angry at her wanting to come with us? Be with her grandkids?

This terrifies me more than anything. Is that where I'm headed? Where we're all headed? Are we going to lose the ability to look out for anyone but ourselves? What does my response to my own mother say about what we can expect from our friends? From our compatriots on the other side of the country? From the rest of the world?

Gav reaches across the kitchen counter for my hand.

"Go over. Sort them out," he says. There's a tremor in his voice I haven't heard before. "Family's got to stick together."

He meets my gaze steadily, even though his eyes are swimming. His folks are in Brisbane, twelve hundred kilometers north. He may never see them again.

• • •

Jessie's quilt is not only remarkable for surviving the catastrophic asteroid impact of 2017 and the chaos of the subsequent decades. What makes this artwork so special is that the fabrics it has been constructed from provide us with a unique window into the lives of Australian families in the early 21st Century. We may never know anything about Jessie, or her family, or where in Australia she lived her early life. But in the scraps of clothing that Jessie's mother has pieced together, we are able to see glimpses of Jessie's childhood. And something more: This quilt is also a clear statement of a mother's love for her daughter; a statement that has transcended a period of the grimmest global adversity, to survive to the present day. We can only speculate upon the story of the little girl for whom this quilt was constructed, and hope that, like her quilt, she was a survivor.

HEAVEN COME DOWN

Ben H. Winters

Pea rises slowly on unsteady legs, her body reeling, her flesh tingling, as her mind fills with the impossible voice of God.

NOW it says, booming like cannon fire, rolling thunder, deeply melodic like the notes of the organ—NOW WE CAN BEGIN.

Imagine! Imagine how she feels to hear it now—to hear at last, after lifelong absence, to hear in her mind the overpowering unmistakable majestic voice of almighty God.

When at last she has found her feet she stands bewildered and shivering, looking all around her, down beyond the fence line into the bubbling firepits of the outskirts, back toward the shabby towers of the city. She does not see God, as she knows she will not. Even as she looks, bewildered and tearful, she knows that He is invisible, heard but never seen. This is how He was always described by everyone she knew, for all of Pea's life, while she pretended: God is everywhere and nowhere. Not to be seen, only to be known.

She doesn't see Him, but at last—at long, long last!—she is hearing Him, hearing Him speaking, hearing His deep rolling voice like the waves of an endless ocean.

YOU ARE READY FOR ME NOW CHILD, AS I AM FOR YOU.

That voice! Confident and strong. A bear; a saint; a gentle and condoling giant. God's voice after a lifetime of its absence is a lush breeze tickling the surface of a placid pond. It soothes her and it enlivens her, after the ravishment and confusion and fear of the last two days. She tilts her head up and smells the sulfurous bubbling odor of the outskirts. She is still standing at the fence, where she and Robert were dragging the bodies for disposal. They had set themselves the task of disposing of all of the corpses, the bodies of everyone in the world but them, one at time. And then suddenly Robert attacked her, tried to add her body to their number, and just as suddenly she found incredible powers inside of herself, and she used them, by wild instinct, to send him over the edge, to his own burning drowning death.

All of it now seems like a dream from which she has awakened. God's voice is a new day. God's voice is a curtain rising.

THE NEW WORLD CAN BEGIN, says God, and His voice is a bell tolling a new day. Now Robert is gone and everyone is gone and it's only her, her alone—thirteen years old and the last person in the world, alone at last with the God she's waited on for so long.

YOU ARE WHOLE NOW AND THE WORLD CAN BEGIN, says God, His voice like deep glorious bells tolling.

And Pea whispers, "What do you mean?"

WORK, CHILD. IT IS TIME TO GET TO WORK.

A shiver of joy rushes through her. *Yes of course. Yes it is time to get to work.*

She turns away from the outskirts fence and starts to make her brisk way back to the city.

• • •

Yesterday morning everybody died. Everybody had heard the word of God in their ear, for all of their lives, everybody except for Pea. God some years ago had begun telling the people of the world when and how they were to "go through," and yesterday everybody obeyed. Now only Pea is left, and she makes her way back through the world that has been left behind, back toward the barren city, feeling stronger and stronger, surer and surer with each step, more powerful as she goes.

Because at last God is speaking to her too. No—not to *her too*. To her, *only*.

CHILD, He says, and she stops and closes her eyes and tilts her head back as if to receive the glow of the sun.

EVERYTHING IS BROKEN.

Pea feels a rush of unease. *Broken?* She wrinkles her brow and blinks. The word is frightening, and she isn't sure what He means. But God only says BROKEN again, a note of heavy grief coating His mighty voice.

Broken.

When she re-enters the city limits she sees at once what He means. It is not that everybody is dead, and that the world is empty. The world has *always* been broken, that's what Pea can see now—it's always been broken, and Pea has never noticed it before.

She continues to walk, this way and that, turning left or right at the intersections, stepping around the empty vehicles and under the awnings of empty shops. God does not tell her where to go. She wanders of her own will. *Broken.* She finds herself standing under the shadow of a skinny brown tree in a small traffic island in the dead center of the city. She sees how small the world is, how small it always has been. The world she had thought of as complicated and enormous—the whole world!—now feels pint-sized, a toy landscape. A simple grid.

And it's *broken.* The buildings are decrepit. The buildings are tall and glass walled, but they are tilting and the glass is streaked and stained. Doorway beams sag. Cornices are jagged at their edges, where bits of stone have fallen away. The statues of the founders, which stand slightly tilted here and there, presiding over deserted street corners, are rusted, covered in bird shit.

The world that Pea has always loved, the only world she has ever known, is revealed to her as it always has been: worn and old.

LET US BEGIN.

"Begin—begin to what?"

But God just repeats Himself: LET US BEGIN.

Pea smiles. It's a tiny little smile, almost a giggle, and after all Pea is still a child—for all that she has experienced and is experiencing now, Pea is just a kid. Last week she was running around the yards, arguing with her parents, alternating giddy wildness with sulky preteen irritation. Just last night Robert snuck into her bedroom and confessed his crush, and would have kissed her, had she let him.

Another life—another time.

CHILD—DEAR CHILD—

It's not a command. God is not insisting. It is a loving suggestion, a sweet urging. There is only one answer. To begin. And so Pea begins.

Let's call this the morning of the first day.

Pea surveys the leaning brown towers one by one. She stops across the road from Building 32. She remembers her friend Arno, who lived here. She was a funny sweet girl, with big laughing eyes. (Dead now. Everyone is dead.) The building is empty. The door hangs half open. A pane of glass in one of the first-floor apartments is cracked down the middle like a lightning bolt.

As Pea watches, a drift of rust comes loose from a fifth-floor balcony and tumbles down like dirty snow, all the way to the ground.

MY CHILD… says God, and she blinks and then begins:

She stares at the unsightly brick pile of Building 32, and then with a surge of that same unexpected power she felt when Robert attacked her, she holds up her hands toward the building, palms out and fingers splayed, and the structure begins to crumble—slowly first, brick by brick, pane by pane, and then faster, stones and sheets of glass sliding down and smashing down, the foundation collapsing inward layer by layer with a series of reverberant booms. Pea gives a girlish gasp and brings her hands up to her mouth, in awe of what's happening, astonished by the beautiful devastation she has wrought.

A moment later it is done: Building 32 has collapsed in upon itself, and dust billows outward from the ruin.

PEA, says God with pleasure, and Pea whoops and hops up and down, wide-eyed, girlish, and inside of her mind God laughs, a warm grandfatherly laugh.

She wheels around. In an island in the center of the road, across from where Building 32 had stood, is a statue that Pea remembers from her visits with Arno, a statue she never loved: a mother and child, holding hands and looking up searchingly at the empty sky. Pea makes a kind of snorting noise and concentrates her mind on the statue for a second or two until it smokes and then bursts, first the woman and then the girl, like popping kernels of corn. The pieces of burning metal leap up into the air and then tumble down but do not hurt her. A flock of small birds, startled by the noise, wheel off and scatter into the sky.

Pea's eyes widen with pleasure. Just down the road is Building 34, its yellowed paint peeling around the corners of the front door. Pea focuses her eyes upon it and raises her hands.

• • •

And so it goes, all of the first day and into the night—and into the second day and into second night, this is how it goes. Pea working unceasing, never tiring, never slowing. God is always with her, never issuing instructions, only gentle praise. She simply walks about, from the downtown area outward through the winding streets, building by building, tree by tree, working her will on the ugly old world. She works according to her own instincts, leaving certain buildings alone, razing whole blocks when the mood strikes.

And then, by the end of the second day Pea is no longer destroying, but creating.

Still using only her mind and her spirit, still never stooping, never breaking a sweat, she clears the ruins of the buildings she has brought down, and begins to bring up new structures in their stead. She goes back to the site of Building 32 to start, when the idea hits her, and where the worn ugly old glass tower had stood she imagines a twisting glass palace with exactly one hundred rooms, each one a different color, and no sooner does she think of it than it is so.

She returns to all of the rubble fields she has made and fills them with new constructions. Each one is a marvelous structure, architected from her merriest imagining. Here a gingerbread house; here a stately mansion; here a child's dollhouse scaled up to human size. Where thick and squat Building 19 had stood there rises a great climbing tree of a building, with rooms tucked away inside of it like squirrel-holes in tree knots.

Pea claps her hands with delight. She spins. The world, the new world rises up around her.

YOU ARE DOING WELL, says God, and Pea beams. YOU ARE MY POWERFUL CHILD.

His voice is rich and calm. It is a vast starry horizon, stretching out silver before her glittering eyes.

• • •

And on the third day, at last, Pea comes to The Center, a massive circular cathedral with many glass windows and many doors. She sighs and crosses her arms, feeling somewhat uneasy. It is hard to believe that Pea spent her childhood, spent her whole life, in thrall of this lousy glass-eyed building. And why? Because it was this building and the people inside of it that her parents were always so fearful of, because if the Center workers were to have discovered that Pea was deaf—that she could not hear the Word of God—they might have taken her away. They might have insisted to Pea's parents that they leave her behind.

Well everyone is gone now. The Center workers, Pea's parents, everyone is gone. Only Pea is left. Pea smiles a crooked smile. She tilts her head and raises a finger, and the Center bursts open from the inside, and when the dust clears she rebuilds it in the shape of a birthday cake, with no doors, a form to be admired but never entered.

She stands then, trembling, fearful for the first time that God will be displeased at what she has done to His church.

PERFECT, he says. BEAUTIFUL.

Pea unclenches. She closes her eyes. "Thank you," she says.

She carries on. Third day into the fourth. Building by building, site by site, she makes the ugly old world better than it was.

• • •

The world had always looked like this. As long as Pea had been alive. She had never seen it, but it had always looked like this. Ever since it was settled, by the grandfathers' grandfathers' grandfathers' generation. They who had been left behind by the others, the ones who had journeyed on, in search of a habitable planet. This group, Pea's ancestor's group, they were to *wait here*, to *make do*, until the others returned.

But the others had never returned. Year after year, decade after decade, the founders had done as instructed. They had *waited here*, they had *made do*.

And just when despair might have begun, the voice of God started coming. Jennifer Miller in Building 14 first heard the voice of God, and then others did, and then everyone did. There was never any reason to struggle, to make the world beautiful and habitable, because God had told them the future, and the future was short. Soon they would all go through. This was something Robert had always been pointing out; something that had saddened and angered him about the God-days—how after Jennifer Miller, after the voices started, everyone became so enamored of the death to come that they forgot to be alive. Everyone was so busy waiting for heaven to come down, they stopped seeing the world, and the world had thus been slowly falling to bits.

It had made Robert so frustrated. Pea smiles now to think of him, sputtering and sighing and adjusting his glasses on his nose.

It really was a shame that he hadn't lived for this, to see how Pea was taking their old world and making it shine. Making it glorious after all.

Pea notices a hideous vehicle dock at the end of a row of towers, and the structure disintegrates, all at once, into a cloud of dust, and when the dust clears there is a field of grass, just as Pea had pictured it in her head, dotted with great green trees dripping with bright yellow flowers.

This is all that Robert had wanted, after all, she thinks sadly. To make things look nice. To make their world a beautiful world.

And now, as Pea surveys her newest creation, a shadow falls across her heart.

It is almost sundown now—sundown on the third day. Pea has not heard God for hours.

Along with that small and frightening realization comes a new voice. Soft, soft. She almost can't hear it.

be careful

Pea's body tightens. She hunches forward, cocks her head to one side, as if to hear better, even though the voice is inside of her, even though she hopes it won't speak again. But it does speak—

be smart

It's a gruff whisper, a rusted knife-edge, jagged and cold.

be warned

Pea doesn't like it. Unease roils her stomach, in part because she can't tell who or what this voice is. The voice of God had been so obvious, so self-evident. She had been waiting for it all her life, and then suddenly there it had been. But *this* voice, this voice is unfamiliar; it has a raspy quality, a darkness that hovers about it like a deep red mist.

do not trust it says. *do not*—

And then nothing.

Pea breathes in the deserted street, surveying what she has done thus far. She waits to hear God, hoping he will fill the silence, but there is nothing now—only silence in the lonely world.

She goes about her work, resolutely, deciding for now to ignore this new voice. She marches on, bites her lip, narrowing her eyes. She finds her own old building, Building 49, the one where she was born and raised, where her parents died, where she and Robert dragged them out of the kitchen and down the tower stairs. She blinks her eyes and turns the building into a vast play structure, with slides and ladders and swings.

• • •

She feels, right away, when she wakes on the morning of the fourth day, that everything has changed.

There are still many buildings to go, many ugly tilting electrical poles to be dealt with, but Pea feels fitful and restless. She still has the power, but no longer the glory. She just ducks her head toward whatever building she intends to bring down, just sighs and watches as it tumbles. The three previous days she has felt magical, powerful, glorious, and now she feels like a drudge, like some sort of supernatural construction worker. Boom! A building falls. Pow! A new one rises from its footprint. And again. And again.

"What for?" she thinks, and then she says it out loud. "Why?"

COME, says God.

And Pea, less trusting than she was, less in love with the voice of God, says "Where?"

COME NOW.

"Where?"

God leads Pea's footsteps back to the outskirts, back to the edge of the built world. Along the fence line, where Robert had tried to kill her and she killed Robert instead. Where first she heard the voice, and it brought her to her knees. She understands that God *knows*—of course He knows, for He is God and knows everything—He knows that she is growing weary, growing skeptical. Some new miracle is in the offing, and it tightens the fibers of her gut. She arrives at the outskirts and sets her eyes on the bubbling sulfurous pools beyond the fence, and feels the power surge through her and watches in astonishment as the bubbling noxious deadly surface bubbles up and evaporates and disappears into the air. It pops and fizzes as it raises off the earth, and there is a strong smell and then no smell at all—and there, revealed at the bottom of the sea floor are the bodies of

Pea's parents. Her mother and father, who had argued over her and coddled her and tried to protect her for all the days of her life.

The bodies are not decayed, but whole. Though they have been lying at the bottom of the consuming red sea they look like they've been asleep.

BEGIN.

"But—"

MY DEAR BEGIN.

no

That other voice, the low contrarian, makes itself louder, gets agitated.

no—

She ignores the protesting voice. She can't help herself. She focuses on the dead bodies on the floor of the sea and angles her head, tilts her chin, narrows her eyes—and she melts the fence, and she keeps staring, and the ground groans and rises miles of red seafloor rising upward until it levels with the abutting beach and it is one vast field of earth, and she keeps staring and the bodies rise and walk toward her.

Pea's body fills with fear. She stumbles backward.

no says the protesting voice—*no, you know better*—while God says NOT ALONE, YOU NEEDN'T BE ALONE—and the shambling corpses of her dead parents raise their hands to her, and their flesh is restored but their eyes are all white, nothing but white.

No says the hidden voice and now Pea screams with it, "No!" and shakes her head violently and screams and lets the power cease flowing, and watches as the bodies of her parents slump to the ground like the corpses they were and always had been.

In the pause that follows there are no voices, there is no sound at all, and everything begins to drain out of Pea: her faith and her joy and her spirit. It burbles downward in her like water funneling out of a tub. Pea shuts her eyes and life is a dream, but she opens her eyes because it's not a dream. It's all real, and she has to find out what is happening.

"Who are you?"

God doesn't answer.

you see—do you see—

"Hush," she tells the secret voice, the contrary voice. She again addresses the one that came as God—that came to everyone as God. The voice that doomed her parents and her people. "What *are* you?"

YOU MUST UNDERSTAND, the voice begins, and then it hesitates— it *hesitates!*—and in that hesitation Pea feels her last drop of hope drain away. Her last vestige of faith. The last chance that it really was God singing to her, coaching her and coaxing her along. It's gone. God, if God is real, would never hesitate. God needs never consider what to say next. Pea looks at the bodies of her mother and father, dead now for good. Dead now for real. She feels lonesome in the way that a person can only really feel lonesome when they've accepted that God isn't real and death is forever.

The voice that isn't God and never was God says it again: YOU MUST UNDERSTAND—

. . .

As she is told the story, Pea walks one more time through the world.

It's remade now. It's hers.

She skirts between alleys that she has repaved in pink limestone, trails sidewalks she's dotted with flowering trees.

Eventually, as the full and terrible impact of what the voice is telling her sinks in, she no longer wants to look at it. She wants things to be how they were, but they'll never be the same again.

She stops in the center of the lonely city and lowers her body into what used to be a black iron bench and is now a love seat, and she looks up at the remade skyline and waits for Him to be done.

. . .

Everybody fled the old world together. The doomed old world, the dying world. Everybody, those that still lived, they crowded onto ships, they took children by hands, they took what resources remained and set off in search of a new place to be.

The doomed species of a doomed planet sailing away together, fleeing scared into the stars.

When they had to, they split themselves into two groups: One group that sailed on, and one that stayed behind. Stayed behind here, on Pea's own world, a desolate and just-barely-livable world.

The others went forward and kept on, kept searching. They had promised that they would return, one day, when they had found a real place. They had promised they'd return for those left behind.

Years passed. Generations gave way to generations. Those who had been left behind never gave up hope. They scanned the skies. They built their shabby little world, made what structures they were able to. Drew water, constructed a grid. They did the best that they could, always waiting.

All of this Pea knew already. Her ancestors were the ones who had been left behind on this sad little world. This was the world of her grandparents, the waiting world, the weary world. A world that had by that time given up already, given up on scanning the stars for the returning Others. No wonder it had been so easy for Pea to destroy. No wonder everything had come apart so easily. It wasn't made of good stuff. It was a drywall world, of plaster, a tent city floating in a scrap of universe, year after year.

But now the voice goes on, to the part that Pea doesn't know, that she couldn't have known. He tells her of the other ones, who ventured further while Pea's grandparents' grandparents struggled and scraped.

These other ones, they floated forward and fought and experienced great traumas and great chapters of violence—until at last they found an extraordinary place to rest.

"Stop," Pea says softly.

All of it was sliding into place in her mind, all of it was making sense. Disparate pieces coming together to make a whole idea.

"Stop saying *they,*" she says. "Say *we.*"

The voice, after a pause, complied. The voice obeyed her, like she had obeyed the voice.

WE. WE FOUND OURSELVES AN EXTRAORDINARY PLACE TO REST.

Not only was the planet they had found habitable, it seemed to function as a kind of battery, a radiant and living thing on which the long-suffering people could feast and thrive. The people settled there, and they grew. While the ones they had left behind teetered and scraped, their cousins underwent impossible feats of evolution. Generation by generation, they achieved wild leaps in potential. Disease was eradicated. They fought no more wars. Death was destroyed. Their population grew and grew.

and then you know what

"I do," she whispers.

then you know what happens next

This smaller voice Pea of course now recognizes as not external but internal—it's her, it's just her, her own good sense, pointing out what she always should have known. She writhes in her body, knowing what is coming, fearful of what is coming.

But the story continues, getting closer now to the nub of it, the horrible center.

These others are now a race apart, a different species. They have grown so quickly, and so spectacularly. They need *space*. They need endless space. No one ever dies, and logically, algorithmically, they know that they need all the space that they can find. They need all the space that there is. And so they set out across the universe, filling the skies of distant planets with the lights of their ships, one by one. Destroying populations at a sweep, seizing worlds instantly.

Except for one.

"Ours," whispers Pea.

"Yes," says the God voice, a voice that is suddenly smaller, more intimate, more conversational. A voice that has sidled up beside her, almost intimate. She understands at once that this voice can be anything it wants to be. Be or do anything. "Our ancestors deserved more. Our cousins."

For their cousins the conquerors devised a wild idea. A hoax—a con—a mercy.

"We gave them this gift of God. They were to have not just death, but a reason to die." God's voice, no longer booming or rolling, but cajoling, explaining. "Not just death, but a purpose in dying. A calling! A benefice!"

Pea keeps her eyes closed. She feels tears burn paths down her cheeks. All of it. All of her life. Everything and everyone she'd known—

"Think of it, dear child. Other planets we destroyed in a sweep, but your people—our people—got two generations of knowing that God was waiting for them. Two generations without terror, without regret. Two generations looking upward and onward instead of into misery."

Pea is crying, alone but not alone on this ridiculous love seat she has created, and she is ashamed because she isn't crying for her parents, and she isn't crying for her world—she is crying for herself. "What about me?" she says now. "Why am I different? Why did I escape?"

"We don't know, Pea. It had taken the rest of us many generations, on a different kind of soil and under a different kind of sun, to become what we were. And here you were, all along. Like a fairy caught under glass. You were here all along. You are special, Pea."

She stands up. "I don't want to be special."

"You are one of us, Pea."

"I don't want to be one of you."

LOOK! The voice booms again. It is a hive of voices, a thousand voices. LOOK!—and Pea rockets up into the air, and she doesn't know if she's doing it or if it's being done to her, but the thousand voices fill her head again, LOOK!

She hovers in the air and can see all that she has done, in three days, she has rebuilt every building, remade every surface. She has borne a whole dead planet into a living world.

YOU HAVE BUILT YOUR OWN FUTURE, DEAR CHILD.

"No—"

Pea misses her parents. She misses the world as it used to be. But the future is here, it's coming now, the future is always rushing closer—the future was starting already—the sky was filling with lights, and the lights revealed themselves to be ships, the undersides of ships crowding the horizon.

And then the future begins.

AGENT NEUTRALIZED

David Wellington

afety glass cracked, and the driver's side window caved in. The biker brought his wrench back for another blow, and shards poured in through the suddenly open window, dust and wind blinding Whitman for a second as he fought to control the van and keep it on the road. In the back seat, Bob screamed, while up front in the passenger seat Grace fumbled with the shotgun clipped to the van's dashboard.

The biker's face was tattooed like a Japanese demon. He shoved his wrench back into a pannier on the side of his motorcycle and reached for a machete.

It was all Whitman could do to keep the van on the road. Ten years since the end of the world, potholes and broken asphalt made driving hazardous at any time. With a lunatic trying to kill him and six more of them in the rearview, Whitman was driving way too fast. One bad bump in the road and they would spin out, or fishtail to a stop at the worst possible time.

"Glove compartment," Whitman said, though he wasn't sure if Grace would hear him over the boy screaming in the back. "Glove compartment!"

He tried to push the biker off the road—the van might be a lumbering hulk at these speeds, but it weighed a lot more than Demonface's patched-together bike. He veered hard, right into the bastard, but it was no use. The biker had to grab both handlebars for a second but he was a lot more maneuverable than the van. He swerved away, avoiding the collision with ease.

"Glove compartment!"

Grace finally seemed to process what he was saying. She popped open the glove compartment and a heavy revolver fell out. She caught it before it bounced away, then stared at it like she'd never seen a gun before.

Maybe she hadn't—Whitman knew nothing about her, nothing that the plus sign tattooed on the back of her hand couldn't tell him. He'd picked her—and Bob—up at Atlanta the day before. He was supposed to drive them to a medical camp in Florida. There hadn't been much conversation since then.

Through his window he saw Demonface grab the machete again. The bike had no trouble matching speeds with the van, no matter how hard Whitman leaned on the gas.

"What do I do?" Grace demanded.

Whitman didn't get a chance to answer. The machete came chopping down, the blade slicing deep into the rubber lining of the empty space where Whitman's window used to be. He shoved himself back in his seat and the tip of the machete just missed cutting off the end of his nose.

Cubes of broken glass danced and fell from his shirt. Up ahead was the on-ramp to Route 75. Maybe it would be safer up there—he knew the government had pushed most of the abandoned cars off the main roads. Maybe—

The machete had cut deep into the window frame. Demonface had to wrench it free, a tricky thing to do while also controlling his motorcycle. The blade came loose, but the bike skidded across the road, falling back a full car length.

Whitman took the on-ramp at high speed, leaning into the curve as the van reared up on two wheels, then fell back on its suspension with a sickening crunch. Up ahead the road stretched out straight and clear forever, six lanes wide and completely empty. Even the road surface was in better shape, with barely a pothole to be seen.

Behind them the bikes came roaring up the ramp, seven of them riding in formation. Whitman saw their leader riding up front, a guy in a leather jacket with deer antlers sewn up and down the arms. Demonface was right next to him.

Even as he watched, Demonface poured on the speed and surged ahead, clutching his machete across his handlebars. He was coming in for another attack.

In the back, Bob kept screaming. The kid hadn't said a word all night, literally not one word. Now he wouldn't shut up.

Demonface came up alongside the van again. Whitman could see him grow huge in his wing mirror. He was grinning, his own white teeth visible inside the demon's row of fangs.

"Give me—" Whitman started to say, but he didn't get a chance to finish.

Demonface was riding right next to him, at his window, machete in hand. Then Grace leaned across Whitman's body, obscuring his view.

She pointed the revolver right at the bastard's face and pulled the trigger.

The noise and the flash of light rendered Whitman senseless. He tried to hold the wheel straight, but his head was full of smoke. Grace dropped the revolver in his lap, and he felt the hot barrel graze his knee.

He fought to recover, to see again at least—his hearing would be gone for a while, he knew. He blinked and rubbed at his eyes and finally got a bleary view of the road ahead. He straightened out the van before it could plunge into the concrete median strip.

Then he looked back and saw the bikers falling away, slowing down and letting the van rush forward and away from them.

Demonface's bike was still sliding over the road, its wheels racing as it clattered to a stop. The biker himself lay motionless on the blacktop, one arm twisted over his head.

• • •

A month ago—ten years after the Crisis began, shortly after the world ended. Time didn't mean what it used to.

There was music in the trees. Softly playing, patriotic songs. The trees were fake. The music was there to cut the silence.

A mile underground, seven hundred miles away. States between then and now, track-less lengths of wasteland and wilderness. Distances were so much longer than they had been.

Whitman dozed on a comfortable wooden bench, waiting his turn. Overhead, some-thing that felt like the sun burned down on his face. Except, of course, it wasn't the sun. It was a bank of floodlights high in the bunker roof.

They had moved Washington underground. The vaults below the capital had been built long before, built to withstand a nuclear apocalypse. More than safe enough for this particular Crisis. They'd brought down everything they needed, food and water and a nuclear generator. Staffers and pages and clerks. The business of government had to continue—somebody had to be in charge.

"They're ready for you, Mr. Whitman," a page said, a young woman in a blazer and a modest tweed skirt. She smiled at him when he opened his eyes.

He stood up—a little too fast. He heard movement behind him, rubber-soled boots squeaking on simulated flagstones. The jangling sound of an assault rifle being unlim-bered from its strap.

He turned and looked behind him. The soldier there never smiled. He did his best to stay out of Whitman's line of sight, but he was always there. Everywhere Whitman went in the Washington bunkers—to the bathroom, when he slept—the guard was there, because Whitman had a tattoo of a plus sign on the back of his hand.

There was no test for the prion disease that turned people into zombies. No symptoms to warn you when it was coming. It could incubate in your head for twenty years and then just one day, out of the blue, you would snap. Your eyes would fill with blood. You would forget your name; you would attack any living thing you saw.

Or—you could be perfectly fine. You could be completely clean, live out your whole natural life and never succumb. You just never knew. Once you had the tattoo on your left hand, it didn't matter.

The guard followed Whitman as he walked down toward the Capitol dome. Not as nice as the old one, the above-ground one, he thought. This dome was made of concrete and wasn't even painted. It was designed to survive even if the entire bunker came crashing down around it, a million tons of rock.

Inside, it looked much like the old Senate floor. Rows of desks turned inward toward a big podium. The desks were empty today, but five senators sat at the podium. Whitman recognized three of them. The other two were very, very young.

One of them, a man with white hair and gold-rimmed glasses perched on top of his head, had his own honor guard. A soldier stood behind him with an assault rifle, waiting. The senator had a plus sign on his hand just like Whitman's. Apparently no matter how powerful you might be, the tattoo still made people nervous. A great democratizer, that tattoo.

A table stood in front of the podium, covered in loose papers and manila folders and two microphones on flexible stalks like the eyes of a crab. Two men were already sitting there. One of them—the lawyer assigned to Whitman's defense—stared at the floor, his mouth a set line. Whitman had seen plenty of people like that. People who survived the Crisis but couldn't handle what came next. People who couldn't forget what they'd seen.

The other man turned as Whitman approached. Whitman couldn't help but be surprised. It was Director Philips, Whitman's old boss at the CDC. He'd heard the man had killed himself.

Pink scar tissue covered one side of Philips' head. His ear was missing. Aha, Whitman thought. He had enough medical training to recognize a self-inflicted gunshot wound. So Philips had tried to kill himself—tried and failed.

Whitman could sympathize. He'd tried lots of things in his life, and failed. Now he was going to get to tell a select committee how badly he'd fucked up.

He was ready. He actually wanted this.

It meant closure.

• • •

Whitman stood on the gritty shoulder of the road, keeping one eye on the trees twenty yards away. There could be zombies out there. But he had to check the van, make sure it wasn't going to conk out at the worst possible moment.

The painted government seal on the driver's side door was scratched to hell, and his window was a complete loss. The tires seemed alright, though, and when he bent low to look at the undercarriage, he found only a few dents and scrapes.

They'd been lucky. As fast as he'd been driving over those rough roads, they could've cracked an axle.

When he straightened up, he nearly jumped out of his shoes. A figure with long stringy hair was walking toward him. It was only Grace, though.

"I told you to stay in the car," he said.

She shrugged, then nodded at Bob sitting in the back seat. The kid was still screaming, though he'd grown hoarse and it wasn't quite as deafening.

"I'm not like him," Grace said.

Whitman took a deep breath. He had a pretty good idea what was coming. When he'd picked these two up, back in Atlanta, he'd been aware they were both positives. Positives weren't allowed to live inside a proper city.

Being positive didn't mean you were actually infected. At least that's what every one of them told themselves.

"My friend Heather and I found a zombie in this underground mall. We weren't supposed to be there, but... look, it bit Heather. I get that. They took her away and I don't know what happened to her."

Whitman could probably guess. Heather wouldn't have been a positive, then. She'd been a confirmed infected. Only one thing happened to people like that.

"I ran away. I know that was... cowardly," Grace said. She sounded like she'd prepared this speech well in advance. "I know it was wrong. But I never even got close to the zombie. It didn't touch me."

Whitman nodded. He supposed he had to hear her out.

"The police wouldn't even listen, they just tattooed me and locked me up. They don't know all the details. I know they were just trying to be careful. But I'm not at risk." She gave him a hopeful smile. "I'm really not. Please. You can just take me back. Tell them I'm clean." A little shake of her hair, which probably worked great on boys her age. "Please," she said.

"I don't make the rules."

"I shouldn't be out here!" she said. "It's dangerous—those bikers would've killed us, they would've... what they would've done to me—"

"You'll be safe at the medical camp," he told her. He pulled open the driver's side door and jumped back inside. "You coming?"

She stood there for a while, her face a mask of disbelief. She must have really thought she could talk her way out of this. Finally, she turned and looked back the way they'd come.

"Those bikers—"

"They were after our water, our food, our gasoline," Whitman told her. "They must've been following us for a while."

"They're not going to give up, are they?" she asked. "They'll kill us."

Whitman shrugged. "They didn't have any guns, or they would've used them. I guess after ten years there aren't any bullets left out here. That gives us a chance. Plus, we've got a head start now. The sooner you get in the van," he told her, "the sooner we get to Florida."

She got in the van.

• • •

"Once we walled in the cities," Director Philips droned on, "zombie incidents fell by a considerable degree. New infection rates are down nearly ninety-nine per cent..."

Even the senators looked bored as the Director droned on with his endless report on the progression of the Crisis. Whitman barely listened to any of it. He knew the numbers. As the CDC's ranking field agent, he'd been responsible for collecting most of them. The last few years had been a blur as he traveled around the country interviewing what passed for medical personnel, overseeing the administration of the hospital camps, working with the army to get a sense of how many zombies were still out there, hiding in the wilderness.

It had been depressing work, if vital.

"Outside the cities, looting has become endemic," Philips went on. "The vast majority of people surviving outside of protected communities make their living by foraging. Of perhaps greater concern is the appearance of so-called road pirates. Gangs, organized to a lesser or greater degree, who prey on the looters and even government convoys..."

Whitman had seen the pirates, though only from the window of a helicopter. Packs of scavengers. He'd pitied them, looking down from that height. They were only doing what they had to if they wanted to survive, he supposed. He'd assumed the army would put a quick end to such nonsense, but it seemed they had more important things to do.

"Food stocks continue to be a problem, though the agricultural worker program has made considerable advances in that regard. The key seems to have been adequate policing of the countryside around the farm complexes..."

Plantations, in other words. Out west, whole communities had been conscripted to work the fields. Battalions of soldiers watched over them, keeping them safe from zombies—and making sure they couldn't run away.

"I believe that completes my report. I want to thank the committee for allowing us this chance to speak about—"

"Horseshit," Whitman said.

The senators stirred in their chairs. Philips fell silent. Even the braindead lawyer sitting next to him twitched his head around as if looking for the cause of the disturbance.

Whitman was surprised at himself. He hadn't meant to interject. Maybe his tolerance for obfuscation was just at its end.

"Mr. Whitman, we will have order in this chamber," the white-haired senator insisted.

"Fine," Whitman said. Well, in for a penny, in for a pound. "I just thought we could all save a little time if we skipped the pleasantries. We all know you didn't bring Philips and me here to talk statistics. We could just as easily have submitted those in writing."

"Then why," the white-haired senator asked, smiling like a shark, "do you believe we asked for this face-to-face meeting?"

"It's obvious, isn't it?" Whitman asked. "You want someone to blame for the end of the world."

• • •

When night fell, he had no choice but to pull over.

"We'll take turns sleeping," he said.

Grace protested—she wanted to keep driving through the night—but Whitman knew better. "Nothing out here shows lights at night," he said. "The merest flicker, and the zombies would be all over us."

"So we drive without headlights," she suggested.

He laughed. "Sure. Then we blow out a tire on something we can't see. Or run into a tree trunk that fell across the road. One accident like that, and we're walking to Florida."

Eventually, she agreed to go to sleep. Whitman took the first watch.

Not that there was anything to watch. Outside the van, the moonless night was just a flat plane of black, as if someone had spray-painted over their windows. He forced himself to stay awake, punching himself hard in the thigh at one point just to clear his head.

At some point, he realized he was being watched.

He turned around and saw Bob's eyes, just two smudges of pale gray in the unrelieved blackness.

"Can't sleep?" he asked.

The boy blinked at him.

"I'm sorry you got scared back there when those bikers came at us," he told the kid. He didn't know what else to say. "I didn't want to scare you."

"My mom said you would keep me safe."

It was the first thing Bob had said to Whitman, other than to give his name.

"She said to obey you."

"Who, me specifically?" Whitman asked.

"She said they would send a man. Then she just cried."

Jesus, Whitman thought. He imagined the scene. The mother, probably on the far side of a pane of glass, looking at her child—her potentially infected child. How could she give him up?

But of course they wouldn't have given her a choice. They would've taken the boy away the second they realized he was a positive. And who knew? Maybe she had looked at the tattoo on little Bob's hand and maybe—maybe she hadn't put up much of a fight.

Everyone knew the risk. Everyone knew the rules.

Whitman tried to keep Bob talking. It would help pass the time, help keep him awake. He asked the boy how he'd become positive, but Bob didn't seem to understand. So instead he tried to talk about the future.

"You know where I'm taking you?"

The boy just blinked.

"It's a camp. Not exactly like a summer camp, though. There's no archery or making lanyards or anything, but—"

"I don't know what a summer camp is," Bob said.

Oh. Of course he didn't. Bob was maybe ten years old. The Crisis began ten years ago. There hadn't been summer camps in a long time.

"A camp. I'll be safe there," Bob said, because his mom had told him so, no doubt.

"That's right. You'll be safe from zombies and... and bikers. They'll feed you and make sure you don't get sick."

Which was about all Whitman could promise.

"You like baseball?" he asked, to change the subject.

Bob blinked. Maybe they didn't have baseball in Atlanta anymore, either.

After a couple hours, Whitman woke Grace up so she could take a watch. When he opened his eyes again, it was dawn and pink light smeared across the roof of the van.

"Anything to report?" he asked Grace.

"I thought maybe I heard engines, once," she told him. "Except I'm not sure. Maybe it was just animals or something, growling in the trees."

Whitman put the van in gear and moved out.

• • •

"It's the business of this committee to hear a lot of reports," one of the senators said. Whitman didn't even look to see which one. He was watching his lawyer, the one they'd assigned to his case. He realized he'd never even caught the man's name.

The lawyer's eyes were glazed over, and his mouth was open in a rictus of horror. Whitman could only wonder what he saw, what moment of the Crisis he was reliving.

"What we hear disturbs us," another senator said. "Director Philips presented the most optimistic data we've heard in a while. He didn't mention the outbreaks of cholera and hantavirus in the cities of the Southwest. He didn't say anything about the nutritional deficiencies we see—pellagra, beriberi, even childhood blindness."

"You can hardly blame us for that," Philips said.

The senator wasn't done, however. "We were very alarmed to hear about conditions inside the so-called hospital camps. The camps are beyond overcrowded. Positives are herded inside and all but forgotten. They are given some food and clothing, yes—"

"Now, now," the white-haired senator broke in. "We're talking about people who might be zombies, here. The resources we have should always go first to healthy people. People who can live productive lives."

"Nevertheless. Medical care is non-existent in the camps. The guards refuse to even touch the inmates. Riots and violent altercations kill more of them than zombie outbreaks ever could."

Whitman turned and looked at the podium. The senator who had been talking had flecks of spittle on his lips, and his eyes burned with outrage.

"Mr. Whitman, you speak of blame. We're more interested in justice. You don't think the people of America—the people we represent—deserve better than this? You don't think they have a right to know who was responsible for the Crisis?"

He might have answered, if he wasn't interrupted by a sudden strangling noise.

Whitman swiveled around to see the lawyer jerk spasmodically upright in his chair. At first he thought the man was having a seizure. A clear, lucid light came into his eyes, though, and he stood up, his chair squeaking across the floor.

"Senator," he said. "Senator, I—I object to this line of… of questioning," he announced. "You can't suggest that my clients were personally… personally…"

Everyone waited. Time stretched out, but the lawyer didn't come up with any more words. Eventually, he sat back down.

"Director Philips was responsible for all CDC operations when the first zombies were discovered. It was his set of recommendations," the senator went on, "presented to the President in the first days of the Crisis, that led to the formation of the hospital camps, those prisons for the sick. That led to hundreds of thousands of healthy people dying because he did not prepare us for just how quickly the prion infection would spread."

The white-haired senator cleared his throat and leaned forward. "On the other hand, it was Mr. Whitman who recommended the partition of the cities. Who suggested that we wall off our urban areas, stranding millions of Americans out in the wilderness."

"Saving millions more," Whitman said, but it came out as barely a whisper.

"The position of this committee is that the two of you are responsible for the incredible suffering and hardship that ensued from your recommendations. We would like to bring official charges today that will give the American people some peace of mind, some relief. Some closure."

The five of them, the senators, stared down at them from the podium. They looked so damned indignant. So sanctimonious. Whitman wanted to shout imprecations in their faces.

It was Philips who broke the silence, however.

"If I may," he said, weakly. Then he stood up and said it again, nearly shouting. "If I may!"

"Go ahead, Director," the too-young senator said.

"I have just one point to make in defense," he told them.

Whitman wondered why he bothered.

"Just one point," Philips said again. He took a deep breath. Then he looked down at the table in front of him and said, "It was Mr. Whitman who came up with the plus sign. He was the one who created the idea of positives."

Whitman was too shocked to even laugh.

· · ·

The sun beat down on a road surface almost as pristine as the one he remembered from his youth—a stretch of concrete and asphalt wide and clear like a manmade river, pointed right in the direction he wanted to go. Say what you like about the world before the Crisis, they'd built well; they'd built to last. He didn't see a single abandoned car or significant pothole for miles.

It couldn't last.

It wasn't anything he saw that warned him, it was something he felt. A kind of rumbling in his stomach, a little like hunger, a little like nausea. Soon, he could hear it, but he told himself it was the engine of the van making that noise.

Right up until he couldn't deny it. Until he saw the motorcycles in his mirrors.

"They're—they're coming for us again," Grace said, in a whisper. She swiveled around in her seat, her arms everywhere, one elbow hitting him in the side of his head as she turned to look through the rear window.

He glanced back and saw Bob looking back at him. Just watching him. *I'm supposed to keep you safe,* he thought. *Your mom told you I would.*

The bikes roared as they surged down the road straight toward the van. Now that he had a chance to actually look at them, he saw they were ragged junk. Pieces of dozens of different bikes strapped together, mismatched components hammered and beaten until they joined up. Only the leader's had a headlight, and it was broken. Many of them didn't even have mudguards.

Crazy. You had to be crazy to ride a bike like that. Which might explain how they dressed—like the leader, with antlers sewn on his sleeves like armor. One of the others had a pair of baby dolls hanging around his neck, their long blond hair tied together behind him. What was that even supposed to mean?

They came up fast, black smoke belching from their exhaust pipes. Babydolls had a sledgehammer that he brandished over his head. Antlers twisted his throttle and came racing ahead of the pack. He came up even with Whitman, though a full lane away. Whitman supposed he didn't want to get shot.

Antlers gestured with one hand, telling Whitman to pull over.

Not much chance of that. Whitman shouted for Grace to get the shotgun. Then he veered toward Antlers, thinking maybe he would get lucky and knock the biker off the road. No dice—Antlers just swerved away, a big shit-eating grin all over his face.

That was when Babydolls attacked. Whitman had been too focused on the leader to see the other bike coming up on the passenger side. Babydolls smacked the side of the van with his hammer and the whole frame rang like a bell. Grace screamed, but she had the shotgun off the dashboard, cradled in her hands.

Whitman craned around trying to see what was going to happen next. Babydolls had his head down, below the level of their windows, but Whitman could just see the curve of his back. "Shoot him," he told Grace, pointing through her window. "Don't let him get any closer."

She raised the gun, but Whitman grabbed the barrel. "Roll down your window first," he told her.

Meanwhile, Antlers took a long knife off his belt. He veered in toward the van, the tip of his weapon pointed not at Whitman's broken window but at the left front tire. Whitman wanted to swear. If he slashed the tire, at this speed, the van would spin out and probably roll over half a dozen times before it came to a stop.

He waited until Antlers got close, until he could almost have reached out his window and grabbed the bastard's arm. Antlers lifted his knife and started to bring it down.

Two things happened at once. Grace fired her shotgun, screaming into the noise. Whitman twisted his wheel hard over to the left.

The van briefly went up on two wheels. There was a screeching sound as the deer antlers bit into the van's paint job. Whitman expected the pirate leader to go flying, to fall off his bike, but apparently he was too skilled for that—instead he recovered, leaning deep into a turn and spinning around until he was riding the other way. When the van's four wheels touched the pavement again, Whitman glanced over to his right and saw Babydolls receding, slowing down and falling back. There was blood on his face, but he was smiling, blinking one eye to keep it clear.

"I got him," Grace said, whooping. "I got him!"

Except he was still alive, and still in control of his bike. Whitman expected the two of them to catch up and make another run any second now.

Except—they didn't. They fell back and rejoined their pack. Kept pace with the van but didn't try to catch up to it, just stayed a set distance behind. Out of range of firearms.

Antlers still had that shit-eating grin.

"Seatbelts," Whitman said. "Get your seatbelts on!" Then he poured on the speed, potholes be damned.

• • •

They took Philips and Whitman to a waiting room, a pleasant little chamber just off the Senate floor. There was a fridge full of cold water in plastic bottles and a basket full of cookies in individual foil wrappers. After the MREs he'd been eating for the last few years, Whitman just stared at the little snacks, amazed such things still existed. He had the urge to fill his pockets with them. Then he looked back and saw his personal guard standing there, unsmiling. Waiting to shoot him if he went symptomatic. Always watching.

Philips, on the other hand, wouldn't look at him. The Director curled up in a padded chair, almost in a fetal position. He covered his scarred face with one hand as if he expected Whitman to hit him.

Well, that would probably feel pretty good, honestly. Whitman wasn't a violent man by nature, but the years since the Crisis had required him to gain some skill in that regard. He could probably break the Director's jaw before the soldier pulled them apart.

He chuckled to himself.

"I'm sorry," Philips said. "I'm so sorry."

"What, for selling me out back there?" Whitman asked. He considered what to say next. What he came up with surprised him a little. "Don't worry about it."

Philips uncurled a little. "I'm—"

"They'll probably be happy with one sacrifice," Whitman said. He tore open a cookie and took a bite. Oatmeal raisin. Never his favorite, but it was free. "Crucify me. Hold me up as an example. What do you think, a quick firing squad, or will they drag me through New York in chains, first?" He laughed. "Maybe it'll make some people feel better. That's what we swore to do, right? As medical professionals? Relieve suffering."

Philips shook his head. "I have to say—you're being awfully good about this."

"I'm exhausted."

Philips licked his lips. "I'm so sorry…"

"I feel sorry for you."

"Can I ask why?"

"Because if they do just take me, and leave you alive—you're the one who has to keep fighting. You know the funny thing about the end of the world?"

"I… no," Philips said.

"There is no such thing. The world doesn't end. There's always more work to be done, more digging out the rubble. More fucked-up shit to live through. Well," he said, taking a deep breath, "I'm done. Let me have my ending. Let me have some peace, for a change."

The senators kept them waiting for a good half hour. Plenty of time to decide questions of life and death, these days.

• • •

"What the hell are they doing back there?" Whitman asked. In his rearview, the bikers had fallen well back, barely increasing their speed at all as the van outpaced them.

He needed to concentrate on the road. One bad patch of asphalt, and this chase could end very, very badly. "Grace," he said, "keep an eye on them. I need to watch—"

"Mr. Whitman?" Bob asked from the backseat.

"Not now, Bob," he said, a little louder, a little harsher than he'd meant to. The road ahead looked well-maintained, but he knew from long experience that—

"Mr. Whitman," Bob said again.

Had he seen it coming? It didn't matter.

Up ahead, a long curving ramp cut away from the highway. Whitman didn't bother looking at it, being far too busy looking for road obstructions he might have to negotiate. So he didn't see the truck coming up the ramp at high speed.

It was a semi rig, a big rusting hulk of a vehicle eleven feet high with six bald tires that smoked as they bit into the asphalt. Mounted across its grille was a snowplow blade dented and bent from repeated collisions.

It slammed into the front of the van at thirty miles an hour. If it had hit them a split second later it would have sliced right through the passenger compartment, killing all of them instantly. Instead it just pancaked the van's engine, blew out both front tires, and turned the windshield into a storm of flying glass daggers.

Whitman flew forward, the shoulder strap of his seat belt cutting deep into his armpit, crushing his chest so he couldn't breathe. He felt like he'd been picked up and dropped from a height, like he was dangling from his belt as a planet of metal and glass and plastic came rushing toward him. His head bounced off the steering wheel, and a high-pitched scream roared through his head. He couldn't see anything, couldn't feel his own body.

For a long time he could hear nothing, see nothing. He couldn't move, couldn't think... little by little the world came back to him.

The first thing he heard was Bob screaming behind him.

It shook him up. Woke him, a little. He looked around, trying to figure out where he was. Why he hurt so much.

Straight ahead, through the place where the windshield used to be, he saw the tall curving shape of the snowplow, now thoroughly embedded in what remained of the van. Beyond that he could see the cab of the semi rig. Its windshield was gone, too, though it hadn't shattered as cleanly as his. The driver of the rig hung half in, half out of that frosted plane of glass. Blood poured out of him. He was very clearly dead.

Whitman turned, looking for Grace, but he couldn't see her. The impact had torn off the passenger side door, and he saw the road surface beyond, littered with glass and twists of broken metal. He couldn't see her or any part of her.

Bob was still screaming.

He wrestled with his seat belt. Somehow got it loose. He pushed open his door and wriggled out of the wreckage, dropped to his feet on the road. He pulled open the side door and saw Bob unhurt but very upset, staring at him with wide eyes.

Bob stopped screaming. Which allowed Whitman to hear something else.

Motorcycle engines, coming closer.

• • •

"Mr. Whitman, they'd like to see you now," the page said. She was still smiling.

Whitman knew better than to think that was a good sign. He tried to stand up but found that his knees had frozen. They wouldn't do it down here, he thought. They wouldn't want to disturb the senators with the noise of a gunshot. No. They would take him up to the surface, first.

"It's best not to keep them waiting," the page said, her smile dimming just a bit.

• • •

It hurt to breathe. Whitman was pretty sure he'd broken a rib or two. He found just lifting his head was agony. He turned and saw Antlers racing toward him, head bent down low over his handlebars. Was he expecting Whitman to start shooting?

Too bad. Whitman hadn't thought to search the wrecked van for the revolver or the shotgun. He stood there unarmed, waiting to be killed.

It wasn't going to be quick. Antlers tore by him at speed. Something very hard struck him across the back of his legs, and Whitman fell down onto the road. He tried to grab the side of the van, tried to pull himself back up to his feet, but before he could manage it, Antlers swung back around and hit him again, this time in the side. He flopped forward into the van, almost on top of Bob.

He didn't know if the kid was screaming or not, now. He couldn't hear anything over the rush of blood in his ears.

Where was Grace? Did they already have her? Did they pull her unconscious and bleeding out of the wreckage? Whitman cursed himself for worrying about her when his own life was about to end. Surely there were better uses of his mental capacity in this, the last few seconds he had left.

Once he'd caught his breath, he could hear again. He wished he couldn't. He heard a motorcycle engine putter out, then heavy footfalls come rushing toward him.

He turned just in time to see Antlers right behind him, raising a hammer over his head. Whitman rushed forward and grabbed the bastard's arms, nearly impaling himself on a spiky bit of antler. The biker pushed back against him, but now that they were face to face Whitman realized how thin the man was, wasted away by malnutrition and hard living out here in the wilderness. He had a wiry strength, but Whitman bore down on him just by pure mass. He knocked the biker to the ground and kicked him hard—which probably hurt Whitman more than it did Antlers. He felt something tear in his abdomen, and he nearly collapsed on top of the biker.

He heard a shotgun blast behind him and whirled around. Through the van's broken windows, he could see Grace on the other side of the vehicle. She had the shotgun up, and she blasted away again, and then he heard screaming. A grown man screaming his life away.

"That's right! That's right!" Grace screamed. Bikers jumped on their motorcycles and roared away, none of them willing to take her on.

"Grace," Whitman said, trying to shout. It didn't quite work. "Grace—reload."

"What?" she asked.

"I said—"

Except he didn't get to repeat himself. Antlers had gotten back on his feet. He wrapped an arm around Whitman's neck and pulled him backwards, pressing hard until black spots danced in Whitman's vision.

He couldn't breathe—couldn't move—couldn't fight back. His body begged for air, but he had none to supply. He felt his consciousness dwindling away, vanishing.

Then a roar of noise and a shockwave went past his face, burning his cheek, and Antlers let go. Whitman bent over, gasping, wanting very much to sit down. To just die. But he had to know.

He turned first to look at Antlers. There wasn't much left of the biker's head. He turned next to look into the van.

Bob still had his seatbelt on. Nobody had told him to take it off. The boy was curled forward with his whole body braced around the revolver, which looked enormous in his tiny hands.

• • •

He was brought to a pleasant office with wood-paneled walls and a massive desk. Behind it sat the white-haired senator. And, of course, his guard, who looked as grave and deadly as Whitman's own.

"We've made our decision," the senator said. He waved for Whitman to sit down. "I'm going to do you a favor here and just speak honestly, if that's alright."

"Absolutely," Whitman said. As long as he didn't have to stand up when he heard the death sentence, he thought he would be okay.

"It didn't come down to justice, or anything like that. It came down to the fact that your job—overseeing the quarantine, setting up the hospital camps—is essentially

complete. Director Philips still has plenty more to do. If he can isolate the prion and find a vaccine, well. That would be handy, wouldn't it?"

Whitman knew enough about the disease to understand that would probably never happen. Still. He wasn't here for debate. Just sentencing.

"You were right, we need a scapegoat. And you're it. I'm sorry."

Whitman nodded. He looked down at his hands in his lap. His left hand with its tattoo. Had that made a difference? Maybe.

"I understand," he said, meekly. His bravado had deserted him. "So what's next? A quick firing squad? Or do I go on an apology tour first?"

The senator grunted. "You think we're going to kill you?"

"Isn't that why I'm here?" Whitman asked.

"No. Oh, I'm sure some of my colleagues would like that. But no. Your name will go down in history as the man who bungled the Crisis. Part of the official record. But honestly, we don't have enough people left to throw any of them away."

Whitman looked up in surprise. "So—what's going to happen to me?"

"A very serious demotion, to start with. Your salary is going to take quite a hit. But we've got a new job for you. There are still new positives being discovered all the time. We can't very well keep them in the cities where they might spread the infection. They need to be taken to the hospital camps, God help them. Somebody has to be in charge of that. Transportation and the like."

"I don't understand," Whitman said.

"We're giving you another chance," the senator told him. "A chance to make amends."

• • •

The bikers didn't come back for their dead. Maybe they were scared off permanently.

The van was totaled. Surprisingly, the semi rig ran just fine. It took some work extricating the snow plow blade from the van, but in the end they had a vehicle again. Even if it stank inside like home-made liquor and road pirate blood.

Between them, Whitman and Grace figured out how to drive the thing. Within a couple of hours, they were cruising down the highway at a steady twenty miles an hour, Bob curled up in a little bunk behind the cab.

Grace had fallen asleep too by the time Whitman pulled off the highway, just over the Florida line. He drove another couple of miles to a place he'd only ever seen on satellite maps.

It wasn't a city. It wasn't big enough to be a village. He thought it might've been a country club, before. It had a high fence and a parking lot full of patched-together cars. Snipers up on the gate waved them through.

Inside the lot, he saw people dressed in outlandish clothes working on the cars. Women in furs and floppy hats wrestled with carburetors. Men with blue hair or dressed in suits with torn shoulders changed oil filters.

The truck's brakes squealed as he pulled to a stop. The noise woke Grace and she sat up slowly, looking around with bleary eyes. "This isn't a hospital camp," she pointed out.

"No," Whitman told her. "It's a place we can trade some of our water for gasoline, though."

"Who are these people? Road pirates?"

He shook his head. "Looters. They work their way through old suburban subdivisions, finding what food and supplies they can get out of old houses. It's a living, I guess, if you can't score a place in a walled city."

Grace's brow furrowed. "What're we doing here? We have some gas left."

Whitman turned to look at her. He tried to smile. It had been a long time since he'd done that. "We're here to give you a choice. You and Bob both."

He parked the rig and let the engine rumble itself to sleep. "I'll take you to the hospital camp if that's what you want. It's safe there, more or less. Not very comfortable, though—and it's a twenty-year sentence. You have to stay there until you can prove you're not infected."

She didn't appear as though she liked the idea.

"Otherwise—you can start over here. Get to know the looters. Figure out how they survive. You can have this rig and everything in it. That ought to get you started. The only thing I ask is that you and Bob stick together. He can handle a gun, but he's too young to even understand what's happening to him."

Grace stared at him. "Why?"

"Because I think you might have a better chance here."

"No—I mean, why are you doing this? Giving me a choice. Your job is to take us to the camp."

Whitman shrugged. "I've seen you two can look after yourselves. I know what it's like in those camps—and what it's like here. Don't think I'm giving you any good options. Life here is going to be tough, and you might not make it. But you won't be a prisoner. You'll be free to move about as you please." He lifted his hands, dropped them again. "I guess that's something, right?"

Grace ran her fingers through her hair. Clearly she had a lot to think about. "What about you? What happens to you if I say yes?"

"I'll call for a government helicopter to pick me up. I still have a job." There would always be more positives who needed rides. There was no end to that demand. Always more work. The world never did end, it seemed.

He took the keys out of the ignition. Held them out to her.

"What do you say?" he asked.

GOODNIGHT EARTH

Annie Bellet

Karron leaned over the rail of her boat, the *Tarik,* and watched the meteor shower from its reflection in the river below. The bright streaks of light looked like underwater fireflies and the Ring more like a soft blue disk, a monochromatic rainbow that ruled their lives in constant reminder of how broken the world was.

"Water, water, everywhere," she murmured to herself, the words half-forgotten, something she'd read in the Covenant Archive a world—and a lifetime—ago. In their case implanted at the top of her spine, her nanos stirred with the memory.

The *Tarik* rode low in the Missip river as it tacked up the shoreline. She was a smaller boat, fifty feet and built with a shallow draft for sailing rivers and canals. Usually she carried only Karron and Ishim, and whatever cargo they'd bartered for, bought, or stolen.

The ship wasn't equipped to handle six people on board. Karron glanced at their passengers where they huddled on makeshift beds around the steam stack toward the aft of the ship. A man and woman, who had provided what were probably fake names, and two kids. A week ago now they'd appeared on a small dock upriver from Looston, asking about getting around the Covenant checkpoints between Looston and Ria, a good two week journey if they did it straight. No papers for the kids, the woman, Jill, said.

Plausible enough story, and their Covenant coin would spend all along the river. The thirty gallons of pure water they'd offered as bonus had decided it. Karron and Ishim would smuggle the four up to Ria, where Nolan, the man, said his parents and jobs were waiting.

In the pale earthlight coming off the Ring, Karron could almost make out the little family's faces. The adults appeared asleep under their blankets, but the two kids were awake, their dark eyes glinting. Oni, the boy, was supposedly seven years old, and his sister, Bee, was four. They were well behaved, the two kids. Creepily so. Quiet as fish lurking in the rocks, and as nimble as Button, the ship's cat.

Karron bit her lip and glanced to the fore where Ishim stood keeping the ship steering smoothly through the dark water. She hadn't told him her suspicions about the children. Her thoughts were impossible, and she knew as well as he that even if she was right about what they were, there was nothing she nor Ishim could or would do about it.

She'd always been too curious. Her instructors at the Academy had always said so in varying tones of annoyance or amusement.

Curiosity killed the cat, she thought, turning over the phrase in her mind, a phrase from the old times, before the Ring, before the sky broke and war came to the world.

"Satisfaction brought it back," she whispered. She had to know.

Creeping over the deck—the shush of wind in the mainsail and the lap of water against the hull covering any sound she might have made—Karron approached the sleeping passengers. She brought her finger to her lips and saw both children nod. The adults to either side of them didn't move, apparently asleep.

She knelt in front of Oni and reached for his head. He didn't flinch, didn't even seem to breathe as she slid her hand around the back of his neck and felt the base of his skull.

The hard knot was there, distinct and familiar beneath her trembling fingers. Oni reached up and touched her arm. Karron bent her head and let him feel her own knot for himself. Bee's tiny hand replaced Oni's.

"Not your aunt and uncle," Karron whispered, her mouth moving but hardly any sound coming from her throat. The kids would hear her, if they were like she was.

"No," Oni whispered back. "Help us?"

"How?"

"Kill them. They are going to sell us."

She shook her head. "Not my problem," she whispered.

"You are like us," the boy said. Beside him, Jill stirred, and all three of them froze until she settled again.

"Not anymore," Karron lied.

For a long moment they sat in silence, watching one another. Then Karron crept away, her heart in her throat, and went back to her own blanket. Her head buzzed and her adrenaline spiked and the nanos at the base of her skull woke up, reacting to her heightened emotions. She took careful, slow breaths and forced herself to calm.

War Children, they'd been called. The program was dead, dismantled and torched fifteen years ago. She thought she'd been in the last generation, the last raised in the crèche in Deecee. Genetically altered, infested with nano-tech that even the Covenant didn't understand, trained from the day they could walk to hunt, kill, be soldiers at the front of the Covenant peace-keeping forces.

She'd seen the Academy burn, seen her fellow Children burn with it. Only a few escaped that she knew of and many of them had been hunted down or gone insane. If Ishim hadn't pulled her from the river, she would have died as well.

It was luck and staying calm and quiet that had kept the nanos from driving her insane, kept her from being caught. She'd told Ishim what she was, but he didn't seem to care. Karron had warned him if she went crazy, he'd have to put her down.

"If you go crazy, will I even be able to kill you before you get me?" Ishim had asked.

Karron had looked away. They both knew the answer was no. No one man alone could take out a War Child.

Now there were three of them on this boat, though what training the two kids had, Karron didn't know. At Oni's age, she'd already run her first mission. Was there a program again? Why were these kids traveling with the suspiciously normal-seeming man and woman who Oni said were going to sell them? Sell them to whom?

Too many questions get smugglers killed, Ishim would say. Karron stared up at the Ring and pushed the questions away as stones fell out of the sky, flamed bright, and died away.

• • •

The Missip branched into a hundred waterways as the Zouri joined up with it. Ishim and Karron knew many of those ways. Which ones were patrolled by Covenant boats or led to Covenant settlements, which ones were dead ends, which were safe for a boat with a shallow draft to pole down or steam up. Reeds and willow branches shivered in the cool spring air as they tacked west and north along one of these myriad of ways. By afternoon they would join up with a bigger branch of the Zouri and in another week they'd be able to steam toward Ria, the worst of the checkpoints and danger zones.

Ria itself was controlled by a Baron, one of the gang leaders set up by the Covenant to keep a semblance of order on this side of the Missip. Long as the trains ran on time and the tithes got paid, Covenant didn't seem to care what else happened or how the Barons went about their lives.

Ishim was catching a nap and Karron had the wheel as she guided the ship, keeping the boat turned so the big sail held a bellyful of wind. This way would narrow too much for sailing soon and they'd have to break out the poles or risk the racket of the steam engine for a while. They'd decide when Ishim woke, probably with a shared glance, a look at the river conditions, and a nod. A decade and a half relying on each other made words irrelevant. Karron smiled to herself as a Kingfisher dove into the water ahead. Sometimes they'd go weeks without words.

Not like their passengers. Nolan and Jill talked to each other a lot and sometimes attempted to engage Ishim or Karron in small talk, more and more as the days went by. They said idle things mostly. When they spoke to each other, they used Esper instead of Covenant. Their accents in that tongue put them from the south, maybe from as far as Nawlins. She and Ishim never sailed too far south. Too many sharks and crocodiles, too much heat, unstable weather, and biting insects. Too many Covenant Peace Keepers. The north was safer.

Nolan had insulted Karron and Ishim the second day in Esper, calling Ishim a night pig and Karron his little white slut. Ishim didn't speak Esper and Karron had decided not to respond, curious as to why the man went off on them with such a pleasant tone and a smile on his face. She'd figured he was trying to see if she spoke the language. Her training was still there, lurking beneath her skin like the nanotech. So she said nothing, just shook her head as though she had no idea what he was saying.

This morning they'd been whispering about a broken bridge. Their excitement, the anticipation they couldn't keep out of their body language, it scared Karron. Felt to her like the thick heat before a bad storm, air crackling with energy as the world held its breath.

War Children. She hadn't told Ishim. No way to tell him without chancing being overheard. The kids had stayed aft all morning, crouched together and watching the world with dark, quiet eyes that didn't quite meet hers when she risked looking their way.

Wherever they'd come from, wherever they were going, they weren't her crèche, her brothers and sisters. Not her problem. Killing took her away, took her to the warm place it was hard to come home from. She wouldn't go there for strangers. She couldn't.

The children as she'd known them were gone. These kids? Not. Her. Problem.

The wheel beneath her hands creaked and started to splinter. She forced her grip to relax.

Ishim woke, and they shared a quick meal of flatbread and dried fruit. Supplies were low and it hadn't rained in a few days. They'd have to start boiling river water soon, or use the precious gallons of filtered water on their passengers. They had filter tabs, but those made water taste awful, and Karron's shit turn to tar, so she avoided them unless it was dire. There was a settlement nearby, just upstream where their Covenant coin would spend. Fresh water, maybe fresh fruit and vegetables. Maybe even game meat. Karron was getting tired of fish and flatbread.

They doused the sails after losing the stern wind as the river narrowed, and pushed the boat with long poles through the smaller canal-like passage that should connect up to the Zouri tributaries. She hadn't sailed this way since the previous summer, and the winter rains and flooding could have changed things. It wouldn't be the first time.

Hours of poling felt good on her muscles, taking her mind off the kids. Something red caught her eye off the port side as she shoved the long pole into the canal bed. Metal, the remnant of a settlement here probably before the Ring, back when Earth had a moon and this whole land was called the United States. Fragments survived even in the wilderness, sometimes rising like the carcass of a long-dead beast from reeds and swamp.

Part of a bridge, Karron realized. She'd seen it before, the broken expanse stretching like an accusing finger pointing over the water. It hadn't been red then. It was painted on the side toward her, bright and fresh.

She went still, pole in her hands nearly forgotten.

Ishim cursed and she made herself turn and look to the starboard side. Nolan had a .38 revolver pointed at Ishim's head. The way the man held it, it was clear he had practice with a gun and was ready to kill.

"Pole over to the bank there by that bridge," Jill said. She stood near the mast, another gun held in one hand, pointed down but with her finger near the trigger.

"Don't do anything stupid," Nolan added.

Karron contemplated doing something stupid. The nanos in her head were angry insects begging to be let free. They buzzed through her, little twitches of muscle and thought which she had tried to euthanize with time and quiet.

Jam the pole into the river, shove the ship hard right. Grab the gaff two steps fore, take five steps, remove gun from man. Throw gaff and rope at woman. Take gun, kill. Two shots.

She ran it in her head ten different ways. Every time, Ishim had a high chance of being shot before she got to the man. She had a high chance of being shot, too, but a bullet or two would only piss her off, not take her down.

The kids stayed aft, crouched on a blanket, staring at the deck. No help there.

Ishim caught her eye and shook his head, his graying braids swinging with the movement. Karron pressed her lips together and nodded. She would wait then; wait for the passengers to screw up. Humans always screwed up.

They poled over to shore. The hull ground into the reeds, and Jill threw a rope up onto the broken bridge. A man rose from above and caught it, tying the ship off. Two more men made their way out of the brush and slogged into the shallows.

"Lower the ladder. This is where you get off," Jill said, motioning with her pistol. Covenant gun, the pointed cross clearly stamped on the barrel.

"I am not leaving my ship," Ishim said. He folded thickly muscled black arms over his chest, chin up. "You want to go somewhere, we'll take you. But I do not leave my ship."

She and Ishim had checked all the bags. They'd made Jill and Nolan stand while they patted them down, too. Where had they hidden the guns?

Karron looked back at the kids. They hadn't checked them. Stupid of her. She should know how dangerous children could be. He hadn't told her, the other night. Karron wondered if the boy would have, if she'd agreed to help. He hadn't said a word, because he knew the man and woman would force her hand if they had guns. It was how a War Child would think, what she would have done in his place.

Oni caught her eye now and mouthed a word of apology, looking decades older than seven. Bee clung to him, staring at the planks, her knuckles white where she gripped Oni's shirt. There was a gun on the ship, next to the steam engine in a hidden compartment. Fat lot of good it would do her now. She had a small knife on her belt. Knife in a gunfight. Not so good either.

All scenarios led to Ishim being shot before she could fight back.

Her mind buzzed, her blood singing the song of death. The song of war.

Memories buried and half-forgotten arose, snapping into place like a joint of out of socket. She'd killed once before to protect the ship, to protect Ishim. She'd come back from the warm rage that time. She could return again from that bright place. She had no choice.

Karron raised her eyes from the kids to the Ring where it slashed the blue skies above, shining white in the sun. She was no more able to stop being a killer than the Ring was able to stop dropping rocks. Hating the Ring for the storms and the fires was as pointless as hating the sun for shining. Hating her nanotech and her training was the same. She could fight it, the way they fought the river to move upstream. But let go, stop for a moment, and she would drift like the ship, going the way nature intended.

Karron set her pole down slowly. It was too long to use as a weapon. She turned to Jill after a glance told her the men on the shore didn't have guns in their hands.

"You think you are the first to try to hijack our ship? Ishim and his brother built this ship with their hands, sweat, and tears. His brother's name is on the hull, his brother's blood in the nails and boards, his hair in the rope and sail." Karron moved slowly to her left. One more step and she'd have the gaffing hook. She kept her eyes on Jill.

"A captain," she continued, knowing Ishim would hear her, knowing he'd understand, "a true captain always goes *down* with his ship."

Oni acted before she could. The boy crossed the deck in a blur of preternatural speed, whipping the blanket into a weapon before him. It caught Jill in the side and threw her off balance. The boy was small, and there wasn't much strength in the blow, but the blanket's momentum shoved her into the mast, distracting the woman for a precious moment.

Karron grabbed the gaffing hook. Ishim dropped to the deck, sweeping his own pole to the side and catching Nolan in the legs with it. Karron sprang and landed on the man. She plunged the pointed end of the gaff into his throat with her right hand even as her left went for the revolver. Blood sprayed from his mouth as a gunshot cracked out over the water.

Bee screamed. Karron wrenched the revolver from Nolan's dying fingers and rolled to the side, pointing the gun where she'd last seen Jill.

Oni was down, holding his hands to his thin stomach, dark blood welling between his fingers. Jill turned, swinging the gun a little wildly. Dimly, at the edge of her battle-focused awareness, Karron saw movement as the man on the bridge jumped to the deck and the other two tried to climb the side.

The revolver was her hand, a metal extension of her killing will. Fifteen years without a gun, and she felt as though time had stood still. She was a Child again, full of light, bright and hot and deadly.

The laughter ringing over the water was her own, echoing back at her as she squeezed the trigger.

One shot for Jill, giving the woman a third eye and a baffled expression before she toppled over. Two shots for the man who had jumped to the deck. One shot for the man climbing over the railing.

Karron gained her feet and ran to the rail. The final man wasn't trying to climb up anymore. He sloshed and slogged to the firmer shore, trying to run. She raised the gun. Two shots left, if the weight was right, if it was as she remembered.

"Karron."

Ishim's voice broke her focus. The big man moved up beside her, carefully making noise and staying out of striking distance.

She kept her eyes on the escaping prey.

"Karron," he repeated. "Look to the sky."

Her arms shook with the effort of holding the gun without firing; Karron forced herself to look up.

"Ringlight," she murmured. "Sunlight. Earthlight. Ringlight. Sunlight. Earthlight." Over and over until the words became nothing but breathing.

Karron lowered the gun.

The man was gone, lost to the brush. She could have hunted him down, but the light was fading inside. She was tired, the buzzing in her head growing quiet as the moment passed.

"Help him," Bee said, the little girl's voice strained but strong.

"They are like me," Karron said. "He'll live. Get powder for the bleeding. He'll live," she repeated. "He is like me."

Ishim went for the first aid kit. Karron went for the bodies. She cut their throats before she hauled them over the side, shoving away her aroused, visceral reaction to the salt and copper scent of blood.

They'd have to scrub the boards. The blood would stain. The coin would buy paint to hide the stains. Karron kept her thoughts flowing, simple, calm thoughts. Lists of things to do. She ignored the kids as long as she could, getting the boat unhooked. Oni would live. Ishim would help him.

Oni slept in a pile of blankets, Bee holding his hand. Ishim and Karron didn't speak, just poled further up the channel. They would skip the settlement.

"He'll need a good meal," she said eventually, as the sun set and painted the Ring orange and pink.

"There's an inlet ahead. I can hunt."

"I'll hunt."

The rabbit was slow and fat on spring grass. Karron used a thrown rock to bring it down. The hard earth beneath her feet felt strange as she made her way back to the river.

Ishim had brought the kids down off the ship and started a fire on the driest bit of land they could find. Oni's color was better, his eyes bright and clear.

"You could have told me about the guns," Karron said as she quartered the rabbit into the small kettle before adding precious pure water to the stew.

"You wouldn't have helped us," Oni said.

"You knew?" Ishim said, looking at Karron, making it clear he was talking about the kids, not about the guns.

"Only last night. They weren't our problem." She lifted a shoulder in a half-shrug. "Smugglers and questions, right?"

"We're your problem now," Oni said with the kind of smug smile only a child used to being the smartest person around could wear.

"And where do you expect us to take you? Ria?"

"We have been paid to take them that far," Karron offered.

Ishim looked at Karron and shook his head with a small smile of his own.

"No," Oni said. "Sanctuary."

Karron laughed, the sound barking from her throat, surprising her. "That's a myth. Hell, we told each other that myth in my crèche."

Sanctuary. A place where they had tech that could take out the nanos. Tech to calm them, make a War Child normal again. A place where no one would make you kill, a place where no brothers or sisters went insane and had to be put down like rabid dogs.

A myth. A bedtime story told by motherless children. Told by killers.

"I have a map," Oni said. "Give me your knife."

Karron drew her knife, trying not to think of the throats it had cut today.

"Wait," Ishim said, reaching for Oni as the boy cut into his own arm with a sure stroke.

Karron caught Ishim's forearm and pushed him back. "He's like me," she said.

Oni pulled a small tube from under his skin. Already his nanos were closing the wound, the blood welling, slowing, and stopping even as she watched. He handed the knife back before opening the tube.

Inside was a map on thin paper. No, Karron saw, not paper. Leather of some kind. So thin that when he held it up in the firelight, the flames shone straight through. Illuminating lines. River lines. Numbers. A small star, done in red ink, like a drop of blood.

"Zouri to James, James to Dakota. Then west, to the Yellowstone and into the mountains. I have coordinates, see those numbers? Not a myth. It's real. The ones who made us, they came from there. We were to be the new generation, the new kind of Child."

"I am Eve," Bee added. "I hate being Eve. Wanna be Bee. Bees can sting."

"Jill and Nolan were from Sanctuary?" Ishim asked.

Karron was silent, still staring at the map, holding her breath, trying to decide if a legend could be real.

"No, they worked there. I don't know what happened. Funding dried up. The Covenant doesn't want more Children, I guess. They ended the program, and we were supposed to be destroyed."

Karron tore her eyes from the map and looked at Oni. "History repeats," she said softly.

"Marta, the woman you call Jill, she stole us. Said a baron would pay for us. She killed the others, but not before Sandy, the woman from Sanctuary, gave me the map and told me how to find it." Oni leaned back against the piled blankets with a pained sigh and carefully rolled up the map.

The stew started to boil over. Karron turned away from the kids, from the map to an impossible place, and settled for dealing with dinner.

Later—her belly full of spring roots and rabbit—she stood at the edge of the river and watched lights smear across the darkening sky. Ishim came up beside her, making no attempt to hide his approach.

"Do we take them to this place, this Sanctuary?" he said.

"*Tarik* is yours," Karron said. She turned and looked at her friend. Her real words were unspoken. *Don't make me decide.*

"We been on the river a long time," Ishim said. "Drifting up and down. Been a long time since I did anything but sail with my grief and try to outrun old memories."

"We are alike," Karron said, her mouth twisting into what felt like a smile. At least on the outside. "I like the river. Sanctuary is a dream, nothing more."

"Maybe it's time we stopped drifting," Ishim said with a too-casual shrug. "Can't just leave two kids on their own. But if you don't want to go, we'll set them down in Ria. That boy is smart as ten men. He'll figure his way and take care of his sister."

Karron nodded and looked back to the sky as Ishim moved back toward the camp. She walked to the very edge of the river. Water soaked through her boots, her toes going numb as she stood on the muddy bank. Oni and Bee. Children like she had been. Like she still was, in the bright moments she couldn't quite seem to escape.

"Water, water, everywhere," she murmured. Bending low, she dug her fingers into the mud and squeezed, feeling the gritty earth slide over her skin.

Sanctuary meant healing, meant being free of insanity, free of the things in her head. Myth. Myth like War Children were becoming a myth. Another generation, and they'd be as forgotten as most of the texts and histories from before the Ring, as much legend as the Archive was legend, as the great Wars would become in thirty or fifty more years.

Ishim was right. She had been drifting on the river. But now she had a brother and sister again. And they had a map. A map to a dream.

Karron bent down and let the river wash the last traces of grit from her hand.

Maybe it was time to dream again.

CARRIERS

Tananarive Due

2055
Republic of Sacramento
Carrier Territories

Nayima's sleep had turned restless as she aged, so the rattling from the chicken coop outside woke her before her hens raised the alarm. The intruder was likely either feline or human, and she hoped it was the former. A cat, no matter how big, wasn't as dangerous as a person.

Nayima ignored the sharp throb in her knee when she jumped from her bed and ran outside with her sawed-off in time to see a hound-sized tabby scurrying away with a young hen pinned in its teeth, a snow globe of downy white feathers trailing behind. The army of night cats scattered in swishing bushes and brittle leaves. The giant thief paused to look back at her, his eyes glowing gold with threat. The cats were getting bigger.

Nayima had been saving that hen for Sunday dinner, but she was too winded to chase the thief. Now both knees throbbed. And her lower back, right on schedule. She fired once into the dark and hoped she'd hit him.

Fucking cats.

The dark was thick to the forsaken east, but to the west she saw the gentle orange glow from the colony in Sacramento, the fortress she would never enter. The town folk had electricity to spare, since their lights never went fully dark anymore. They were building a real-life Emerald City from the ruins, with bright lights and fresh water flowing in the streets—literally, after the levees flooded back in the '20s.

By contrast, her tract, Nayimaland, was two-hundred acres of dead farmland she shared with feral cats made bold because food was scarce—taken by drought, not the Plague. The late State of California had yet more dying to do.

Nayima felt thirsty, but she didn't stop at her sealed barrel to take a scoop. She couldn't guess how long her standing water would have to last. Sacramento owed her water credits, but she would be a fool to trust their promises.

At the rear of the chicken coop, Nayima found the hole the cat had torn in the mesh and lashed loose wires to close it. The hens were unsettled, so she could expect broken eggs. And she couldn't afford to cook one of her reliable laying hens, so she'd have to wait for meat at least another week, until trading day.

By the time Nayima came back to her porch, her two house cats, Tango and Buster, had gathered enough courage to poke their heads up in the window. For an instant, her pets looked like the thief cat, no better.

"It's okay, babies," she said. "One of 'em got a chicken."

Buster, still aloof, raised his tail good night and went to his sofa. But Tango followed her to her bedroom and jumped beside her to sleep. Nayima preferred a bare mattress to the full bed that had been in this room—fewer places for intruders to hide and surprise her. She slept beneath the window, where she could always open her eyes and see the sky. Tango rested his weight against her; precious warmth and a thrumming heartbeat to calm her nerves.

"I can't feed you all," she told Tango. "I'm crazy for taking in just you two." Tango slowly blinked his endless green eyes at her, his cat language for love. Nayima returned Tango's long, slow blink.

• • •

Nayima thought the jangling bells outside soon after dawn meant that a cat had been caught in a cage, but when she went to investigate, she found Raul's mud-painted red pickup slewed across the dirt path to her ranch house. He was cursing in Spanish. His front tire had caught a camouflaged cage, and he was stooping to check the damage. At least a dozen sets of cats' eyes floated like marbles in the dry shrubbery.

"Don't shoot!" Raul called to her. He knew she had her little sawed-off without looking back. "You'll blow off your own culo with that rusty thing one day. ¿Es todo, Nayima?"

Despite the disturbance and his complaining, Nayima was glad to see Raul. He looked grand in morning sunshine. Raul's eyes drooped slightly, giving the impression of drowsiness, but he was handsome, with a fine jaw and silvering hair he wore in two long braids like his Apache forebears. Since reconciliation and the allotment of the Carrier Territories eight years ago, Raul looked younger every time she saw him.

Nayima had turned sixty-one or sixty-two in December—she barely tracked her age anymore—and she and Raul were among the youngest left, so most carriers had died before the territories were allotted. In their human cages.

Captivity had been their repayment for the treatment and vaccine from the antibodies in their blood. They were outcasts, despite zero human transmissions of the virus after Year One. The single new case twenty-five years ago had been a lab accident, and the serum had knocked it out quick.

The Ward B carriers Nayima had barely known still lived communally, or close enough to walk to each other's ranches. But Nayima had chosen seclusion on an airy expanse of unruly farmland that stretched as far as she could see. In containment, she'd never had the luxury of community, except Raul. She had enough human contact on her market trips, where she made transactions through a wall. Or her hour-long ride on her ATV to see Raul, if she wanted conversation. Other people wearied her.

"Sorry—cat problem," she told Raul. "Did it rip?" She had a few worn tires in her shed from the previous owner, but they were at least forty years old.

Raul exhaled, relieved. "No, creo que está bien."

She squatted beside him, close enough to smell the sun on his clothes. She had not seen Raul in at least thirty days. He had begged her to share his house, but she had refused. She needed to talk to him from time to time, but she remembered why she did not want to live with him, and why she had slept with him only once: Raul's persistent recollections about his old neighborhood in Rancho Cucamonga and his grandparents' house in Nogales were unbearable. He always wanted to talk about the days before the Plague.

But after forty years, he was family. He'd been a gangly fifteen-year-old when the lab-coats captured him. Shivering and crying, he had webbed his fingers to reach toward her hand against the sheet of glass.

Nayima missed skin. She felt sorry for the new children, being raised not to touch. She absently ran her fingertips along the dirt-packed ridges in the tire's warm rubber.

"Do you have meat?" she said.

"Five pounds of dried beef," he said. Nayima didn't care much for beef, but meat was meat. "In the back of the truck. And a couple of water barrels."

Water barrels? A gift that large probably wasn't from Raul alone, and she didn't like owing anyone.

"From Sacramento?"

"You're doing a school talk today, I heard. Liaison's office asked me to come out."

Nayima's temper flared. She could swear she'd felt a *ping* at her right temple an hour before, waking her from fractured sleep. The lab-coats denied that they abused her tracking chip, but was it a coincidence she had a school obligation that day? And how dare they send so little water!

Nayima was so angry that her first words came in Spanish, because she wanted Raul's full attention. He had taught her Spanish, just as she had taught him so much else, patient lessons through locked doors. "Que me deben créditos, Raul. They owe a lot more than two barrels."

"You'll get your créditos. This is just…" He waved his hand, summoning the right word. Then he gave up. "Por favor, Nayima. Take them. You earned them." He tested the air pressure in his tire with a pound of his fist. "Gracias a Díos this is okay."

Nayima's shaky faith had been shattered during the Plague, but Raul still held fast to his God. *He told us the Apocalypse was coming in Revelation,* he always said, as if that excused it all. Nayima still believed Sunday dinner should be special, but only to honor the memory of her grandmother's weekly feasts.

Two new orange water barrels stood in the bed of Raul's truck. Large ones. She needed more credits to get her faucets running, but the barrels would last a while. Nayima climbed up, grabbing the bed's door to swing her leg over. She winced at the pain in her knees as she landed. She treasured the freedom to move her body, but movement came with a cost.

"¿Estás bien, querida?" Raul said.

"Just my knees. Stop fussing."

Nayima fumbled with an unmarked plastic crate tied beside the closest barrel.

"Don't open that yet," Raul said.

But she already had. Inside, she found the beef, wrapped in paper and twine. Still not quite dry, judging by the grease spots.

But she forgot the jerky when she saw two dolls, both long-haired girls, one with brown skin, one white. The dolls' hands were painted with blue plastic gloves, but nothing else. They had lost their clothes, lying atop a folded, obscenely pink blanket.

"What the hell's this?" Nayima said.

Raul walked closer as if he carried a heavy sack of across his shoulders. "I wanted to talk to you," he said, voice low. He reached toward her. "Come down. Walk with me."

"Bullshit," she said. "Why is Sacramento sending me dolls?"

"Bejar de la truck," Raul insisted. "Por favor. Let's walk. I have to tell you something."

Nayima was certain Raul had sold her out in some way, she just couldn't guess how. Raul had always been more willing to play political games; he'd been so much younger when he'd been found, raised without knowing any better. So Raul's house had expensive solar panels that kept his water piping hot and other niceties she did not bother to covet. His old pickup truck, which ran on precious ethanol and gasoline, was another of his luxuries for the extra time and blood he was always willing to give the lab-coats.

Nayima climbed out of the truck more carefully than she'd climbed in, refusing Raul's aid. Living in small spaces for most of her life had left her joints irritable and stiff, even with daily exercises to loosen them. If she'd had the energy or balance, she would have shoved Raul down on his ass.

"Start talking," she said. "What have you done?"

"Put the gun down first."

Nayima hadn't realized she was pointing the shotgun at him. She lowered it. "Tell me ahora, Raul. No hay más secretos." Raul's secrets stung more than anyone else's.

"I won a ruling," Raul said.

"About what? Free toys?"

Raul stared out toward the thirsty grasslands. "I have a library portal at my house…" he began.

Of course he did. Toys and gadgets. That was Raul.

Raul went on. "I did some research on… the embryos."

Nayima's cheek flared as if he'd struck her. During Reconciliation, she and Raul had learned that dozens of embryos had been created from her eggs and his sperm, more than they'd known. They had been the cocktail du jour; something about their blood types. Her heart gave a sudden sick tumbling in her chest, as if to drown him out.

"There's a bebé, Nayima," he said, whispering like wind. "One survived."

The world went white. Her eyesight, her thoughts, lost.

"What? When?"

"She just turned four," he said. "She's still in the research compound."

There was a *she* somewhere?

"How long have you known?"

"Six months," he said. "When I got the portal. I saw rumors of the surviving infant, did the research. She's one of ours. They never told us."

Now Nayima's sacrifices seemed fresh: the involuntary harvesting of her eggs, three first-trimester miscarriages after forced insemination, a succession of unviable embryos created in labs, and two premature live births of infants from artificial wombs who had never survived beyond a day. Pieces of her chopped away.

"We can't reproduce," she said.

"But one lived," Raul said. "They don't know why."

"You've known all this time? And you never told me?"

He sighed. "Lo siento, Nayima. I hated hiding it. But I knew it would upset you. Or you might work against me. I didn't want to say anything until I got a ruling. As the biological father, I have rights."

"Carriers don't have rights."

"Parental rights," Raul said. "For the first time—yes, we do."

Nayima despised herself for her volcanic emotions. How could Raul be naïve enough to believe Sacramento's lies? If there was a surviving child—which she did not believe—they would not release their precious property to carriers.

"It's a trick," she said. "To get us to go back there."

Raul shook his head slowly. Impossibly, he smiled. "No, Nayima," he said. "They're sending her to us. To you. She's free under Reconciliation to be with her parents. All you have to do is sign the consent when they come."

Nayima needed to sit, so she ignored her sore joints and sat where she'd been standing, on the caked dirt of her road. The air felt thick and heavy in her lungs.

"No," Nayima said. Saying the word gave her strength. "No no no. We can't. It's a trap. Even if there's a girl…" It was so improbable, Nayima could barely say the words. "And there isn't… But even if there is, why would they offer her except as a weapon against us? To threaten us? To control us? Why do they keep trying so hard to make children from us? She's not from my womb, so she doesn't have the antibodies. Think about it! We're just… reserves for them. A blood supply, if they ever need it. That's the only reason we're still alive."

Raul's eyes dropped. He couldn't deny it.

"She's our child," Raul said. "Ella es nuestra bebé. We can't leave her there."

"You can't—but I can," she said. "Watch me."

Raul's voice cracked. "The ruling says both living parents must consent. I need you with me on this, Nayima."

"I'm an old woman now!" Nayima said. Her throat burned hot.

"And I'm fifty-six," Raul said. "But we had una hija together. The marshals are bringing her here tomorrow."

"You're sending marshals to me?" The last time marshals came to see her in the territories after only nine months, a pack of them had removed her from the house she had chosen and stolen half of her chickens, shooting a dozen dead just for fun. Her earliest taste of freedom had been a false start, victim to a government property dispute.

"Marshals aren't like they were," Raul said. "Things are changing, Nayima." Like he was scolding her.

Raul lowered the truck's bed door and pulled out the plastic crate. He carried it to her porch. Next, he took down the barrels and rolled them to the house one by one. The heavy barrels thundered across the soil.

When he returned, breathing hard, Nayima was on her feet again, with her gun. She jacked a shell into the chamber. "You could've shot me before I did all that work," Raul said.

"I'm not shooting you yet," she said. "But any marshals that show up here tomorrow are declaring war. They might bring her, but they could take her at any time. We're all property! I won't give them that power over me. She's better off dead. I'm not afraid to die too."

Raul gave her a forlorn look before he walked past her and slammed the bed of his truck shut. "I was hoping for some eggs, pero maybe mañana."

"I swear to your God, Raul, I will kill anyone who comes to this house."

Raul opened his driver's side door and began to climb back inside, but he stopped to look at her over his shoulder. He had left his truck idling. He had never planned to stay long.

"She doesn't have a name," he said.

"What?"

"Nobody bothered to name her. In the records, she's called Specimen 120. Punto. Some of the researchers call her Chubby for a nickname. Like a pet, Nayima. Our hija."

The weight of the shotgun made Nayima's arms tremble.

"Don't bring anyone here," she said. "Please."

Raul got in the truck and slammed the door. He lurched into reverse, turned the truck away, and drove. Nayima fired once into the air, a roar of rage that echoed across the flatlands. The shotgun kicked in her arms like an angry baby.

After the engine's hum was lost in the open air, the only sound was Nayima's wretched sobs.

• • •

In her front room, Nayima's comm screen flared white, turning itself on. A minder waited in five-by-five on her wall, as though she'd been invited to breakfast. The light haloing her was bright enough to show old acne scars. Makeup had yet to make a comeback, except the enhanced red lips favored by both men and women. Full of life.

"Hello, Nayima," the minder said. Then she corrected herself: "Ms. Dixon."

Nayima nodded cordially. Nayima's grandmother, born in Alabama, had never stood for being called by her first name, and neither did Nayima—an admittedly old-fashioned trait at a time when numbers mattered more than names.

The minder seemed to notice Nayima's puffed eyes, and her polite veneer dulled. "You remember the guidelines?"

Guideline One and Only: She was not to criticize the lab-coats or make it sound as if she had been treated badly. Blah blah blah and so forth. Questions about the embryo—the *girl*—broiled in Nayima's mind, but she didn't dare bring her up. Maybe the marshals wouldn't come. Maybe she could still get her water credits.

"Yes," Nayima said, testing her thin voice.

"We added younger students this year," the minder said. "Stand by."

Three smaller squares appeared inset beneath the girl's image—classrooms, the children progressively older in each. The far left square held the image of twelve wriggling, worming children ages about three to six sprawled across a floor with a red mat. A few in the front sat transfixed by her image on what seemed to be a looming screen, high above them. Every child wore tiny, powder blue plastic gloves.

Nayima had to look away from the smallest children. She had not seen children so young in forty years, and the sight of them was acid to her eyes.

Hadn't Raul said the girl was four?

Nayima blinked rapidly, her eyes itching with tears.

Crying, she was certain, was against the guidelines.

Nayima willed herself to look at the young, moony faces, braving memories of tiny bodies rotting on sidewalks, in cars, on the roadways, mummified in closets. These were new children—untouched by Plague. Their parents had been the wealthy, the isolated, the truly Chosen—the infinitesimal number of survivors who were not carriers, who did not have the antibodies, but had simply, somehow, survived.

Nayima leaned closer to her screen. "Boo!" she said.

Young eyes widened with terror. Children scooted away.

But when Nayima smiled, the entire mass of them quivered with laughter, a sea of perfect teeth.

Nayima's teeth were not perfect. She had never replaced the lower front tooth she'd lost to a lab-coat she'd smacked across his nose, drawing blood. He'd strapped her to a table, raped her, and extracted her tooth on the spot, without anesthesia.

Nayima had been offered a dental implant during Reconciliation, but a new tooth felt like a lie, so she had refused. In previous classroom visits, she had answered the question *What happened to your tooth?* without bitterness—why should she feel contempt for brutes any more than she would a tree dropping leaves?—until a minder pointed out that the anecdote about her extracted tooth violated the guidelines.

The guidelines left Nayima with very little to say. She chose each word with painful care.

These schoolchildren asked the usual questions: why she had survived (genetic predisposition), how many people she had infected (only one personally, as far as she knew), how many carriers were left (fifteen, since most known carriers were "gone now"). By the fourth question, Nayima had lost her will to look at the children's faces. It was harder all the time.

The girl who spoke up next was not yet eight. Her face held a whisper of brown; a girl who might have been hers. And Raul's.

"Do you have any children?" the girl said.

All of Nayima's work, gone. No composure. No smile. A sharp pain in her belly.

"No, I've never had children," she said. "None that survived."

Nayima shot a pointed gaze at the minder, who did not contradict her. Maybe the minder didn't know about Specimen 120. Maybe a bureaucrat had made up the story to tease Raul.

"Okay," the girl said, shrugging, not yet schooled in the art of condolences. "What do you miss the most about the time before the Plague?"

An easy answer came right away, and it almost wasn't a lie. "Halloween."

When she explained what Halloween had been, the children sat literally open-mouthed. She wondered which part of her story most stupefied them. The ready access to sweets? The trust of strangers? The costumes?

The host looked relieved with the children's enchantment and announced that the visit was over. A flurry of waving blue gloves. Nayima waved back. She even smiled again.

"Don't forget my water credits," Nayima said from behind her happy teeth.

But the minder's image had already flashed away.

• • •

Nayima lined up her contraband on the front table—the sawed-off, a box of shells, an old Colt she'd found in the attic with its full magazine, the baseball bat she kept at her bedside. She'd even found a gas mask she'd bartered for at market. When the marshals came, she would be prepared. In her younger years, she would have boarded up at least her front windows, but her weapons would have to do.

"Raul is the real child," she told Tango and Buster while they watched her work. Buster swatted at a loose shell at the edge of the table, but Nayima caught it before it hit the floor. "He believes every word they say. 'Things are changing,' he says. Believing in miracles. Sending marshals here—to me!"

Tango mewed softly. A question.

"Of course they're not bringing a child here," she said. "A judge's ruling? In favor of carriers? You know the lab-coats would fight to keep her." She shook her head, angry with herself for her weakness. "Besides, there is no child. Babies with carrier genes don't live."

The crate was light enough to lift to the table with only slight pressure in her lower back, gone when she stretched. But she could only roll a barrel slowly, oh-so-slowly, across her threshold. How had Raul managed so easily? She left the second barrel outside. By the time she closed her door again, her lower back pulsed with pain and she felt aged by a decade.

"Lies," Nayima said.

Tango and Buster agreed with frenzied mews.

She would have no Sunday dinner if she died tomorrow, Nayima reminded herself. So she got her cleaver from the kitchen, unwrapped the beef, and began chopping the meat on the table, not caring about dents in the wood. She chopped until she was perspiring and sweat stung her eyes.

Nayima held a chunk with both hands and sank in her teeth. She mostly did not bother with salt in her own cooking, so the taste was overwhelming at first. The cats gnawed at the meat beside her on the table with loud purrs.

"Could there be a child?"

Suppose they'd had a breakthrough, found a way to rewire the genes? But why go through that trouble and expense when other children were being born? The girl must be a failed experiment. A laboratory fluke. Did they need caretakers for a child born with half a brain—was that it? Nayima swore she'd be damned if she'd spend the years she had left tending the lab-coats' mistakes.

"But there is no child," she reminded Tango and Buster. "It's all a lie."

After dark, with her flashlight to guide her, Nayima set her traps for the thief cat with slices of meat and visited the wooden chicken coop Raul had helped her build, as big as her grandmother's backyard shed. She checked the loose wires in the rear, but the hole was still secure. She hadn't collected eggs earlier, so chickens had defecated on some. A few eggs lay entirely crushed, yolks seeping across the straw.

Nayima was exhausted by the time she'd cleaned the nestboxes, scrubbed the surviving eggs, and set them on a bowl in her kitchen for Raul to find later—but she couldn't afford to sleep tonight. The marshals might come at any time.

Nayima fixed herself a cup of black tea from her new water—so fresh!—and sat vigil by her front window with her shotgun, watching the empty pathway. Sometimes her eyes played tricks, animating the darkness. A far-off cat's cry sounded like a baby's, waking Nayima when she dozed.

Just before dawn, bells jingled near the chicken coop. Heart clambering, Nayima ran outside. The food was gone from the first trap she reached, but the door had not properly sprung. Shit.

More frantic jingling came from the trap twenty yards farther. Nayima raced toward it, her light in one hand and her gun in the other.

A pair of eyes glared out at her from beyond the bars.

The cat scrambled to every corner of the cage, desperate to escape while bells mocked him. This was the one. Nayima recognized the monster tabby's unusual size.

"Buddy, you stole the wrong chicken."

Nayima could not remember the last time she had felt so giddy. She carefully lowered her flashlight to the ground, keeping it trained on the trap. Then she raised her shotgun, aiming. She'd blow a hole in her trap this way, but she had caught the one she was looking for.

The cat mewed—not angry, beseeching. With a clear understanding of his situation.

"You started it, not me," Nayima said. "Don't sit there begging now."

The cat's trapped eyes glowed in her bright beam. Another plaintive mew.

"Shut up, you hear me? This is your fault." But her resolve was flagging.

The cat raised his paw, shaking the cage door. How many times had she done the very same thing? How many locks had she tested, searching for freedom?

Could there really be a child?

Nayima sobbed. Her throat was already raw from crying. Never again, she had said. No more tears. No more.

Nayima went to the trap's door and flipped up the latch. The cat hissed at her and raced away like a jaguar, melting into the dark. She hoped he would run for miles, never looking back.

Is my little girl with those zookeepers without even a name?

"But it's all lies," she whispered at the window, as she stroked Tango in her lap. "Isn't it?"

Dawn came and went with the roosters' crowing. Nayima did not move to collect the morning eggs, or to eat any of the beef she and the cats had left, or to empty her bulging bladder. She watched the sky light up her empty pathway, her open gate.

Why hadn't she closed the gate?

Based on the sun high above, it was nearly noon when Nayima finally stood up.

The metallic glint far down the roadway looked imaginary at first. To be sure, Nayima wiped away dust on her window pane with her shirt, although the spots outside still clouded it. The gleam seemed to vanish, but then it was back, this time with bright cobalt blue lights that looked out of place against the browns and grays of the road. Two sets of blue lights danced in regimented patterns, back and forth.

Nayima's breath fogged her window as she leaned closer, so she wiped it again.

Hoverbikes!

Two large hoverbikes were speeding toward her house, one on each side of the road at a matching pace, blue lights snaking across their underbellies. At least it wasn't an army, unless more were coming. Marshals' hoverbikes were only big enough for two, at most.

"You damn fool, Raul," she whispered again, but she already had forgiven him too.

Nayima was too exhausted to pick up her shotgun. She had failed the test with her cat thief, so what made her think she could fight marshals? Let them take what they wanted. As long as she had Tango and Buster, she could start again. She always did.

As the hoverbikes flew past her gate, Nayima counted one front rider on each bike in the marshals' uniform: black jackets with orange armbands. The second rider on the lead bike was only Raul—his face was hidden behind the black helmet, but she knew his red hickory shirt. His father had worn one just like it, Raul had told her until she wanted to scream.

"Nayima!" Raul called. He flung his helmet to the ground.

The hoverbike Raul was riding hadn't quite slowed to a stop, floating six inches above the ground, so Raul stumbled when he leaped off in a hurry. The marshal grabbed his arm to help hold him steady while the bike bobbed obediently in place.

"Querida, it's me," Raul said. "Don't worry about the marshals. Please open the door."

Nayima stared as both marshals took off their helmets, almost in unison, and rested them in the crooks of their arms. One was a young man, one a woman, neither older than twenty-five. The man was fair-haired and ruddy. The woman's skin was nearly as dark as her own, her hair also trimmed to fuzz. Had she seen this man during an earlier classroom visit? He looked familiar, and he was smiling. They both were. She had never seen a marshal smile.

The marshals wore no protective suits. No masks. They did not hide their faces or draw weapons. Even ten yards away, through a dirty window, Nayima saw their eyes.

Nayima jumped when Raul banged on her door. "Nayima, ella está aquí!"

"I don't see her." Nayima tried to shout, but her throat nearly strangled her breath.

Raul motioned to the woman marshal, and she dismounted her hoverbike. For the first time, Nayima saw her bike's passenger—not standing, but in a backward facing seat. A child stirred as the woman unstrapped her.

It couldn't be. *Couldn't* be. Nayima closed her eyes. Had they drugged her meat? Was it a hallucination?

"Do you see, Nayima?" Raul said. "Ven afuera conmigo. Please come."

Raul left her porch to run back to the hoverbike. Freed from her straps, a child reached out for a hand for Raul's help from the seat. Raul made a game of it, lifting the child up high. Curly spirals of dark hair nestled her shoulders. For an instant, the child was silhouetted in the sunlight, larger than life in Raul's sturdy upward grasp.

The girl giggled loudly enough for Nayima to hear her through the window pane. Raul was a good father. Nayima could see it already.

"Now you're going to meet your mamí," Raul said.

Nayima hid behind her faded draperies as Raul took the girl's hand and walked to the porch with her. When she heard the twin footsteps on her wooden planks, Nayima's world swayed. She ventured a peek and saw the girl's inquisitive face turned toward the window—dear Jesus, this angel had Gram's nose and plump, cheerful cheeks. Raul's lips. Buried treasure was etched in her delicate features.

Jesus. Jesus. *Thank you, Dear Lord.*

Nayima opened her door.

IN THE VALLEY OF THE SHADOW OF THE PROMISED LAND

Robin Wasserman

"So it was, and so it is written:

And fire rained from the sky, and Abraham died, and all his brethren, and all that generation of the world were burned away."

Isaac had really thought writing the bible would be easier.

"And Isaac saved the children of Abraham and led them to the promised land.
And Isaac took Julia and Ellen for his wives and begat Joseph and Thomas.
And Joseph begat Simon who begat Noah and Reuben and Thomas begat Paul and Israel and Luke. And the children of Abraham were fruitful, and increased abundantly, and multiplied, and the land was bountiful, and the LORD was pleased and gave them his favor, and the children of Abraham filled the land."

The scribe falls silent, waiting; Isaac keeps his eyes closed, lets the words echo. Steeples his gnarled hands, draws a rasping breath, hocks up the phlegm.

Life is phlegm, now. Most likely death will be, too, a slow drowning in his own bed, gurgling and frothing. A death unfit for a patriarch. A voice, now, unfit for a patriarch, this phlegmy croak, but the scribe is of no use either, his thin warble that of a boy still proud of the peach fuzz on his balls, trying to prove himself to the sovereign Father. Failing.

"Again," Isaac snaps, and the boy, with his stuttering rhythm, reads back the morning's work.

And Isaac saved the children of Abraham.
And the children of Abraham filled the land.

Isaac likes the sound of these words, the roll and crest of them. He likes the tense of them, the tide sweeping the children's struggles into the past, smoothing its edges, blurring its sharp, painful lines. Between each verse, the fine-grained memories: brighter, for Isaac, than the details of his breakfast meal or his great-grandchildren's names. The burn of frostbitten fingertips in an ashen winter, the paperwhite crinkle of skin preserved too long from the sun. No room, in this new bible, for the names of the traitors who chose death over the Lord's command, the whores who stole away with their soft curves and gentle voices, the plump breasts and fertile wombs meant to belong to Isaac, leaving him to women like Julia and Ellen and Shirley and Kate, too fat or too old or too angry. Abandoning him to Kate's womb, all dried up, and Shirley's tongue so sharp no one could blame her hands for tying the noose, silencing it for good. Julia's inability, for so many years and so many daughters, to finally give Isaac a deserved son.

Isaac took Julia and begat Joseph. He appreciates the tidiness of it. The act of taking, his spindly thirteen-year-old limbs crushed against Julia's bulk, her meaty fingers on his spurting organ as he finally became a man—third try's the charm, her tears and his, their murmurs overlapping, *God's will God's will God's will,* let it be done, please God let it be done, and eventually, fifteen seconds later, seven years later, three daughters later, it was.

Isaac still thought, then, that the woman he'd loved would return from the wilderness, to save him as he had once saved her. He assumed the Lord would return her to the fold, because Isaac desired it.

It never happened. Isaac never found anyone worthy of replacing her, and the voice he'd once heard so clearly never spoke to him again. In body and spirit, Isaac was left alone.

Here is another bible he could write, testament of Isaac, son of Abraham.

And then the father abandoned the son, charged him to be a man before his time and lead his people through the dark times.
And then the son was left by those he loved, the father and the whore and the LORD his God.
And then the son led his people, and pretended at a voice he could no longer hear.
And the people were sheep and the son was a liar and they were fruitful and multiplied.

He will die soon, and his truth will die with him. His children and grandchildren and great-grandchildren, all those born after the skyfall, too young to mourn electricity or indoor plumbing, too trusting to question his version of the past, these are the ones who will build a future Isaac will never see. This week he will mark his birthday, and his Children will mark it for him, with pageants and jubilation, and Isaac will pretend to enjoy it, but he knows holidays are the present's way of embalming the past. This celebration of the birth of their savior doubles as an invitation to the grave; it would perhaps be less embarrassing for all if Isaac did as his forefathers had done and recede into ink and memory.

He will not begrudge them for it. Every man is ultimately a Moses, denied access to the future's promised land. Still: when the scribe finishes his reading, Isaac tells the bright-eyed young man that he's done an abominable job, that he's no longer of use in this task, that God has determined his place is in the pastures, where his back will knot and his skin will burn and the stink of cowshit will flavor every breath and bite, and once the boy has slunk away, pretending, pathetically, at gratitude for God's will, Isaac allows himself a smile.

• • •

"Well?" The strange man broadcasts impatience like a bad actor, stubby fingers tapping at tree trunk leg, lips pursed ducklike around rotting teeth. "What's it going to be?"

"Give me a minute, I'm thinking," Isaac says, hocking his phlegm, and Isaac is thinking, thinking *who* and *where* and well *what?*

Isaac is thinking that it's happening ever more often now, the amnesiac fogs that settle over him, shrouding the passage from present to future.

Isaac is thinking that God has finally returned to him, that in these sunblind spaces, God is speaking to him once again, and Isaac need only learn to hear.

He has his tricks. He knows how to observe, where to find the clues. This room is his room, the main living space of the small cabin in which he's dwelled ever since the children ventured out of their compound and back to the land. As they spread down the mountain, the children of Abraham reclaimed the homes left behind by a generation of dead. They buried rotting bodies in vegetable gardens and claimed brick split levels and ranch houses for their own. It was a temporary solution. The old world was tainted, Isaac taught them that. Living among its luxuries risked too much, and so as decades passed, they felled trees and cut beams and erected homes of their own.

Isaac sits in a chair taken from the compound, modest wood frame and fraying cushion, the chair that's suited him for sixty years. The stranger with the bald spot and the bulbous nose spills over the edges of his own narrow chair and grunts, "Yes or no, Dad?" and like that, his features resolve themselves into sorry familiarity. Isaac nods at his eldest son, guessing at *yes.* Judging from the subsequent scowl on Joseph's face, he has answered well.

Joseph is Isaac's eldest son and presumptive successor. He is also, unfortunately, a moron.

To be fair, dullness proliferates in the newer generations. These children of the skyfall are hardened to the laws of nature but softened to everything else, shaped by the slow, singular pace of their lives. However dimly, Isaac remembers the speed of the world before: fingers skimming across a keyboard, eyes lighting from one window to the next. He remembers tiny people skipping back and forth across a screen with rocket launchers and grenades, pocket universes born and extinguished behind the glass. He remembers that nothing ever seemed as important as the next thing, that there always was a next thing, on screen and off, that even the longest hours of boredom were crowded with claims on his attention. These new children—always children no matter how prematurely aged by sun and fieldwork—they can be absorbed entirely by the slow creep of clouds across the sky or the nut-cracking of an earnest squirrel. Isaac once watched a girl, already old enough to be married off, lose an hour to the study of a single blackbird as it flitted from branch to branch and, eventually, massacred a nest of worms. They're undemanding, these children of the new world. Isaac leads, but will never understand.

Joseph, on the other hand, is ravenously demanding, born with the entitlement of the eldest son and groomed for such by his mother, both of them too thickheaded to notice how thickheaded they were.

"I still say we just toss 'em to the wolves," he says now, "or have a little fun with them," which is how Isaac is able to reconstruct out the question that has been lost to the fog, Joseph no doubt referring to the pen where they keep the pilgrims who stumble across their borders. Their fate is left to Isaac's whim. Depending on mood, he will grant them an audience and perhaps a refuge or summarily return them to the wilderness from whence they came. Joseph hates outsiders on general principle. In his youth—before Isaac caught wind and shut it down—the boy played a gladiatorial game that pitted one pilgrim against another in mortal combat, this in the early days when survivors straggled in starving and half-dead, tear-stained at the sight of other human faces. He's not simply a dullard, Isaac's oldest son. He's a brute.

Isaac tries to love him, as he tries to love Thomas, younger and craftier, but sometimes he worries he's expended his lifetime quantity of love on the original generation of Children, loving them enough to save them or loving them *because* he saved them, loving most the ones who left him by death or by choice, because if the end of the world has taught him anything, it's that the most precious things are those most easily lost, and vice versa.

He tries to love his sons, but mostly he loves how little they love each other, the Jacob and Esau of it all, the spectacle of their scrabbling for the Father's finite affections. All that happens, has happened before; God ensures that and Isaac avails himself of its comforts and certainties. He has been Noah and Abraham and even Isaac, and endured all. Survival and success depend on little more than recognizing the nature of one's story and following the script. And in this story, in the story of sons, love is beyond the point; the point is fatherhood and leadership, the point is the obligations of blood and filial obedience, the point is he is the Father and they are his sons, and someday his Children will be their Children. Someday, he will be gone, and though the blame for that sits squarely with God, it's hard not to hold it against the sons who will remain.

He gives very little thought to his daughters.

• • •

Isaac's father once told him, during their months together, that all stories are the same two stories. "Either someone goes on a journey," Abraham said, "or a stranger comes to town. And trust me, people, fucking lazy as they are, like the second one a lot better. Why do you think the New Testament's so much more popular than the old one?"

"What about my story?" Isaac asked him. "My story is both stories."

Isaac was the stranger who came to town, small hand tucked inside his mother's, left practically on the doorstep of a man he'd never seen by the woman he'd never see again. Because of Isaac, they'd all gone on a journey, the father, the son, and the Children. God had warned Abraham of the end of the world, but Isaac was the one who understood how to survive it. Because of Isaac they dispensed with their worldly belongings, they learned to shoot and trap and hoard, they built themselves a modern-day ark, and when the sky fell, and Abraham followed God's command to venture alone into the wilderness—the stranger, no longer so strange, takes a journey— Isaac and the Children were safe, and saved.

In this new world, there is only one story.

The Children take no journeys. They live here, in the valley of the shadow of the promised land. Those who choose to leave cease to exist. When a stranger comes to town, he learns quickly to leave his stories of the world, and his journey, behind.

This stranger is Isaac's younger son. He kneels, as he's been warned to do, at the old man's bunioned feet, and says, "I've come a long way to find you."

Isaac coughs. "I don't need to hear about it." He's too tired and too busy to be wasting time on etiquette lessons, and wonders whether perhaps Joseph didn't have the right idea after all.

The stranger has scrappy red hair and a raking scar on his forearm, claw marks from some brush with the angry wild. He looks familiar to Isaac, but then, these days, everyone looks either familiar or strange, faces of his blood dissolving into inchoate shape and line, faces like this one pretending at being known. Like the fogs, this is God's hand at work. God showing him who to trust.

His younger son, his favored son, stands at the stranger's side. Unlike Joseph, Thomas enjoys the company of newcomers. He collects their stories, and Isaac allows it: Stories need a repository, and better one son than all the Children.

Thomas nudges the young man. "Show him."

The man reaches into a shapeless coat, pulls out something tattered that Isaac recognizes as a photograph.

Isaac had all the photographs burned long ago.

He takes this one in his hands, rests it flat against his palms, lets himself remember photographs, their laminate paper, their lie of permanence, that time can be fixed and people too, and then he takes in the faded face smiling up at him, and should know better than to believe this trick of the eye, whether it be divine message or practical joke, but how can he help but believe, because resting in his palms is the face of his mother.

• • •

"What?" Isaac says.

He's horizontal.

"Dad?"

"Dad, are you okay?"

These two boys—men now but boys forever—stand over him. These two boys must be his sons, and he must love them, but it's the third face that Isaac fixes on, the stranger come to town, and Isaac remembers that often, in the old bible, the stranger come to town was an angel, a divine flunky sent to test the righteous. Then Isaac remembers what this stranger has brought him.

"What?" he says again.

"Dad, you faded out on us again."

"Should we get the doctor?"

Isaac remembers hospitals. White robes bustling with self-importance across a TV screen. He remembers medicine, and clean sheets, and anti-bacterial soap, and old men, men much older than he is now but looked so much younger, and will not let himself curse God, who allowed his own son only thirty-three years upon the Earth.

He wants to say: *Leave me.*

He wants to say: *Take this burden from my shoulders. It's your turn to save yourselves.*

"What?" he says, and hates the sound of his voice and the spittle that lands on his chin.

"Rest, Dad." Thomas puts an arm around the stranger and ushers him away. Joseph sits by the bed, takes Isaac's hand in his hairy fingers. They are alone.

Thomas and Joseph hate each other, always have. Isaac prefers it that way.

"Who was that woman in the picture, Dad?"

The Children call him Father; his sons and daughters call him Dad. No one calls him Isaac anymore, and sometimes Isaac can almost remember the days before he gave himself the name, can almost remember the boy he was before he was chosen.

"Hannah found an extra store of chocolate. She's making a cake for your birthday. Your favorite. Isn't that great, Dad?"

Hannah is either one of Isaac's daughters or one of Joseph's wives, he can't be bothered to remember.

"Great," he manages.

"You remember it's your birthday coming up, right?"

The irony of it, the way Joseph treats *him* like a simpleton.

He shoulders himself upright, leans against the wall, fixes Joseph with a gaze that, years before, might have frozen the boy's blood. He will tell Joseph to keep his brutish hands off the stranger, and while he's at it, keep his brutish organ in his pants because there are enough little dolts running wild, everyone pretending not to notice their green eyes and Joseph-like cowlick in stubbornly curly Joseph-like hair. Joseph will hear that Isaac is not dead yet, nor his infant to mother and manage, that Isaac knows what his son is trying to do: rally support among the Children, make decisions for them without consulting Isaac, decisions that he speaks of as "distracting trifles" and a "waste of your time." He will tell Joseph that when the time does come, it will be Thomas who takes the mantle of leadership and Joseph's birthright, and he will do so with his father's blessing—and once that's settled, Isaac will summon Thomas and tell him that his softhearted, muddle-headed ways and unhealthy obsession with the past are slow-acting poison and that unless he toughens up, Joseph has Isaac's blessing to send him into the wilderness. He'll set brother against brother, just the way the Lord likes it. This is a good plan, he thinks. Smart.

"Joseph," he says. "Son."

"Yeah, Dad?" Joseph squeezes his hand.

"Where am I?" Isaac says. "Who are you?"

• • •

The dark of night.

Isaac remembers when stars were blotted out by the lights of man. The Children know this from history lessons, and shudder to think of it.

Isaac misses his nightlight, and the warm glow of a screen.

The stranger is in his cabin, and Isaac wonders if he invited the young man in and forgot. Just in case, he acts hospitable, offering the stranger a cup of tea.

"It's the middle of the night," the boy says.

Isaac shrugs.

"I'm sorry, I shouldn't be in here," the boy says, "I know that, but…" and Isaac thinks now perhaps he hasn't been invited in, and Isaac should act accordingly, but then there's the matter of the photograph.

In the dark, he feels young again.

"I need to tell you a story," the boy says.

"I guess you do," Isaac says.

• • •

My grandfather raised me, the boy says. Until he died, at least. Then no one raised me. But that's not the story. I mean, not *this* story.

His name was Abraham, the boy says, and pauses for Isaac to say something, but Isaac only waits.

He survived what you call the skyfall, the boy says. He was driving south, toward the ocean, and he almost drowned when the tidal waves came, but he didn't, and when so many people died but he lived, he decided to be a better man. He fell in love. He married my grandmother, and they had my father, and then my father had me, except he died before I was born. My mother right after. Plague year. I don't know if you had that here.

He didn't tell me any of this 'til later, the boy says. I didn't ask. We didn't talk much about what came before. Like you people, I guess.

I was still a kid when he died, the boy says. When he was getting toward the end, that's when he told me where he came from. Who he was before. That he was a liar, that he'd made up one last lie and it came true, and maybe that was okay, because he'd saved a bunch of people—his Children, he called them, which confused the hell out of me at first. He said he didn't feel so guilty about lying to them, because it made them happy, and he guessed it pretty much kept them alive—they thought the end was coming and they prepared for it, and then it actually *did* come and they must have lived, but he felt guilty about the other thing, about his son. Lying to him. Leaving him behind. Letting him believe God told him to do it.

I asked him why he never went back to this kid, since he knew where to find him, if he didn't want to see whether the kid had survived, maybe apologize for being such a shit, not that I said that to his face, but we both knew that's what he was. And he told me he guessed being a good man was harder than it looked, and he'd used all his goodness up on me and my dad and my grandma. She's dead, too. Long time ago. That's not important.

Before he died, he gave me the picture, and I figured it would be a picture of the son, but he said he didn't have one of those. Barely knew the kid. This was a picture of the kid's mother, and maybe it would come in handy someday, if I wanted it to. He didn't tell me how. He wasn't big on telling people what to do. That made more sense to me after he told me about the Children. A lot of things made more sense.

What are you looking for, Isaac asks him, like he doesn't know, and the kid says, *You.*

• • •

The boy's name is Kyle, as his dead father was named Kyle, and that in itself gives the lie to his tall tale, because what kind of name is *Kyle* for a child of Abraham?

Kyle would have Isaac believe that his father was a fraud. That the miracle of prophecy that saved the Children from extinction, was a co-incidence. That God had never spoken to him, never spoken to Isaac, that Abraham had spoon-fed his son the same bullshit he'd dumped on his Children, that he locked them into and himself out of the doomsday compound not because God refused him access to the promised land, but because he was a fraud who'd abandoned his son to responsibility, packed a suitcase of cash, and got the hell out of dodge. That he had survived, had married, had bred, had regretted, but had never returned. Could have returned, but never did.

And the father duped the son, and made him believe.
And the son wasted his life on a fantasy, and taught his Children to worship his father, who was a piece of shit, and the LORD laughed and laughed.

It makes for a ridiculous story.

A story that doesn't explain the miracle.

Maybe, Isaac thinks, Abraham mistook God's warning for coincidence, or maybe he lied to this new child about lying to the old one.

Kyle doesn't know anything about Isaac's mother, or where she went. This is fine. Isaac has already solved the puzzle of his mother: By leaving him, she saved him, which meant God must have intended—commanded—her to do it, just as He did Abraham.

Isaac doesn't believe the boy, cannot and *will not* believe him, tells the boy not to speak of it again and certainly not to anyone else, and the boy agrees, so that in the morning, when Isaac is awoken by the screech of birds and his own insistent bladder, he's left to wonder whether the story was a dream.

The story cannot be true and the boy cannot be what he claims, but Isaac lets him stay, even gives him a bed in Thomas's home.

"What do you want from me?" Isaac asked him, in the middle of the night, or maybe imagined it.

"I don't want anything," Kyle said, sounding as if he'd never considered desire.

"Then why are you here?"

Kyle shrugged. "I had to go somewhere. Figured this would be interesting. An adventure, you know?"

Isaac doesn't know, because Isaac's life hasn't allowed for the luxury of adventure. It's things like this, children seeking danger for danger's sake, that prove to him the end of the world has come and gone. Sometimes he misses it.

He thinks he told Thomas to invite Kyle to stay with him.

But maybe Thomas decided for himself, told Isaac after the fact. He can't remember.

Joseph doesn't like it either way, Isaac knows that. Neither do Thomas's wives, not the young pretty one nor the old cranky one, but the children, despite being booted from their bed and forced now to sleep on the floor by the kitchen, delight in Kyle, requesting that he take over Three Questions duty and tuck them into bed.

"I got to ask three questions every night when I was a kid, too," Kyle tells them. "Weird coincidence, yeah?"

"Everybody gets to ask three questions," the youngest one, Jeremiah, says solemnly. "It's the law."

"What are you, dumb? Everyone knows that," says Eli. He takes after his uncle Joseph.

Isaac watches from the doorway, but leaves before the children put forth their questions. This nightly ritual is his decree, but he's never liked to watch. "Stop it with the fucking questions," his mother had said to him, over and over. "What's wrong with you?" she'd asked him, when he couldn't stop, because how did you stop wanting to know? Three questions was the compromise they made, a daily dessert, three questions only once he was safely tucked into his sheets, three questions saved up for the dark before bed, never to be wasted; this was how Isaac learned of the world, how he thinks all children should learn of the world, in the dark, in threes. But he prefers not to see it, because he prefers not to remember. With Joseph and Thomas and the girls, he left the duty to their mothers.

Their mothers are dead now, not that it matters. As Kyle would say, that's not the story.

Days pass. Thomas embraces the stranger. Joseph ignores him. Isaac thinks too much about the past. In daylight hours, he maneuvers himself out of being alone with the boy, but at night, too often, the boy comes to him. The boy, his nephew. Isaac answers his questions about the Children's earlier, harder days, locked up in the compound, waiting for the sky to clear and the land to welcome them home, but asks none of his own. One night Kyle slips into the house and sits beside his bed, says, "Three questions, I really like that. What would yours be?"

In Isaac's dreams, now, he is a child again. A child for real, not the wise man in the boy's body that he had to play after the skyfall, not the boy wonder who received his father's prophecy as if it were a bolt of lightning and, electrified, became someone new. He dreams of the fuzzy time before, when he lived with his mother in a small room over a store, a room that smelled of raw fish and skittered with roaches—the real ones that escaped from couch cushions and through the hole in the toe of a favorite sneaker, and the imaginary ones that crawled over him as he curled up on the futon and tried to sleep. He dreams of his mother's hand pulling out of his, of her whispered promise that she would be back.

"I save my questions for God," Isaac tells Kyle. "I expect I'll get my chance to ask, sooner or later."

"Wait. Isaac—"

Kyle doesn't call him Father, and this is a relief. Once, he tried to call Isaac by the name he had before, the name his mother gave him and the only one his father ever knew. That boy, Isaac told Kyle, is dead. There is precedent: God gave Jacob a new name, too. Every father of a nation deserves a name of his own.

Still, Kyle knew the name.

Kyle knew the name, had the photograph; Isaac is forced to believe the boy is who he says he is, and he grows impatient waiting for God to reveal what the hell Isaac is supposed to do about it.

"Okay, I've got to ask you," Kyle says. "You don't really *believe* all this junk?"

"What junk?"

"You know, this. The miracle. God. That your father prophesied a fucking meteor strike."

"Didn't he?"

"Well, I guess, but it's like they always say about the monkeys and the typewriters, you know. Hamlet."

"What? What about monkeys?"

"You know, because they—never mind. I just want to be clear: You think God saved you? Like, you, specifically."

"I *know* He did," Isaac says, choosing the verb with purpose. This isn't like the time before, where men were resigned to faith. This is the age of miracles. He knows God loves him because God saved him, and he knows God saved him because there is no other explanation. His father taught him this, before Kyle was born, and the years since have proven it. "This surprises you?"

Kyle is frozen. Isaac remembers this expression from Saturday morning cartoons, the coyote who chased his prey straight off a cliff, only falling once he looked down to see no ground beneath his feet. "I figured you just picked up where grandpa left off."

"I did," Isaac says, and will say no more.

• • •

Isaac blows out candles; Isaac eats cake; Isaac sits in the front row and watches his life play out on a makeshift stage. This is the birthday pageant, performed every year for the last ten, inside the compound that has become a museum. One of Isaac's grandsons play Isaac. Joseph plays Abraham. Some of the women play other women.

Kyle sits beside him, and together they watch the past enacted for the present.

"Not for me, the promised land," Joseph-as-Abraham tells the child playing his son. "You shall lead our Children to salvation."

"I shall," the boy says, and the man marches off the stage, his role finished.

The Children are all played by children.

"God has decreed that we marry," the boy playing Isaac tells the pretty girl playing Heather, and Heather drops to her knees and says, "I will never leave you."

"Lies!" the children shout, as is the tradition.

"I promise," the girl playing Heather says, then the lights fall and the boy playing Isaac closes his eyes into sleep, and Heather steals herself away.

"Treason!" the children shout and boo. This is their favorite part.

The pageant speeds through the ten years of confinement, and ends as the Children step through the door of their compound into the new world that awaits them, their skin pale, their faces gaunt, their newborns cradled in their arms, their gratitude to God on their lips and in their hearts.

"Father Abraham had many sons," the children sing. "Many sons had Father Abraham. I am one of them, and so are you."

The first time Isaac saw the pageant, he cried. These days he fights to stay awake, to keep his mind from wandering into the past. He doesn't like coming back to this place, remembering the time when he thought they might never leave it. He doesn't like to watch himself left behind, once and again. He doesn't like to imagine this pageant playing out year after year, even when he's gone.

Sometimes, inside these walls made of old shipping containers and scavenged steel, he imagines this as the tomb it almost was. To seal himself in with his Children by his side, bound to him for all eternity—this was the way death should be. This was the wisdom Moses should have carried from Egypt, along with his people. Isaac has sacrificed his entire life for his Children. How is it just that they should live on while he dies alone?

The Children sing happy birthday, and Isaac senses a curtain about to fall.

"Are you all right?" Kyle says, turning toward him, very close and at the same time shrinking further and further away.

Isaac wants to tell him that he's more than all right, that if Kyle could feel what he feels, the imminence, the *immanence*, of the fog and that certainty, when he's inside its white hot haze, that he's not there alone, then there would be no more need for faith and doubt. Isaac wants to say that the decades he's spent waiting for the Lord to reveal himself, to turn Isaac's decades of bullshit into retroactive truth, have finally given way to revelation, and that Kyle should shut up, everyone should shut up, so that Isaac can fall into the sunblind silence and hear.

• • •

He wakes in Thomas's house.

Isaac has always hated waking alone.

The bedroom is the children's bedroom, the one that Kyle has now claimed for his own, except Isaac can tell from the sound of the dark that the room is empty.

He finds Kyle in the family room.

He finds Kyle on top of Thomas's pretty young wife.

They lie together in the dark, lie together in the biblical sense, and then, when that's finished, lie together still, Kyle's fingers tangled in the pretty young wife's pretty hair.

Isaac watches.

Isaac thinks that he has never smiled like that, after. For him, every time is somehow still the first time, and beneath the pleasure there is pain and something else, less bearable. The emptiness left behind at the moment of release, the sense that he has given something essential away; the anticipation, lying together, sticky and hot and wet, of the inevitable, that she will leave and take it with her.

"It doesn't bother you, brainwashing these kids?" Kyle is murmuring to the pretty young wife. "I mean, they think there's nothing outside this valley. They think the world ended and they're all that's left. They don't want to hear different."

"They're children," she says. "We know what's best for children."

"But *you* know this is all bullshit, right?"

"It doesn't matter."

"Of course it fucking matters," Kyle says, but he says it gently, with a finger tracing the curve of her cheek, like he's telling her that she's beautiful. "It's all lies. And the old man—"

She stops his lips with her hand.

"Father knows best," she says, and looks confused when he starts to laugh.

$$\bullet \ \bullet \ \bullet$$

Maybe, Isaac thinks in the morning, it was a dream, the way his dreams of stabbing his sons, letting their blood run red over his hands, have always been dreams, the way his dreams of his mother and his father returning have always been dreams—the way he sometimes thinks the entire world before was a dream, video games and frozen yogurt machines and skateboards and homework all a collective fantasy that they've dreamed up together.

But if it is a dream, it's one given to him for a reason.

Kyle wants to take a walk with him. But Isaac is an old man, tired and frail—he says. Come sit with me, he says, in the sleeping room of the old compound, where your grandfather and I once slept side by side.

The cots are still there, preserved for posterity, and Kyle perches on one while Isaac takes the other. Isaac remembers museums from before, trooping with his schoolmates through absurdly still rooms, adults frantically shushing them. He remembers a water fight in a bathroom with a cross-eyed boy; he remembers the glory of a dessert cart in the cafeteria, all you can eat; he doesn't remember, has never been able to remember, what was encased behind all those panes of glass, and what was the point. He supposes that this museum will be its own kind of bible someday, telling its story after the storytellers are gone.

"I'm leaving," Kyle says.

Isaac is too old to pretend at surprise. Does anyone ever do anything else? He is an old man, but a cagey one, and he says to Kyle *no, don't*.

"You're my nephew," Isaac says. "You have family here."

Kyle shakes his head. "I don't know what I was looking for, Isaac, but… this isn't it."

"What, then?"

"I miss him, I guess," Kyle says. "My grandpa. Your dad. It's funny, if you think about it. He raised us both. I guess I always thought of us as kind of like brothers, you and me. And maybe I thought—it's stupid."

"What?" Isaac prods, though he is hardly listening, his mind fixed on the word, *brothers*, the shape of things coming clear.

"You came first, you know? I've always been kind of jealous of that. You knew this whole different part of him. Maybe the real him? And he loved you first. Maybe he loved you best, even if he was a total shit to you, leaving you like that."

"As he had to."

"Uh huh. Yeah. The firstborn. That's something. He was a good dad to my dad, I think, but I get the sense he never liked the guy very much. I guess I always wondered… I don't fucking know what I wondered, okay? I thought you'd be more like him, or you'd be more like me, or we could be, like I said, brothers. Family's more than blood, that's what your dad always said. Maybe he was trying to tell me about 'the Children,' or whatever without actually telling me, I don't know. Maybe he was trying to warn me not to come find you. I'm glad I did, though, Isaac. Maybe I needed to know you. Who knows, maybe your God brought me here, wanted you to know me, right?" He holds out his hand. "Brothers?"

All this time, Isaac has been trying to figure out what story he's in, how events are meant to unfold. All this time, he's had it wrong, distracted by the tangle of fathers and sons, nephews and wives.

Brothers.

Two brothers, one favored by his God, the other wandering in cold wilderness, envious and lost. One brother who was a shepherd of his flock and one who was rejected, and dreamed of usurping all his brother possessed: life and land and legacy. One who spoke the truth and one who used deception to gain the advantage, who said walk with me in the field and disguised love as its opposite. Both born to the father of all men, neither his brother's keeper.

He feels foolish that he hasn't seen it before now, and thanks God for this chance to put the ancient story right. This time, in this new world, the righteous brother is not so easily led to the slaughter. This time, the right brother will live.

• • •

Isaac's bible, like its predecessors, is part history and part law. Such are the edicts of Isaac's God:

Children shall ask questions, but only three at a time, and only these three shall be answered.

Man shall join with woman as determined by the will of the Father, and these pairings shall not be put asunder.

Honor thy Father.

Know thy edible mushrooms and berries, for they will sustain you in the wilderness.

Isaac's God is a practical God.

Keep a store of six months' worth of food, dried and canned and preserved from damp.

Keep herds separated, in case of plague.

Keep your weapon in working order and in reach.

Isaac's house has many rooms, and in each room, Isaac has a gun. He keeps one in this compound, too, one the Children know nothing about, cached beneath his old cot, that sacred artifact none of the Children would dare touch.

He hears Kyle saying things like *no* and *wait* and *what are you doing* and again, more than once, *no*, but the voice is a stranger's and the words easily swatted away.

Over them, he hears instead, finally, the word of the Lord.

He can sense the fog descending again, and recognizes it now as his reward for long service and one final, righteous act, and he raises the weapon and prepares for God to welcome him home.

• • •

Thomas and Joseph are the first to find the body. They've been keeping an eye on their father; they've been keeping an eye on the stranger; they know where and when to look.

They were hoping things would turn in this direction, though they were hoping the turn would be tidier.

"Now what?" Joseph asks Thomas. Joseph is older, but Thomas is smarter, and they've both come to terms with this.

"Now we deal with dear old Dad," Thomas says. The old man has always liked him better, and they've come to terms with that, too. Once they did, it made everything easier. As long as they played the roles Isaac set for them, the old man believed he knew his sons.

The stranger who's been fucking Thomas's wife is gutshot and, from the look of things, took a good while to die. Thomas wishes that Isaac had shot him in the groin, and considers doing it now, for good measure.

Joseph, the firstborn, who actually loves his father, wishes the old man hadn't pissed his pants. It's an undignified way for him to go.

"Where am I?" the old man says, kneeling in the puddle of blood.

He got old fast, their father. Or maybe they were just so used to seeing him as he began, too young, that they didn't notice the change until it was too late.

He got old fast, but not fast enough. Thomas feels like he's been waiting for this moment forever.

The old man holds out the gun, flat on open palms. "Who are you?" he says.

Finally, and too late, Thomas thinks: The right question. He's never known them, or wanted to, so certain was he that because they were his sons and his blood, they were whatever he imagined them to be. That as his creation, they were his to shape to his whim. Thomas remembers being small, stumbling up the hill after his father, Joseph following behind, kicking his brother's shins when he thought no one was looking, because Joseph was dumb enough to think people ever stopped looking. Their mothers down in the valley, having abandoned them to a rare moment alone with their father, who wanted to show them their legacy. "This is where we lived, before God gave us the promised land," Isaac told them, then pushed them inside one of the compound's small rooms and locked them into the dark. "Can you imagine it?" he shouted through the door. "Closed behind these walls for a decade, wondering if the Lord had left us enough world to return to." Their father left them in the dark for a day and a night: A lesson in captivity and faith. Joseph screamed and kicked the walls and wet his pants. Thomas abided, quiet and calm, retreating to an even darker room in his mind. He's always been good at waiting. By the time their father finally let them out—"Breathe deep, boys! Now you understand how grateful you should be for fresh air, for sky!"—Joseph was a wild creature, and stayed that way. Thomas knew enough to smile and thank his father for the field trip, and has been the favorite ever since.

That the old man thought a few hours in a dark room could do the job, allow the children of the new generation to see through the eyes of the one that came before—that he thought this necessary? His father, Thomas thought then, and thinks now, is a fool. He can't see his own stain. The Earth has been purified, and its people along with it, but Isaac still bears the taint of the world before, and the years between. There was a reason Moses and his people spent forty years wandering the desert—it gave the old ones, the ones warped by an unholy life of servitude and false idols, the chance to die. Thomas has always thought it was gracious of Moses, at least, to do so on schedule.

"We should get this done before he snaps out of it," Thomas says.

"Maybe this time he won't?"

"All the more reason."

The brothers don't agree on everything. Joseph wants to see the world beyond the valley, wants his children's and his grandchildren's futures uncircumscribed by the duties of blood and power. Thomas wants to rule.

They agree, however, on this.

"Do we make it look like he did it to himself?" Joseph asks.

The idea is tempting, but Thomas needs his father's legacy to loom. He shakes his head. "He did it," he says, stepping on the stranger's chest, bearing down like the man can still feel pain, and if only it were possible. "Assassination. Self-defense. A good story."

They'll need to adjust the pageant next year, write a new closing act. Joseph will write it. He's always liked a good story.

The old man is peeing again. Joseph looks away. Thomas laughs.

"I don't know about this," Joseph says, nervous now that the time has come, nervous despite how long they've been waiting. At least the old man won't die alone. He knows his father would have hated that. "What about God?"

"God loves killing," Thomas points out.

Brother killing brother, Joseph thinks. Yes. Fathers killing sons, husbands killing wives, gods killing soldiers, generations, cities—yes, all of that. But sons killing fathers? "I had to read that fucking bible as much as you did," Joseph says. "Patricide is a no."

"What does the old man always say? We're writing a *new* bible now. Correcting the mistakes of the old one. Brave new world."

The old man is crying.

"This is fucking embarrassing," Thomas says.

Joseph wishes he could have heard the stranger's story. Thomas knows, but refuses, as usual, to share. Joseph stole the stranger's photograph from his father's bedside. He likes the look of the woman in it, the smile that can't imagine the world could end. She looks innocent, the way his father looks now, even though he had imagined it best of all.

"I loved you best," their father says, talking to neither of them. Talking to me, Joseph imagines, but lacks the will to make himself believe. Talking to his father or his lost whore, Thomas thinks, someone he loved before he forgot how. Maybe to his Lord, that monster in the sky to whom they're all supposed to be grateful. Gratitude and fear, this is the old man's recipe for love. Thomas has no talent for either, and when he looks to the sky, he's never seen the beauty his father goes on about, never appreciated its capacious blue. The sky is where death comes from, everyone knows that. The sky fell once, can fall again, and because of that, Thomas owes it obedience. But not gratitude, and not love. He owes no one that.

The old man blinks rapidly, spittle frothing at weathered lips, then says, "What?"

"Third question," Thomas tells him, and takes the gun from his father's willing hands. "That's enough."

THE UNCERTAINTY MACHINE

Jamie Ford

May 1910

When the end of the world came and went, the accidental prophet Phineas Kai Rengong sat in his lavishly appointed comet shelter wrapped in robes of red silk that had been bathed quite literally in the tears of his followers. And in that moment of stifling calm he asked himself the most important question posed to any great Daoist master: *What the hell am I gonna do now?*

Phineas rubbed the stubble on his cheeks. He was now trapped thirty feet below the streets of Seattle's Pioneer Square, alone, save for the lifeless bodies of the curvaceous twins who had enjoyed his company the night before. Both had eaten snow-skinned mooncakes laced with pure opium as Halley's Comet, the great and terrible Broom Star, had crossed the night sky and the Earth roared and the building shook. Now in the glow of his oil lamps and a single battery-powered tungsten bulb that somehow remained unbroken, the girls' figures, arms and legs akimbo, looked like unfinished sculptures, their long dark hair a tangle of shimmering cobwebs; their eyes—still open, stared back at him accusingly. He wished he'd known their real names. He'd jokingly called them *Yin* and *Yang*, because one was hot and one was cold, one was bold while the other was retiring. And now his bed servants were both gone. So young, so innocent—well, somewhat. But at least his secret (one of many) had died with them. To his radicalized followers, Phineas was a eunuch, a self-inflicted condition that was expected of all Daoist Anarchist leaders. Like the philosopher *Wunengzi,* the ultimate Master of Non-Potency, self-castration was seen as a token of piety, the ultimate destruction toward a reorganized peace—a sign of greatness. But… well… Phineas had never gotten around to that odious task. A procrastination that he'd been thankful for twice last night.

As the foundation of the building creaked and settled once again and dust rained down through fingerling cracks in the ceiling, soiling his rugs from Persia and Turkey, Phineas stared at the collapsed doorway to his bunker. A ruin of concrete occupied the space where a golden door had once been hinged, and upstairs, his lavish apartment was surely demolished. He frowned and chewed his lip as he regarded the broken window to the light well that had been his only means of seeing the reflected sky. The polished silver mirrors that lined the walls of the shaft had shattered and the well had filled up with brick and rubble. He sighed and pursed his lips disapprovingly as pulverized mortar poured in like sand to the bottom of an hourglass, slowly counting down to the moment when Phineas' air would become scarce and then nonexistent.

He waited in minutes of silence that stretched into hours. He tried to distract himself by rereading for the umpteenth time passages from books by the philosopher Jean Reynaud and the skeptic Chuang Chou, gifts, translated into English. But Phineas couldn't stop worrying about his followers, wondering who, if any, had survived the comet's poisonous tail. And more importantly: When would they rescue him?

To his minions, Phineas was *Yueguang Tongzi*. A great scientist and the Prince of Moonlight predicted in the Sutra on the Extinction of the Dharma. And his people, they considered themselves members of the *Way of Former Heaven,* poor slaves who had fallen off the wheel of reincarnation and had been stuck here forever when the wheel began moving again. But the leaders among his followers were affiliates of the White Lotus Society—a triad with dreams of an anarchist revolution. If they knew Phineas was nothing but a charlatan, they didn't let on. They sailed along in his boat of falsehood, adrift on a sea of lies, paddling in the same ruinous direction.

"The future is a deep river, flowing," his predecessor, Professor Franz Der Ling had explained. "I have found a way to navigate the bends, the rapids."

Phineas had thought the late Professor Ling to be a madman, a raving lunatic who rambled on and on about Gaussian reduction, polynomial interpolation, and the Greek island of Antikythera—just another intellectual prisoner banished to the stockades of Hong Kong where Phineas had been sentenced to nine months for selling phony treasure maps. Another jailed respite in his long history of arrests for schemes and petty crimes against the Crown of Britannia who had smashed China's Celestial Empire long before he'd been born. And during his many stints behind bars he'd been locked up with liars and thieves, smugglers and spies, but never an innocent man. Or a genius.

Professor Ling happened to be both.

"My invention has made me an exile in my own country," The professor had said. "The British think I'll use it to rally the people, to incite a rebellion, or call down the Golden Horde from the Steppe. So when you get out, you must find it for me—use the device and tell me my fate. When will I ever be free?"

Phineas closed the book in his lap and walked to the sturdy bank vault that had been added to his comet shelter years ago. He entered the combination that only he knew, turned the handle, and opened the iron door with both hands. Inside was his most prized possession, its secret location in the Chinese countryside gifted to him by the professor. The machine was the size of a hatbox, but made from silver, gold, and curious alloys inscribed with Chinese characters describing *zhou yi*.

When Phineas had first laid eyes on the device, he had no idea what it was, though he recognized the word *change*. He'd hoped the machine was an auto-abacus, the kind of pinwheel calculator that Chinese clockmakers had tinkered with in hopes of predicting lottery numbers. But Professor Ling had been an adjunct of the Royal Laboratory of Psychical Research so Phineas assumed the thing must be some kind of automatic writing machine, something from the burgeoning field of pyschography.

Now as Phineas sat with the device on his lap and opened the lid, he marveled at its intricate construction just as he had all those years ago. He stared in awe at the countless iron gears, the copper wiring, and scores of spinning tumblers carved from yarrow root with calligraphic writing on four sides, all driven by an ornate silver handle.

"My invention can predict the future," Professor Ling had said as his wild eyes flashed beneath matted hair that hadn't been washed or cut in a decade. "But because the machine uses the primitive, subconscious mind, it can never interpret the operator's *own* future. You must use it on my behalf!"

Phineas had no intention of returning the device. Though he remembered skeptically asking the box when the professor would be free, turning the handle, and observing how the word *tsum yut* appeared.

"Yesterday?" He'd muttered. *So much for the future.*

It was only after Phineas learned that Professor Ling had died the day before, only then did he realize that the old man's invention did indeed speak the truth. The professor had created a difference engine based on the ancient Book of Changes. But instead of divulging sixty-four vague answers left up to interpretation, his device broke those answers into four-thousand and ninety-six specific words.

Professor Ling had forged an I-Ching machine.

...

Three nights had passed since the apparition of the Broom Star, and Phineas began to worry. He still had brass bottles of oxygen (though he felt an occasional draft, which was chilling, yet comforting to have a meager source of air), tins of canned salmon and caviar, canisters of sea biscuits and pilot bread, crates of apples, pears, and lychee, and stores of water as well as casks of fine wine made from rice and barley, enough to last a month—two if he rationed. But where were his followers? His devotees, many of them silver miners, were men with ashen skin experienced in plumbing the noxious pits beneath Mount Rainier. Surely they'd risen up by now and were employing their steam drillers, working their way toward his rescue as planned.

Two years ago the I-Ching machine had predicted that the Vile Star would cleanse the Heavens, that the great comet would bring death to all but the very rich and the very poor. That the sky wanderer would poison those above, drain the Pacific, and would cause drops of iron to rain on Britannia for a full day. Upon hearing the news, some of Phineas' followers had given him everything to build this shelter—their homes, their possessions, (even their daughters), making them destitute and Phineas wealthy beyond measure, a faithful gesture to ensure everyone's survival, a win-win in his mind.

Phineas held the machine and asked, "Are my beloved followers alive?" As he waited and then turned the handle he desperately wanted to ask *when will they rescue me*, but he knew that asking about himself was folly. He'd tried once, out of curiosity, and the machine returned an error message: *Cuowu*. Now as he listened to the whir of the gears and tumblers, he thought about his followers until the machine settled on the Chinese words for *Healthy* and *Strong*.

Phineas breathed a sigh of relief. He'd rarely, if ever, doubted the machine, but then the device had never predicted something as imperious as the end of the world. He asked again, "Are my followers, especially my lieutenants, the ones I hand-picked to lead in my absence, are they guiding my people? What are they doing?" He knew his question was somewhat muddled, but as Professor Ling had once said, *"Diction is less important than intent. The machine interprets the beating of your heart, the quaking of your thoughts."*

This time the machine said: *Gathering.*

Phineas smiled. Sensing an imminent rescue, he looked around the room. There was still a certain morbid decorum to be had. With that in mind, Phineas dragged the bodies of the twins to the vault and sealed them inside. Then in a magnanimous gesture, one foretelling his release, he opened the copper cages of his collection of mockingbirds, whippoorwills, and nightingales. Their even songs had comforted him. Their singing reminded him that the world had kept on spinning, that despite the comet which shook and poisoned the world, the sun was still rising and falling, days and nights were passing unmolested. But while the birds sung, chortled, whispered and flit about—none left their cages. Their wings had been clipped long ago. That's how Phineas felt as he sat in his chair and waited, wondering how long his oil lamps would last.

• • •

After ten days, Phineas decided it prudent to only eat one meal a day. Though a grumbling stomach only stoked his fears as he would occasionally bang a golden spittoon on the walls, hoping to be heard, screaming at the ceiling until he was exhausted.

Now in the awful silence, he huddled in his blankets and furs of Russian sable as he watched a trickle of fetid water seep down the wall.

It's… raining. I have water. I have air.

He hadn't predicted that, though he hadn't asked. He also hadn't asked about the loyalty of his followers, because he couldn't ask something that benefited him directly, but moreover, why would he need to? The machine had never been wrong—or so he'd thought. In the early years, Phineas was unsure of how to use the device, for what purpose and to what end, so he'd found work as a village matchmaker—the most legitimate scam he knew. Most intermediaries were numerologists, superstitious old crones who used birthdates and astrology to assuage conflicts of interest between families. When Phineas showed up with his machine, marriage became a science (though an imperfect field of knowledge if ever there was one).

In the beginning, Phineas' predictions connected peasant families, but eventually he was being paid handsomely to bind sons and daughters of the rich and powerful merchant class. He delighted in his calling, because if people married and were happy, his wisdom seemed infallible. But if wives failed to produce a son, or accept a husband's concubine, if there was discord, that contention was usually seen as a sign of the couple's hidden weaknesses, their vices, not his. His fame spread from Guangzhou to Nanchang, until a young girl rebuffed the cousin whom she'd been betrothed to and ran away. Her absence drew the ire of the British Territorial Minister who had her arrested along with the entire village, which had been declared unruly, given English courtesy names and sold to the West—Phineas included. But to his surprise (and sincere delight) his reputation had preceded him. He arrived in the West, not as a village scryer as the British described him, but as a prophet like *Lao Tzu*, one of the great masters reborn. And the girl's disobedience became a parable of what would happen to those who disregarded his predictions.

Because of his lofty status, Chinese merchants spared no expense to smuggle him to the Underground, a hidden part of Seattle, for his safety, with everything given to him.

He was treated as a god.

• • •

A month later, Phineas scraped the last of the canned fish into his mouth with his dirty, unclipped fingernails and drank the briny oil. His only question as he sat in the pitch black, overcome by the smell of the twins' decaying bodies and his own bodily waste was: *Will I starve first or go completely mad?*

He tossed the empty can into the darkness of the room and heard it clatter among garbage and the shattered lamps, which had since run out of fuel. He crawled to the battery powered light and switched it on. He only used the simple bulb to operate the I-Ching machine, to ask what day it was as he scratched what he thought was the correct date onto the wall with a jewel-encrusted letter opener. He'd twice forgotten to reset the pulley on his mantle clock (and once let it run down on purpose because of the incessant ticking) so now his chronological bearings were off by a few hours, but in the darkness, the isolation, did it really matter? Now as he slept, his dreams seemed like wakefulness and his waking hours, an endless nightmare.

His only hopeful, productive activity was the three minutes each day that he allowed himself to use the battery powered light to operate the machine. In those fleeting, precious moments, the device became a periscope to the city above, a telegraph of questions and answers, his gear-driven silver-handled radio to the outside world.

Throughout the week he'd asked a litany of questions, none of which seemed helpful. Yes, his followers were doing well. And yes, his survival predictions had come true—living underground in the mines had spared them. The most affluent of the rich had survived as well, with tinctures of colloidal silver, but many more were gone. Yes, the survivors were fighting each other in the streets, the Luddites were smashing the machine-works because few science ministers had survived and those who had lived, unfortunately had left their servants to die. Revolution was happening. But his followers had left the heart of the ruined city. That answer had been crushing, pressing in like the walls around him. Somehow he'd been forgotten, or worse, deemed unnecessary. He prayed to all the gods he could remember that his people were battling above, waging a war and when the fighting stopped he'd be rescued, but as each day passed…

Phineas heard himself laugh hysterically as his voice boomed off the walls and he realized how much he sounded like Professor Ling. He started crying as he pulled out fistfuls of hair and rocked back and forth as he asked the machine one final rhetorical question for the day, "What do nightingales taste like?"

He saw the word, *Cuowu*, and turned out the light.

• • •

Three months later, as near as he could tell, Phineas' greatest regret was not preserving the bodies of the twins. He'd long since run out of food. And if he had misgivings about subsisting on human flesh, those had passed, lost somewhere in the lucid dreams he now had about sucking the raw meat from the last of his precious mockingbirds.

"I wasted the twins. Who knew that lapse in judgment would be my undoing," he muttered to himself as he picked at scabs along his scalp.

Phineas guessed that he hadn't eaten in weeks. His battery powered light had run out, so now he lived in perpetual darkness, trying to remember the days, to count them, feeling the numbers he'd scratched on the wall, occasionally waking up and adding another tic mark. But he still had rice wine in abundance and the alcohol soothed as the sugar sustained him. He regularly drank until he lost consciousness, waking up, imbibing more, vomiting, crawling, finding a dry place in the darkness to collapse, repeating the cycle again and again. It was better than sobriety, which made for unpleasant madness.

Though occasionally he'd be clear-headed enough to remember the I-Ching machine. He'd feel his way through the pitch and the filth and find that device, cradling the cold metal box like a long lost child. Sometimes he'd sit for hours, the machine in his lap, as he asked questions and talked to Professor Ling's cursed invention like a friend, turning the handle, receiving revelation and outright hallucinations. But in blackness that had become his world, he was never able to read the answers.

It was during one of those manic sessions that he thought he'd died, passed through the veiled, onion-skin of reality and slipped into the ether as he saw a flickering glow that grew into a light as bright as the sun. The heavenly orb blinded him as he called out to his rescuers, tears flowing down his greasy, soiled cheeks.

But in the silence, his eyes finally adjusted. And he saw that the sun was merely the burning coil of the tungsten bulb. He reached out and touched the lamp with the dead battery, turning it off and on. Yet, the light remained. Twitching, he unscrewed the bulb and it glowed in his hand, even brighter still, as he became aware of the chamber of horrors that his comet shelter had become. Phineas could feel the hum of electricity in the air, on his arms, and the fine hairs on the back of his neck. The World Wireless

System was still functioning, but more importantly, someone was using a Tesla coil, beaming spark-excited voltage in his direction, which could only mean one thing.

Finally, someone was searching for him.

Or perhaps, just the machine. Maybe that's all they wanted. His lieutenants, the men with lotus tattoos, had waited for him to expire, to take it from his lifeless grasp. As fearful, angry, vicious thoughts clogged his reason his prison became a fortress, his tomb became his castle. And his followers became traitors, worse, they became fallen foot soldiers. The terrible enemy was coming, the Mongols had risen up again, but instead of wearing cloaks sewn from field mice the hordes were arriving in great steam-driven airships sewn from the skin of their conquered dead. They would come in waves, they would search, but they would never find him. The British wouldn't find him. Neither would the boastful Americans. He'd never allow it. He'd smash the machine—he'd destroy the professor's creation if he had to.

Holding the glowing bulb like a torch, he rested the machine on his lap. He wiped grime off the metal and asked in a breathless panic, "Will someone *else* ever use this beautiful device. Could the I-Ching ever be attuned to another. Will they come digging to claim this clever machine." Phineas cranked the handle, listened to the gears thrum with clockwork precision, and watched the lettered tumblers spin and spin and spin… until the static charge in the room faded as quickly as the light.

The answer, his answer came, as he smiled in the darkness.

MARGIN OF SURVIVAL

Elizabeth Bear

In darkness, Yana waited. To her left, the sea was the smell of spent oil and a blackness broken by the slow hiss of phosphorescent breakers. If she squinted at the horizon, she could just make it out—a line as level as if it had been planed, pimpled with the tops of aquaculture rigs. To her right, the beach stretched rocky, rusty, and bleak up to an undercut bluff that she knew was there only because of suggestion and memory. It was a narrow margin of survival between the proverbial devil, and the equally proverbial sea.

The aquaculture domes were within sight, trailing rich constructed biomes of mussels and kelp through the richly nutritious, bitterly cold water. She could swim out to them and spare herself the risks. If she were a stronger swimmer; if she were not already weak with hunger; if it weren't for the waves and the rip current; if she had a drysuit; if she had some way to keep the mussels from spoiling before she got them home to Yulianna; if she could guarantee there weren't snipers or booby traps or guards.

Yana counted under her breath until the light came again.

Thirty-five, thirty-six. And there it was once more, a beam like a stroking finger. It crossed the black water, lanced over her head, bathed the bluff in brilliance, and moved on. On the horizon, she watched the shine of the Svet nezhyti, the Zombie Light, dim as it swept away again. The thing loomed out there in the night, unmanned, forgotten, possibly leaking reactor coolant—but automated. Still doing the job it had been set to do, decades or maybe a century ago. And it had illuminated enough of the stretch of beach before her that, crouched, she could scurry to the next rock without breaking her ankle.

Her stomach clenched, but Yana had become a connoisseur of clenching stomachs. This wasn't early hunger, which could endanger one with plunging blood sugar, unexpected weakness, and dizzy spells. Nor was this true starvation, when the stored resources were exhausted and the will began to revolve around food and only food, when the body grew frail and riddled with sores.

This was, rather, the comfortable middle ground of hunger—where the body had adapted to privation, where it was working hard to utilize stored resources, rather than grabbing and cannibalizing anything at hand. What a falconer called "sharp set," where the bird is ready and eager to hunt, lean—but also physically capable.

Another kind of margin. Another narrow edge to balance on.

Yulianna had been worse off, which was why Yana was here alone. Because when their supplies started to get low, Yulianna had set her jaw and refused food, refused water—starving herself so that Yana would have more. That was when Yana had realized that she would have to go out and seek supplies. They would need to go south, go inland. For that, they needed portable rations—and gear. Boots. Warm clothing.

Yana wanted to worry, but she wouldn't let herself. Her sister would be fine. She'd left Yulianna most of the remaining food. And the gun.

If she pulled this off, neither she nor Yulianna would have to be any kind of hungry—or cold, or badly dressed—for a good long time.

But first she had to survive the rest of the night.

Yana reached over her shoulder and patted the neck of the crowbar tucked into the loop of her large frame pack. She waited for the light, waited for the darkness, and darted to the next shelter. She wasn't worried about being spotted by anyone in the Zombie Light; there *was* no one in the Zombie Light. It had been empty for the devil knew how long, mindlessly spinning away on its reactors.

The people—and cameras, and infrared sensors—she wished to avoid were those in the bunker at the top of the bluff, overlooking the sea.

Unfortunately, they were *also* the people who had the food.

A basic conflict in desires, as her economics tutor would have said. Before he starved, or was torn apart by feral dogs, or went cannibal and was put down, or whatever the hell had killed him.

She might have made an effort to find out—she'd liked him—if there had been any chance of the news being good, and if there'd been any chance of her finding out some kind of definitive answer. But she'd learned a long time ago that the news was *never* good, and that it was generally best not to ask too many questions.

You never liked the answers once you got them.

He, too, might have had a couple of trenchant comments to make about margins. Margins of survival. Margins of safety. Margins of profit. The world was right up against the edge of all of them now.

Maybe it was teetering back, Yana told herself. Maybe things were starting to get better.

She was finally close to the bluff. One disadvantage of the bunker's position, from the point of view of the bunker's inhabitants: It held a commanding view of sea, strand, genetically-engineered kelp-tangle aquaculture clusters, and distant undead lighthouse, but the edge of the bluff cut off their line of sight to the beach immediately below. There had been motion detectors down here once, not too long ago… but after the Eschaton, the end of the world—here in the future—entropy took its toll and things which had once been cheap and disposable could not be replaced. Manufactured objects that had been designed to be thrown away were not simple to repair.

It was Yana's advantage, and a delightful little scrap of irony.

She bounced on her toes like a runner warming up before a race. When the light swept past again, she scrambled up the steep, overhung-in-places bluff. Her fingers scraped at crumbling stone; roots gave when she grabbed at them. Though she was strong and fit and practiced and not *too* hungry, her forearms ached with a deep muscular soreness by the time she dragged herself over the edge.

There was no time to lie there panting and collecting herself. She wriggled to her feet and crouched, balanced on her toes and fingertips, waiting to discover if she'd been seen.

The blind eye of the robot lighthouse swept past once, twice, while Yana held as still as a toad that hopes not to be noticed. She thought, over and over like a short penitent prayer: *I am stone.* The illumination within the bunker never flickered. No hue, no cry. No sign of life.

They were probably in there enjoying a pleasant supper of hot soup and bread, she thought bitterly—a mistake. Her stomach growled, and she felt faint. She waited for one more pass of the light, gathered herself, and when the welcome darkness embraced her again, sprinted toward the back of the bunker, running not by sight but by the remembered outlines of the land.

She made it. Pressed against the base of the bunker, she paused and listened intently for alarms and excursions. Nothing. Had the infrared sensors given out long ago, along with everything else? Had she been skulking for no reason?

Or was it simply that no one was watching them, and all the artificial systems had long since degraded, ground down, and failed?

She knew the bunker wasn't deserted. She'd seen shapes moving around it as recently as her last scouting visit, a mere few days ago. But they went inside at night, sealed themselves up. And that was why night was the safest time for her to strike.

She didn't expect to break in. The bunker was pre-Eschaton tech, and she might have about as much luck prying a clam open with her torn and ragged fingernails. It'd be safer to try to swim out to those aquaculture rigs, and that was nearly certain death. But her careful spying had revealed that while the *bunker* was probably impregnable by any means within Yana's reach, the people who lived there didn't store everything within its walls.

There were outbuildings. Low, dug-in, camouflaged with rocks so they looked like part of the outcropping the bunker was built into; they huddled behind it like so many slanting boulders. There, by those storage sheds— there, Yana thought she could probably break in. And there was food there. She'd seen men rolling the barrels of mussels from the aquaculture rigs along the beach, hoisting them up the bluff with pulleys and cables. She'd seen them hauling up baskets of seaweed, too. And more mysterious large, soft-looking sacks of things, all carried from small boats moored far out to sea—too far to swim.

She imagined flour, bacon. Oatmeal. *Sugar.*

Her stomach growled again. She swallowed the bitter bilious flavor of her hunger and propped her hands on her knees.

There was a little more light here. It filtered down from the floodlights above, and the dark sky was brightening. Not with dawn, not yet. With rich drapes and swirls of electric green and arctic blue aurora.

Sprinting—and potentially falling—wasn't worth it, here. By the glow of the Northern Lights, Yana picked her way along the edge of the path that led from the bunker's great steel door around to its rear. She didn't walk *on* the path because it was scattered thickly with bivalve shells—clam, oyster, mussel—and she knew they would crackle and crunch under her feet.

She moved crouched over, as much to get her eyes closer to the ground as to disguise her silhouette. It was a good thing, too, because it kept her from tripping into the trench beside the entrance to the sheds. There were three of them, side by side, two-thirds buried underground and then more earth and stones heaped on the roofs.

She drew up sharply, found the stone steps leading down, and paused. If she, herself, were going to set a booby trap, this is where she would do it.

Someone moaned in the darkness below.

Yana froze. She felt like a damned startled rabbit. For an instant, she thought bitterly of what it had been like to walk tall, mostly fearless. To have a full belly and time to think, read, plan. Then she acknowledged the thought, let it pass through, and refocused her attention on the actual, critical, possibly life-threatening matter at hand.

There was a person in the darkness below.

And that person was hurt.

Well, most likely. She could construct all sorts of conspiracy theories and worries about decoys and traps, but Occam's razor suggested that somebody else had been attracted by the presence of food, and had either triggered a trap or just—in the dark—stumbled into the gaping hole in the ground.

Yana risked bending down, dropping her hand below the line of the ground, and squeezing her fingers tightly, briefly, on the activator of her minilume. It glowed with a pleasant cool light, illuminating a bare pit or trench paved in flagstones and featuring a fieldstone retaining wall to keep it from collapsing in on itself. On the far side were the doorways to the three sheds or root cellars. They were all closed.

Yana heard the moan again.

This time, she had been listening. Waiting. She thought the sound emanated from the leftmost of the sheds, which was the one closest to the sea. Another quick squeeze on her lume, and she saw that each shed had a small casement window about four feet off the ground. The three windows were not identical. They had obviously been constructed from whatever materials were available, then hinged to a custom-built window frame when the time came to install them in the sheds.

The one on that leftmost shed was propped open at the bottom.

As if in response to her light, Yana heard a brief intake of breath. The moaning stopped.

Silence.

She hadn't seen anything that looked like a trap in her brief glimpses. Now, though, she palmed the lume and waited for her eyes to adapt. She moved her head from side to side, scanning—looking with her peripheral vision, which was sometimes better in the dark.

There. A faint silvery runnel reflected the glow of the night sky. Elongated, razor-thin, like when sunlight splayed along a length of spider-line: a tripwire strung across the bottom riser of the stairs.

All right, Yana thought. So if you saw that and wanted to avoid it, what would you do next? You'd drop down, right, over the edge on the opposite side?

Yana waited for the lighthouse beam and matched it with a quick flicker of her lume, peering down into that pit. The big flagstone at the far end of the pit had a funny, plasticky shine to it. And it was suspiciously clean, without the scraps of dead grass and litter of sand that marked the other flagstones. Plenty of birdshit, but some of the shit had a sort of funny, elongated splatter pattern.

The flagstone was on hinges. It was designed to drop whoever jumped down onto it into an oubliette. Or possibly into a pit of hungry tiger sharks and rotating knives, which would probably be more efficient in the long run, and probably just about as much fun. No need to haul any prisoners—or bodies—out of a hole in the ground that way. You'd save on rigging pulleys.

She checked again, but those were the only two traps she saw. The moaning had stopped completely, as if the moaner were biding their time, or simply playing dead.

Yana shrugged, checked her pack straps, made sure the lume's loop was fast around her middle finger, and walked slowly down the stairs, pausing to step over the tripwire as gingerly as a cat walking through deep snow before testing the pit-bottom with one toe. It held. She shifted her weight onto it.

It held, still.

All right then, she thought, and lifted her trailing foot high over the wire.

She'd need something noisier than her crowbar to get through any of these doors quickly. Though she could probably shatter the frames. But that one down on the end, with the open window...

The window wouldn't have been wide enough for her to wriggle through before the Eschaton. Hell, she wouldn't have had the strength to boost herself up to it. She'd been a comfortable, wide-hipped graduate student then, and not the lean predator she was now. Yulianna had always been the skinny one—the hot one—back in the day, and Yana had been the smart one. Because most people were too blind to notice that her sister was just as smart as Yana was.

She missed that margin of safety. Hell—insulation, stored food—it was probably the reason she'd survived this long.

She flashed her lume again and inspected the window ledge for imbedded glass and razor blades and the like. She craned her neck to see upward, to check for any sign of, oh, something like a guillotine suspended on the other side of it. She poked the crowbar in, just to be sure.

Nothing.

"Lazy," she said.

In fairness, she supposed, the bunker folks came in and out of this place every few minutes during the day. Even in the post-apocalyptic world, you wouldn't want your toddlers playing around guillotines.

She hooked the window open with the crowbar and waited.

Nothing. Nothing but the sound of the sea.

"Hey," she called softly through the window, with a preparatory glance toward the stair. If somebody in there were inclined to raise the alarm, she could hoof it out of here pretty quickly. She'd just have to remember to hurdle that tripwire. She could shine the light in and take a peek, but to see in she'd have to silhouette herself against the sky. And the light was a bullet-magnet, if the person inside were armed and inclined to open fire.

Talking was safer. It didn't require line of sight.

"Hey," she stage-whispered again, having the peculiar sensation that the darkness was listening. "Is there somebody hurt in there?"

A pause, and then a cautious voice. "Not badly hurt," a woman replied. "I'm tied up, though. What's your name?"

"Yana," Yana said. "Yours?"

"Yulianna."

Yana stopped dead, brought up sharp. It was her sister's name.

This was not her sister's voice or phrasing, though, and she forced herself to take a breath and continue on. "Are there any traps? If I come through the window?"

"No," Yulianna said. "It's safe. They propped it open so I could breathe, but it's cold in here. Are you here to steal food?"

"Is that what happened to you?"

"Sort of," the woman said. "Here, let me get out from under the window."

There was a scraping sound and a couple of thumps. "Ow," the woman said.

"I'm coming in," Yana warned. She jumped up, got her belly on the window frame, and slithered through. The hard part was not falling on her face on the floor, but she managed a sort of controlled slide and caught herself with her hands. Her feet hooked the window frame. Carefully, she unhooked them one at a time and brought them down to the floor, then stood.

"I'm going to make a light," she said, and squeezed her lume.

She'd turned the ring around so the bright part was inside the curve of her hand, so the lume mostly shone through her flesh, producing a macabre effect. Even that was enough light that the woman on the floor winced and turned her face away, which told Yana how long she'd been sitting in the dark. The stranger didn't shield her eyes with her hands because she couldn't; her wrists were zipped to her ankles with plastic ties.

The woman couldn't have been as hungry as Yana and her sister were. She still had some flesh on her bones, not just sinew and ropy muscle. Her hair was red, and shoulder-length, though it seemed patchy and staring as if she'd been ill. Or perhaps it was just matted from sleeping on the dirt floor, or from lack of general care.

"What did you steal?"

"Mussels," the woman said. "From the frames. The aquaculture. I dove for them." She looked defensive. "They were from before the Eschaton, and just sort of got left there. A little engineered ecosystem of kelp and shellfish."

"Huh," Yana said. She gave her lume two quick short squeezes so it would stay on without her attention. Impressed despite herself, she said, "Did you have a drysuit?"

"Just a lot of practice," the woman said.

Yana tried to think of her as Yulianna. But the dry hair, the shadows under bruised skin… she couldn't look at them, and think that name. It was a common name. But every time Yana tried to wrap that name around this stranger, her mind sheered off.

So she said instead, "Is that really… stealing?"

"They thought so," the woman said, jerking her chin at the door. "You know, this is a great conversation, but maybe you could… untie me?"

"Right," Yana said. "Do you solemnly swear not to decapitate me or something?"

"I do so swear," the woman said, with mock gravitas.

Yana knelt beside her, pulled her clam knife from the sheath in her boot, and jerked the short razor-sharp blade through the plastic straps.

"Ahh," the woman said. She flopped her hands against her chest as if they were wet feather-dusters. "Devil take it," she said. "Nothing. Feels like a couple of hot squid on the ends of my arms. I hope I don't get gangrene."

Then she moaned sharply, bit her lip to stem the noise, and curled up around the arms, rocking back and forth with her face distorted by pain. "Ow, that hurts. Ow, ow, pancakes! Ow."

Yana watched, thinking there was nothing she could do for her except bear witness. It made her uncomfortable to watch the other woman's pain, so she turned her back. She played her lume over the barrels and crates and shelves, spotting food, gear—

"Is any of this booby-trapped, do you know?"

"Ah, ah. Don't touch the two-way radios, owww!"

But the *ows* were getting softer. Finally, Yu… the *woman* made a sound that was probably a sigh expressed through gritted teeth and rolled forward onto her hands and knees.

"Anoxic pain," she said. "Wow, that was not fun."

"You're a doctor?" Yana asked, interested. That was useful.

"Biologist," the woman said. "Marine."

Well, that explained the swimming.

"Right," Yana said, examining the shelves. She needed valuable things, trade goods. Travel equipment. And food. There was a metal box labeled "wind-dried fish" that reeked promisingly. She grabbed that and opened it. Stuffing papery pieces of whitefish into her mouth, she started chewing, then filled up one of the side compartments in her pack while the pungent flavor flooded her mouth with saliva. The texture was a bizarre combination of leathery, spongy, and crisp. This was just protein, though, and you'd starve to death on only that. She handed the box over to the woman—since her hands seemed to be working now—and found a bag of dried apples next to it. She appropriated the whole thing. They were old, stiff and brown. Probably not pre-Eschaton, though. Dried fruit wouldn't last *that* long.

Trade goods.

"Fat," Yana said.

The other woman was now chewing on her own slice of fish. She rubbed her hands through her hair, where her fingers stuck in the mats. She wriggled them free, then rolled a cat's cradle of shed strands down her fingers, wadded it up and tossed it away. There was sea salt still crusted on her skin and along the hems of her clothing, and it seemed to be causing purple sores around her hairline.

Yulianna, Yana thought, and turned away.

"There's salted blubber up there," the woman said. "And some pemmican."

Yana was grateful for something plausible to do with her hands. "You inventoried the place in the dark?" Yana found the clothing, packed neatly in old crates along the back wall. She rummaged through it, finding warm wool trousers that would fit Yulianna—*her* Yulianna, who was thinner than this one, thinner still even than Yana was—base layers, technical fleece. She took what was warm and light.

Yana found sugar and flour, too, and took a five pound bag of each. She layered clothing on; she'd put her pack back on *after* she dealt with the window. Rooting around in the clothes, she located a second rucksack—army issue, old, the canvas worn through in small fraying squares—and began to pack a load for the other woman, too.

"I've been here two days," the woman said. "Some light gets in in the daytime." She had made it up to kneeling and was working one of her feet flat in front of her. Grabbing the ledge of a shelf, she stood.

Yana was ready to catch her, and she did stagger. But once she was up, she seemed pretty stable. She looked around. "It's hard to see in here."

"Sorry," Yana said. "I've just got the one lume. Here."

She handed the woman the bag. "Can you manage that?"

The woman hefted it, winced, and started to struggle into the straps before glancing at the window and deciding that she would wait until they were outside, as well. "I'd better. We're taking a lot to travel light."

"I have to bring food back," Yana said. "For my sister."

The woman raised her eyebrows, then gave Yana a nod after she'd thought about it for a while. "Good girl. What else are you looking for?"

"Trade goods," Yana said. "Something valuable." She was starting to feel the pressure of time. Surely somebody would come to check on the prisoner soon. Or worse, notice the lights moving around in here. But they couldn't forage in the dark.

"Well." The woman stepped aside with a magician's flourish.

Yana stared. Behind where the woman had been standing was a shelf holding dozens of jars of clear liquid. Yana snatched one up—they were all mismatched, old jam jars and who knew what; the one in her hand had once held marmite, by the shape of it—and unscrewed the top. She didn't get it all the way off when the smell hit her.

"Alcohol."

The woman nodded, smiling tight.

"Grab as much as you carry," Yana said.

Loaded up, the woman with her sister's name stepped toward the door while Yana killed the lume. The woman was still limping slightly but didn't complain, and seemed to be loosening up somewhat. She reached the door and tested the handle.

The door swung open with an oiled click.

Yana shrugged the pack up her arms. "Good. Just as glad not to do the window again."

She stepped forward, but the woman stopped Yana five steps from the bottom of the stairs. "Careful," she said. "There's a monofilament a couple of centimeters over the wire you can see."

A horrible shock of realization settled in Yana's stomach. The expression must have registered even in the semi-dark. "Missed it on the way in?"

"I think I might be sick."

"Don't do that," the woman said. "You look like you need that fish on the inside. How do you still have your feet?"

"I stepped really high."

"Well then," the wrong Yulianna said. "You know how high to step on the way out, don't you?"

They were very careful climbing up the stairs. When they came to the top, Yana shifted her pack. It was heavy with wrapped glass jars, and she could already tell that the weight would be a problem. But she was fed now. She was strong. All she had to do was get it back to Yulianna.

Her Yulianna.

She looked over her shoulder at the woman.

"I'm going west along the coast," she said.

"I have nowhere else to go," the woman answered. "May I come with you?"

Yana paused. The woman was strong, capable. Despite getting caught, if she'd been diving for mussels as far out as the aquaculture cages, she really must be a powerful swimmer. Yana still didn't think she could have done it herself without drowning. Or dying of hypothermia.

"We'll decide that later," Yana said, after only a brief hesitation. "For now, let's put as many kilometers between this place and ourselves as our legs can manage."

The woman threw a hateful glance over at the bunker, though all they could see from here was the back slope of it, like a rubble-strewn hill. The Zombie Light swept across them again.

"Yes," she said. "Let's."

They couldn't run in the dark with the heavy packs. And they certainly couldn't down-climb the bluff. So they crept inland, staying low, though Yana's body complained about the belly full of food she'd stuffed into it before leaving the shed, or cellar, or whatever it was. A palpable mist rolled in from the ocean as dawn approached. They blundered through it, picking their way, following the sound of the sea to stay oriented. They had to be wary of terrain, walking so nearly blind.

Yana's body finally managed to assimilate the food. The lack of fat was a blessing now; she thought if she had eaten anything richer, she would have vomited. And it was good that she was recovering some of her brains along with the calories—she hadn't realized how much the hunger had affected her—because about an hour into the walk she decided that she should probably ask the woman a few questions before she brought her down on her unsuspecting sister.

The end of the world, at least, provided for a plethora of conversational openings. "So," she asked the woman. "What have you been doing since the apocalypse?"

"Stealing," the woman said. She patted her hip; it wasn't exactly ample, but she wasn't the next thing to skin and bones, the way Yana was. "Or the army dogs would call it that, anyway, but you saw how much food they had just piled up there. And what gives them the right to claim that aquaculture farm as if somebody didn't build and maintain it beforehand?"

Yana contemplated her accent. "You're not from near here."

"I've been camped near the lighthouse for about three months."

Which was a non-answer.

"I was a graduate student before," Yana said. "Economics."

The woman smiled. "An academic."

Yana nodded.

"I was a biologist. Wait, I told you that already. So. *You* say apocalypse," the woman continued, doubling back in the conversation. "*I* say opportunity."

"The world," Yana said harshly, "has *ended.*"

The woman shrugged. "It's not the first time." She smiled. "The Black Death, for example. That was an apocalypse. Or the smallpox epidemics in the Americas. Some evidence suggests that at one point our species died back to around two thousand individuals. *Two thousand individuals.* There were fewer of us than there are whooping cranes. Well, *were* whooping cranes. After they bounced back, I mean. Who knows if there are any left now?"

They were clambering down to the beach at last, to walk in the mist that glowed pink with incipient sunrise. The woman paused and studied Yana's face in the strawberry glow. "What I'm saying is, give it time. It's hard now, I know. Still hard. The margins are slim, incredibly tight. But we've survived worse. And in another ten, twenty, ten thousand years… it will turn out to have been good for all of us. Except the ones who died. Infinite possibilities for everyone now. Like the Black Death."

"I don't understand," Yana said.

The woman coughed, then turned to spit the result on the beach. It gleamed blackly in the night-sky glow.

"Empty ecological niches are an opportunity for evolution," she said. "As surely in human society as in the natural world. We'll have an opportunity as a species to become so much more than we are now. To improve. Evolve, as we haven't evolved in millennia. And that's what matters in the long run. Species survival. Species development. Who knows—maybe we'll finally take that next step, become something transhuman."

"What about…" Yana pointed to herself, the other woman. The sweep of abandoned rocks on the strand. "… the casualties?"

You're creepy, she didn't say.

"Awful, isn't it?" The woman coughed. "And yet, life finds a way. This is hardly even an extinction event, compared to some of them." She cast her hands out wide, staggered, caught herself before she stumbled into the sea. She put her hand to head as if it ached. "And you and I have already outcompeted our rivals simply by surviving. When we start to push back from this crisis, there will be a world of opportunities."

"You're pretty cocky for somebody who was hogtied in a root cellar fifteen minutes ago."

"There weren't any roots in that cellar," the woman said. She turned to walk backwards, smiling at Yana while the sun rose and filtered through the mist over Yana's shoulder, lighting the woman's hair up in shades of incredible flame.

"We can stick together," Yana said, suddenly, feverishly hopeful. "The three of us. We'll be safer. We can go someplace. You're right, of course you're right. We're young, we can work. Somewhere there's got to be a community, doesn't there?"

"Maybe we should walk south to Africa," the woman said with a smile. "That's always been where the waves of human evolution come from."

The stranger's face seemed more bruised under the salt. In the morning light, as the mist burned off, Yana could see the purple stains spreading under translucent skin. Her steps began to drag, but when Yana said they should rest, she shook her head. "It's not much farther, right? I'll rest when we get there."

She hitched her pack straps away from the bones of her shoulder as if they hurt.

They walked another two kilometers, but the woman was soon staggering. She hemorrhaged before they reached the broken highway that marked the place where Yana must turn landward.

The blood gushed from her—nose, mouth, down the insides of her trouser legs—as she doubled over and clapped her hands across her face as if she could somehow stuff it back inside, keep her life from running out.

Yana went to her, lifted off her pack, held her head, and tried to calm her when she begged through blood. At last she lay still, and Yana laid her down, composed her hands, smoothed her shedding hair back, and laid pebbles on her lids to close her wild, wild, white-ringed eyes.

She wanted to stay and pile the beach rocks over her in a cairn. But somewhere, her own Yulianna needed her. And there were untold riches in her bag.

She picked up the woman's pack too, and strapped it across her chest despite the blood. She was bloody herself, from her attempts to help, though she washed as much as possible off in the sea. It might have been a hemorrhagic fever, some mutant disease. But Yana wasn't too worried about that.

She remembered what the woman—*Yulianna, call her Yulianna*—had said, about camping among the rocks near the zombie lighthouse.

The reactors must be leaking after all, then.

Yana looked back once, while she still thought she should be able to see the stranger's body. It wasn't there, though, and Yana wondered if the tide could have so quickly rolled up the margin between sea and shore and reclaimed it.

She and her Yulianna would have to move on. Once Yulianna was strong enough. Once the food did its magic. They had two packs, trade goods now. Clothes for hiking in.

It was only a few kilometers more. Yana followed the highway on its long curve away from the beach, not leaning as far forward as she might have to make the climb because of the unbalanced weight of the packs. She saw just the stones and the sky.

There had been fewer people every year, since the Eschaton. Now Yana wondered if there were any at all, except her and Yulianna, and the army men holed up in the bunker. Maybe they were all that was left in the whole world.

Probably not.

But maybe.

They would do what the biologist had suggested, Yana decided. They would walk south. To Africa. They would be part of the future of humanity. The next step in evolution. If they were tough enough to survive.

If they could prove their fitness. It could still turn out to be a good thing for everyone.

Yana wondered how many thousands of kilometers it was, to get to Africa. Once, it would have been easy to look that up.

She turned off the road at the moss-covered boulder that was shaped roughly like a giant tortoise, and picked her way around to the tumbledown old fishing shack that looked like it was about to melt into the landscape. If you even happened to notice it, weathered gray as it was and wedged between two great, wind-break stones, you'd never think it anything but a ruin.

She paused, assessing, as the shack came into view. It seemed undisturbed. It was considerably more sound than it appeared—they had made all their structural improvements on the inside. They had spent the first summer after the Eschaton reinforcing, insulating, and weatherproofing it—but leaving the exterior treacherous and abandoned-looking.

It had mattered more at first. When there had been more people.

Yana's feet hurt. Her shoulders burned. She hurried down the little dip to the shack, wishing she could call out for Yulianna but too careful to give their position away that easily. Besides, she wasn't worried. Yulianna would be fine. She'd left Yulianna the gun.

The quiet and the closed door were good signs. Peaceful signs.

She broke into a trot, careful of the gravel underfoot. If she shattered her ankle, it would not get a chance to heal. She paused by the boulder, listened. Everything quiet, everything good.

She stepped up to the shack's little crooked door, which was better hinged than it seemed to be, and tapped lightly. The latch string was out, but she still called, "Sweetheart? It's me, don't shoot," softly before she opened the door.

It glided on the hinges she had oiled, and she stepped inside.

It took a moment for her eyes to adjust to the dimness. She used that time to shrug out of both packs and set them down by the table made of planks resting on salvaged plastic crates. Jars wrapped in cloth knocked against one another, muffled. She straightened up with relief and turned.

Yulianna was on the plank bed, curled on her side as she always slept, the blanket pulled up to warm her. The rifle leaned against the wall beside the bed, in exactly the position where Yana had left it. That was good, very good; Yulianna hadn't even needed to move it.

Yulianna watched Yana with her gray eyes as Yana came in. Yana picked up the bag of dried apples and a canteen of water and went to sit beside her.

"Hey, sweetie," Yana said. She rested her hand on Yulianna's shoulder and stroked her faded, straw-stiff ginger hair back from her cool, firm brow. "I got food. Will you eat some?"

She placed a piece of apple in her own mouth and chewed, then carefully scooped the moist pap into the corner of Yulianna's lips. She gave her a little water, but it ran out between her teeth.

"Sweetie," Yana said, "You have to swallow. There's fish too, beef jerky. Some pemmican. So much food, we'll get fat. And I have trade goods. We can find a town."

Yulianna didn't answer. She stared ahead unblinking.

Yana wiped the corner of her sister's eye, and the skin crumbled. She pulled her hand back and resolutely reached for another bite of apple.

"You have to get strong," she said, stroking her sister's hair again. The stiffness was bad today, she thought. "You have to eat. You have to get strong. So we can travel. So we can be the ones who make it."

She leaned down and kissed her sister's cheek, rubbing soft lips against hard, papery skin.

Yulianna made no answer.

JINGO AND THE HAMMERMAN

Jonathan Maberry

-1-

Kind of hard to find yourself when everything's turned to shit.

Kind of hard, but when it happens… kind of cool.

That's what Jingo was trying to explain to Moose Peters during their lunch break. Moose liked Jingo, but he wasn't buying.

"You are out of your fucking mind," said Moose. "Batshit, dipso, gone-round-the-twist monkeybat crazy."

"'Monkeybat'?" asked Jingo. "The hell's a—"

"I just made it up, but it fits. If you think we're anything but ass deep in shit, then you're off your rocker."

"No man," said Jingo, stabbing the air with a pigeon leg to emphasize his point, "*your* problem is that you don't know a good thing when you see it."

Moose took a long pull on his canteen, using that to give himself a second to study his friend. He lowered the canteen and wiped his mouth with a cloth he kept in a plastic Ziploc bag in an inner pocket of his shirt. He was careful to not dab his mouth with the back of his hand or blot it on his shirt.

Jingo handed him a squeeze bottle of Purell.

"Thanks," said Moose in his soft rumble of a voice. The two of them watched each other sanitize their hands, nodded agreement that it had been done, and Jingo took the bottle back. Moose stretched his massive shoulders, sighed, shook his head. "Not sure I get the 'good' part of things, man."

Jingo, who was nearly a foot shorter than Moose, and weighed less than half as much, got to his feet and pointed to the crowd of people on the far side of the chain link fence. "Well, first," he said, "we could be over there. I don't have a college degree like you and I haven't read all those books, but I'm smart enough to know that they got the shit end of the stick. Tell me I'm wrong."

Moose shook his head. "Okay, sure, they're all fucked. Everyone knows they're all fucked. Fucked as fucked will ever get, I suppose."

"Right."

"But," said Moose, "I'm not sure that sells your argument that we have it good."

"I—"

"Just because we're on *this* side of the fence doesn't sell that to me at all, and here's why. Those poor dumb bastards are fucked, we agree on that, but they don't *know* they're fucked. At worst, they're brain-dead meat driven by the last misfiring neurons in their motor cortex. At best—at absolute best—they're vectors for a parasite. Like those ants and grasshoppers, with larvae in their brains or some shit. I read about that stuff in Nat Geo. Either way, the people who used to hold the pink slips on all those bodies have gone bye-byes. Lights are on but no one's home."

"You going somewhere with that?" asked Jingo as he rummaged in his knapsack for his bottle of cow urine.

"What I'm saying," continued Moose, "is that although they're fucked they are beyond *knowing* about it and beyond caring. They're gone, for all intents and purposes. So how can you compare us to them?"

Jingo found the small spray bottle, uncapped it and began spritzing his pants and shirtsleeves. The stuff had been fermenting for days now and even through his own body odor and the pervasive stench of rot that filled every hour of every day, the stink was impressive. Moose's eyes watered.

"We're alive, for a start," Jingo said, handing the bottle to Moose.

The big man shook his head. "Not enough. Give me a better reason than us still sucking air."

"A better reason than being alive? How much better a reason do we need?"

Moose waggled the little bottle. "We're spraying cow piss on our clothes because it keeps dead people from biting us. I don't know, Jingo, maybe I'm being a snob here, but I'm not sure this qualifies as quality of life. If I'm wrong, then go ahead and lay it out for me."

They stood up and looked down the hill to the fence. It stretched for miles upon miles, cutting this part of Virginia in half. Their settlement was built hard against the muddy banks of Leesville Lake, with a dozen other survivor camps strung out along the Roanoke River. On their side of the fence were hundreds of men and women, all of them thinner than they should be, filthy, wrapped in leather and rags and pieces of armor that were either scavenged from sporting goods stores or homemade. Dozens of tractors, earthmovers, frontend loaders and bulldozers dotted the landscape, but most of them were near the end of their usefulness. Replacement parts were hard to find. Going into the big towns to shop was totally out of the question. Flatbeds sat in rows, each laden with bundles of metal poles and spools of chain link fencing.

On the other side of the fence, stretching backward like a fetid tide, were the dead. Hundreds of thousands of them. Every race, every age, every type. A melting pot of the American population united now only in their lack of humanity and their shared, ravenous, unassuageable hunger. Here and there, stacked within easy walk of the fence, were the mounds of bodies. Fifty-eight mounds that Moose and Jingo could count from the hill on which they'd sat to eat lunch. Hill seventeen was theirs. Six hundred and fifteen bodies contributed to the composition of that hill. Parts of that many people. Though, to be accurate, there were not that many whole people even if all the parts were reassembled. Many of them had already been missing limbs before Jingo and Moose went to work on them. And before the cutters did their part. Blowflies swarmed in their millions above the field and far above the vultures circled and circled.

Moose shook his head. "If I'm missing anything at all, then please tell me, 'cause I'm happy to be wrong."

-2-

As they began prepping for the afternoon shift, Jingo tried to make his case. Moose actually wanted to hear it. Jingo was always trying to paint pretty colors on shit, but lately he'd become a borderline evangelist for this new viewpoint.

"Okay, okay," Jingo said as he wrapped the strips of carpet around his forearms and anchored them with Velcro, "so life in the *moment* is less than ideal."

"'Less than ideal'," echoed Moose, smiling at the phrase. "Christ, kid, no wonder you get laid so often. You could charm a nun out of her granny panties. If there were any nuns left."

Quick off the mark, Jingo said, "What's the only flesh a zombie priest will eat?"

"Nun. Yeah, yeah. It's an old joke, man, and it's sick."

"Sick funny, though."

Moose shook his head and began winding the carpet extensions over the gap between his heavy gloves and leather jacket. It was nearly impossible to bite through carpet, and certainly not quickly. Everyone wore scraps of it over their leather and limb pads.

"Okay, okay," conceded Jingo. "So that's an old joke. What was I saying?"

"You were talking about how life sucks in the moment, which I'll agree about."

"No, that was me getting to my point. Life sucks right now because we're all in a transitional point."

"'Transitional'?"

"Sure, we're in the process of an important change that will shift the paradigm—"

Moose narrowed his eyes. "Where's this bullshit coming from?"

Jingo grinned without shame. "Books, man. You're always on me to read, so I've been reading."

"I gave you a couple of Faulkner novels and that John Sandford mystery."

"Sure, and I finished them. They were okay, but they didn't exactly speak to me, man. What's Faulkner got to say about living through a global pandemic? Nah, man, I needed something relevant."

"Uh huh. So… who've you been reading?"

The little man's grin got brighter. "Empowerment stuff. Dr. Phil, Esther Hicks, Don Miguel Ruiz, but mostly Tony Robbins. He's the shit, man. He's the total shit. He had it all wired right, and he knew what was fucking what."

"Tony Robbins?"

"You know, that motivational—"

"I know who he is. Or was. But, c'mon, he was all about business and taking charge of your career. Not sure what we do qualifies as a 'career.' I mean, I could build a stronger case for this being all of us working off our sins in purgatory. If I believed in that sort of thing, which I don't. Neither do you. So, tell me exactly how Tony Robbins' books—or *any* empowerment books—are useful for anything except toilet paper?"

"You say stuff like that because you haven't read them," said Jingo. "Empowerment is what it's all about. Look, history goes through good and bad moments. Transitional moments, you dig? Going from what was to what will be."

"I understand the concept of transition," said Moose, reaching for his reinforced cervical collar.

"Right, so that's what this is." Jingo gestured widely to include everything around them.

"A transitional period?"

"Sure."

"That's how you're seeing this?" Moose asked.

"It's what it is. The world as we knew it is gone. We know that. We all know that. The plague was too big and it spread too far. Too much of the systems we needed—what do you call that stuff? Hospitals and emergency services and shit? People we're used to being able to call—?"

"Infrastructure," supplied Moose.

"Right. The infrastructure's gone, and that means the world we *knew* is gone. And it's so totally gone, so completely fucked in the bunghole that we can't put it back together the way it was."

"Is that a Tony Robbins quote?"

"You know what I mean." Jingo picked up the two football helmets and handed one to Moose. "Everything that was is for shit. Right now things are for shit, too, but in a different way."

Moose hooked the chinstrap in place and adjusted his helmet. The visor was scratched and stained, but he could see through it. "Not in any version of a good way."

"No, but that's what I mean by transitional." He picked up the sledge-hammer, grunting with its weight and handed it to Moose. "The world's still changing."

"Changing into what?"

Jingo pulled his machete from the tree stump where he'd chunked it before lunch. He slid it into the canvas scabbard on his belt.

"Into something better."

"Better?" Moose snorted. "Look around, brother, 'cause that's setting the bar pretty low."

"Sure, but that means that things can only keep getting better."

"Jesus."

The shift whistle blew and they began walking down the hill toward the gate.

-3-

Because neither of them had premium skills, they worked cleanup. Before the plague, Jingo—born James Go—had been a third-generation Chinese American who mostly fucked around on trust money left to him by his software developer dad. He had some school, even a degree, but not a lot of what he'd studied had stuck. It was only when the trust was beginning to dry up that Jingo had started reading self-help and empowerment books to try and grab the future by the horns. The apocalypse had mostly, but not entirely, short-circuited that process. He knew that he would never be a great man or a great doer of things, but he had plans.

Michael 'Moose' Peters was different. He'd been a high school football coach and health-ed teacher. A college graduate with a degree in education, a constant reader and small-scale social activist in his community. Unlike Jingo, Moose had been a family man, but his wife and two sons were long gone. Taken by the first wave of the plague as it swept through Bordentown, a narrow spot on the map in Western Pennsylvania. Bordentown was notable only for being next door to Stebbins, where the plague began. Some of the guys working the fence thought that was kind of cool, and it gave him low-wattage celebrity. A few of the men, though, seemed to hold it against him, as if proximity to the outbreak somehow made him part of the problem.

Neither of their skill sets were of prime use. They weren't doctors, scientists, military, police, EMTs, or construction workers. Neither of them could cook, sew, hunt, or survey the landscape. Nobody was playing football anymore, and Moose didn't think it would make a comeback. It was as extinct as accounting, software development, infomercials, TV producing, the real estate industry, reality show competitions, taxi service, pizza delivery, cosmetic surgery, valet parking, car detailing, investigative journalism, secret shoppers, and ten thousand other things Moose could name. Putting together a list of useful skills was easier and quicker. A lot of people, including movie actors, famous models, politicians, CPAs, advertising executives, pet therapists, comic book writers, professional athletes, lawyers, and many, many more were now part of a mass of unskilled labor. Some were so unsuited to the survival of the collective that they were quietly shoved out of the gate at night. Those who made the cut, like Jingo and Moose, survived because they had—if nothing else—muscle.

Both men were fit. Jingo was small and fast and had good stamina. Moose was huge and strong and could work all day. Neither of them complained. Neither was overtly insane, at least not in any way that made them a security risk or a danger to their co-workers.

They worked support for the fence project. More highly-skilled men built the fence. Less skilled men washed dishes and clothes. Those without even those basic skills threw parts on the mounds. Everyone worked. Idlers were starved out or pushed through the fence. Same for thieves, especially food thieves. Steal someone's meal and you become a meal for the dead beyond the fence. Courts and lawyers had all died off, too.

Jingo and Moose worked as a team. Jingo was a cutter and Moose was the hammerman.

As they passed through the fence they nodded to each other and set right to work. The process was simple. First came the cover-men, who were the most heavily armored. They worked in teams of two, with each team holding a folding table in front of them like a wide shield. Five sets of cover-men pushed out into the crowd of the dead to create a kill-zone. Then Jingo and Moose, along with two other two-man teams, worked the cleared area. The shield opened and closed, opened and closed, allowing a few of the dead in at a time. The cutters of each team went in low and fast, cutting hands off at the wrists with their machetes and then chopping the outside of one leg to make the infected fall. The hammermen followed, swinging sledgehammers down on the dead skulls. Even though Moose and the others who wielded hammers were big, they used the lightest-weight sledges—for speed and to keep from fatiguing.

The dead never learned from the deaths of their fellows, so it was all rinse and repeat.

Stackers then dragged the corpses—in whole and in parts—off the kill zone and began a mound. When the mound became too big for the shield wall to contain it, they pushed forward to occupy a new plot of land.

Working in teams like his, two-dozen men could take down five hundred of the dead per shift. There were forty shield walls running at any time, round the clock, every day. The landscape was littered with thousands upon thousands of mounds from Taylor Ford Road all the way to Slush Branch. It never stopped.

Rest only came when there was such heavy rain that floodwaters made it impossible for the clumsy dead to approach the chain link fence. And if they hit a zone where the dead were so densely packed that the fence itself was in danger of being overwhelmed, the shift foreman would call all the teams inside and send the bulldozers out. Twenty dozers could clear pure hell out of a field.

But that was hard on the machines. The pulped flesh clogged worse than mud, and it meant having each dozer stripped and cleaned. That would take them out of commission for days. The risk reward ratio meant that it was usually men out there doing the job.

Men like Jingo and Moose.

"Let's rock and roll," said Jingo. He said it every single time they went out, and every time he made it sound like they were about to do something fun. It amazed Moose. He wondered, though, if his friend's happy-puppy enthusiasm was a front. There were guys like that, people who relied on the fake-it-til-you-make-it approach to handling life. The let-a-smile-be-your-umbrella crowd. Moose knew several guys like that, and he'd seen what happens when the rain came down so hard that their umbrellas collapsed. Behind some of those smiles was a mask of shrieking terror. Once their illusion was shattered they were left in pieces. Suicides were not uncommon. There was even one smiling, happy guy who went so far off the rails that he took a sledge and smashed the shackles on a forty-yard wide section of fence before the guards cut him down. By then a wave of the dead had swarmed into camp, and when all the shooting and cutting was over the collective was down fifty-six workers.

Not that Moose feared Jingo would go out that way if something ever wiped the smile off his face. But he'd break. They all broke.

At times Moose wanted to shake the little guy, or maybe slap some sense into him. Get him to stop daydreaming about how good things were going to be. But what would be the benefit of that? Even Moose had to admit that Jingo's optimism made their life easier. It was a skill set more important than his ability to swing a machete.

He'd break, though. In the end they all broke. Moose had left his own optimism behind in a lovely little cottage in Bordentown, behind doors that were stained with the blood of everyone he ever truly loved.

A transitional period? No, as he saw it, the global paradigm had already shifted and it had stripped the clutch, blown out the tires, and was rusting in the sun. Dead and unfixable.

"Yeah," he said to Jingo, "let's boogie-woogie."

The shield teams pushed out, and Jingo raced behind them to claim his spot. He was a lefty and he liked the club-and-cut method of using his padded right forearm to parry the grabbing hands of the dead and then a waist-twisting cut to "blunt" the arms. That was easiest to do if he took up station on the left-hand side of the opening. He won his spot, chopped and won a double as both of a dead woman's hands flew off with one cut, then he pivoted and put a little pizzazz into a squatting leg cut that he'd labeled his "Crouching Tiger" move. Moose had his sledge in a rising arc before the infected was even falling, and so the ten-pound weight followed her down and stroked the top of the skull.

The trick was not to make the rookie move of burying the mallet in the skull. Hard as hell to pull out. All that suction from the brain. A deep grazing hit along the top of the head worked well, and it did enough damage to the motor cortex that it shorted them out nicely. Moose seldom had to swing twice on the same target. Not more than two or three times in a shift, and usually only when he was getting tired.

Jingo was good, too. Months and months of practice had honed his skills so that more often than not he got his doubles, and sometimes caught the angle just right to cleave completely through the knee joint. If he hit the sweet spot the knee fell apart. Hit it wrong and the wide, flat machete blade got stuck in bone. Jingo always carried a back-up cutter and several short spikes for emergencies, but he seldom had to use them.

They worked the pattern in silence for a while, but soon the moans of the dead got to them and Jingo picked up the thread of their earlier conversation.

"Sooner or later we're going to run out of zombies," he said.

"How do you figure that, genius? Last I heard there were something just shy of seven billion of our life-impaired fellow citizens."

Jingo laughed at that even though it wasn't the first time Moose had made the joke. "Sure, sure, but they're spread all over the world. Big damn planet."

"Got our fair share here."

Jingo cut the hands off a man in an Armani hoodie and dropped him in front of Moose. "Right, but look how many we're taking off the board. I heard the guys working the fence in North Carolina are taking down fifty thousand a day. A *day.*"

"First off, that's horse shit."

"No, I heard it from—"

"And second, there were three hundred and twenty million people infected. There's, what, thirty thousand of us working the fences? Maybe less. Call it twenty-five thousand and change."

"So?"

Moose smashed a head and paused to blink sweat from his eyes. He had grease around his eyes to prevent sweat from pooling, but it happened. Couldn't wipe it away because he had black blood and bits of infected meat clinging to his clothes, from fingertips to shoulders. They'd all seen what happened to guys who made those kinds of mistakes. Some of them were out here among the moaning crowds.

"So, it's going to take just shy of forever to clear out the dead."

"Well, in his book, Tony said that solving small problems results in small personal gains. It's only when you conquer your greatest challenge that you achieve your greatest potential."

"Uh huh."

"Absolutely," said Jingo, cutting a corpse down without even looking at it.

He was very good at that. They all were. Peripheral vision and muscle memory were their chief skills. Jingo sometimes joked that he could do the job blindfolded. Between the rot of undead flesh and the constant moans they made, you'd have to be an idiot to have one sneak up you. A lot of people agreed with that, including Moose, though Moose never took his eyes off the infected. Never. He looked at the face of everyone who came through the shield wall. Even the ones he didn't finish himself. It was part of his personal ritual and he never shared the meaning of it with anyone. For him, though, it was crucial to his own spiritual survival to see each face and recognize—however fleetingly—that the infected were people, to never lose sight of the respect owed to the fallen. They had each died in pain and fear. Each of them had been part of a family, a household, a community. Each of them had expected to have futures and lives and love. Each of them had been unfairly abused by the plague. It had stolen their lives from them and it had turned them into monsters.

Moose could not and would not accept that as the final definition of what each of these people were. They would always be people to him. Dead, sure. Infected, yes. Dangerous, of course. But still people.

Jingo was different. Maybe it was part of his *faux* optimism, but he rarely looked at any face, and like a lot of the guys in the collective, Jingo tended to refer to the infected as zombies, zoms, stinkers, rotters, grays, walkers, stenches, fly-bait, wormers, and any of the other epithets common since the plague. Moose had long ago decided that Jingo was afraid to do what Moose *had* to do—which was connect with the humanity, however lapsed, of those they killed. Jingo couldn't afford that kind of cost. And Moose knew that if his friend ever spent that coin, it would break him.

That thought saddened him. Jingo was a bit of an idiot at times, and he was far from the sharpest tool in the woodshed, but he had light. The kid definitely had light, and the world had become so god damn dark.

So, as they worked through the afternoon, Moose encouraged Jingo to talk, to expostulate and expand on his new theory. To elaborate on his latest theory on what would be his ticket out of the hell of the now and into a brighter future. However fictional or improbable it might be. So what if the kid had become a post-apocalyptic Professor Pangloss? Who knows, maybe this was the best of all possible worlds, with a promise of greater possibilities tomorrow.

Skewed logic, sure, but Moose figured, what the fuck. Listening to Jingo was a crap-ton better than listening to his own moody and nihilistic thoughts. Maybe the kid was saving them both from that fractured moment when they'd lose their shit, cover themselves with steak sauce and go skipping tra-la out among the hungry dead.

"It all comes down to what we believe," said Jingo as he chopped down two more of the dead. Hands flew into the air and legs buckled on severed tendons, dropping them right in Moose's path. Whack, chop, fall, smash. Rinse and repeat. "That's what Tony Robbins wrote about. I mean… what's a belief anyway? I'll tell you, man, it's a feeling of certainty about what something means. What we need to do is make sure that we shift what we believe to align with what we want to happen."

"Okay," said Moose, playing along, "and how do we do that?"

"Well… I'm just reading those chapters now, but from what I've read so far, it's all about taking an idea you have to find things that support it. That gives the idea what he calls stability. Once an idea is stable like that, you can go from just thinking about it to believing in it."

Moose saw Jingo's blade flash out and take the delicate hands from the slender wrists of what must have once been a truly beautiful woman. Even withered he could see that she had been gorgeous, with a full figure and masses of golden hair. The blade swept down and cleaved through a leg that had slipped out through a long slit in a silvery gown. Moose swung his sledge at her head and silently said what he always said.

I'm sorry.

"So, Tony said that the past doesn't equal the future, and I figure that our present doesn't either. We know things have to change. Either we're going to wipe out the rotters and rebuild, or we won't. I'm thinking we will because even though they outnumber us, we're smarter and we can work together. Once we finish the fences, we're going to start planting crops. This time next year we'll be eating fresh veggies, and maybe even steak."

Moose almost made a comment about the challenge of finding useful seed that wasn't the GMO stuff that grew into plants that wouldn't breed. They'd have to find seeds that had never been genetically-modified, and how would they know? How would they test that stuff?

He almost said it, but didn't.

Whack and chop, fall and smash.

Jingo said, "Tony wrote a lot about how there's no such thing as failures, only outcomes. So, we shouldn't look at all this as us having fucked up. It happened, so we need to sack up and deal and move past it. We need to make the future we want rather than moan and cry about the way it is."

His face was alight with the promise of what he was saying, but Moose wasn't fooled. He could see the doubt, and the panic it ignited, right behind the sheen of those bright eyes.

"Okay," Moose said, keeping the kid on track, "tell me how we go about getting to this shiny new future? 'Cause personally I'd love to get there."

That was exactly what Jingo needed to hear, and he went on a long, convoluted rant about the seven steps to maximum impact.

"What Tony said," began Jingo, "is that we're always living in uncertain times and that change is constant. Mind you, he was writing this before the zombies, but the world was for shit then, too. Exactly the same, only different. Instead of rotters we had all those wars, the dickheads on Wall Street, climate change, the right and left waving their dicks at each other, everyone in the Middle East losing their *damn* minds, churches hating on each other, all that shit. It was fucked six ways from Sunday, and yet some people were able to get along. And more than along, they were able to keep their eyes on the prize. People were even making some nice bank all through when the economy went into the pooper. Why? Well, that's the secret. Tony says that what we need are charismatic leaders…"

The rant went on because Jingo was completely in gear now. He wasn't even flicking a sideways glance at the dead. His blade moved like it was laser-guided. Never missing, never faltering. And Jingo never got within nibbling distance of any of the infected. It was impressive, and Moose could feel himself get a little bit of a charge out of the message. The rise of a charismatic leader was something he'd read about in college. Of course that was a broad description that included everyone from Gandhi to Hitler to Jim Jones. Charisma didn't mean the same as personal integrity.

As Jingo spoke and Moose hammered, he suddenly saw something that was so strange, so impossible that he instantly felt as if the whole world had slipped from the harsh certainty of reality into one of Jingo's delusional fantasies. It froze Moose, bugged his eyes wide, dropped his jaw, and seemed to infuse the world with far too much of the wrong kind of light.

It was a dead man. An infected. He was very tall—six and a half feet or better. He wore the soiled remnants of a very expensive suit. He had a prominent jaw and laugh lines carved into his face, though he was not laughing at the moment. His mouth opened and closed as the dead man bit at the air, like all of them did, as if they were already chewing on the flesh they craved. The man staggered through the gap in the shield wall and lunged for Jingo.

"No!" cried Moose, but the little man's machete snapped out, cutting through thick wrists, sending diamond cufflinks flying into the air. Jingo pivoted, still looking at Moose, still talking about the process of change through charismatic leadership as his machete sliced through the tendons of the walking dead. The infected fell at Moose's feet, handless arms reaching, mouth chewing at the dirt, thousand-dollar shoes skidding in the mud in a clumsy attempt to rise. Jingo did not even glance down. Not for a second.

"Tony's probably out there somewhere right now," he said, "putting together a community of smart people who have their shit wired tight. He's the kind of guy who is definitely going to be there when we build our better world. And don't laugh, Moose, but I'm going to be right there with him. You and me. Fuck this world, man. It's all about optimism and *knowing* that better times are coming because we're going to make them come. You got to see the logic in that, dude. You with me or do you think I'm just blowing smoke out my ass?"

Moose looked down at the infected man. At the face he'd seen on TV and on book covers. The odds were insane. Moose didn't know if this was God's way of taking a final shit on everyone. Or if the Devil was driving the bus. Or if the world was simply so fucked that the impossible was going to be on the menu from now on.

The absolute insanity of the moment made the ground under his feet feel like it was crumbling. But the sledgehammer was heavy and real in his hands.

Jingo glanced at him and grinned. "You with me or not, bro?"

Moose swung the sledge up and down, destroying the face. He raised his sledge and swung it again, crushing the skull.

"Yeah," he said, "I'm right here with you."

Jingo laughed and swept out with his machete. He continued talking about the pathway to the better future, to the best of all possible worlds.

Moose raised his dripping sledgehammer, sniffed to clear his nose of tears, bit down on the scream that wanted to claw its way out of his throat.

Whack and chop, fall and smash.

THE LAST MOVIE EVER MADE

Charlie Jane Anders

People tossed around words like "collapse of civilization" and "post-apocalyptic," but really everything was the same mess as always. Only without any soundtrack, since the whole world had gone deaf, and with a "militia" of guys in red bandanas swarming around killing everyone who got in their way, and putting loads of "undesirables" into prison camps. But civilization, you know, has always been a relative thing. It rises, it falls, who can keep track?

So some kind of sonic weapon had gone off the wrong way, and now absolutely everybody in the world had lost their hearing. Which was a mixed curse, sort of. Sneaking up on people was suddenly way easier—but so was getting sneaked up on. The fear of somebody sneaking up behind me and cutting my throat was the only thing that kept me from being bored all the time. I always thought noise was boring, but silence bored me even worse. And if you walked up behind someone, especially a member of the red-bandana militia who were keeping order on our streets, you had to be very careful how you caught their attention. You did not want a red bandana to think you were sneaking up on them. And often, you'd find a whole street of stores that were there yesterday were just burned-out husks today, or bodies piled in an odd assortment, like corpse origami.

I found myself sniffing the air a lot, for danger or just for amusement. If anyone had still been able to hear, they probably would have been doubled up laughing, because we were all going around sniffing and grunting and mumbling in funny voices as soon as we had no clue how ridiculous we probably sounded.

Almost every corner seemed to have red bandanas standing on it, looking bored and desperate for someone to fuck with them.

But meanwhile, I was *Entertainer Explainer's* New Talent of the Month, because I'd managed to avoid getting murdered in an amusing fashion, and the video had gone mega-viral. I was seeing my own face on shirts and on people's phablets more and more often. Our film showed the part where Reginald, the wild-eyed mustache dude in the Viking helmet, was chasing me around and trying to tear my arms and legs off, but not the aftermath, where Reginald got pulverized and lit on fire by the red bandanas. (That part, maybe, not as funny.) In any case, Sally and I were suddenly kind of famous, and we had to clear out our freezer to make room for all the meat and casseroles and stuff that people kept bringing over.

Everybody was bracing themselves for the next thing. We still believed in money, kinda-sorta, even after a ton of people had lost their savings and investments in the big default spiral. We didn't *not* believe in money, let's put it that way. We still had electricity and cell phone service and Internet, even though many parts of the country were on-again, off-again. The red bandanas and the rump government needed a cellular network as bad as the rest of us, because they needed to be able to organize, so until they figured out how to have a dedicated network and their own power sources, they would make sure it kept running for everyone. We hoped so, anyway.

Sally and I spent hours arguing about what sort of movie we should make next. All of my ideas were too complicated or high-concept for her. I wanted to do a movie about someone who tries to be a gangster but he's too nice—like he runs a protection racket but never collects any money from people. Or he sells drugs but only super-harmless ones. So the other gangsters get mad at him, and everyone has to help him pretend to be a real gangster. And he does such a good job he becomes the head gangster, and then he's in real trouble. Or something.

Anyway, Sally said that was too complicated for people right now; we had to shoot for self-explanatory. Some of the film geeks wanted us to make a movie *about* the fact that everyone was deaf, but that seemed like the opposite of escapism to me—which I guess would be trapism, or maybe claustrophilia.

Sally was all about recapturing the Vikings-and-Samurai glory, like maybe this time we could have Amish ninjas who threw wooden throwing stars. I was like, Amish ninjas aren't high concept? I was happy to keep debating this stuff forever, because I didn't actually want to make another movie. Whatever part of me that had let me turn calamity into comedy had died when I fell out of a window on top of Reginald and watched him die on fire.

Snow fell. Then hail, then sleet, and then snow again. Things felt dark, even during the day, and I felt like my sight, smell, and touch were going the way of my hearing. Only my taste burned as strong as ever. Everything was salty, salty, salty. You could slip and break your leg in a ditch and nobody would know you were there for days and days.

This was going to be a long winter.

• • •

"ROCK MANNING. WE NEED YOU."

I stared up at the giant scrolling light-up banner over Out Of Town News in Harvard Square. I blinked the snow away and looked a second time. It still looked like my name up there.

Okay, so this was it, the thing my school therapist had warned me about back in fifth grade: I was going narcissistophrenic and starting to imagine that toasters and people on the television were talking to me. It was probably way too late to start taking pills now.

But then a guy I had met at one of our movie shoots saw it too. He tugged my sleeve and pointed at the scrolling words. So unless he and I were both crazy the same way, it really did say my name up there.

A bus zipped past. (They'd gotten a few buses running again.) The big flashing screen on the front didn't say, "WARNING. BUS WILL RUN YOU OVER. GET OUT OF THE WAY" as usual. Instead, it said, "ROCK MANNING, YOU CAN MAKE A CONTRIBUTION TO REBUILDING SOCIETY." I grabbed the guy, whose name was Scottie or Thor or something, and pointed at the bus for more independent confirmation that I wasn't losing it. He poked me back and pointed at a big screen in the display window of Cardullo's delicatessen, which now read, "ROCK MANNING, COME JOIN US." I grabbed my cell phone, and it had a new text message, much the same as the ones I was seeing everywhere. I almost threw my phone away.

Instead I ran toward the river, trying to outrun the words. Over the past few months since everyone went deaf, I'd seen the screens going up in more and more places, and now all of a sudden they were all talking to me personally. Computer screens on display at the big business store, the sign that normally announced the specials at the Mongolian buffet place—even the little screen that someone had attached to their golden retriever's collar that would let you know when the dog was barking. They were calling me out.

I got to the river and ran across the big old stone bridge. In the murky river water, the letters floated, projected from somewhere in the depths: "WHY ARE YOU RUNNING? WE THOUGHT YOU'D BE FLATTERED."

When I got to the other side of the bridge, Ricky Artesian was waiting for me. He was wearing a suit, and instead of the red bandana, he had a red handkerchief in his breast pocket, but otherwise he was the same old Ricky from high school. He held up a big piece of paper:

"Relax, pal. We just need your help, the same way we needed you once before. Except this time we're going to make sure it goes right."

As if I would ever forget the time I got blackmailed into helping Ricky's crew make a propaganda movie—that was the start of me losing my mind. As our movies had gotten more popular, Sally had gotten paranoid that terrible early film, in which I played a heroic red bandana, would turn up online and ruin our credibility. But I was pretty sure it was lost forever.

Ricky had a couple other guys in suits behind him, also clearly red-bandana honchos. I thought about jumping off the bridge, and kept looking over my shoulder at a dark shape below me. The river had defrosted but still looked chilly. I looked over the edge again, tossed a mental coin and jumped.

The loose boat was right where I thought it was. It had drifted down-river from the Harvard boathouse, and I landed in the stern without capsizing it all the way. I righted the boat and found the oars. Someone had either forgotten to chain it up, or had vandalized the chain. I slotted the oars into their nooks and started to row. I'd never sculled before, but how hard could it be?

After half an hour of rowing as hard as I could, and going in the same circle over and over while Ricky watched from overhead, I wondered if I'd made a mistake. I texted Sally that I was in a boat trying to escape and didn't know how to row. She Googled rowing. She said I needed to straighten out and row the same amount with both oars, and then maybe I'd stop going in circles. Also, go with the current. Meanwhile, Ricky and his friends were grabbing a big, scary-looking hook.

I tried to figure out what the current was. It took me a long while to find a drifting leaf and figure out I should go the same way. I tried to row in that direction, but the boat kept veering and swerving. Then I saw a bench right in front of me that looked like someone was supposed to sit facing the other way. So maybe part of the problem was that I was sitting backwards? I got myself all turned around, but I lost my grip on one of the oars and it floated away, much faster than my boat had gone so far. At this point, the hook snagged my boat, and a moment later I was a landlubber again.

"Hey Rock," Ricky said. I was up to about ten percent accuracy with my lipreading. He held out his hand, and I took it out of reflex.

We all went for burgers at this little diner nearby, which had survived everything without changing its greasy ways. I admired that. It even had a little jukebox at each table, and the red checkered vinyl tablecloth with stray burn marks from when you could still smoke indoors. Ricky smoked, because who was going to tell him not to?

"i think it's great you're still doing the same thing as in high school," Ricky's laptop screen said. He swiveled it around and typed some more, then turned it back. Now it said: **"you found something that worked for you, and you stuck with it. that's kool."** I nodded. If Ricky had been talking instead of typing, he probably would have made this stuff sound like compliments. He typed some more: **"you know i always liked you."** The other two guys didn't try to say anything, or even read what Ricky was typing; they just ate their burgers and stared out the window at the handfuls of students who were crawling back to Harvard.

I didn't try to contribute to the conversation either, I just read whatever Ricky typed. He hadn't touched his burger yet. He told me about how he'd moved up in the world since high school, and now he was working for some pretty juiced-up people in government, and everything was really under control. You would be surprised, he said, at how under control everything was.

I nodded and half-smiled, to show that I knew what he meant, but really I didn't think I would be that surprised.

I thought about the oar that had gotten away from me, floating down-river toward freedom, as fast as it could go. Where would it end up?

Ricky said I shouldn't worry about a repeat of what happened last time. We were both older and more experienced, and he'd gotten smarter since then. But the thing was, he said, people were still in shock—almost like little children, right now. And they needed their cartoony entertainment to keep their minds off things. So here was the deal: he would get us resources—resources like we couldn't imagine, like our wildest dreams were this tablecloth and the actuality was up there on the ceiling. And in return, we would just portray authority in a kind way. Nothing too heavy, like everyone wearing the bandana or any army uniforms or anything. Just occasionally we see that the militia and Army are trustworthy, and the people in charge have everyone's best interests at heart, etc. Most of the time, we'd have a free hand.

I had to get up and go wash my hands so I could type on Ricky's laptop. I didn't want to get his keyboard greasy. Then it took me a minute to hunt and peck: **"sally wont go for it she thinks you killed her boyfriend which duh you did."**

I swiveled it around before I could think twice about what I'd just typed.

Ricky's eyes narrowed. He looked up at me, and for a moment he was the legbreaker again. I thought he was going to lunge across the booth and throttle me. Then he typed: `"the robot guy?"` I nodded. `"that was a situation. its complicated, and many people were to blame."`

I tried really really hard not to have any expression on my face, as if it didn't matter to me one way or the other. I ran out of hamburger, so I ate my fries slow, skinning them and then nibbling at the mashed potatoes inside. Everything smelled meaty.

`"tell u what, just dont tell sally im involved,"` Ricky typed. `"just tell her the government wants 2 support your work."`

It was easy for me to agree to that, because I knew my face was a giant cartoon emoticon as far as Sally was concerned, and she would know within seconds that I was hiding something.

Ricky didn't threaten to break parts of us if we didn't go along with his plan, but he didn't need to, and he only made some gauzy promises about payment. He did say he could get me some rowing lessons.

• • •

It took me two hours to find Sally. I almost texted her, but I had a bad feeling about my cell phone.

She was in a group of film students building a giant ramp that looked as if they were going to roll a mail cart into a snowbank. She saw me and then turned away to watch her pals slamming boards together. I nudged her, but she just ignored me. I remembered she'd said something about this movie they wanted to make about a guy who works in the mailroom and discovers a hidden doorway that leads to Hell's interoffice mail system, and he has to deliver a bunch of letters to demons before he can get out. High fuckin' concept. Anyway, she was pissed that I'd been blowing her off for weeks, so now I couldn't get her attention.

Finally, I wrote just the name `"ricky a"` on my cell and shoved it in front of her without pressing send. Her eyes widened, and she made to text me back, but I stopped her. I grabbed a pad and a pen and wrote down the whole story for her, including the signs in Harvard Square. She shook her head a lot, then bit her lip. She thought I was exaggerating, but the guy who'd seen the signs showed up and confirmed that part.

"We're so small time," she wrote in neat cursive under my scrawls. "Why would Ricky care?"

Under that, I wrote: "1. He remembers us from hi skool, unfinished biz. 2. He likes us and wants to own us. 3. He hates us and wants to destroy us. 4. those guys are scared of losing their grip & they think we can help."

It was a cold day, and I'd gotten kind of wet trying to escape in a Harvard boat, plus the sun was going down, so I started to shiver out there on the lawn in front of BU. Some students were straggling back in, just like at Harvard, and they stared at the set, abandoned half-finished against one wall. Sally gestured for her gang to get the ramp to Hell's mailroom back into storage.

We piled ourselves into the back of the equipment van, with Zapp Stillman driving, and headed for the Turnpike, because the sooner we got out of town the better.

We got about half a mile before we hit the first checkpoint. There were soldiers with big dragonfly helmets standing in front of humvees, blocking off most of the lanes of Storrow Drive, and between the soldiers and the swiveling cameras on stalks, there was no way you would get past their makeshift barricades. They were checking everybody coming in and out of the city, and a hundred yards past them stood an exoskeleton thingy, or a mecha or whatever they call it, with thighs like Buicks and feet like dumpsters. I couldn't really see its top half from my hiding place in the back of the van, but I imagined piston elbows and some kind of skull face. The kind of people who built a mech like this would not be able to resist having a skull face. My brother Holman had probably piloted one of these things in Central Asia or Central Eurasia, someplace Central. The pilots of these things had a high rate of going A.U.T.U., because of all the neural strain. This one wasn't moving, but it was cranked up and operational because you could see the ground shivering around it, and there were fresh kills nearby: Cars still smoking, a few unlucky bodies.

Our van turned onto a side street as fast as possible, and we swerved back toward Boston University. By the time we got back there, Janelle had found some forum posts about the cordoning off of several major cities. It was part of a sweep to round up certain radical elements that threatened the shaky order: you had the red bandanas inside the cities, and the army outside.

We were still in the van, parked on a side street just off Dummer St., sheltered by a giant sad oak that leaned almost to the ground on one side. You could put a tire swing on that oak and swing underground and maybe there would be mole people. Mole people would be awesome, especially if they had their own dance routine, which I just figured they probably would because what else would you be doing stuck underground all the time?

I wasn't sure if we should get out of the van, or if someone would spot us, but Sally went ahead and climbed out, and Janelle followed. I got out and stood on the sidewalk, shrugging in a sad ragdoll way. Sally stomped her foot and gritted her teeth. She tried some sign language on me, and I got the gist that she was saying we were trapped—every way out of the city would be the same thing. I just looked at her, waiting for her to say what we were going to do, and she looked weary but also pissed. This not-talking thing meant you really had to watch people, and maybe you could see people more clearly when you couldn't hear them.

I studied Sally. She had the twitch in her forearms that usually meant she was about to throw something. She had the neck tendon that meant she was about to yell at someone, if yelling were still a thing that happened. Her mouse-brown hair was a beautiful mess bursting free of her scrunchie, her face so furious it circled back around to calm. Biting her tongue, the better to spit blood.

She wrote on her phone: **"the army outside + red bandanas inside. occupation. city is screwed. we r screwed. trapped."** She erased it without hitting send.

I took the phone and wrote: **"red bandanas + army = opportunity."**

She just stared at me. I didn't even know what I had in mind yet. This was the part of the conversation where I would normally start spitballing and suggesting that we get a hundred people in koala costumes and send them running down the street while someone else dropped hallucinogenic water balloons from a hang glider. But I couldn't spitball as fast with my thumbs.

I paused and thought about Ricky, and the other bandanas I'd met, and how they were so desperate to be someone's hero that they were even willing to ask someone like me for help representing them. I thought about Holman, and how much he looked down on civilians, even before he got the A.N.V.I.L. socket in his skull. I thought about how Ricky and his guys had engineered a clusterfuck at that peace protest, making the cops think the protestors were shooting at them so the cops shot back. I thought about how the bandanas weren't leaving the city, and the army wasn't coming in.

"i think I have a bad idea," I wrote.

• • •

All my life, there had been a giant empty space, a huge existential void that had needed to be filled by something, and I had never realized that that thing was the Oscar Meyer Wienermobile.

With its sleek red hot-dog battering ram surrounded by a fluffy bun, it was like the Space Battleship Yamato made of bread and pork, made of metal. This MIT student named Matt had been suping it up with a high-performance electric engine and all-terrain wheels, just saving it for the right occasion. And somehow, Janelle had convinced Matt that our little adventure was it.

The tires were the perfect mud color to match the lower part of the chassis, which Matt had rescued from a scrapyard in Burlington. The chassis had a tip as red and round as a clown's nose on either side of the long, sleek body. This baby had crisscrossed the country before I was born, proclaiming the pure love of Ballpark Franks to anyone with half an eye. Just staring at it made me hungry in my soul.

All around us, Sally's film-student minions were doing engine checks and sewing parachutes and painting faces onto boomerangs and inflating sex-dolls and making pies for the pie-throwing machine. The usual, in other words. I felt an emotion I'd never felt before in my life, and I didn't know how to label it at first. Sort of like excitement, sort of like regret—but it wasn't either of those things. It was lodged down where I always pictured my spine and my colon shaking hands. I finally realized: I was afraid.

People had told me about fear, but I had never quite believed it existed in real life. I watched Zapp Stillman blowing up a blow-up doll, and something wobbled inside me. I had felt guilt and self-loathing, especially after Reginald, but now I felt worry-fear. Zapp saw me looking at him and gave me a cocky little nod. I nodded back.

Sally was busy studying a big road map with Janelle, charting the escape route and where we were all going to rendezvous if we made it out of town. Sally had taken my vague arm-wheeling notion and turned it into an actual plan, which would let us escape to the Concorde Turnpike and make for Walden Pond, that place where Henry David Thoreau had built a comedy waterslide two hundred years ago. And then maybe head west. Find a quiet place (so to speak) to wait things out. Sally handed her magic marker off to Janelle and came over to stand with me.

"What changed your mind," she wrote in ballpoint on a pad, "about doing more stunts? You were ready to quit, before."

I took the pad and pen. Chewed the cap. Wrote: "Ricky won't leave us alone. We gotta blow town and this is the only way. Plus this is different than just making another weird movie. If this works, maybe we ruin the red bandanas' day. Maybe we ruin their whole week even. PAYBACK." That last word, I underlined three times. Sally took the pen back from me and drew little stars and hearts and rainbows and smiley faces around it, until it was the most decorated "PAYBACK" you've ever seen.

One of our lookouts shone a flashlight, and Janelle nodded, and Sally and I got stuffed into a little cubby under the floorboards with no light and almost no air, with all the cameras and filming equipment on top of us. We were scrunched together, so her knee was in my face and my left arm dug into her side. Every few moments, the floor over us shuddered, like someone was knocking things around. Sally shivered and twitched, so I gripped her tighter. I was starting to freak out from the lack of light and air and entertainment options, but just as I was ready to wobble myself silly, Janelle and Thor (Scottie?) lifted the lid off and pulled us out.

• • •

So. *Ballpark Figure* was the last movie we ever made, and it was probably one of the last movies anybody ever made. It was a mixture of fiction, reality and improv, which Zapp Stillman said was pleasingly meta—we were counting on the bandanas and the army to play themselves in the story, but I was playing a fictional character, and so were Janelle and Zapp. My character was Horace Burton, the last baseball fan on Earth who had been heartbroken since the MLB shutdown and who was driving his giant hot dog vehicle to try and find the world's greatest baseball players, in a *Field of Dreams*-with-lunch-meat kind of thing. Janelle was a former hot dog mascot who had turned Vegan but still wanted to keep dressing up as a hot dog, now just a meatless hot dog. And Zapp was some kind of coach. We filmed a sequence of the three of us piling into our hot dog car with some animated cue-card exposition, and posted it online with minimal editing, as a kind of prequel to the actual movie, which we promised would be posted live and streaming, right as it happened, on our video tumble.

By the time we were ready to leave town, an hour before dawn, the *Ballpark Figure* prologue had been up for a few hours, and we had a few thousand people refreshing our vumble over and over. I had slept a few hours, but Sally hadn't slept at all and Janelle was guzzling really terrible coffee. Sally wasn't going to be in the hot dog, she was going to be one of the people filming the action from—I hoped—a safe distance, using Matt's remote-controlled camera drones, which I had insisted on. If nothing else came of this but Sally getting somewhere safe where she could start over, I could count that the biggest win ever.

As we rolled into the middle of the street and cranked the hot dog up to its maximum speed of fifty miles per hour, I had time as I clambered out onto the outermost front reaches of the metal bun to obsess over the contradiction between Horace Burton and myself. Horace's goal, in this movie, was to take his hot dog out onto the open road and find the lost spirit of baseball. Horace didn't want any trouble—but I, meanwhile, had no goal *other than* trouble, and (if I were being honest) no plans after today.

How was I going to play that, in a way that preserved the integrity of Horace and his innocent love of sportsmanship? In fact—I reflected, as I raised a baseball and prepared to hurl it at the shaved head of the red bandana standing on the nearest corner in front of a shuttered florist—that might be the reason why people root for the comic hero after all: the haplessness. This fresh white baseball was emblazoned with a slogan about bringing back the greatest game, and the story called for Horace to toss them out as a promotional thing, and to hit a militia member in the head purely by accident. So it was important for the story that I not look as though I were aiming. But I also couldn't afford to miss. Horace is a good person who just wants to bring joy to people, and he gets caught up in a bad situation, and the moment you think Horace brought this on himself through meanness or combativeness, that's the moment you stop pulling for him.

The baseball hit the teenager in the jaw, over the neatly tied red cloth that looked too big for his skinny neck, and he whipped around and fired off a few shots with his Browning Hi Performance, while also texting his comrades with his free hand.

I tried to wear a convincing look of friendly panic, like I hadn't meant to wake a thousand sleeping dogs with one stray baseball, and danced around on the front of the hot dog so hard I nearly fell under the wheels. I slipped and landed on my crotch on the very tip of the hot dog, then pulled myself back up, still trying to toss out promotional baseballs and spread goodwill, and it occurred to me for the first time that I had spent so much time worrying that I was going to hurt someone by accident, it never even occurred to me that I would finally reach a point where I would decide to cause harm on purpose.

Our hot dog had red bandanas chasing us, with two motorcycles and some kind of hybrid electric Jeep. I had no idea if anybody was still shooting at me, because I couldn't see anyone aiming a gun from where I stood on one foot and I couldn't see any bullets hitting anything—

—until a bullet hit me in the thigh just as the hot dog swerved without slowing and we released the blow-up dolls in their makeshift baseball uniforms. The blow-up dolls flew behind us, and I saw one of them hit a motorcyclist right where the red bandana tucked under his round white helmet, so that he lost his grip on his handlebars and went somersaulting, and I felt the blood seeping through my pants like maybe it had missed the bone but hit an artery and I was cursing myself for forgetting to bring a giant comedy bottle of ketchup to squirt at people, because ketchup is like fake blood only more cheerful, when Ricky Artesian climbed on top of the third car of the five that were now chasing us and held up a big flatscreen TV that read "YOU MADE YOUR CHOICE ROCK TIME TO PAY." And another bullet tore through my side just as the hot dog made another sharp turn and we disappeared into the tunnel from the abandoned Back Bay T extension project.

The hot dog came to a stop in a dark hutch Xed in by fallen rusted steel girders, just as one of our bready tires gave out and the whole vehicle slumped on one side, and our support crew set about camouflaging the Wienermobile with rocks and planks. Janelle climbed out of the cab and came over to show me the vumble, the insane number of hits we were getting right now and the footage, in a loop, of me hurling baseballs at the red bandanas.

Janelle noticed that I was pissing blood from my leg and my side, and started trying to get me to lie down. Just then a message came through from Sally, who was still masterminding the filming from a remote location: **"theyre not taking the bait."** The bandanas were staying on their side of the line and not trying to chase us into the army barricades like we'd hoped.

I slipped out of Janelle's grasp—easy when you're as slick as I was, just then—and leapt onto Zapp's bicycle. Before anybody could try to stop me, I was already pedaling back up the ramp the way we'd come, past the people trying to seal and camouflage the entry to the tunnel, leaping from darkness into the light of day. I raced close enough to Ricky Artesian to make eye contact and hurl my last baseball—absolutely coated at this point with my own blood—at his pinstripe-suited torso. And then I spun and tore off in the direction of Storrow Drive again, not looking back to see if anyone was following me, racing with my head down, on the ramp that led up to the Turnpike.

My phone thrummed with messages but I ignored it. I was already reaching the top of the ramp, all thoughts of Horace Burton, and lovable fall guys in general, forgotten. The checkpoint was a collection of pale blobs at ground level, plus a swarm of men and women with scorpion heads rushing around tending their one statuesque mecha and a collection of mustard-colored vehicles. My eyesight was going, my concentration going with it, and my feet kept sliding off the pedals, but I kept pedaling nonetheless, until I was close enough to yank out my last limited edition promotional baseball, pull my arm back and then straighten out with the hardest throw of my life.

Then I wiped out. I fell partway behind a concrete barrier as Ricky and the other bandanas came up the ramp into the line of fire. I saw nothing of what came next, except that I smelled smoke and cordite and glimpsed a man with the red neck-gear falling on his hands and rearing back up, before I crawled the rest of the way behind my shelter and passed out.

• • •

When I regained consciousness, I was in a prison camp, where I nearly died, first of my wounds and later of a fiendish case of dysentery like you wouldn't believe. I never saw Sally again, but I saw our last movie, once, on a stored file on someone's battered old Stackbook. (This lady named Shari had saved the edited film to her hard drive before the Internet went futz, and people had been copying *Ballpark Figure* on thumb drives and passing it around ever since, whenever they had access to electricity.)

The final act of *Ballpark Figure* was just soldiers and red bandanas getting drilled by each other's bullets until they did a terrible slamdance, and I have to say the film lost any of its narrative thread regarding Horace Burton, or baseball, or the quest to restore professional sports to America, not to mention the comedy value of all those flailing bodies was minimal at best.

The movie ended with a dedication: "To Rock Manning. Who taught me it's not whether you fall, it's how you land. Love, Sally."

THE GRAY SUNRISE

Jake Kerr

Don Willis is forty five years old and has just finished loading his grocery cart. He bypasses the cash registers but pauses at the entrance. A man and woman are fighting over a can of baby formula, blocking the doors. The man punches the woman in the face, grabs the formula, and shoves his overloaded cart through the doors to the parking lot.

A mass of bodies surge forward, their own overloaded carts banging together as they are pushed through the bottleneck. The woman is gone by the time Don makes it to the doors. He takes care not to slip in the puddle of blood she left behind.

• • •

Donnie Willis is ten years old and watching a TV show, long forgotten, about rich people doing rich things, and there is a feature about a yacht. It is majestic, with billowing white sails, and colorful flags that adorn a line from the cabin to the bow. Donnie scrambles closer to the TV, as if he could crawl through the screen and onto the boat, surrounded by the sea, the sun, and the beach.

"That's the home I want," he tells his dad, who walks over, kneels down next to him, and smiles. He squeezes Donnie's shoulder and asks, "What do you like about it?"

Donnie explains about the flowing sails, the blue water, the freedom of being alone, the golden beach, and—more than anything—the excitement of being free under the sun and the sky and how he could sail anywhere. "That's a good dream, Donnie. Don't let go of it. Live your life in a way to achieve it, and you'll never regret it."

Falling asleep that night, Donnie dreams of waking up before the dawn, standing on the deck of his yacht, and watching the sun rise, the sound of seagulls and waves and flapping sails his only company.

• • •

It's too late. The bags of groceries are shaking in Don's arms. *Please don't make it be too late.* Even without official confirmation, the word is spreading everywhere that the asteroid is going to hit North America. Escape is their only hope. He rushes up to his son's room. They have no time. How desperate will people be?

He walks into Zack's room. His son is playing a video game, looking bored. "Son, I'm sorry. You know what's going on, and I'm afraid we don't have much time. We need to start packing."

Zack shoots him a glance but pays most of his attention to his video game. "Is this about the asteroid?"

"What kind of question is that?" Don walks over, grabs the VR controller from his son's hand, and tosses it on the bed. "Of course this is about the asteroid. We need to get to safety. We're leaving tonight on the *Southern Cross.*"

"God, Dad. You know I hate your boat."

Don stares. "What do you mean 'I hate your boat?' We need to get away, Zack!"

His son shrugs.

Closing his eyes, Don gets his anger and fear under control. "Zack, this is not a game. We don't even have time to track down your mom or my family in Austin. We need to get to safety *now.*"

"Sure, Dad. Whatever." Zack moves to put his VR controller back on.

"Whatever? Do you have a better idea?" He had worked two full-time jobs over ten years to achieve his dream, and that dream would now save their lives, and Zack's response was *"whatever?"*

Zack shrugs. "I just assumed we'd die."

Don's anger collapses under the casual acceptance in his son's voice. "Zack, we can make it. You know that, right?"

A painful pause and then Zack replies, "I guess."

"Think of the future, Zack." Don sits down next to his son. "We *can* get away, and we *can* survive." Zack nods, but there isn't much heart in it. "Think of the future, son. Where do you want to be? What do you want to do? We have to put all this—" Don taps the controller. "—behind us." His son's face is still blank, emotionless. "Don't you have a dream?"

"I don't know." A nonchalant shrug. "To live. I guess."

• • •

Donnie is sixteen and gets through the pain of junior high by clinging to his dream. The yacht is no longer under his feet; it is moored in the middle of the bay, white and majestic. The sails are furled up and the mast and mooring are elegant in their angles and geometry, a different beauty than the billowing sails. The sky is a sun-washed blue, and the sun itself is bright enough that he can't really judge its size. It is high above, a background piece that shines light on the new additions to his dream: The girls in bikinis arrayed in front of him on large beach towels with bright blue, white, and yellow patterns.

It is just him and them. They don't have names, but it doesn't matter to Don. They adore his yacht, his private beach—and him.

He hasn't met the girl of his dreams, so these girls are like the sun, the beach, the sea, and the yacht itself—abstractions of what could be. Don looks at the yellow bikini bottom of one of the girls. It is tugged up and reveals her butt in a way that is so much better than a thong, revealing what is supposed to be hidden.

Donnie knows his dream will come true some day. He just knows *it.*

• • •

Don has never seen the marina so full of people. He walks past old dusty boats that had been in long-term storage being cleaned and prepped for use. Larger boats are being loaded with supplies. There is activity at every slip, and the water is crowded with boats heading out to sea.

He stops and holds his hand out in front of Zack. There is a stranger loading up Don's sailboat.

"Zack, go back to the truck and bring my rifle."

Zack nods, drops the big military-style duffelbag, and rushes back up the cement path.

He returns a minute later and hands his father the thirty-ought-six. "I loaded it," he adds.

"Stay here and watch the supplies," Don says.

"What's he doing?"

"He thinks he's stealing our yacht."

Don checks the chamber as he strides toward the slip. No one notices him, their attention all on the same thing—loading up and getting out. There is a man tossing a few plastic bags onto the back of the boat. There is a small pile on the boat and a larger pile on the dock.

"Okay, buddy," Don says. The man glances up mid-throw to see Don pointing the rifle at his chest. "Just drop that and get the rest of the bags and toss them back to the dock." The man looks scared, but doesn't seem desperate enough to do anything stupid.

"Just loadin' up my boat!" The man smiles and tosses the bag onto the back of the *Southern Cross.* "I know you're probably worried and all, but no need to be stealin' a man's boat." The man reaches for another bag, but stops as Don walks forward.

Don knows at that moment that the world has irrevocably changed. There is no room for debate or weakness. He has a way out for him and his son, and there is no room for discussion, explanation, or negotiation. The stranger holds up his hands. Before he can say anything else, Don swings the stock of the rifle around and slams it into the side of the man's face.

He stumbles backward, his hands against his head, a stream of red flowing through the fingers of his left hand. He screams, hysterical and shrill, "You fucker! This is my boat! I found it!" He steadies and lowers his hands. He has a gash across the left side of his forehead, but his eyes are clear.

"Take one step, and you're dead." Don points the rifle at the man's chest again. The man moans but doesn't move. "Is anyone on the boat?"

"No. I'm waiting on my family." The response is slow and grim.

"Grab your stuff and get out."

"C'mon, man. I have kids. Maybe we can both take the boat. The owner ain't even here."

"*I'm* the owner," Don replies, not that it matters. The world has changed. Motioning with the barrel of the rifle toward the boat, he repeats, "Get your stuff."

The man gathers up his bags from the boat and tosses them with the others on the dock. They appear to contain clothing. Don tries not to think about how big the man's family is. *Not my problem.*

After the man clears out, Don and Zack finish loading up the boat. He had hoped to take another trip out to stock up on supplies, but in light of what had just happened, he decides to just head for the open seas after they stow what they have.

The sailboat isn't huge, but it is comfortable, with a single cabin big enough for two. There are two large padded benches that could act as beds, and a storage area in the hull below.

Don starts to organize things—boxes of food, bottles of water, suitcases, and bags of recently bought supplies. He opens the wooden hatch that leads to the storage area below decks and grabs a plastic container full of painkillers, antacids, bandages, and a desalination kit—all still inside their grocery bags. He takes a step when he hears a shout from behind the boat.

Putting the crate down, Don grabs the rifle leaning against the door frame and walks out. Zack has his hands up. There are two men, their attention focused on Zack. One has a pistol pointed at him.

"Just get going, kid. There's no reason for you to get hurt." The man nods over his shoulder up the cement walkway to the parking lot. "Just walk away." Both look like normal middle-aged men—jeans, tennis shoes, a polo shirt, one has glasses, the other is balding. The only thing out of place is the pistol.

Don puts the rifle to his shoulder and aims at the man with the gun. He is the shorter one and is wearing what looks like surgical scrubs. On another day he'd just be some guy checking on his boat on his way to the hospital, but on this day he is like everyone else, desperate. And he has a gun aimed at Don's son.

The world has changed. Now there are no options. No negotiations. No discussions to be had.

The sun is high in the sky. The sea is calm. The boat barely moves. Don pulls the trigger. The rest is nothing but image and sound. A spray of red. A shout. Zack stumbling toward the boat. Released ropes. Shouts. Zack taking the rifle from Don and holding it steady as he points it toward the crowd gathering on the slip. The slapping sound of ropes and sails. White filling the sky. Steady movement out into a chaotic bay full of sails and froth and boats avoiding collisions only because they are all heading in one direction—the open sea.

• • •

It's Don's junior year in college, and the nameless girls in the dream have become a single girl, a classmate named Kiko, and she sways on the deck in a black bikini to the smooth sound of Latin jazz, her hands twisting above her head and reaching toward the sun. Don watches, a beer in one hand. The sky is a pale blue with streaks of white clouds.

The girl would fade from Don's dream, replaced by someone new, but everything else would remain: The yacht, the open sea, the sun, and the sound of mellow guitar chords matching the flowing sails and the gentle rocking of the boat.

• • •

"Oh my God, Dad. Do we have to hear more jazz?"

The music draws Zack from staring at his phone. For once Don is thankful for annoying his son. Zack had called his girlfriend before the ship had left cell phone range, and as her voice faded, he was left just staring at the screen.

"I like it." Don elbows his son, hoping to draw his attention from the dead man lying in his own blood on the dock, his girlfriend's final words, and the uncertainty of a future they haven't even started to grasp. "Come to think of it, I just put it on repeat."

"Argh. It's like from the dark ages."

Don smiles and thinks of bare feet dancing across a gleaming deck. He glances at Zack, whose lips are set in a thin line as he stares into the distance, the phone hanging from his hand.

"You're right. We should listen to your music. What do you want to hear?"

Zack turns to him and shakes his head. "I'm just kidding, Dad. You know I don't care about music."

Don wonders if Zack cares about anything. He was apathetic when he was at home with his girlfriend, surrounded by friends. Here on the boat it seems to be even worse.

"Maybe we should start playing Salsa or music like that," Don says. "I was thinking we could eventually dock in Rio. You could go dancing with some Brazilian girls." He smiles, hoping it doesn't seem forced.

Zack looks at his phone and then shakes his head. "Play whatever you like, Dad."

"Well, if Salsa dancing isn't your thing, what else would you like to do when we get back to civilization? Where would you like to live? That kind of thing." When Zack doesn't reply, Don adds, "It's good to think about the future."

"I'll think about it when I have one." Zack turns away and looks toward the horizon, the sun is bright, and the sky is blue.

• • •

They are South of the Sargasso Sea and approaching Barbados, searching for better fishing. The trouble is that after the asteroid impact, South American countries had set up heavily armed coast guards to keep undocumented refugees out. The orders were shoot to kill, and the only thing that saved Don on a few occasions was that the patrol boats were relatively small and stayed near the coast. He and Zack had been fired upon several times, and each time Don turned back out to the Atlantic and pursuit ended quickly.

Zack grabs the binoculars from the shelf under the dash and pulls them up to his eyes. His finger adjusts the focus. "Trouble."

Don takes the binoculars from his son, and focuses on the horizon. It's a small boat approaching fast. "Shit." Don doesn't need a closer look to know that it's a performance speedboat. The rich kids in the fast boats were the worst. Heavily armed, they weren't guarding the coast so much as hunting Americans. "What's it doing this far out?" Don mutters as he hands the binoculars to Zack and adjusts the tack for them to sail dead East and back out to open ocean. "Speedboat," Zack notes from behind the binoculars, "Two or three on board. Hard to tell with them bouncing over the waves."

Don nods. "Reef the sails. We can't outrun them, so I'll have to scare them."

"Why don't I close haul, and beat us East?"

"No. We can't outrun them. Just keep her steady."

Zack slams his fist on his thigh. "If we make progress they may just leave. If we just float here we're sitting ducks!" Before Don can reply, he adds, "Wait, you don't think I can beat this, do you?"

Don stands up, and pauses before replying. He had been waiting weeks for his son to express any hope, and here it is, only expressed through desperation. He grabs Zack's arm. "Listen. I *know* you can sail this boat, but I need us to appear like we're not afraid. So just keep us steady. If it doesn't work, you'll know, and I trust you that you can beat us East."

Zack nods, lips pursed. Don grabs the rifle and heads out to the stern.

The wind is strong, and the sea is choppy, but soon the boat is floating in relative calm. Zack is doing a good job working the sail. Supporting himself against the transom, Don lifts the rifle and hopes that the rich kids don't expect them to be armed. Surprise is what he needs.

The yacht crests a wave, and the pursuing boat is much closer than he had expected. *Damn, that's a fast boat.* There are three young men sitting behind a glass windshield. The boat drops over a crest, and Don thinks he can see weapons in the hands of two of them.

Wrapping the sling around his forearm, Don lifts the rifle and waits for a clear shot. He is good with a rifle, having spent nearly every summer hunting in South Texas with his grandfather. He is fairly certain he could take out at least one of the men before they consider the sailboat a threat.

Another crest, and he has his shot. The young men are close enough together that hitting one of them was possible even if his aim was off to the left or right.

Sudden inspiration hits, and Don fires to the right of the three men, shattering the windshield but not hitting anyone. Hitting the wide windshield is not only an easier shot, he hopes that the reality of shattered glass in their faces from an armed opponent would scare them without inciting any desire for revenge, the kind of revenge that would burn if he had killed one of them.

Don peers down the barrel, thankful for his Marksmanship merit badge. He looks for the boat. It takes a moment, and there it is. It breaks starboard and turns away from them.

Don stands, slings the rifle over his shoulder, and yells back to the cabin. "Time to close haul, Zack!"

As he steps down into the cabin, Zack asks, "Did you shoot one? They peeled off and turned away."

Collapsing onto the padded bench, Don lets out a deep breath and lets his son work the controls. "Don't let up. You're doing good. We need to get out of here."

Zack glances over his shoulder at his dad. "So you killed one?" His voice is shaky, and Don fears it's from excitement.

"No," he says. "Enough people have died already."

• • •

Don is thirty-five. There are no longer bikini-clad women dancing in his dream. He had married and divorced Maria by then. He doesn't know what went wrong, but it doesn't matter—his dream has no room for the instability of relationships.

He traded the sway of tanned bodies on the beach for the gentle rocking of the Southern Cross, *moored in a virgin bay, white sand nearly surrounding the boat. The water is so clear he can see manta rays gliding along the seabed.*

With age comes comfortable familiarity. The following no longer changes: He gets up early and watches the Milky Way slowly fade from the sky as he sits at the bow of the boat. The sun climbs slowly in the distance, spreading a glittering carpet of diamonds across the caps of tiny waves. His son is there, asleep below.

Don closes his eyes and smells the salt water and listens as jazz music harmonizes with the sound of gulls, canvas sails, and lapping waves.

• • •

The Milky Way is gone, buried under a shroud of gray ash. Still, Don spends each morning on the deck of the *Southern Cross* hoping to catch the sunrise. He glances at his watch. Daybreak was thirty minutes earlier, and the horizon is charcoal rather than black. He squints, but there is no sun. The only difference between day and night is the shade of the oppressive gray draped from horizon to horizon. Shards of black glass surround the boat, an angry sea that hasn't been calm or blue in months. He rubs his face with his right hand and stands up, bracing himself against chaotic waves. He heads below deck to wake up Zack. It's another day. One no brighter, no clearer, no better than the one before.

• • •

The first storm comes when the asteroid hits. It's as if the Earth shudders in pain. As the harsh winds blow and the seas thrash, Don is convinced that the yacht will be dashed to pieces. But after hours of being hurled up, down, and sideways, the seas quiet, and he and Zack nurse their cuts and bruises and take stock of the damage.

The winds blew out the windows, which they repair with plywood pried up from the bilge flooring, and Don repairs the jib without much difficulty. The biggest loss was their rainwater-catching basin, which was ripped free and blown out to sea. They replace it with one of their plastic storage bins.

They are better prepared for the next few storms, but the two of them emerge from each one injured and bruised, the boat battered. The worst is when Don dislocates his shoulder. He does his best not to scare Zack, but he is wracked with pain for hours after a loose flogging line rips his arm out of its socket, with each crashing wave grinding his dislocated arm against the surrounding bone.

After the seas calm, Zack takes charge with a sense of purpose that Don has only seen in glimpses between long periods of depression and quiet. He sets his foot on Don's ribs and pulls hard on his father's arm. Don's scream ends with a loud pop and then silence.

Don has spent so much energy keeping Zack positive that his own oppressive depression, seeping into his consciousness little by little, surprises and overwhelms him as they face yet another storm.

The timing of the growing storm couldn't be worse. He and Zack are weak from lack of food. They've drifted South again searching for fish, but the ocean water is thick with the ever-present dirt and ash that falls from the sky, an obscene black snow that poisons everything.

Don is thinking that the fish have finally learned that there is nothing of value near the surface. *Maybe the time is right to try a landing. Certainly the government of Brazil or Guyana would not turn them away so long after the impact?* But first he has to survive the storm.

It's the worst yet, a gale or maybe even a full-blown hurricane. Don tries to steer the ship by hand, but quickly gives up as the thrashing waves and raging winds are coming from every direction. Zack stumbles into him, and Don is surprised not to see terror in his son's eyes. They are grim, but it is a grimness borne of resolve, not powerlessness.

They hold on to whatever they can, their only goal not to break any bones as they are tossed around the cabin. The ship rolls nearly on its side as a steep wave lifts it into the air.

Don holds his breath, hoping the boat doesn't split in two. As the ship rolls in the opposite direction, he falls back against one of the benches. He breathes out, and the ship slams into another wave, tossing both Zack and Don against the other side of the cabin.

There is a loud crack, and Don looks over to Zack, expecting to see a broken bone or his twisted body. But Zack looks fine. Taking a deep breath to shout, Don yells, "Did you hear that?" thinking that perhaps the mast had finally snapped.

But not before he can get two words out, a searing pain in his chest staggers him. The pain is so great that he can barely see as he clutches at whatever will keep him anchored to the cabin. He feels a hand grasp his arm. It is strong, steady, a grip that won't let go.

The boat rolls, and Don falls against something hard. He screams. And everything goes dark.

• • •

Don is celebrating his fortieth birthday alone, but he is not lonely. The Milky Way fades, and as the sun rises in the distance, he watches dolphins jump from the ocean, welcoming the day with a primal enthusiasm. The bay is as beautiful as ever, but this time there are other boats, and the sandy beach has people lounging on it. He is holding an ice-cold glass of lemonade as the sun's rays bathe him. The harmonies of Latin Jazz weave among the sounds of vibrant voices, flapping flags, and ice tinkling in his drink. Don presses the cold glass against the side of his face, the condensation flowing in rivulets down his cheek.

• • •

It's not the pain that wakes Don but the cold. He shivers and opens his eyes. Zack is there, his face in shadow, a glowing Coleman lantern sitting on a crate to his left and filling the tight space with light. "Dad, are you okay?"

"I'm fine." His voice is a whisper. Don looks around. He is in the bilge. It is cramped, but he is comfortable He is covered in a blanket and surrounded by pillows. The sails and crucial spares have been moved, creating a space for him. He puts his elbow down to lift himself from the berth, but his chest screams in agony. He lets out a groan through clenched teeth.

"You broke some ribs. I moved you here in case another storm comes." Zack talks while he gently pushes Don back down onto the blankets. "The storm ended shortly after you blacked out."

Even with his face in shadow, Don can tell his son is proud of himself. He reaches out and squeezes his arm, ignoring the pain. "That's good, Zack. You did good."

"I'm sorry it's cold." Zack pauses and then continues, "I used all our heating packs. I was worried about you." He sounds like a father breaking bad news, not a son wondering if he's made a mistake.

With the sun blocked by dust and ash, the temperatures have plummeted, even in the Caribbean. Snow is not uncommon, and freezing temperatures at night are the norm. There is a difference between dangerous cold and uncomfortable cold. Don realizes the blankets are warm enough and that Zack wasted the heating packs.

"Thank you, Zack." Though Zack's face is still in shadow, it can't conceal his smile.

• • •

Don has been stuck below deck for a few days. It's dark and feels colder. An oppressive hopelessness takes hold of him as he listens to Zack walk along the deck above him. He closes his eyes, trying to imagine the bay, the sunrise, and his yacht. There are glimpses of the scene, but he can't grasp them, like reaching for a pen under a couch that slips further away each time his fingers brush against it. He strains to raise himself but is overwhelmed by pain and despair. He thinks of his son. Their lack of food. His injury. The cold. The storm.

"Zack!" he yells, ignoring the pain in his chest.

His son scrambles down through the hatch. "What is it, Dad?"

"What time is it?"

"Six."

"When's dawn?"

"Seven something."

"Help me up."

His son objects, but Don knows with a clarity that doesn't exist anywhere else in his mind that he needs to see the sunrise. If he can just see the sun cresting the waves, he will be able to look ahead, to know that all is not lost.

"We tried this, Dad. We need to wait for the rib to heal more. You're in too much pain."

"Help me up!"

"Dad, we tried this yesterday."

"—and the day before. I know." Don's voice is strained. "Now help me up."

His son pauses, shakes his head, and puts his arm behind his father's back. He lifts him gently, and Don grunts, tears forming in his eyes. Zack gently lowers him to the blankets.

"No! I need to get out of here."

"It's okay. Don't worry. You will." Zack squeezes Don's shoulder. "The fish are back, Dad. The storm got them active. We'll be okay. Don't worry. I'll take care of it. You just rest here." Zack turns and heads back up the ladder.

The muted light through the square hatch does little to change the oppressive darkness. This isn't just his present. It is his future.

"Zack!" Don cries out, desperation in his voice.

His son rushes down again. "Are you okay?"

Don doesn't answer at first. He knows the answer. His dream is dead. There are no more sunrises. The yacht is black with ash and dirt. The ocean will never be blue again.

"Yeah. I'm fine." He tries to hide the bitterness in his voice. He adds in a whisper, "We'll make it."

"I know, Dad."

Don doesn't know how to respond. He is the one who doesn't think they will make it. Before he can say anything, Zack adds, "We'll be hitting shore soon."

Of all the things his son could say, this is the one that Don least expects. "Wait—" Don gathers his thoughts, preparing to object or, at least, understand. *Where did this thought come from?* But before Don can speak, Zack interrupts him.

"The storm, Dad. It nearly sank us. I was on the manual bilge for six hours. Had to plug a seacock. We nearly lost her. But—" Zack pauses. His words are spoken not with fear, but with a calm confidence. "—the winds, they cleared the clouds—it's no longer raining ash. And the sea… the fish are back."

"That's good, Son, but—"

"No, Dad. This is important." Zack looks up, an intensity in his eyes. He isn't listening to Don. He is no longer the boy more interested in playing his VR game than escaping the asteroid. His words come out in a rush. "I want to help rebuild. I want to help others get back on their feet. I don't care where. I really don't care how. I just want to help make things normal again." Zack takes a breath and sighs. "Is that crazy?"

Don takes a breath, even as pain pierces his side. He knows the right words. He has practiced them countless times before, and yet never had the opportunity to use them. "You're right, Son. It is important." Don turns his head away from his son, and says, his voice steady, "That's a good dream. Don't let go of it."

• • •

Zack tells Don that he is charting a course for São Luis. Don still can't move much. He's worried that he may have hurt his back or that he has internal injuries. He keeps his concerns to himself as Zack outlines various rebuilding plans. He listens intently, adding commentary every once in a while, but this is Zack's dream, and Don knows the importance of staying out of the way.

The next morning Zack asks, "Dad, do you think you can make it up on deck?"

Don's breath catches in his chest, the question a sudden light shone on a dark truth—Don feels better but is afraid to face another dead sunrise. He is living through his son's dream. His is dead. "Still too much pain." Zack nods and heads topside.

After three days, Zack stops asking.

• • •

Don loses track of time. It is days later, but he isn't sure how many. Zack climbs down and sits next to his father. "I know something is wrong, Dad."

"Nothing's wrong." Don tries to sound nonchalant.

"Then why won't you come up to the deck?"

"There's just no reason for me to be up there."

"I think there is."

"There isn't. I told you. It's okay. I'm just healing. There's nothing wrong."

"Dad." Zack's gaze is piercing as he looks at Don. "There's a reason for you to be up there." Don prepares another objection, but Zack stands up and reaches for Don's arm, adding, "Sunrise is in ten minutes."

He grabs his father's arm. Don hesitates, but realizes that it's pointless to resist. This new look in his son, he once understood it. It is forceful. Hopeful. His son has found his dream. That Don's is gone doesn't matter. He needs to support his son even if it pains him. Isn't that what a good father would do?

Zack puts his arm around him, lifts him up, and helps Don up the steps. *When did he get so big*, Don thinks.

"We're facing West," Zack says, "so just sit at the stern and watch. You can make it."

Don focuses on his feet and doesn't look up as he walks slowly to the helm seat at the stern of the boat. There isn't much pain, but Don knew there wouldn't be—it wasn't the pain that kept him inside. Zack helps him sit, and is quiet as Don closes his eyes and takes a few breaths. *I'm doing this for Zack*, he thinks.

• • •

Don opens his eyes and grips the side of the boat to steady himself.

The sky is black, and there are pinpoints of white. Some of them sparkle. He looks left and right. There are no gray clouds of dust. Don looks at his son. "Where are we?"

"The North Equatorial Current runs South now, Dad. It's already taken us around the Eastern tip of South America. Didn't you notice it getting warmer?" Zack is smiling broadly.

Don answers, "No," but doesn't think of what he is saying; he is lost in the brightening sky in the distance. The water sparkles as a yellow glow peeks above the horizon. His heart beats faster.

Zack grabs his dad's arm. "Oh, before it's too late. Look up there!" Zack is pointing high in the sky. Don looks up at a bright group of stars. "It's the Southern Cross!"

A sob escapes as Don gazes upon the constellation above him. He turns to the sun rising in the distance. The ocean is a deep blue, not black or ashen gray.

Don glances at Zack. His son is beaming; his dream of rebuilding has already begun.

• • •

Don is on the beach, sitting in a weatherbeaten chair, the wood warped and the paint flecking away. Still, it is comfortable and solid. It's a good chair. *The Southern Cross* is docked off the pier, the sun glinting off the glass windows of the cabin. It needs a new paint job, but Zack did an admirable job making it presentable. Zack. He is at the edge of the surf with Inez, the two of them sharing a single set of earbuds and dancing to some song that Don can't hear. He doubts it's jazz.

But that's okay. This isn't his dream.

THE GODS HAVE NOT DIED IN VAIN

Ken Liu

I can prove now, for instance, that two human hands exist. How? By holding up my two hands, and saying, as I make a certain gesture with the right hand, "Here is one hand," and adding, as I make a certain gesture with the left, "and here is another."

—G.E. Moore, "Proof of an External World," 1939.

Cloud-born, cloud-borne, she was a mystery.

• • •

Maddie first met her sister through a chat window, after her father, one of the uploaded consciousnesses in a new age of gods, died.

<Maddie> Who are you?

<Unknown ID> Your sister. Your cloud-born sister.

<Unknown ID> You're awfully quiet.

<Unknown ID> Still there?

<Maddie> I'm… not sure what to say. This is a lot to take in. How about we start with a name?

<Unknown ID> ¯_(ツ)_/¯

<Maddie> You don't have a name?

<Unknown ID> Never needed one before. Dad and I just thought at each other.

<Maddie> I don't know how to do that.

<Unknown ID>

So that was how Maddie came to call her sister "Mist": the pylon of a suspension bridge, perhaps the Golden Gate, hidden behind San Francisco's famous fog.

Maddie kept the existence of Mist a secret from her mother.

After all the wars initiated by the uploaded consciousnesses—some of which were still smoldering—the reconstruction process was slow and full of uncertainty. Hundreds of millions had died on other continents, and though America had been spared the worst of it, the country was still in chaos as infrastructure collapsed and refugees poured into the big cities. Her mother, who now acted as an advisor to the city government of Boston, worked long hours and was exhausted all the time.

First, she needed to confirm that Mist was telling the truth, so Maddie asked her to reveal herself.

For digital entities like Maddie's father, there was a ground truth, a human-readable representation of the instructions and data adapted for the different processors of the interconnected global network. Maddie's father had taught her to read it after he had reconnected with her following his death and resurrection. It looked like code written in some high-level programming language, replete with convoluted loops and cascading conditionals, elaborate lambda expressions and recursive definitions consisting of strings of mathematical symbols.

Maddie would have called such a thing "source code," except she had learned from her father that that notion was inaccurate: He and the other gods had never been compiled from source code into executable code, but were developed by AI techniques that replicated the workings of neural networks directly in machine language. The human-readable representation was more like a map of the reality of this new mode of existence.

Without hesitation, Mist revealed her map to Maddie when asked. Not *all* of herself, explained Mist. She was a distributed being, vast and constantly self-modifying. To show all of herself in map code would take up so much space and require so much time for Maddie to read that they might as well wait for the end of the universe. Instead, Mist showed her some highlights:

< > **Here's a section I inherited from our father.**

((lambda (n1) ((lambda (n2...

As Maddie scrolled through the listing, she traced the complex logical paths, followed the patterns of multiple closures and thrown continuations, discovered the contours of a way of thinking that was at once familiar and strange. It was like looking at a map of her own mind, but one where the landmarks were strange and the roads probed into terra incognita.

There were echoes of her father in the code—she could see that: a quirky way of associating words with images; a tendency to see patterns that defied the strictly rational; a deep, abiding trust for a specific woman and a specific teenager out of the billions who lived on this planet.

Maddie was reminded of how Mom had told her that there were things about her as a baby that defied theories of upbringing, that told her and Dad that Maddie was *their* child in a way that transcended rational knowledge: the way her smile reminded Mom of Dad even at six weeks; the way she hated noodles the first time she tried them, just like Mom; the way she calmed down as soon as Dad held her, even though he had been too busy with Logorhythms's IPO to spend much time with her during the first six months of her life.

But there were also segments of Mist that puzzled her: the way she seemed to possess so many heuristics for trends in the stock market; the way her thoughts seemed attuned to the subtleties of patents; the way the shapes of her decision algorithms seemed adapted for the methods of warfare. Some of the map code reminded Maddie of the code of other gods Dad had shown her; some was entirely novel.

Maddie had a million questions for Mist. How had she come to be? Was she like Athena, sprung fully-formed from her father's mind? Or was she something like the next generation of an evolutionary algorithm, inheriting bits from her father and other uploaded consciousnesses with variations? Who was her other parent—or maybe parents? What stories of love, of yearning, of loneliness and connection, lay behind her existence? What was it like being a creature of pure computation, of never having existed in the flesh?

But of one thing Maddie was certain: Mist was her father's daughter, just as she had claimed. She was her sister, even if she *was* barely human.

• • •

<Maddie> What was life in the cloud with Dad like?

Like her father, Mist had a habit of shifting into emoji whenever she found words inadequate. What Maddie got out of her response was that life in the cloud was simply beyond her understanding and Mist did not have the words to adequately convey it.

So Maddie tried to bridge the gap the other way, to tell Mist about her own life.

<Maddie> Grandma and I had a garden back in Pennsylvania. I was good at growing tomatoes.

<Maddie> Yep. That's a tomato.

< > I know lots about tomatoes: lycopene, Cortéz, nightshade, Mesoamerica, ketchup, pomodoro, Nix v. Hedden, vegetable, soup. Probably more than you.

< > You seem really quiet.

<Maddie> Forget it.

Other attempts by Maddie to share the details of her own life usually ended the same way. She mentioned the way Basil wagged his tail and licked her fingers when she came in the door, and Mist responded with articles about the genetics of dogs. Maddie started to talk about the anxieties she experienced at school and the competing cliques, and Mist showed her pages of game theory and papers on adolescent psychology.

Maddie could understand it, to some extent. After all, Mist had never lived in the world that Maddie inhabited, and never would. All Mist had was data *about* the world, not the world itself. How could Mist understand how Maddie *felt?* Words or emoji were inadequate to convey the essence of reality.

Life is about embodiment, thought Maddie. This was a point that she had discussed with Dad many times. To experience the world through the senses was different from simply having data about the world. The memory of his time in the world was what had kept her father sane after he had been turned into a brain in a jar.

And in this way, oddly, Maddie came to have a glint of the difficulty Mist faced in explaining her world to Maddie. She tried to imagine what it was like to have never petted a puppy, to have never experienced a tomato filled with June sunshine burst between the tongue and the palate, to have never felt the weight of gravity or the elation of being loved, and imagination failed her. She felt sorry for Mist, a ghost who could not even call upon the memory of an embodied existence.

• • •

There was one topic on which Maddie and Mist could converse effectively: the shared mission their father had left them to make sure the gods didn't come back.

All of the uploaded consciousnesses—whose existence was still never acknowledged—were supposed to have died in the conflagration. But pieces of their code, like the remnants of fallen giants, were scattered around the world's servers. Mist told Maddie that mysterious network presences scoured the web to collect these pieces. Were they hackers? Spies? Corporate researchers? Defense contractors? What purpose could they have for gathering these relics unless they were interested in resurrecting the gods?

Along with these troubling reports, Mist also brought back headlines that she thought Maddie would find interesting.

< > Today's Headlines:

○ **Japanese PM Assures Nervous Citizens That New Robots Deployed for Reconstruction Are Safe**

○ **European Union Announces Border Closures; Extra-European Economic Migrants Not Welcome**

○ **Bill to Restrict Immigration to "Extraordinary Circumstances" Passes Senate; Majority of Working Visas to Be Revoked**

○ **Protestors Demanding Jobs Clash with Police in New York and Washington, D.C.**

○ **Developing Nations Press UN Security Council for Resolution Denouncing Efforts to Restrict Population Migration by Developed Economies.**

o Collapse of Leading Asian Economies Predicted as Manufacturing Sector Continues Contraction Due to Back-Shoring by Europe and the US

o Everlasting Inc. Refuses to Explain Purpose of New Data Center

< > You still there?

< > ??

< > ???????????

<Maddie> Calm down! I need a few seconds to read this wall of text you just threw at me.

< > Sorry, I'm still under-compensating for how slow your cycles are. I'll leave you to it. Ping me when you're done.

Mist's consciousness operated at the speed of electric currents fluctuating billions of times a second instead of slow, analog, electrochemical synapses. Her experience of time must be so different, so *fast* that it made Maddie a little bit envious.

And she came to appreciate just how patient her father had been with her when he was a ghost in the machine. In every exchange between him and Maddie, he probably had had to wait what must have felt like eons before getting an answer from her, but he had never shown any annoyance.

Maybe that was why he had created another daughter, Maddie thought. *Someone who lived and thought like him.*

<Maddie> Ready to chat when you are.

< > Everlasting is where I tracked them dragging those fragments of the gods.

<Maddie> They didn't get any pieces of Dad, did they?

< > Way ahead of you, sister. I took care of burying the pieces of Dad as soon as it calmed down.

<Maddie> Thank you... Wish we could figure out what they're planning over there.

Adam Ever, the founder of Everlasting, Inc. was one of the foremost experts on the Singularity. He had been a friend of Dad's, and Maddie vaguely recalled meeting him as a little girl. Ever was a persistent advocate of consciousness uploading, even after all the legal restrictions placed on his research after the crisis. Maddie's curiosity was tinged with dread.

< > Not that easy. I tried to go through Everlasting's system defenses a few times, but the internal networks are completely isolated. They're paranoid over there—I lost a few parts when they detected my presence on the external-facing servers.

Maddie shuddered. She recalled the epic fights between her father, Lowell, and Chanda in the darkness of the network. The phrase "lost a few parts" might sound innocuous, but for Mist it probably felt like losing limbs and parts of her mind.

<Maddie> You've got to be careful.

< > I did manage to copy the pieces of the gods they took. I'll give you access to the encrypted cloud cell now. Maybe we can figure out what they're doing at Everlasting by looking through these.

• • •

Maddie made dinner that night. Her mother texted her that she was going to be late, first thirty minutes, then an hour, and then "not sure." Maddie ended up eating alone and then spent the rest of the evening watching the clock and worrying.

"Sorry," Mom said as she came in, close to midnight. "They kept me late."

Maddie had seen some of the reports on TV. "Protestors?"

Mom sighed. "Yes. Not as bad as in New York, but hundreds showed up. I had to talk to them."

"What are they mad about? It's not like—" Maddie caught herself just as she was about to raise her voice. She was feeling protective of her mother, but her mother had probably had enough shouting for one day.

"They're good people," Mom said vaguely. She headed for the stairs without even glancing at the kitchen. "I'm tired. I think I'll just go to bed."

But Maddie was unwilling to just let it go. "Are we having supply issues again?" The recovery was jittery, and goods were still being rationed. It was a constant struggle to get people to stop hoarding.

Mom stopped. "No. The supplies are flowing smoothly again, maybe too smoothly."

"I don't understand," said Maddie.

Mom sat down on the bottom of the stairs, and patted the space next to her. Maddie went over and sat down.

"Remember how during the crisis, when we were coming to Boston, I told you about layers of technology?"

Maddie nodded. Her mother, a historian, had told her the story behind the networks that connected people: the footpaths that grew into caravan routes that developed into roads that turned into railroad tracks that provided the right-of-way for the optical cables that carried the bits that made up the Internet that routed the thoughts of the gods.

"The history of the world is a process of speeding up, of becoming more efficient as well as more fragile. If a footpath is blocked, you just have to walk around it. But if a highway is blocked, you have to wait until specialized machinery can be brought to clear it. Just about anyone can figure out how to patch a cobblestone road, but only highly trained technicians can fix a fiberoptic cable. There's a lot more redundancy with the older, inefficient technologies."

"Your point is that keeping it simple technologically is more resilient," said Maddie.

"But our history is also a history of growing needs, of more mouths to feed and more hands that need to be kept from idleness," said Mom.

Mom told Maddie that America had been lucky during the crisis: very few bombs had struck her shores and relatively few people had died during the riots. But with much of the infrastructure paralyzed across the country, refugees flooded into the big cities. Boston's own population had doubled from what it was before the crisis. With so many people came spiking needs: food, clothing, shelter, sanitation...

"On my advice, the governor and the mayor tried to rely on distributed, self-organizing groups of citizens with low-tech delivery methods, but we couldn't get it to work because it was just too inefficient. Congestion and breakdowns were happening too frequently. Centillion's automation proposal had to be considered."

Maddie thought of how impatient Mist had been with her "slow cycles," and she imagined the roads packed with self-driving trucks streaming bumper-to-bumper at a hundred miles an hour, without drivers who had to rest, without the traffic jams caused by human unpredictability, without the accidents from drifting attentions and exhausted bodies. She thought of tireless robots loading and unloading the supplies necessary to keep millions of people fed and warm and clothed. She thought of the borders patrolled by machines with precise algorithms designed to preserve precious supplies for the use of people with the right accents, the right skin colors, the luck to be born in the right places at the right times.

"All the big cities are doing the same thing," said Mom, a trace of defensiveness in her voice. "It's impossible for us to hold out. It would be irresponsible, as Centillion put it."

"And the drivers and workers would be replaced," said Maddie, understanding finally dawning on her.

"They showed up on Beacon Hill to protest, hoping to save their jobs. But an even bigger crowd showed up to protest against *them.*" Mom rubbed her temples.

"If everything is handed over to Centillion's robots, wouldn't another god—I mean a rogue AI—put us at even more risk?"

"We have grown to the point where we must depend on machines to survive," said Mom. "The world has become too fragile for us to count on people, and so our only choice is to make it even more fragile."

· · ·

With Centillion's robots taking over the crucial work of maintaining the flow of goods into the city, a superficial calmness returned to life. The workers who lost their jobs were given new jobs invented by the government: correcting typos in old databases, sweeping corners of streets that Centillion's robots couldn't get to, greeting concerned citizens in the lobby of the State House and giving them tours—some grumbled that this was just a dressed-up form of welfare and what was the government going to do when Centillion and PerfectLogic and ThoughtfulBits and their ilk automated more jobs away?

But at least everyone was getting a paycheck that they could use to buy the supplies brought into the city by the fleet of robots. And Centillion's CEO swore up and down on TV that they weren't developing anything that could be understood as "rogue AI," like the old, dead gods.

That was good, wasn't it?

Maddie and Mist continued to gather pieces of the old gods and studying them to see what Everlasting might want with them. Some of the fragments had belonged to her father, but there were too few of them to even dream of trying to resurrect him. Maddie wasn't sure how she felt about it—in a way, her father had never fully reconciled to his existence as a disembodied consciousness, and she wasn't sure he would want to "come back."

Meanwhile, Maddie was working on a secret project. It would be her present to Mist.

She looked up everything she could online about robotics and electronics and sensor technology. She bought components online, which Centillion drones cheerfully and efficiently delivered to her house—straight to her room, even: she kept the window of her room open, and tiny drones with whirring rotors flitted in at all hours of the day and night, dropping off tiny packages.

< > What are you doing?

<Maddie> Give me a minute. I'm almost done.

< > I'll give you today's headlines then.

- o **Hundreds Die in Attempt to Scale "Freedom Wall" near El Paso**

- o **Think Tank Argues Coal Should be Reevaluated as Alternative Energy Fails to Meet Promise**

- o **Deaths from Typhoons in Southeast Asia Exceed Historical Records**

- o **Experts Warn of Further Regional Conflicts as Food Prices Soar and Drought Continues in Asia and Africa**

- o **Unemployment Numbers Suggest Reconstruction Has Benefited Robots (and Their Owners) More Than People**

- o **Rise of Religious Extremism Tied to Stagnating Developing Economies**

- o **Is Your Job at Risk? Experts Explain How to Protect Yourself from Automation**

<Maddie> Nothing from Everlasting?

< > They've been quiet.

Maddie plugged her new creation into the computer.

<Maddie>

The lights near the data port on the computer began to blink.

Maddie smiled to herself. For Mist, asking Maddie a question and waiting for her slow cycles to catch up and answer was probably like sending snail mail. It would be far faster for her to investigate the new contraption herself.

The motors in Maddie's creation spun to life, and the three wheels in the base turned the four-foot-tall torso around. The wheels provided 360° of motion, much like those roving automatic vacuum cleaners.

At the top of the cylindrical torso was a spherical "head" to which were attached the best sensors that Maddie could scrounge up or buy: a pair of high-def cameras to give stereoscopic vision; a matched pair of microphones to act as ears, tuned for the range of human hearing; a sophisticated bundle of probes mounted at the ends of flexible antennae to act as noses and tongues that approximated the sensitivity of human counterparts; and numerous other tactile sensors, gyroscopes, accelerometers, and so on to give the robot the experience of touch, gravity, presence in space.

Away from the head, near the top of the cylindrical body, however, were the most expensive components of them all: a pair of multi-jointed arms with parallel-elastic actuators to recreate the freedom of motion of human arms that ended in a pair of the most advanced prosthetic hands covered in medical-grade plastiskin. The skin, embedded with sensors for temperature and force, were said to approach or even exceed the sensitivity of real skin, and the fingers modeled human hands so well that they could tighten a nut on a screw as well as pick up a strand of hair. Maddie watched as Mist tried them out, flexing and clenching the fingers, and without realizing it, she mirrored the movements with her own fingers.

"What do you think?" she said.

The screen mounted atop the head of the robot came to life, showing a cartoonish pair of eyes, a cute button nose, and a pair of abstract, wavy lines that mimicked the motion of lips. Maddie was proud of the design and programming of the face. She had modeled it on her own.

A voice came out of the speaker below the screen. "This is very well made." It was a young girl's voice, chirpy and mellifluous.

"Thank you," said Maddie. She watched as Mist moved around the room, twisting her head this way and that, sweeping her camera-gaze over everything. "Do you like your new body?"

"It's interesting," said Mist. The tone was the same as before. Maddie couldn't tell if that was because Mist was really pleased with the robotic body or that she hadn't figured out how to modulate the voice to suit her emotional state.

"I can show you all the things you haven't experienced before," said Maddie hurriedly. "You'll know what it's like to move in the real world, not just as a ghost in a machine. You'll be able to understand my stories, and I can take you on trips with me, introduce you to Mom and other people."

Mist continued to move around the room, her eyes surveying the trophies on Maddie's shelves, the titles of her books, the posters on her walls, the models of the planets and rocketships hanging from the ceiling—a record of Maddie's shifting tastes over the years. She moved toward one corner where a basket of stuffed animals was kept, but stopped when the data cable stretched taut, just a few centimeters too short.

"The cable is necessary for now because the amount of data from the sensors is so large. But I'm working on a compression algorithm so we can get you wireless."

Mist moved the swiveling screen with her cartoonish face forward and backward to simulate a nod. Maddie was grateful that she had thought of such a thing—a lot of the robotics papers on robot-human interactions emphasized that rather than simulating a human face too closely and falling into the uncanny valley, it was better sticking to cartoonish representations that exaggerated the emotional tenor. Sometimes an obviously virtual representation was better than a strict effort at fidelity.

Mist paused in front of a mess of wires and electronic components on Maddie's shelf. "What's this?"

"The first computer that Dad and I built together," said Maddie. Instantly, she seemed to have been transported to that summer almost a decade ago, when Dad showed her how to apply Ohm's Law to pick out the right resistors and how to read a circuit diagram and translate it into real components and real wires. The smell of hot solder filled her nostrils again, and she smiled even as her eyes moistened.

Mist picked up the contraption with her hands.

"Be careful!" Maddie yelled.

But it was too late. The breadboard crumbled in Mist's hands, and the pieces fell to the carpet.

"Sorry," said Mist. "I thought I was applying the right amount of pressure based on the materials used in it."

"Things get old in the real world," said Maddie. She bent down to pick up the pieces from the carpet, carefully cradling them in her hand. "They grow fragile." She looked at the remnants of her first unskilled attempt at soldering, noticing the lumpy messes and bent electrodes. "I guess you don't have much experience with that."

"I'm sorry," said Mist again, her voice still chirpy.

"Doesn't matter," said Maddie, trying to be magnanimous. "Think of it as a first lesson about the real world. Hold on."

She rushed out of the room and returned a moment later with a ripe tomato. "This is shipped in from some industrial farm, and it's nowhere as good as the ones Grandma and I grew back in Pennsylvania. Still, now you can taste it. Don't talk to me about lycopene and sugar content; *taste* it."

Mist took the tomato from her—this time her mechanical hands held it lightly, the fingers barely making an impression against the smooth fruit skin. She gazed at it, the lenses of her cameras whirring as they focused. And then, decisively, one of the probes on her head shot out and stabbed into the fruit in a single motion.

It reminded Maddie of a mosquito's proboscis stabbing into the skin of a hand, or a butterfly sipping nectar from a flower. A sense of unease rose in her. She was trying so hard to make Mist *human*, but what made her think that was what Mist wanted?

"It's very good," said Mist. She swiveled her screen toward Maddie so that Maddie could see her cartoonish eyes curving in a smile. "You're right. It's not as good as the heirloom varieties."

Maddie laughed. "How would you know that?"

"I've tasted hundreds of varieties of tomatoes," said Mist.

"Where? How?"

"Before the war of the gods, all the big instant meal manufacturers and fast food restaurants used automation to produce recipes. Dad took me through a few of these facilities and I tried every variety of tomato from Amal to Zebra Cherry—I was a big fan of Snow White."

"Machines were making up the recipes?" Maddie asked. She had loved watching cooking shows before the war, and chefs were artists, what they did was *creative*. She couldn't quite wrap her head around the notion of machines making up recipes.

"Sure. At the scale these places were operating, they had to optimize for so many factors that people could never get it right. The recipes had to be tasty and also use ingredients that could be obtained within the constraints of modern mechanized agriculture—it was no good to discover some good recipe that relied on an heirloom variety that couldn't be grown in large enough quantities efficiently."

Maddie thought back to her conversation with Mom and realized that it was the same concept that now governed the creation of ration packets: nutritious, tasty, but also effective for feeding hundreds of millions living with a damaged grid and limited resources.

"Why didn't you tell me you've tasted tomatoes?" Maddie asked. "I thought you were—"

"Not just tomatoes. I've had every variety of potato, squash, cucumber, apple, grape, and lots of other things you've never had. In the food labs, I tried out billions of flavor combinations. The sensors they had were far more sensitive than the human tongue."

The robot that had once seemed such an extraordinary gift now seemed shabby to Maddie. Mist did not need a body. She had been living in a far more embodied way than Maddie had realized or understood.

Mist simply didn't think the new body was all that special.

● ● ●

- o Expert Report Declares Nuclear Fallout Clean Up Plan in Asia Unrealistic, Further Famines Inevitable

- o Japan Joins China and India in Denouncing Western Experts for "Scaremongering"

- o Indian Geoengineering Plan to Melt Himalayan Snow for Agricultural Irrigation Leaked, Drawing Condemnation from Smaller SE Asian Nations for "Water Theft"

- o Protestors in Italy and Spain Declare "African Refugees Should Go Home": Thousands Injured in Clashes

- o Australia Announces Policy of Shooting on Sight to Discourage "Boat People"

- o Regional "Resource Wars" May Turn Global, UN Special Commission Warns

- o White House Stands Firm Behind "NATO First" Doctrine: Use of Military Force Is Justified to Stop Geoengineering Projects That May Harm Allies or US Interests

Mom was working late most nights now, and she looked pale and sickly. Maddie didn't have to ask to know that reconstruction was going worse than anyone expected. The war of the gods had left so much of the planet's surface in tatters that the survivors were fighting over the leftover scraps. No matter how many refugee boats were sunk by drones or how high the walls were built, desperate people continued to pour into the US, the country least damaged by the war.

Protests and counter-protests raged in the streets of all the major cities day after day. Nobody wanted to see kids and women drown in the sea or electrocuted by the walls, but it was also true that all the American cities were overburdened. Even the efficient robots couldn't keep up with the task of making sure everyone was fed and safe.

Maddie could tell that the ration packets were going down in quality. This couldn't go on. The world was continuing its long spiral down toward an abyss, and sooner or later, someone was going to conclude that the problems were not solvable by AI alone, and we needed to call upon the gods again.

She and Mist had to prevent that. The world couldn't afford another reign of the gods.

While Mist—possibly the greatest hacker there ever was—focused on testing out the defenses around Everlasting and figuring out a way to penetrate them, Maddie devoted her time to trying to understand the fragments of the dead gods.

The map code, a combination of self-modifying AI and modeling of human thinking patterns, wasn't the sort of thing a programmer would write, but Maddie seemed to have an intuition for how personality quirks manifested in this code after spending so much time with the fragments of her father.

In this manner, Maddie came also to understand Chanda and Lowell and the other gods. She charted their hopes and dreams, like fragments of Sappho and Aeschylus. And it turned out that deep down, all the gods had similar vulnerabilities, a kind of regret or nostalgia for life in the flesh that seemed reflected at every level of organization. It was a blind spot, a vulnerability that could be exploited in the war against the gods.

"I don't have a weak spot like that in my code," said Mist.

Maddie was startled. She had never really considered Mist one of the gods, though, objectively, she clearly was. Mist was just her little sister, especially when she was embedded in the cute robot Maddie had built for her, as she was now.

"Why not?" she asked.

"I am a child of the ether," said Mist. And the voice was now different. It sounded older, wearier. Maddie would almost have said it sounded *not human*. "I do not yearn for something that I never had."

Of course Mist wasn't a little girl, Maddie berated herself. She had somehow allowed the cartoonish trappings she had created for Mist, a mask intended to help Mist relate to her, fool her. Mist's thoughts moved at a far faster pace, and she had experienced more of the world than Maddie had ever experienced. She could, at will, peek through billions of cameras, listen through billions of microphones, sense the speed of the wind atop Mount Washington and at the same time feel the heat of the lava spilling out of Kilauea. She had known what it's like to gaze down at the world from the international space station and what it was like to suffer the stress of kilometers of water pressing down upon a deep-sea submersible's shell. She was, in a way, far older than Maddie.

"I'm going to make a run at Everlasting," said Mist. "With your discoveries, we're as ready as we'll ever be. They might already be creating new gods."

Maddie wanted to tell Mist some words of comfort, assuring her of success. But really, what did she know of the risks Mist was undertaking?

She wasn't the one to put her life on the line in that unimaginable realm inside the machine.

The features on the screen that served as Mist's face disappeared, leaving only a single emoji.

"We'll protect each other," Maddie said. "We will."

But even she knew how inadequate that sounded.

• • •

Maddie woke up with a start as cold hands caressed her face.

She sat up. The small bedside lamp was on. Next to her bed was the squat figure of the robot, whose cameras were trained on her. She had fallen asleep after seeing Mist off, though she hadn't meant to.

"Mist," she said, rubbing her eyes, "are you okay?"

The cartoonish face of Mist was replaced by a headline.

o Everlasting Inc. Announces "Digital Adam" Project

"What?" asked Maddie, her thoughts still sluggish.

"I better let him tell you," said Mist. And then the screen changed again, and a man's face appeared on it. He was in his thirties, with short-cropped hair and a kind, compassionate face.

All traces of sleep left Maddie. This was a face she had seen many times on TV, always making reassurances to the public: Adam Ever.

"What are you doing here?" asked Maddie. "What have you done to Mist?"

The robot that had housed Mist—no, Adam now—held up his hands in a gesture intended to calm. "I'm just here to talk."

"What about?"

"Let me show you what we've been working on."

• • •

Maddie flew over a fjord filled with floating icebergs until she was skimming over a field of ice. A great black cube loomed out of this landscape of shades of white.

"Welcome to the Longyearbyen Data Center," Adam Ever's voice spoke in her ears.

The VR headset was something Maddie had once used to game with her father, but it had been gathering dust on the shelf since his death. Adam had asked her to put it on.

Maddie had known of the data center's existence from Mist's reports, and had even seen some photographs and videos of its construction. She and Mist had speculated that this was where Everlasting was trying to resurrect the old gods or bring forth new ones.

Adam told her about the massive assembly of silicon and graphene inside, about the zipping electrons and photons bouncing inside glass cables. This was an altar to computation, a Stonehenge for a new age.

"It's also where I live," Adam said.

The scene before Maddie's eyes shifted, and she was now looking at Adam calmly lying down on a hospital bed, smiling for the camera. Doctors and beeping machines were clustered around the bed. They typed some commands into a computer, and after a while Adam closed his eyes, going to sleep.

Maddie suddenly had the sensation that she was witnessing a scene similar to the last moments of her father.

"Were you ill?" she asked hesitantly.

"No," said Adam. "I was in the prime of health. This is a video recording of the moment before the scan. I had to be alive to give the procedure the maximal chance for success."

Maddie imagined the doctors approaching the sleeping figure of Adam with scalpel and bone saw and who knew what else—she was about to scream when the scene shifted mercifully away to a room of pure white with Adam sitting up in a bed. Maddie let out a held breath.

"You survived the scan?" asked Maddie.

"Of course," said Adam.

But Maddie sensed that this wasn't quite right. Earlier, in the video, there were wrinkles near the corners of Adam's eyes. The face of the Adam in front of her now was perfectly smooth.

"It's not you," said Maddie. "It's not you."

"It *is* me," insisted Adam. "The only me that matters."

Maddie closed her eyes and thought back to the times Adam had appeared on TV in interviews. He had said he didn't want to leave Svalbard, preferring to conduct all his interviews remotely via satellite feed. The camera had always stayed close up, showing just his face. Now that she was looking for it, she realized that the way Adam had moved in those interviews had seemed just slightly odd, a little uncanny.

"You died," said Maddie. She opened her eyes and looked at the Adam, this Adam with the smooth, perfectly symmetrical face and impossibly graceful limbs. "You died during the scan because there's no way to do a scan without destroying the body."

Adam nodded. "I'm one of the gods."

"Why?" Maddie couldn't imagine such a thing. All of the gods had been created as a last measure of desperation, a way to preserve their minds for the service of the goals of others. Her father had raged against his fate and fought so that none of the others had to go through what he did. To choose to become a brain in a jar was inconceivable to her.

"The world is dying, Maddie," said Adam. "You know this. Even before the wars, we were killing the planet slowly. There were too many of us squabbling over too few resources, and to stay alive we had to hurt the world even more, polluting the water and air and soil so that we might extract more. The wars only accelerated what was already an inevitable trend. There are too many of us for this planet to support. The next time we fight a war, there won't be any more of us to save after the nukes are done falling."

"It's not true!" Even as she said it, Maddie knew that Adam was right. The headlines and her own research had long ago led her to the same conclusion. *He's right.* She felt very tired. "Are we the cancer of this planet?"

"We're not the problem," said Adam.

Maddie looked at him.

"Our bodies are," said Adam. "Our bodies of flesh exist in the realm of atoms. Our senses require the gratification of matter. Not all of us can live the lifestyle we believe we deserve. Scarcity is the root of all evil."

"What about space, the other planets and stars?"

"It's too late for that. We've hardly taken another step on the moon, and most of the rockets we've been building since then have been intended to deliver bombs."

Maddie said nothing. "You're saying there is no hope?"

"Of course there is." Adam waved his arm, and the white room transformed into the inside of a luxurious apartment. The hospital bed disappeared, and Adam was now standing in the middle of a well-appointed room. The lights of Manhattan shone beyond the darkened windows.

Adam waved his arm again, and now they were inside a voluminous space capsule. Outside the window loomed a partial view of a massive sphere of swirling bands of color, and a giant red oval slowly drifted among the bands like an island in a turbulent sea.

Once more, Adam waved his arm, and now it wasn't even possible for Maddie to understand what she was seeing. There seemed to be a smaller Adam inside Adam, and yet a smaller Adam inside that one, and so on, ad infinitum. Yet she was somehow able to see all of the Adams at once. She moved her gaze around the space and felt dizzy: space itself seemed to gain an extra level of depth, and everywhere she looked she saw *inside* things.

"We could have all we ever desire," said Adam, "if we're willing to give up our bodies."

A disembodied existence, thought Maddie. *Is that really living at all?*

"But this isn't *real,*" said Maddie. "This is just an illusion." She thought of the games she used to play with her father, of the green seas of grass that seemed to go on forever, of the babbling brooks that promised infinite zoom, of the fantastic creatures they had fought against, side by side.

"Consciousness itself is an illusion, if you want to follow that logic to its conclusion," said Adam. "When you put your hand around a tomato, your senses insist that you're touching something solid. But most of a tomato is made up of the empty space between the nuclei of the atoms, as far from each other, by proportion, as the stars are apart. What is color? What is sound? What is heat or pain? They're but pulses of electricity that make up our consciousness, and it makes no difference whether the pulse comes from a sensor touching a tomato or is the result of computation."

"Except there is a difference," the voice of Mist said.

Maddie's heart swelled with gratitude. Her sister was coming to her defense. Or so she thought.

"A tomato made up of atoms is grown in a distant field, where it must be given fertilizer mined from halfway across the world and dusted with insecticide by machines. Then it must be harvested, packed, and then shipped through the airways and highways until it arrives at your door. The amount of energy it takes to run the infrastructure that would support the creation and delivery of a single tomato is many times what it took to build the Great Pyramid. Is it really worth enslaving the whole planet so that you can have the experience of a tomato through the interface of the flesh instead of generating the same impulse from a bit of silicon?"

"But it doesn't have to be that way," said Maddie. "My grandmother and I grew our tomatoes on our own, and we didn't need any of that."

"You can't feed billions of people with backyard gardens," said Mist. "Nostalgia for a garden that never existed is dangerous. The mass of humanity depends on the fragile, power-intensive infrastructure of civilization. It is delusion to think you can live without it."

Maddie remembered the words of her mother. *The world has become too fragile for us to count on people.*

"The world of atoms is not only wasteful, it is also limiting," said Adam. "Inside the data center, we can live anywhere we want and have whatever we want, with imagination as our only limit. We can experience things that our fleshly senses could never give us: live in multiple dimensions, invent impossible foods, possess worlds that are as infinite as the sands of the Ganges."

A world beyond scarcity, thought Maddie. A world without rich or poor, without the conflicts generated by exclusion and possession. It was a world without death, without decay, without the limits of inflexible matter. It was a state of existence mankind had always yearned for.

"Don't you miss the real world?" asked Maddie. She thought of the vulnerability that existed at the heart of all the gods.

"We discovered the same thing you did by studying the gods," said Adam. "Nostalgia is deadly. When peasants first moved into the factories of the industrial age, perhaps they also were nostalgic for the inefficient world of subsistence farming. But we must be open to change, to adaptation, to seeking a new path in a sea of fragility. Instead of being forced here on the verge of death like your father, I *chose* to come here. I am not nostalgic. That makes all the difference."

"He's right," said Mist. "Our father understood that, too. Maybe this is why he and the other gods gave birth to me: to see if their nostalgia is as inevitable as death. They couldn't adapt to this world fully, but maybe their children could. In a way, Dad gave birth to me because, deep down, he wished *you* could live here with him."

Mist's observation seemed to Maddie like a betrayal, but she couldn't say why.

"This is the next stage of our evolution," said Adam. "This isn't going to be a perfect world, but it is closer to perfect than anything we've ever devised. The human race thrives on discovering new worlds, and now there are an infinite many of them to explore. We shall reign as the gods of them all."

● ● ●

Maddie took off her VR set. Next to the vibrant colors inside the digital world, the physical world seemed dim and dull.

She imagined the data center teeming with the consciousnesses of billions. *Would that bring people closer, so that they all shared the same universe without the constraints of scarcity? Or would it push them apart, so that each lived in their own world, a king of infinite space?*

She held out her hands. She noticed that they were becoming wrinkled, the hands of a woman rather than a child.

After the briefest of pauses, Mist rolled over and held them.

"We'll protect each other," said Mist. "We will."

They held hands in the dark, sisters, human and post-human, and waited for the new day to come.

THE HAPPIEST PLACE...

Mira Grant

*"To all that come to this happy place: welcome.
Disneyland is your land. Here age relives fond
memories of the past, and here youth may
savor the challenge and promise of the future.
Disneyland is dedicated to the ideals, the dreams,
and the hard facts that have created America,
with hope that it will be a source of joy and
inspiration to all the world."*

—Walt Disney

The Disneyland generators were intended to keep the Park's lights on during municipal power outages and emergency situations. They were never meant to power the entire Park for weeks on end, and one by one, they were giving up. Generator #3 had been showing signs of strain for three days. It fought long and valiantly, but in the end, entropy won. Generator #3 died at 6:15 AM on Monday morning, filling the air with the hot stink of biodiesel and exhaust. The other generators whined, struggling to pick up the slack. It was a lost cause. The techs on duty knew it but still grabbed their tools, ready to fight a battle that was already over.

In the Hall of Presidents, the lights flickered before going out. Amy—who most people called "the Mayor of Main Street" these days, despite her best efforts at rejecting the title—ran outside in time to see the brass streetlights that ringed Town Square die, leaving the area in darkness. She stood in the doorway, frozen with fear. People began to emerge from the surrounding buildings, exclaiming in dismay. Amy didn't move. Even when someone shouted, "It's dark all the way to the Castle!", she didn't move.

It was finally happening. After eighteen months of struggle, sacrifice, and pain, the lights were going out in Disneyland.

• • •

It began with the sniffles.

First the sniffles, and then a mild cough, the sort of thing that wasn't enough for most people to justify staying home from work or keeping the kids out of school. From there, it developed into severe congestion, breathing difficulties, and finally, a cascade of third-stage symptoms that seemed to come without warning, sometimes developing over the course of an afternoon. Bronchial inflammation, rash, fever, all building to internal hemorrhaging and multiple organ failure. Most people who got sick were dead inside of a week, and most people got sick. There were no final statistics published on this epidemic, but if Amy had been asked to guess, she would have said that nine out of every ten people caught the H13N3 flu. And of those nine, at least eight died, leaving two out of every ten people still standing—and one out of every two people weak, sick, and shaky.

It was no wonder things had collapsed as fast as they did. People who were on vacation died in unfamiliar hotel rooms and hospital beds, wondering how things had gone so very wrong. Others staggered their unsteady ways to the places where they remembered being happy. Amy would always remember the last guest to walk up to the gates of Disneyland. He was a little man, old enough to have been coming to the Park since it first opened, and his nose wouldn't stop running.

She'd been standing on the train tracks above Town Square with a telescope stolen from Walt's apartment, watching the plaza for signs of movement, when he'd come shuffling into view. She was at the gate to meet him by the time he arrived. It had been two days since she had shown up for her shift in Guest Relations. She hadn't left the Park since then. None of the Cast Members who had been well enough to come to work had gone any further than the plaza.

"Hello, miss," he'd said, voice thick with phlegm. "I know it's irregular, but I couldn't find my Annual Pass this morning. The wife, she always has them with her. Is there any way… is there any way you could see fit to let me come inside?"

"Welcome home," she'd replied, and unlocked the gate for him. He hadn't tried to touch her as he shuffled past her into the Park, and she'd been grateful.

His body had been found on a bench in New Orleans Square about six hours later. The Cast Member who found him said that he looked peaceful. It only bothered Amy a little that she'd never learned his name.

"What do you mean, we can't fix it?"

"I mean, we can't fix it." The chief engineer was a patient man—he had to be, when everyone on his work detail was untrained. He had two mechanics and one Imagineer, but Clover spent most of her time being hauled off to fix malfunctioning animatronics, and that left him with his makeshift crew of car-jockeys and well-meaning custodial staffers. "The piston's shot. We'd need a whole new engine if we wanted to get number three up and running again, and at that point, we might as well wish for a whole new generator, because we're not going to find it."

"There has to be something we can do." Amy forced her hands to stay down by her sides, fighting the urge to clasp them together and beg. "We've lost power to Town Square. Half of Main Street is running on emergency backup. And the Castle—"

"Mayor, I don't know how many ways I can say this. The generator is dead. The engine is fried. We've been pushing them way too hard. These were meant to cover for rolling blackouts, not supply power to the whole complex." The chief engineer shook his head. "Maybe if we shut down Tomorrowland, we can shift some of the load between the generators we still have. That could keep us up and running for another month. Two if we're careful, and if we stop running the dark rides."

Amy stiffened. "You're talking about the Mansion."

"I am. The air conditioning alone—"

"You have to understand why we can't turn off the air conditioning inside the Mansion." The idea was enough to make Amy's flesh crawl. If the Mansion stopped...

"It's July, Mayor. The hottest month of the year, and you're turning one dark ride into an icebox. Now, I know you've got your reasons, but the fact remains, we don't have the power."

Amy paused. "Look—Anthony, wasn't it? Have you been inside the Mansion recently?"

"I don't like closed spaces."

"I thought it might be something like that." She looked away, toward the back lot buildings that the guests were never meant to see, all of them painted that same bland shade of go-away green. A few seconds passed before she looked back to him, eyes hardened with resolve. "I want you to go ride the Haunted Mansion. If you come out the other end and agree that we don't need to run the air conditioning anymore, then fine, I'll listen to you. But if you change your mind, we're going to need to find another way. Do we have a deal?"

Anthony frowned. "You know, I never quite understood how you wound up in charge."

Amy's smile was small, quick, and bitter. "I was the last person alive in Guest Relations," she said. "All I was ever trained to do is make sure that everyone at Disneyland has a magical day."

• • •

At the end of everything, when there was no place left to turn, the Cast Members who survived came home. Custodians and princesses, ride operators and stage show dancers, one after another they came to the gates. Some had shown up while the Park was still technically open—before humanity's season had been declared over for good. They had formed the skeleton crew that kept things running until everyone else could arrive. Amy thought of them as her family. They had done things together, *seen* things together, that could never be unseen. They had done them for each other. They had done them for the children they knew would come, eventually, the orphans of the world that was being born outside their gates. And they had done them for Walt.

He might not have anticipated his Park's future as one of the last strongholds of mankind. But as Amy walked down the access corridor that would lead her back to Town Square, she couldn't help thinking that he would have been pleased by what they'd been doing in his name.

Tiffany and Skylar were waiting in front of the Gallery. As always, Tiffany was dressed in her Guest Relations uniform, so crisp and perfect that she must have spent half her waking hours ironing the creases into her jacket, while Skylar was wearing something she'd looted from one of the stores on Main Street. They were holding hands. Amy felt a brief, sharp stab of envy.

Not everyone made it through with their sister by their side, she thought—not for the first time, and not, she knew, for the last. Her own sister had stopped answering the phone two days after she'd first complained of a sore throat. Nikki was long dead, and all Amy could do to honor her memory was keep on fighting for a future.

"Is it true?" asked Tiffany.

"That depends on what 'it' is," Amy replied. "Use exact terms and phrases and maybe I can calm your mind." That wasn't likely, all things considered.

"Michael said one of the generators blew," said Skylar. "He said it wasn't fixable."

The trouble with being a closed community—there were fewer than five hundred people in Disneyland, and more than half of them were living in the buildings on Main Street and in Adventureland—was that rumors couldn't be controlled: they could only be predicted, and chased down. "We did lose a generator today, but Anthony says we have options," said Amy carefully. "We should be able to run on what we have for three or four days before things become critical. By then, we'll hopefully have located a replacement."

"We can't scavenge any more from California Adventure, can we?" asked Tiffany.

Amy shook her head. "They're down to three generators for the whole park, and they have their own problems to take care of," she said. "If the air conditioning goes out in Ariel's Undersea Adventure…"

Tiffany looked sick. "That would be bad."

"Yes, it would," agreed Amy.

"Is the power still on in the Mansion?" asked Skylar.

"For now." Amy shook her head. "Tiffany, get the rest of Guest Relations and tell them we're having a mandatory meeting at the Big Thunder Ranch tonight. Skylar, can you get Michael to tell the rest of the ride operators?" Between the three of them, Tiffany, Skylar, and Michael knew most of the Park's population by name, and knew where to find them during the day.

The sisters nodded. "Okay," said Tiffany, clearly relieved to have something to do. Skylar looked less eager. The assessing way she studied Amy made it clear she knew something was up. She just had the good grace not to say anything about it yet. Amy smiled, relieved, and watched them walk away down Main Street.

She was lucky; there was no one inside the firehouse. She made it all the way up to the apartment that had belonged to Walt Disney, and was now hers, before she started to cry.

• • •

Amy hadn't intended to wind up in charge of the survivors who took refuge in Disneyland; it was an accident. She'd just been the highest-ranking member of the Guest Relations team still standing when the doors officially closed to the public for the last time, and the only member of management who'd been willing to get her hands dirty along with everyone else. By the end of the first day (an endless string of cleanup and sanitation, until it seemed like none of them would ever be clean again, until they were all family forever, bound by things their hands could not undo), she was already being referred to as "Mayor" by almost everyone. It stuck. People wanted to feel like they still existed in a world with structure, and she was the closest thing they had to a face to put on their new existence.

So she'd tried. She'd tried so damn hard to rise to the level of their expectations, sleeping four hours a night—if that—and racing through the

Park every day soothing out conflicts, streamlining processes, and searching, always searching, for the line between Disney magic and the end of the world. It had been Clover's idea to start running one ride a day to take everyone's mind off things; the generators were designed to power entire Lands. A single ride couldn't overload them. Amy hadn't been sure it would work, but she'd given the okay, and the results had been staggering. People lined up like nothing had changed, and even the act of standing in a line was enough to make them laugh and talk about the old days, finally at ease. It might only last for the duration of one trip through Space Mountain or around the submarine lagoon, but it *worked*.

The Disney magic was still there. All Amy had to do was find the balance between the old world and the new one, and everything would be fine.

Supplies were tight, but Downtown Disney had plenty of stores, and she had plenty of manpower for raiding parties. They'd looted the Disneyland Hotel in the first week, coming away with food, bottled water, medicine, and even fuel for the generators. But it was the pillows that had really sealed her place as the Mayor of Main Street, and honorary regent of Disneyland.

"We can't stay in the hotels; they're too hard to defend, and there's not enough power to waste it on electric locks," she'd said. "That's no reason people should be uncomfortable." The looting crews had carried more than five hundred pillows, almost that many blankets, and nearly two hundred mattresses back to Disneyland. Those Cast Members and guests who had arrived after the comfortable sleeping places had been claimed suddenly found themselves with something soft to put their heads upon. Amy had been virtually canonized that night.

It was a hard existence. It was a strange existence, shuffling through the ruins of a place that had never been intended for this kind of life. But it was what they had, and it was amazing how quickly people had been able to adapt to their strange new circumstances. If the woman they called "Mayor" worked herself to death trying to make those circumstances better, well…

Heavy is the head that wears the crown.

• • •

The Big Thunder Ranch BBQ was one of the larger open-air restaurants in the Park, with picnic-style seating and a stage that had once played host to carefully scripted "hoedowns" intended to amuse the guests. Now, it was stripped of all its faux-Old West charm, and was just a place where the majority of Disneyland's residents could gather without needing to stand, and without forcing their weary Mayor to shout in order to be heard.

Anthony stood at the back, holding the tablet computer used to control the restaurant sound system. It was an odd juxtaposition of modern technology and old-fashioned setting, made stranger by the fact that he was unshaven and wearing overalls that had seen far better days. That was what the end of the world really looked like, Amy thought; like a man in dirty clothes, with equipment straight out of Tomorrowland in his hands.

Maybe a third of the residents of the park had shown up. That was better than Amy had been expecting. They were all survivors, but none of them had volunteered for that honor. They were the ones who hadn't gotten sick, the ones who found themselves marooned on a ride that never ended, and that never gave them an opportunity to get off. Honestly, the fact that even a third of the residents would come to a meeting like this spoke to the Disney spirit. They wanted to help.

Amy took a deep breath, resisting the urge to fiddle with her headset microphone, and said, "You've probably heard the rumors about our power supply. I'm sorry to have to be the one to say this, but they're not unfounded. Generator three has suffered a mechanical failure, and without additional parts, it will not be coming back online. We will be unable to power vital Park services, such as the refrigeration units in New Orleans Square."

The third who had come to the meeting were the ones most likely to understand what that meant. Alarmed looks were passed around the crowd, and a voice from the back shouted, "So what are you going to do about it, *Mayor?*"

That was the trigger for a wave of discontent muttering. Amy let it come, allowing it to wash over her. It cleaned nothing, and left only more anxiety in its wake. "Citizens of Disneyland," she said. There was a new snap to her voice, one that brought the crowd to abrupt silence. It was the tone she had once reserved for members of her staff, reminding them that they needed to worry more about creating magical moments for the guests, and less about who was surreptitiously texting who. "We are at the doorway of a crisis, and I need each of you to consider what you can do to help. Some things are simple. Turn off lights, conserve power whenever possible, do your part. Other things are more complicated." She paused, allowing them to consider her relatively minor requests. They had survived the end of the world, they were living in *Disneyland,* and she wanted them to turn off lights when they left the room? There had to be a catch. Taking a deep breath, she continued:

"There is a hospital facility roughly four miles from here with a generator array of the size and type we need. A party will be leaving Town Square at dawn to cross the city, enter the hospital, and secure the necessary parts to make the repairs. I am assured by the engineering department that we can bring back enough material to keep us functional for the better part of a year." A year was as far into the future as any of them dared to look. A year would take them through most of their water, and virtually all of their food. None of them were farmers. Even if they could convert the landscaped parts of the Park into gardens, it wasn't going to be enough.

But Walt wouldn't have given up. Walt would have fought tooth and nail for that year, for the chance that something might change, and the world might magically come alive again.

Amy looked out at the crowd of battered, weary survivors, trying to guess how many of them would be there in the morning. *Come on, Anthony,* she thought. *They need a tipping point.*

And Anthony rose to the occasion, as he had so many times before: "What about you, Madame Mayor?" he shouted. "Will you be sitting safely in City Hall, waiting for your delivery people to come back?"

"I'll be leading the expedition," said Amy. A low murmur spread through the crowd. She turned away, allowing herself the shadow of a smile. Maybe this would work out after all.

The next morning, fifteen people were waiting for her in Town Square: thirteen citizens, Anthony, and Clover. Tiffany and Skylar walked them to the gates of Disneyland. The sixteen raiders stepped outside. The sisters locked the gates behind them, and they were alone.

• • •

Most of the cars near the Parks had long since been scavenged for parts and fuel, but the Cast Member parking area was relatively untouched—in part, Amy admitted, because she had more respect for Cast Member property, but also because they had known, almost from the start, that one day raids like this would become necessary. Disneyland was designed to stay operational even during a blackout or other civic emergency. It was never intended to operate through an apocalypse.

They split into three teams, each of them taking the largest operational vehicle they could find. Amy wound up sitting with Anthony, Clover, and two others in a red SUV, wondering even as she fastened her seatbelt whether there was any good waiting for them in the silent city streets. Anthony glanced over at her as he turned the key in the ignition.

"It'll be okay," he said.

"Yeah," said Amy, relieved that he'd drawn the wrong conclusion from her face. She turned in her seat, looking out the window, and tried to make her shoulders unknot as the car rumbled to life and Anthony drove them into the deserted streets of Anaheim.

The first thing any of them noticed was the silence. It was almost a physical thing, so heavy across the deserted city that it felt as if it should have been visible, an obstacle they could see and drive around. The engines of their borrowed cars were obscenely loud, and Amy couldn't shake the feeling that they were violating something sacred by even being here.

They passed the first body when they were less than a block from the parking lot. It was—it had been—a woman in a flowered dress. She was slumped over on a bus stop bench, so dried out by the weather that she might as well have been mummified. The bodies came quickly after that, until everywhere that Amy looked there was another one sprawled in the street or sitting on a patch of sidewalk, their empty eye sockets turned up at the sky. Crows perched on the wires overhead, watching with casual fearlessness as the cars went rolling by.

"It was never about the meek inheriting the earth," said Clover, sounding disgusted. "The whole thing went to the scavengers."

Amy, who had been dealing with reports of coyotes skulking in the landscaped underbrush of the Jungle Cruise for weeks, said nothing, and they rolled on.

The piles of bodies continued to thicken for a while, and then began to vanish as gradually as they had appeared. The last was a man, lying face down in the gutter outside the hospital gates. Anthony stopped just outside the parking lot, frowning.

"What is it?" asked Amy.

"Look." He indicated the lot.

She looked.

The hospital should have been mobbed during the crisis. Not only patients, but staff and family members should have clogged every available parking space. Instead, half the lot was empty, allowing them a clear line of sight to the glass-fronted Admissions Building. Amy squinted. Nothing was moving on the other side of the glass.

"Do we go in?" asked Anthony.

"I don't think we have a choice." If there were people living in the hospital complex, maybe they could make a deal. Some generator parts for Park tickets, or for food, or for a share of the bedding they'd scavenged from the Disneyland hotels. Whatever the cost, they had to try, because if they lost one more generator, they were going to lose a lot more than a few lights.

Anthony seemed to have been thinking much the same, because he didn't argue. He just nodded, and said, "All right," and rolled on into the parking lot.

• • •

They waited outside their borrowed SUV until the other teams were parked and ready. The volunteers assembled in a loose crowd on the sidewalk, most of them looking substantially less sure of themselves than they had when still safely behind the gates of Disneyland. Amy felt like she should be making some sort of inspirational speech, but all she could really manage to do was clutch her promotional Mickey Mouse tote bag full of scavenging gear and try not to let them see how terrified she was.

The parking lot was the problem. It was too empty. Even the lots at Disneyland weren't that empty, and the Park had been virtually deserted by the last days of the outbreak.

Anthony and Clover moved to stand at what had become the de facto head of the group. They made a curious pair, the short, slender man and the hulking, freckle-faced woman. There was no better engineering team in the Disney complex.

"You know what we're here for," said Anthony. "We're not sure exactly where in the building it will be located, but structurally, assume you're looking for 'down.' Basements, lower levels, engineering rooms tucked into non-load-bearing parts of the foundation. If you find something, use your walkie-talkie, and call us. If you're too deep for the signal to get through, move until it can, and call us. Clover and I will come as fast as we can, and we'll figure out where to go from there."

"If you see signs that people are living in the building, or have been living there recently, do not scavenge anything other than generator parts," said Clover. "The lights aren't on inside, so we can safely assume that either there's no one here, or that anyone who *is* here doesn't have the technological skills to get the generator up and running." Unspoken went the cold, simple fact that if someone didn't know how to operate the resources they had, they couldn't be allowed to keep them. Disneyland needed the generator. Disneyland was going to have it.

"Does anyone have any questions?" asked Amy. She didn't really have anything to add, but she felt she should be seen to be taking part in the process—it would be good for morale if she was involved. Also, talking helped, at least a little bit. It drew attention away from the blind eyes of the building in front of them, where maybe their salvation would be found.

No one had any questions. Two by two, they turned and made their way to the door. Clover was the first to reach it. She tried the handle, then nodded to herself and turned to mouth 'It's unlocked' to the others, using the sort of exaggerated lip motions that used to allow them to communicate across restless crowds and during fireworks shows. Pulling the door open, she stepped inside, her partner beside her. They were visible through the window as they crossed the lobby unmolested and without signs of trouble. Then they vanished into a hallway, and were gone.

That was the cue for everyone else to risk going inside. Amy found herself paired off with Anthony, who smiled at her encouragingly, almost like he could hear the frantic pounding of her heart, and led the way into the lobby.

It was cool and dark inside. The air smelled of old bleach and softly settling dust. It was the smell of dead places. Amy had grown all too familiar with it since they had started being forced to make the difficult decision to let parts of Disneyland close down. They needed the power. They couldn't keep everything alive. And this building… this building wasn't alive. She took a breath, gripped the strap of her tote bag a little harder, and walked on into the dead zone.

Footsteps echoed more loudly than they should have, like the quality of the air had changed in the absence of people. It was like walking the service corridors at Space Mountain. Amy tried to focus on the comparison. This hospital was just another ride that needed maintenance, allowed to wind down and sit fallow until the people could return. Anthony walked beside her without saying a word, and the soft crackle of voices from his walkie-talkie accompanied them down, down, down into the depths of the hospital.

"We found a maintenance room, but it's empty—just some tools and a broken boiler."

"No signs of human habitation in the cafeteria. We got some spices."

The reports came in one after the other, along with Clover's calm, impassive recitation of the medical supplies they'd managed to obtain from a locked storeroom—including a substantial supply of Lactaid, which they'd been needing at the Park for quite some time. Amy and Anthony continued to travel downward through the halls, accompanied by their own echoing footsteps.

Finally, Anthony stopped in front of a plain wooden door. It looked just like all the others to Amy, but something about it clearly meant more to him. "Here," he said, and turned the knob. The door swung open easily, revealing the generator inside.

Amy clasped her hands together, eyes shining. They could save the Park. They could save everyone.

"Clover, we're on the second basement level; get your team down here. We have visual." Anthony smiled as he clipped his walkie-talkie back to his belt. "Well, Madame Mayor? Let's get our hands dirty."

• • •

It took almost half an hour to free the generator parts they needed, along with a few more that Anthony and Clover insisted on taking "just in case." Everyone was relaxed and happily burdened down with what they had scavenged as they walked out of the hospital.

Perhaps that was why the ambush was so effective.

Gunmen appeared from behind the cars on either side of the parking lot and opened fire on the startled citizens of Disneyland when they were halfway to their vehicles. In the screaming and chaos that followed, Amy saw four people go down, one with half his face blown away, one with four bleeding bullet holes in her stomach. Anthony grabbed her arm. She put her head down and kept running, forcing her feet to move as terror tried to root them to the spot.

Clover was already at the car. She wrenched the doors open, and the others piled inside, accompanied by a hail of bullets.

"Is anyone hit? Is everyone all right?" demanded Amy, as Anthony shoved the keys into the ignition and the SUV roared to life. She twisted in her seat. Three more vehicles were following, leaving six people dead or dying on the ground. *Oh, God. Please don't let this have been for nothing. Please...*

"Clover?" said Anthony.

"We've got all the parts we need," said Clover.

"Oh, thank God." Amy closed her eyes. Now that she wasn't running for her life, she could feel the dull pain of the gunshot wound in her side. She clasped her hand over it, trying to stop the blood. The SUV roared through the silent streets, chewing up the miles between them and Disneyland. "What do you suppose they wanted, if they weren't living in the hospital?"

"Some people may be afraid to go into medical facilities," said Clover. "Letting us go in, and then taking whatever we found, would have been the logical compromise."

"I hate logic."

"Sometimes I hate logic, too."

They drove on.

• • •

The raiders didn't pursue them to Disneyland, perhaps content to pick over the bodies of the fallen. Anthony drove straight through Downtown Disney to the central plaza. "Security can stop me if they want to," he said, and laughed—a wild, bitter laugh that was the only real sign of how much the encounter had disturbed him.

Amy opened her eyes when the SUV stopped. Tiffany and Skylar were running toward them across the plaza, the gates of Disneyland standing open. She smiled and opened the door, almost falling out before she caught herself on the frame. Tiffany and Skylar stopped, eyes wide and horrified. Amy looked down at herself.

"Ah," she said. "I suppose that's rather a lot of blood."

"What?" said Anthony, turning to her. He paled. "Oh, God, Amy…"

"There wasn't time. Done is done." She undid her seatbelt, climbing down from the SUV before her legs buckled and sent her sprawling on the bricks. Tiffany and Skylar moved to help her up. She clung to their arms, distantly sorry about the bloody handprints she was leaving. "We got the parts," she informed them. "We can fix the generator."

"Amy…" whispered Tiffany.

"Get me inside," said Amy.

With Tiffany on one side of her and Anthony on the other, the Mayor of Main Street allowed herself to be half-led, half-carried back into the Park that had become her home.

• • •

Anthony was the one who loaded her into a wheelchair from Guest Relations and pushed her through Adventureland to New Orleans Square. People peered out at them from shops and seating areas, but no one approached. Amy chuckled. Even living through the end of days hadn't made most people any less squeamish about a little blood.

"You don't have to do this," Anthony said. "We just scavenged…"

"I've lost too much blood. I'm not letting you waste the resources." The world was going pleasantly fuzzy around the edges. "Just get me to the Mansion."

"Amy…"

"I'm still Mayor, aren't I?" She smiled. "Do as you're told."

"You're an imperious bitch sometimes, you know that?"

"I do." There was a small bump as Anthony turned the wheelchair and began pushing it up a gentle slope. Amy didn't need to open her eyes to see the artfully crumbling mansion in front of them, or the overgrown yard.

"Do you need me to carry you inside?"

"All riders must transfer past this point." Amy grabbed the armrests and pushed, struggling to get to her feet. When she finally opened her eyes, everything was gray… but she had a little more in her. "Thank you, Anthony. Keep the lights on."

"Anything for you, Madame Mayor," he said. He was crying. She wanted to stop and comfort him, but there wasn't time; she needed what little strength she had left if she wanted to make her way into the ride.

With a final smile, and a jaunty wave, Amy climbed the two low brick steps and walked into the Haunted Mansion, where the doors to the elevator—the famous "stretching room"—were standing ready. She stepped inside. There was a click behind her as Anthony pressed the hidden button, and then the voice of the Ghost Host was welcoming her to find a way out.

No way out, she thought. *Not even* your *way.*

The prerecorded spiel ended, and the door opened in the wall, allowing a gust of frigid air to escape. Aware that she was leaving a trail of blood behind her, Amy staggered through the queue area to the moving walkway, which was still moving; alone of all the rides in Disneyland, the Haunted Mansion never stopped.

The Doombuggies sailed regally by, waiting for passengers. Amy lurched into the first to pass, grabbing the bar and using it to drag herself to the far side of the small black carriage. Then she closed her eyes, and let the Mansion carry her on into the dark.

The smell wasn't as bad as she'd expected. That would be the air conditioning doing its job, lowering the Mansion's ambient temperature to something akin to a walk-in freezer. The citizens of Disneyland went about their lives never considering how many people had died there, or in the Plaza, or in the open spaces of Downtown Disney, the promenade connecting the Parks to the hotels. Those bodies had to go somewhere. It was a health hazard otherwise.

The power could never go out in the Haunted Mansion.

By the time Amy's Doombuggy reached the graveyard scene, she could barely feel her legs. She grabbed her safety bar and pushed with all her strength, finally lifting it enough to bring the whole ride to a halt. She slid out of the buggy and onto the narrow path they had left open between the graves, between the stacked piles of bodies. She pushed the safety bar back down. The ride resumed, and Amy walked on into the dark until walking ceased to be an option.

There was an open space between a pile of bodies and a tombstone. That would do. Sitting down, she closed her eyes, and finally, after the long months of struggle and fear, allowed her shift to end.

"The difference in winning and losing is most often not quitting."

–Walt Disney

IN THE WOODS

Hugh Howey

A sliver of light appeared in the pitch black—a horizontal crack that ran from one end of April's awareness to the other. There was a deep chill in her bones. Her teeth chattered; her limbs trembled. April woke up cold with metal walls pressed in all around her. A mechanical hum emanated from somewhere behind her head. Another body was wedged in beside her.

She tried to move and felt the tug of a cord on her arm. Fumbling with her free hand, April found an IV. She could feel the rigid lump of a needle deep in her vein. There was another hose along her thigh that ran up to her groin. She patted the cold walls around herself, searching for a way out. She tried to speak, to clear her throat, but like in her nightmares, she made no sound.

The last thing April remembered was going to sleep in an unfamiliar bunk deep inside a mountain. She remembered feeling trapped, being told the world had ended, that she would have to stay there for years, that everyone she knew was gone. She remembered being told that the world had been poisoned.

April had argued with her husband about what to do, whether to flee, whether to even believe what they'd been told. Her sister had said it was the air, that it couldn't be stopped, so a group had planned on riding it out here. They'd brought them in buses to an abandoned government facility in the mountains of Colorado. They said it might be a while before any of them could leave.

The body in the dark by April's feet stirred. There was a foot by her armpit. They were tangled, she and this form. April tried to pull away, to tuck her knees against her chest, but her muscles were slow to respond, her joints stiff. She could feel the chill draining from her, and a dull heat sliding in to take its place—like the tubes were emptying her of death and substituting that frigid void with the warmth of life.

The other person coughed, a deep voice ringing metallic in the small space, hurting her ears. April tried to brace herself with the low ceiling to scoot away from the coughing form, when the crack of light widened. She pushed up more, grunting with the strain, and even more light came in. The ceiling hinged back. The flood of harsh light nearly blinded her. Blinking, eyes watering, ears thrumming from the sound of that noisy pump running somewhere nearby, April woke with all the violence and newness of birth. Shielding her eyes—squinting out against the assault of light—she saw in her blurry vision a man curled up by her feet. It was her husband, Remy.

April wept in relief and confusion. The hoses made it hard to move, but she worked her way closer to him, hands on his shins, thighs, clambering up his body until her head was against Remy's chest. His arms feebly encircled her. Husband and wife trembled from the cold, teeth clattering. April had no idea where in the world they were or how they got there; she just knew they were together.

"Hey," Remy whispered. His lips were blue. He mouthed her name, eyes closed, holding her.

"I'm here," she said. "I'm here."

The warmth continued to seep in. Some came from their naked bodies pressed together, some came directly through her veins. April felt the urge to pee, and her body—almost of its own volition, of some long-learned habit—simply relieved itself. Fluid snaked away from her through one of the tubes. If it weren't for the too-real press of Remy's flesh against her own, she would think this was all a dream.

"What's happening?" Remy asked. He rubbed his eyes with one hand.

"I don't know." April's voice was hoarse. A whisper. "Someone did this to us." Even as she said this, she realized it was obvious, that it didn't need saying. Because she had no memory of being put in that metal canister.

"My eyes are adjusting," she told Remy. "I'm going to open this up some more."

Remy nodded slowly.

Peering up, April saw a curved half-cylinder of gleaming steel hanging over them, a third of the way open. She lifted a quivering leg, got a foot against the hinged lid, and shoved. Their small confines flew open the rest of the way, letting in more light. Flickering bulbs shone down from over-head. The lamps dangled amid a tangle of industrial pipes, traces of wire, air ducts, and one object so out of place that it took a moment to piece together what she was seeing. Suspended from the ceiling, hanging down over their heads, was a large yellow bin: a heavy-duty storage trunk.

"What does that say?" Remy asked. They both squinted up at the object, blinking away cold tears.

April studied the marks of black paint on the yellow tub. She could tell it was a word, but it felt like forever since she'd read anything real, anything not fragmented amid her dreams. When the word crystallized, she saw that it was simply her name.

"April," she whispered. That's all it said.

Before they could get the bin down, she and Remy had to extricate themselves from the steel canister. Why had they been put there? As punishment? But what had they done? The IVs and catheters were terrible clues that they'd been out for more than a mere night, and the stiffness in April's joints and the odor of death in the air—perhaps coming from their very flesh—hinted at it having been more than a week. It was impossible to tell.

"Careful," Remy said, as April peeled away the band that encircled her arm, the band that held the tube in place. It tore like velcro, not like tape. Were they put away for longer than adhesive would last? The thought was fleeting, too impossible to consider.

"What's that around your neck?" Remy asked.

April patted her chest. She looked down at the fine thread around her neck and saw a key dangling from it. She had sensed it before, but in a daze. Looking back up at the bin, she saw a dull silver lock hanging bat-like from the lip of the bin.

"It's a message," April said, understanding in a haze how the key and the bin and her name were supposed to go together. "Help me out."

Her first hope was that there was food in that bin. Her stomach was in knots, cramped from so deep a hunger. Remy helped her pull her IV out and extract her catheter, and then she helped with his. A spot of purple blood welled up on her arm, and a dribble of fluid leaked from the catheter. Using the lid of the metal pod for balance, April hoisted herself to her feet, stood there for a swaying, unsteady moment, then reached up and touched the large plastic trunk.

It'd been suspended directly over their heads, where they would see it upon waking. A chill ran down April's spine. Whoever had placed them there had known they would wake up on their own, that there wouldn't be anyone around to help them, to explain things, to hand them a key or tell them to look inside the chest. That explained the paint, the thread, the pod cracking open on its own. Had she and Remy been abandoned? Had they been punished? Somehow, she knew her sister had been involved. Her sister who had brought them into the mountain had locked them away yet again, tighter and tighter confines.

Remy struggled to his feet, grunting from the exertion of simply standing. He surveyed the room. "Looks like junk storage," he whispered, his voice like sandpaper.

"Or a workshop," April said. *Or a laboratory*, she thought to herself. "I think this knot frees the bin. We can lower it down."

"So thirsty," Remy said. "Feels like I've been out for days."

Months, April stopped herself from suggesting. "Help me steady this. I think… I have a feeling this is from Tracy."

"Your sister?" Remy held on to April, reached a hand up to steady the swaying bin. "Why do you think that? What have they done to us?"

"I don't know," April said, as she got the knot free. She held the end of the line, which looped up over a paint-flecked pipe above. The line had been wrapped twice, so there was enough friction that even her weak grip could bear the weight of the bin. Lowering the large trunk, she wondered what her sister had done this time. Running away from home to join the army, getting involved with the CIA or FBI or NSA—April could never keep them straight—and now this, whatever this was. Locking thousands of people away inside a mountain, putting her and Remy in a box.

The bin hit the metal pod with a heavy *thunk*, pirouetted on one corner for a moment, then settled until the hoisting rope went slack. April touched the lock. She reached for the key around her neck. The loop was too small to get over her head.

"No clasp," Remy said, his fingertips brushing the back of her neck.

April wrapped a weak fist around the key and tugged with the futile strength of overslept mornings.

The thread popped. April used the key to work the lock loose. Unlatching the trunk, there was a hiss of air and a deep sigh from the plastic container, followed by the perfume scent of life—or maybe just a spot of vacuum to stir away the stale odor of death.

There were folded clothes inside. Nestled on top of the clothes were tins labeled "water" with vials of blue powder taped to each. Remy picked up the small note between the tins, and April recognized the writing. It was her sister's. The note said: "Drink me."

A dreamlike association flitted through April's mind, an image of a white rabbit. She was Alice, tumbling through a hole and into a world both surreal and puzzling. Remy had less hesitation. He popped the tins with the pull tab, took a sip of the water, then studied the vial of powder.

"You think your sister is out to help us?" Remy asked. "Or kill us?"

"Probably thinks she's helping," April said. "And'll probably get us killed." She uncorked one of the vials, dumped it into Remy's tin of water, and stirred with her finger. Her sister wasn't there to argue with, so April skipped to the part where she lost the argument and took a sip.

A foul taste of metal and chalk filled her mouth, but a welcome wetness as well. She drank it all, losing some around the corners of her mouth that trickled down her neck and met again between her bare breasts.

Remy followed suit, trusting her. Setting the empty tin aside, April looked under the clothes. There were familiar camping backpacks there, hers and Remy's. She remembered packing them back at her house in Maryland. Her sister had just said they were going camping in Colorado, to bring enough for two weeks. Along with the packs were stacks of freeze-dried camping MREs; more tins of water; a first aid kit; plastic pill cylinders that rattled with small white, yellow, and pink pills; and her sister's pocketknife. It was Remy who found the gun and the clips loaded with ammo. At the bottom of the case was an atlas, one of those old AAA road maps of the United States. It was open to a page, a red circle drawn on it with what might've been lipstick. And, finally, there was a sealed note with April's name on it.

She opened the note while Remy studied the map. Skipping to the bottom, April saw her sister's signature, the familiar hurried scrawl of a woman who refused to sit still, to take it easy. She went back to the top and read. It was an apology. A confession. A brief history of the end of the world and Tracy's role in watching it all come to fruition.

"We've been asleep for five hundred years," April told her husband, when she got to that part. She read the words without believing them.

Remy looked up from the atlas and studied her. His face said what she was thinking: *That's not possible.*

Even with the suspicion that they'd been out for months or longer, five hundred years of sleep was beyond the realm of comprehension. The end of the world had been nearly impossible to absorb. Being alive out along the fringe of time, maybe the only two people left on the entire Earth, was simply insane.

April kept reading. Her sister's rough scrawl explained the food situation, that they'd miscalculated the time it would take for the world to be safe again, for the air to be okay to breathe. She explained the need to ration, that there was only enough supplies to get fifteen people through to the other side. She could almost hear her sister's voice as she read, could see her writing this note in growing anger, tears in her eyes, knuckles white around a pen. And then she came to this:

The people who destroyed the world are in Atlanta. I marked their location on the map. If you are reading this, you and whoever else are left in the facility are the only ones alive who know what they did. You're the only ones who can make them pay. For all of us.

I'm sorry. I love you. I never meant for any of this, and no one can take it back— can make it right—but there can be something like justice. A message from the present to the assholes who thought they could get away with this. Who thought they were beyond our reach. Reach them for all of us.

—Tracy

April wiped the tears from her cheeks, tears of sadness and rage. Remy studied the gun in his hand. When April looked to the atlas, she saw a nondescript patch of country circled outside Atlanta. She had no idea what it was her sister expected her to do.

"Did you hear that?" Remy asked.

April turned and stared at the door that led into the room. The handle moved. It tilted down, snapped back up, then tilted again. As if a child were trying to work it, not like it was locked.

"Help me down," Remy said. He started to lift a leg over the lip of the pod.

"Wait." April grabbed her husband's arm. The latch moved again. There was a scratching sound at the door, something like a growl. "The gun," April hissed. "Do you know how to use it?"

• • •

A branch snapped in the woods—a sharp crack like a log popping in a fire. Elise stopped and dropped to a crouch, scanned the underbrush. She looked for the white spots. Always easiest to see the white spots along the flank, not the bark-tan of the rest of the hide. Slipping an arrow from her quiver, she notched it into the gut-string of her bow. *There*. A buck.

Coal-black eyes studied her between the low branches.

Elise drew back the arrow but kept it pointed at the ground. Deer somehow know when they're being threatened. She has watched them scatter while she took careful aim, until she was letting fly an errant shot at the bouncing white tail that mocked hunters of rabbit and venison alike.

The bow in her hand was Juliette's, once. Elise remembered back when it was made that she couldn't even draw the bow, that her arms had been too weak, too short, too young. But that was a forever ago. Elise was nearly as strong as Juliette now. Strong and lean and forest swift. No one in the village had ever caught a rabbit with their bare hands before Elise, and none had done it since.

She and the deer studied one another. Wary. The deer were learning to be scared of people again. It used to be easy, bringing home a feast. Too easy. But both sides were learning. Remembering how to find that balance. To live like the people in Elise's great books had once lived, with prey growing wary and hunters growing wise.

With one motion, Elise steered the bow up and loosed the arrow with more instinct than aim, with more thought than measure, with six years of practice and habit. The buck reared its head, shook its horns, took a staggering leap to one side, and then collapsed. The heart. They only went down like that with an arrow to the heart. To the spine was faster, and anywhere else might mean half a day of tracking. Elise was too competent with a bow to gloat, wouldn't need to tell anyone how the deer went down. When you ate an animal not from a can but from the flesh, everyone who partook could read the hunt right there on the spit, could tell what had happened.

"Careful," she could hear her brother saying whenever she brought home a deer and provided for her people. "Keep this up, and you'll be mayor one day."

Elise drew out her knife—the one Solo had given to her—and marched through the woods toward her kill. Her quietude was no longer a concern. The hunt was over. But this was a mistake that she too often forgot, that a soft pace was always prudent. Juliette had taught her this. "The hunt is never over," Juliette had said once, while tracking a doe with Elise. "Drop your guard, and what changes in an instant is *who* is doing the hunting."

Elise was reminded of the truth of this by another loud noise to her side. Again, she dropped to a crouch. And again, something was watching her. But this time, it was the most dangerous animal of them all.

• • •

April was ready for anything to come through that door. It could be her sister, a mountain bear, a stranger intent on doing them harm. Open to all possibilities, she still wasn't prepared for what appeared.

The battle with the latch was finally won—the door flew open—and some creature entered on all fours. Some half-man, half-beast wildling. The creature sniffed the air, then spotted April and Remy perched inside the steel pod, huddled there beside the large plastic tub.

"Shoot it," April begged.

"What *is* that?" Remy asked.

"Shoot it," she told him again, holding onto her husband's arm.

The beast roared. "FEEF-DEEN!" it growled, with a voice almost like a man's. "Feef-deen!"

And then it was in the air, jumping at them, yellow teeth and white eyes flashing, hands outstretched, hair billowing out wildly, coming to take them.

Remy aimed the gun, but the beast crashed into them before he could pull the trigger. Hair and claws and teeth and snarling. Remy punched the animal, and April tried to shove it away when yellow teeth clamped down on Remy's hand. There was a loud crunch—and her husband screamed and pulled his hand away, blood spurting where two of his fingers had been.

From his other hand came a flash and a roar. Remy flew back into April, who knocked her head against the open lid, nearly blacking out. The animal slumped against the edge of the pod, a clawed hand splayed open, before collapsing to the floor.

"What the fuck!" Remy shouted. He scrambled after the pistol, which had flown from his grip. His other hand was tucked under his armpit, rivulets of blood tracking down his bare ribs.

"Your hand," April said. She pulled one of the clean, folded shirts from the bin and made her husband hold out his hand. She wrapped the shirt as tight as she could and knotted the ends. Blood pooled and turned the fabric red. "Is it dead?" she asked. She braved a glance over the lip of the pod. The beast wasn't moving. And now that she could study it, she saw that it wasn't half-beast at all. It was mostly man. But naked, covered in hair, a scraggly beard, sinewy and lean.

Remy straightened his arms and pointed the gun at the door, his bandaged hand steadying his good one. April saw that there was another beast there. Another person on all-fours. Less hairy. A woman.

The woman sniffed the air, studied them, and then peered at the dead man-creature. "Feef-deen," she said. She snarled, showing her teeth, and her shoulders dipped as she tensed her muscles and readied for a leap. Remy, bless him, didn't allow her to make the jump. The gun went off again, deafening loud. The woman collapsed. April and Remy watched the door, frozen, and after an agonizing dozen throbs of her pulse, she saw the next one.

"How many bullets do you have?" she asked Remy, wondering where he learned to shoot like that, if it were as easy as he made it seem.

He didn't answer. He was too busy lining up his shot. But this next creature, another woman, studied the room, the two dead creatures and the two living ones, and made the same noise but without the rage. Without the snarling.

"Feef-deen," she said, before turning and wandering off. Almost as if satisfied. Almost as if all were right with the world.

• • •

"Who goes there?" Elise asked. She watched the shapes beyond the foliage—it appeared to be two men. Pressing an arrow into the dirt, she left the shaft where she could grab it in a hurry, and then withdrew another from her quiver and notched it onto the bowstring. She drew the string taut but kept the arrow aimed to the side. "Rickson? Is that you?"

"Hello," a voice called. A woman's voice. "We're coming out. Don't shoot."

A couple stepped around a tree. Elise saw that they were holding hands. They kept their free palms up to show that they were empty. Both wore backpacks. Both looked like they'd been living in the bush for ages, like the people who'd made it out of Silo 37 a few years ago. A thrill ran through Elise with the chance that these were new topsiders.

"Where are you from?" she asked. The couple had stopped twenty paces away. They looked rough. And there were only two of them. Elise recalled how back when she lived in Silo 17, every stranger was to be feared. But the people who dared to free themselves from their silos ended up being good people. It was a truth of the world. The bad people stayed right where they were.

"We've been… underground for a long time," the man said.

He didn't give a number. Sometimes they didn't know their number. Sometimes they had to be told by finding their silo on a map; there were fifty of them, the silos, buried underground. Elise fought the temptation to flood this couple with too much all at once. When she was younger, that had been her way. But she was learning to be more than quiet just in the hunt, to be as soft of tongue as she was of foot.

"Are you alone?" she asked, scanning the woods.

"We met another group northwest of here," the man said. He must've run into Debra's scouting party, which had been gone for a week. "They told us the people in charge lived by the coast. We've been looking for them for a long time. A very long time. Can you take us to your city?"

Elise put her notched arrow away and then retrieved the one she'd left in the dirt. "It's a village," she said. "Just a village." The memory of where she used to live, in one of those fifty silos, all cut off from each other, seemed forever ago. That life had grown hazy. Time formed some gulfs that not even recollection could span.

"Do you need help with the deer?" the man asked. "That's a lot of food."

Elise saw that he had a knife on his hip and that both of them bore the shrunken frames of the famished. She wondered what he could possibly know about deer. She'd had to consult her books to learn about deer, how to hunt them, how to clean them, how best to cook them. Maybe he too had pages from his silo's Legacy, that great set of books about the old world. Or maybe his silo had a herd of them.

"I'd love the help," she said, putting away the other arrow, comfortable that these people meant no harm and also that she could take the both of them with her bow or knife if she had to. "My name's Elise."

"I'm Remy," the man said, "and this is my wife April."

Elise closed the distance between them. She shook their hands one at a time, the woman's first. As she shook the man's she noticed something strange about his hand. He was missing two of his fingers.

• • •

Elise and Remy carved the choice cuts of meat and wrapped them in the deer's stripped hide. Elise secured the bundle with bark twine from her pack, and hung the bundle from a thick branch. The couple insisted on carrying the meat, resting it on their shoulders. Elise walked ahead, showing the way back to camp.

She resisted the urge to badger the couple with questions about their silo, how many were left there, what jobs they held, what level they lived on. When she was younger, she would have talked their ears off. But Juliette had a way about topsiders. There were unspoken rules. The people of the buried silos joined the rest when they were ready. They spoke when they were ready. "We all have our demons," Juliette liked to say. "We have to choose when to share them. When to let others in on the wrestling."

Elise often suspected that Juliette was holding out the longest. She had been their mayor for years and years. No one hardly voted for anyone else. But there was something in the woman's frown, a hardness in her eyes, a furrow in her brow, that never relaxed. Juliette was the reason any of them escaped from the silos, and the reason there was something to escape to for the rest. But Elise saw a woman still trapped by something. Held down by demons. Secrets she would never share.

The night fires were times for sharing. Elise told the couple this as they approached camp. She told them about the welcome they would receive, and that they could say as much or as little as they like. "We'll take turns telling you our stories," Elise said. "I'm from Silo 17. There are only a few of us. There are a lot more from Silo 18. Like Juliette."

She glanced back at the couple to see if they were listening. "Like I said, you don't have to say anything if you don't want. Don't have to say what you did or how you got here. Not until you're ready. Don't have to say how many of you are left—"

"Fifteen," the woman said. She'd barely said a word while the deer was being cleaned and packed. But she said this. "There were fifteen of us for the longest time. Now there are only two."

This sobered Elise. She herself had come from a silo that only offered five survivors. She couldn't imagine a world with just two people.

"How many are you?" Remy asked.

Elise turned her head to answer. "We don't count. It's not *really* a rule, but it's basically a rule. Counting was a touchy subject for a lot of our people. Not for me, though. Well, not the same. I came from a silo with very few people. You didn't count so much as glance around the room and see that your family is still there. We have enough people now that there's talk of setting up another village north of here. We're scouting for locations. Some want to see a place that used to be called the Carolinas—"

"Carolinas," Remy said, but he said it differently, with the i long like "eye" instead of "eee." Like he was testing the word.

"It's Carolinas," Elise said, correcting him.

Remy didn't try again. His wife said something to him, but Elise couldn't make it out.

"Anyway, that's the sort of thing we vote on now. We all vote. As long as you can read and write. I'm all for the second village, but I don't want to live up there. I know these woods here like the back of my hand."

They reached the first clearing, and Elise steered them toward the larder where they dropped off the meat. Haney, the butcher's boy, grew excited at the sight of the feast and then at the strangers. He started to pester them with questions, but Elise shooed him away. "I'm taking them to see Juliette," she said. "Leave them alone."

"Juliette's the person in charge here?" the woman asked.

"Yeah," Elise said. "She's our mayor. She has a place near the beach."

She led them there, skirting the square and the market to keep from being waylaid by gawkers. She took the back paths the prowling dogs and mischievous children used. Remy and April followed. Glancing back, Elise saw that April had removed the bag from her back and was clutching it against her chest, the way some parents cradled their children. There was a look of fear and determination on her face. Elise knew that look. It was the hardened visage of someone who has come so far and is near to salvation.

"That's her place," Elise said, pointing up into the last two rows of trees by the beach. There was a small shelter affixed to the trunks with spikes and ropes. It stood two dozen paces off the ground. Juliette had lived inside the Earth and upon the ground, but now lived up in the air. "I'm trying to get to heaven," she had told Elise once, joking around. "Just not in a hurry."

Elise thought that explained why Juliette spent so much time out on the beach alone at night, gazing up at the stars.

"There she is," Elise said, pointing down by the surf. "You can leave your bags here if you like."

They elected to carry them. Elise saw them fixate on Juliette, who was standing alone by the surf, watching the tall fishing rods arranged in a line down the beach, monofilament stretching out past the breakers. Farther down the beach, Solo could be seen rigging bait on another line. Charlotte was there as well, casting a heavy sinker into the distance.

Elise had to hurry to catch up with Remy and April. The couple seemed drawn toward Juliette. On a mission. But the woman had that pull on plenty of people. Sensing their presence, the mayor turned and shielded her eyes against the sun, watching the small party approach. Elise thought she saw Juliette stiffen with the sudden awareness that these were strangers, new to the topsides.

"I got a buck," Elise told Juliette. She nodded toward the couple. "And then I met them in the woods. This is April and Remy. And this is our mayor, Juliette. You can call her Jules."

Juliette took the couple in. She brushed the sand from her palms and shook each of theirs in turn, then squeezed Elise's shoulder. A strong wave crashed on the beach and slid up nearly to the line of rods. The tide was coming in. The couple seemed not to be awed by the sight of the ocean, which Elise thought was strange. She still couldn't get used to it. As for them—they could only stare at Juliette.

"Are you in charge of all this?" April asked.

Juliette glanced down the beach toward Solo and Charlotte for a moment. "If you came from a place with a lot of rules and great concern over who is in charge, you'll find we're not so strict here." Juliette rested her hands on her hips. "You both look hungry and tired. Elise, why don't you get them fed and freshened up. They can look around camp when they're ready. And you don't have to tell us your story until you want—"

"I think we'll say our piece now," April said. Elise saw that she was the talkative one now. Remy was holding his tongue. And there was anger in their guises, not relief. Elise had seen this before, the need to vent. She shuffled back a step but wasn't sure why. Maybe it was because Juliette had done the same.

"Very well—" Juliette started to say.

"We aren't here to be saved," April said. She continued to clutch her bag to her chest, like it was a raft keeping her afloat. "We aren't here to live with you. We died a long time ago, when everything was taken from us. We've been dead and walking for years to get here and to tell you this. You didn't get away with it."

"I'm not sure I—" Juliette began.

April dropped her bag to the sand. In her hand was a silver gun. Elise knew straight away what it was. There were three of them in camp that the men used to hunt; Elise hated the way they spooked the wildlife.

This one was different… and trained on Juliette. Elise moved to stand in front of the mayor, but Juliette pushed her away.

"Wait a second," Juliette said.

"No," April said. "We've waited long enough."

"You don't understa—"

But a roar cut off whatever Juliette was about to say. A flash and an explosion of sound. She fell to the beach, a wild wave rushing up nearly to touch her, all so sudden and yet in slow motion. Elise felt her own body stir, like a deer that knows it's in mortal danger. She sensed the whole world around her. Saw Solo and Charlotte stir down the beach and start running.

Felt the heat of the sun on her neck, the tickle of sweat on her scalp. Could feel the sand beneath her feet and hear the crying birds. There was an arrow in her hand, her bow coming off her shoulder, a gun swinging around, a man yelling for someone to stop, Elise wasn't sure who.

She only got half a draw before the arrow slipped from her fingers. She loosed it before the trigger could be pulled again. And the shaft lodged in the woman's throat.

More screaming. Gurgling. Blood in the sand. Remy moved to catch his wife. Elise notched another arrow, swift as a hare. By her feet, Juliette did not stir. The man reached for the gun, and Elise put an arrow in his side, hoping not to kill him. He roared and clutched the wound while Elise notched another and knelt by her wounded friend. The man regrouped and went for the gun again, murder in his eyes. For the second time that day, Elise put an arrow through an animal's heart.

The only people moving on the beach were Solo and Charlotte, running their way. Elise dropped her bow and reached for Juliette, who lay on her side, facing away from Elise. Elise held her friend's shoulders and rolled her onto her back. Blood was pooled on Juliette's chest, crimson and spreading. Her lips moved. Elise told her to be strong. She told the strongest person she'd ever known to be extra strong.

Juliette's eyes opened and focused on Elise. They were wet with tears. One tear pooled and broke free, sliding down the wrinkled corner of Juliette's eye. Elise held her friend's hand, could feel Juliette squeezing back.

"It'll be okay," Elise said. "Help is coming. It'll be okay."

And Juliette did something Elise hadn't seen her do in the longest time: She smiled. "It already is," Juliette whispered, blood flecking her lips. "It already is."

Her eyes drifted shut. And then Elise watched as the furrow in her mayor's brow smoothed away, and the tension in Jules's clenched jaw relaxed. Something like serenity took hold of the woman, and the demons everywhere—they scattered.

BLESSINGS

Nancy Kress

We move by night, silently, widely separated. It's impossible to know how much the enemy can detect. Their technology is, of course, better than ours. But we have had many successes. We will have more. And we will not give up.

• • •

"Jenna? You awake yet?"

Nothing. I raise my voice.

"Jenna!"

She emerges from her bedroom, my sweet daughter, sleep-tousled hair and dream-wide eyes. "I'm sorry, Dad—I overslept! I'll be ready in five minutes!"

I pour two more coffees, one for her and a half-cup for me. Four minutes later I hand her the ceramic mug; she drinks it as we walk to the lab. People smile and greet us as we pass, and Jeanette Foch—whose son brought her down from Quebec twenty years ago and who still speaks no English—murmurs, "Tres belle, tres belle." At twenty Jenna is prettier than her mother was, prettier than my mother, much prettier than my grandmother, whose faded picture hangs on the wall of our bungalow. My grandparents, Sophie and Luke Ames, once saved this settlement from horrors I can't bear to think about, during the first years of the Blessing. Their photograph used to hang in the Common Hall, but of course nobody else could bear to think about what Sophie and Luke did, either, so the picture stays in a drawer.

I don't know how my people survived the constant violence during the early years of the Blessing.

Jenna stops to greet more people. Old Mr. Caruthers has his breathing mask on today. CO_2 is 1.9% and falling. A generation ago, it looked like all of us might have to wear breathing masks.

Jenna kneels by his wheelchair. "Are you taking your pills, Mr. Caruthers?"

He nods, although I'm not sure he understands. I make a note to remind his granddaughter yet again about his zinc and iron. Kay Caruthers is among the sweetest people in New Eden, but not all that bright.

Unlike Jenna, I think, and then chastise myself for ridiculous pride. Jenna's intelligence and beauty are no more my conscious work than is Kay's dimness, and comparisons only undermine Mutuality.

In the lab, Dant23 greets me by waving a tentacle. I'd forgotten that he is observing today. The Dant—who look like a cross between a flower and an octopus—show up on a semi-regular schedule. Five tentacles where we have arms and legs, an elongated head that on top flares into segments that resemble petals, skin the color of prominent human veins. But they are DNA-based—panspermia is the usual conjecture—and they can breathe our atmosphere. Which is, of course, why they're here.

Humanity owes them a debt we can never repay. Sharing our planet does not even come close. Without the Blessing, we wouldn't have gotten the runaway CO_2 caused by sociopathic industrialization under control. We wouldn't have stopped interpersonal violence and that most unthinkable of acts, war. We wouldn't be free people, living in peace and Mutuality. The Dant remade us.

We cannot, however, talk to them. They understand us, but their speech is pitched too high for human ears. All that we have learned from them has been by demonstration, gesture, pantomime. It is enough; it is more than enough.

Jenna kisses Dant23's cheek and says, "Good morning! How are the children?"

Dant23 nods and waves a tentacle. After more ritual greetings, we get down to work. I look at the new plant samples in the greenhouse.

Overnight, they've all died.

• • •

We choose our destinations carefully. Never small villages, although most of the planet now lives in small villages. And of course not the cities, unlivable and abandoned. We pick large settlements: harder to attack, but that's where the targets are.

Usually.

• • •

Jenna stares at the dead soybeans; this was her experiment. But I know she won't cry. Unlike Zane and Sarah, my other two apprentices, Jenna can summon a sort of steeliness that sometimes worries me. Once, when she was small, I actually saw her hit another child in a dispute over a toy. *Hit* him! He froze immediately, of course, in normal Extreme Involuntary Fear Bradycardia—but she did not. Even now, the memory makes me shudder.

Genes are strange things. Even with the inhibiting compounds now tightly woven into our DNA from the Dants' Blessing, we are individuals.

Jenna says, "I'll start the plant analyses."

Zane, who has come into the lab, says, "I'll help."

She smiles at him. He smiles back. They make a plan to divide the work and I turn to my own experiments, which are not doing much better than Jenna's. The wheat plants look normal, but CO_2 levels have changed their physiology, and they contain thirty percent less iron and twenty-two percent less zinc than preserved samples from forty years ago.

At least, I think those are the percentages. I nurse along my decades-old absorption spectrophotometer. So much sophisticated equipment on Earth is either falling apart or newly manufactured in ways that do—that must—protect the environment and the living things within it. The trade-off is worth it. Doing no harm comes first. Mutuality comes first. I don't understand how pre-Blessing humans tolerated their world. Manufacturing chemicals leaching into the soil and water, people sickened and dying by the greed of others, whole landscapes destroyed by dangerous mining practices, toxic work environments.... .

I breathe deeply, before I get overwhelmed.

But, still, our equipment is inadequate. I remember computers; there were still a few around when I was a boy, running on cannibalized parts. We could not do now what Ian McGill did fifty years ago: describe the genetic changes that confer the Blessing. There are no gene sequencers left. Nor can we communicate the results of our scientific work to each other as easily as could McGill. But I have seen the great pile of shameful trash outside Buffalo, before the whole area was proscribed: dead computers, gasoline-powered cars, airplane fuselages, frivolous electronics, all costing innocent lives and destroying the Earth. Never again.

Jenna finishes her tests and scowls. "This batch of soy shows more zinc and iron, but the plants couldn't live with the CO_2 level. And the batches that can live with it are still starving us of key nutrients!"

"We'll cross-breed again," Zane says.

"It never does any good!" Jenna's scowl deepens. "Without enough zinc and iron…"

She doesn't finish; she doesn't have to. Nearly everyone is already suffering the symptoms of reduced micronutrients: anemia, weakened immune systems, and reduced hormone production.

Jenna hurls the tray of useless plants to the greenhouse floor. Zane shudders.

• • •

We come together after dark, to plan. The village in the valley is not large, but it is important for its size. There is a scientific facility, a small soap manufactury, and a textile mill, all powered by the turbine set into the swift river. Cottages, each with its neat garden. Their windows glow with electric light, but it is torches that illuminate the meadow near the river, where the music comes from. "A dance," Carl says half scornfully, half wistfully.

I train the night-vision goggles on the festivities. The villages are always celebrating something or other. Fools.

"Two of them," I say. "Watching the dancing. I'll do recon. You get into position."

• • •

I watch Jenna dance with Zane, scrutinizing them with a father's eye. His face in the torchlight glows with love. Hers does not. Well, Zane will get over it. Puppy love isn't fatal; desire, even less so. Not that Zane's body—dancing inches away from Jenna, his hand barely touching her waist—expresses much desire. Pre-Blessing people apparently tore themselves apart over sex, which makes no sense. It's just a mild pleasure, like a lovely sunset or a good cup of coffee, and of course it's necessary to produce the next generation. I can't remember the last time I had sex. If the scientific literature is right and the Blessing also created changes in human hormone production, then that's another reason to thank the Dant. We are spared rape, adultery, population overgrowth, and the kinds of violence to Mutuality that I read about in incomprehensible books stored in my grandmother's attic: *Anna Karenina, Lolita, Romeo and Juliet.*

"Larry, do you want to dance?"

Rachel Notting. She's a good dancer. I smile, get to my feet, and move into the circle of dancers—just as a beam of blue light slices down from the sky and explodes beyond the hill.

People scream. A few, the most sensitive, freeze into Extreme Involuntary Fear Bradycardia. Kyra Hanreddy, our mayor this cycle, cries, "Everyone to the community hall! Mutuality!"

People move toward the hall, no one faster than the slowest. Jenna pushes Mr. Caruthers's wheelchair. I help Rachel with her twins. The frozen are soothingly coaxed into normal heartbeats and led forward. Katherine Pacer, an extreme sensitive, is carried stiff as a plank by two men. The Dant have disappeared.

I have seen this before, in another village. Jenna has not. As I walk beside her, carrying a twin sweating and gasping with EIFB, she gasps, "What is it?"

"Alien protection. Probably bears."

She nods, reassured. Dant23 and Dant16 have warned us before when bears, who somehow were made *more* aggressive by the Blessing, are in the area. A Dant ship in orbit chases the bears away. I suspect that the ships actually kill the animals, but I don't want to think about fried and smoking bears.

In the Hall, the Council closes the shutters. Everyone listens for a while, but there is nothing to hear. Eventually the musicians begin again on fiddle and guitar, and the dancing resumes inside. Katherine Pacer unfreezes, watching with dazed eyes, friends hovering over her. Three songs later, Dant23 and Dant16 knock on the door and are admitted. No one asks them anything. We wouldn't understand the answers anyway.

• • •

The bastards got them all. There isn't even anything left to bury. Damn them, damn them to an alien hell in agony and tears.

The supplies and weapons were with the cadre. Hannah's group is only forty miles northwest; I can join them. But all at once I know that I won't.

Hidden under a brush fall, I spend the night silently chanting the farewell song for my dead.

Carl, sixteen years old.

Kaylie, the best shot I ever saw.

Jerome, who ran away from his village at eleven and somehow survived alone until we found him.

Matt, Ruhan, Pedro, Susan, Terry.

Rest in fucking peace.

• • •

I stand in the greenhouse, staring at the tray of crossbred wheat plants. Morning light streams like green water through the uneven glass; there must have been iron oxide impurities in the glassmaker's last firing. The steamy air smells loamy, rich with life.

Jenna comes in. "Oh, it's so hot in here and—Dad? What is it?"

"I ran the tests on the ashing filtrate from this last batch."

"And... ?" Her pretty face wrinkles quizzically.

"The strain is producing ten percent more zinc than either parent plant."

Now Jenna stares at the plants. "Ten percent *more?* But how... ."

"I don't know. If we had a gene sequencer... ."

She grimaces, then tries to console me. "Wheat was never genetically engineered anyway, only crossbred. Do you really need a sequencer? The important thing is the increased nutrition."

"Yes," I say, smiling at her, "of course." And there it is—Jenna's major flaw as a scientist. She is intelligent, meticulous, even inventive. But she is mostly interested in practical results: Of what use is this? Not: Why did this happen?

Why *did* this happen? I have a theory, but no way to test it.

"Dad," she says, "will you run the tests on of my soybeans—tray number eighteen? Julie and Gary and Miguel are getting together a group to hike into the mountains. We'll be back by dark, but they want to leave right away, and they only got around to informing me *now.*"

There is no rancor in the way she says this, only pleasure in the proposed expedition. I think about bears, then remind myself that attacks are less frequent than when I was a boy, that Jenna has tranquilizer darts, that she's not an extreme sensitive. I say, "Of course I'll run your tests. Have fun."

"Thanks!"

Before she can leave, however, the door opens and a stranger limps in. We both smile at him. "Hello," I say, "I'm Larry Travis. Can we help you?"

"Jake Martin," he says. His smile seems strained. Is he ill? "I'm on my way to Bremerville to see my sister, but I hurt my leg. Hoping I can stay here a few days."

"Of course. We have room at our bungalow. This is my daughter, Jenna."

She says, "What's wrong with your leg? Do you need a doctor? I can send for one from Castleton."

"No, ma'am, I just need to stay off it a bit."

"Jenna, take him to the bungalow and get him something to eat. No, wait—you want to hike. Jake, do you mind waiting here about half an hour while I finish up a—"

Jenna says quickly, "I'll take him."

"But you—"

"I'm happy to take him." She smiles again at the stranger, and he says, "Thank you."

As they leave, him leaning a little on her shoulder to favor his left leg, I stare after them. Why did Jenna so abruptly change her mind?

I shrug and begin the dry-ashing procedure on her soybeans.

• • •

No enemies sighted yet. But they're here. I buried my guns in the woods; they can detect metal at close range. Meanwhile, there is this woman, taking me home, collecting some hot food from a refectory, letting me lean on her all the way. I don't need to lean on her, and I think she knows that. She and her father take me in without a second thought—nobody here would harm anyone else. But this woman… How can she be one of the dehumanized, alien-whipped, de-sexed sheep? Her?

She smells like strawberries.

"How did you hurt your leg?"

"Stupid clumsiness," I lie, and she laughs. The laugh sounds confused.

We talk, although it's hard to keep my mind concentrated. She's smart and—like all of them—sweet. But she isn't like all of them.

My cock is like stone.

This woman…

• • •

Dant23 comes in to the lab as I finish the tests. He waves his tentacles at me and I smile. I show him Zane's and my own handwritten notes on the zinc percentages in different wheat strains.

Does he read them? Does he somehow photograph them with his eyes and transmit them to some unimaginable computer somewhere? Does he only pretend to know what they mean? There is no way to tell.

The Dant came down from their ship twenty years ago, when everyone alive from before the Blessing was very old, and we still know almost nothing about them. Not why they chose to help humanity by altering our genes for EIFB. Not why they chose a volcano, of all things, to distribute the molecules that conferred that incalculable boon. Obviously, they wanted to be able to contact humanity without risk of violence to themselves, but we, not them, are the major beneficiaries of their Blessing.

The library at Bremerton has books, very old, with pictures in them that I saw only once, years ago, and still have nightmares about. Worldwide wars. Bodies in trenches. Instruments of medieval torture. Children spitted, women raped, cows slaughtered for meat. People who ate *flesh*.

Dant23 makes a noise, waves a different tentacle, and settles into a corner of the lab to observe.

• • •

She wants it, too, although when I begin, she seems startled at herself. I would bet my rifle that she didn't know she could experience desire like this—how would she know, living here? She's a virgin. Then I'm the one who's startled. I have never known sex like this. She holds nothing back. Not while we do it, not while we talk. And it doesn't seem to occur to her that I might be holding back. Without knowing me at all, she trusts me utterly—not to hurt her, not to lie to her, not to ignore her pleasure.

Is she fucking crazy?

I reach for her again.

• • •

I transfer the soybean filtrate into a beaker and prepare the reagent. But then the ancient spectrophotometer refuses to turn on. The display stays dark. Nothing lights, nothing works, nothing I do repairs it. The thing is finally dead.

I've lost equipment before. But for some reason, this loss affects me profoundly. I sit on a stool and sob like a four-year-old.

Maybe it's the low zinc and iron in my blood. For millions of years, humans absorbed zinc and iron mostly from animal flesh. Barbarianism should not be the price of health.

Or maybe it's not what's in my blood but what's in my head.

Eventually I rise from the stool and splash cold water on my face. I can't stand to be in the lab any longer. It's dusk and music has started by the river, for the second day of the festival. There will be people there, laughter, Mutuality. I make my way toward the bright music, trying to let it overcome the ideas circling, like savage bears, in my bruised mind.

• • •

"There's a dance tonight," Jenna says, "part of the Blessing festival. I know you can't dance but there's a bonfire and music and games and it's fun."

She lies tangled in soft, worn, clean sheets in the last rays of sun slanting through a high window. Her bare breasts rise and fall gently. Her hair is as tangled as the sheets and her eyes are bright, gray flecked with gold.

The enemy might be at the dance.

So far, at least, I've passed as one of these.... "people."

She's talked all afternoon. I know her now. How can she be one of them?

I make myself remember Carl, sixteen years old.

Kaylie, the best shot I ever saw.

Jerome, who ran away from his village at eleven and somehow survived alone until we found him.

Matt, Ruhan, Pedro, Susan, Terry.

• • •

Both Dant16 and Dant23 are at the dance, standing in the shadows beyond the bonfire, observing. What if I showed them the broken absorption spectrophotometer and pantomimed a great need for another? Would they make me one, or the alien equivalent? Can their tech really be so different that they cannot replace ours?

Or do they want us to have, year after year, less and less?

• • •

Jenna says shyly, "I'm going to say something dumb."

We walk toward the river. In the warm twilight she wears only loose pants and a sleeveless tunic of some woven blue cloth. She doesn't notice, or at least doesn't remark on, my long heavy jacket. Her hand moves ceaselessly in mine, like some small fidgety animal.

"What dumb thing are you going to say?"

"I think... that you're different."

I tense. Oh, God, no... what has she noticed? Will she betray me? I don't want to have to—

"You're different because you're like me," she says. "Nobody else here is. Not really."

My free hand moves back from my jacket pocket. I say cautiously, "I am? How?"

"I don't know." Her voice is troubled. "Well, yes, the sex... I never felt any of that wanting before, not like.... Jake, why did I feel like that about you but never before? Who are you, really?"

All at once, to my own astonishment, I want to tell her. But I can't, and I don't want her thinking about my differences from her people. So I pull her toward me and say, to distract her, "Someone who's falling in love with you."

But if it's really to distract her, then why do I say it so softly that maybe I don't want her to hear?

Then I see them under the trees, standing beside Jenna's father.

• • •

Dant16 waves one tentacle, vaguely in time with the music. Dancers stomp and whirl on the flattened grass. The river murmurs, shining in the moonlight, reflecting the bonfire flames. From somewhere comes the sweet odor of wild mint.

How can I be thinking what is gnawing at my brain?

Jenna and Jake come along the path from the bungalows. She tries to pull him toward the dance; he shakes his head, smiling. There's something wrong with his smile but I don't know what. The bonfire behind them haloes both their heads with dancing gold. The fiddles sing; crickets chirp in the grass; the rising moon shines every moment brighter in the darkening sky.

Jenna turns to talk to Kay Caruthers. Jenna looks as if she is introducing Jake, but he is no longer there. He moves quickly toward me, not running but with no sign of his limp. Closer, and I can see his wrong smile. "Hello, Larry," he says, pulls a ceramic knife from his jacket and plunges it into Dant16's forehead.

I can't move. My heart slows and vertigo swoops over me.

Dant23 lets out a shrill, prolonged shriek I have never heard before. He tries to run but Jake pulls the knife from Dant16 and drives it, lightning fast, into Dant23. Both aliens crumple to the grass, oozing foul-smelling liquid.

People rush over, freeze, sway or crumple or stare, eyes wide, mouths gaping, oxygenation and heart rate falling.

All but Jenna.

She runs to Jake and beats him—beats him!—with small, ineffectual fists. "Why? Why?"

He grabs her arms and pins them to her sides. His shoulders shake—this has cost him, too, but not enough. Not nearly enough. "Carl," he gasps, "Kaylie, Jerome, Matt…"

"Why?"

Neither of them show any signs of EIFB. I don't wonder about the reason. I know.

"Listen, Jenna," Jake says. He has control of himself now. He's wrestled her against him so that she cannot strike. "They're the enemy. They fucked up our biology, made us—"

"They made us *better!*"

"No. They made us sheep, passive and fearful so that we won't interfere while they take over Earth. They want our planet."

"They gave us the Blessing! No more violence, no more wars—"

"No more progress, no more discoveries, almost no more sex! How many more generations before humans disappear completely? And all without the violence they can't stand face-to-face, any more than these people can."

"But you—"

"I what?" He holds her more gently now; she struggles less. My breath comes more normally.

Jenna says, "You were able to—*how?*"

"Because I had to. *We* have to—listen, there are more of us. More than you might think. We want the Dant to leave. With enough violence, they *will* leave. We'll convince them that Earth will never be free of humans. If the fuckers don't wipe us out first."

"The Dant don't—"

"Yes," he says grimly, "they do. They laser us from space, like the cowards they are. But we will succeed."

Zane and Ted are coming out of EIFB. Uncertainly, they step toward Jake. He raises his fist and both retreat.

I find my voice. "You don't know what success is."

Jake says savagely, "I know what it isn't."

Jenna—my Jenna, bewildered and upset but not nearly enough frightened—says, "But I still don't understand why the—"

"Jenna, I don't have time for this! Don't you understand? I have to leave now, before whatever trackers these bastards use finds me. I have to go."

They look at each other. I don't understand the look. I have never been in the place they are now: wild, challenging, hot.

I think *No no no no no...*

"Daddy," she says, turning toward me, and I know I've already lost. She hasn't called me "Daddy" for years. "Daddy" was Jenna at three, running toward me to be lifted into my arms. At seven, holding my hands on a walk by a sun-dappled river. At eleven, chin in her hand, listening as I explained crossbreeding plants. Jenna who loved me, not some example of outdated, over-sexed, dangerous "masculinity" with a knife in his hand and an attitude that could destroy the world.

Or remake it.

Tears choke Jenna's voice. "Daddy, I have to go with him." And then fiercely, "I have to *know*. If he's wrong, I'll come back."

She trusts that he would let her go. She trusts everything. He trusts nothing.

Yet they are alike. I know this in ways that Jake, not a scientist, never will. I know it because a crossbred strain of wheat contains far more zinc than either parent plant. Because bear attacks, however terrible, are milder than in my great-grandmother Carrie's day, or my grandmother Sophie's, or mine. Because I've read about regression to the mean, about genetic "throwbacks" that always counterbalance Darwinian selection. About the eternally disturbed, and then restored, balance between predator and prey, violence and cooperation, sex and aggression.

Jenna kisses me. Jake has the grace to say, "Larry, I'm sorry." Then they are running, sprinting hand-in-hand toward the cover of the dark woods.

Around me, the villagers—my people—move, shudder, sob. The bodies of Dant16 and Dant23 lie at my feet. On the horizon, a blue dot appears in the sky, moving fast.

I can't imagine what kind of world Jake and Jenna will make, what kind of world their children will inherit. I don't want to imagine it. But I know, in my bones, that it will come.

ABOUT THE AUTHORS

Carrie Vaughn is the author of the New York Times bestselling series of novels about a werewolf named Kitty, the most recent installment of which is *Kitty Saves the World*. She's written several other contemporary fantasy and young adult novels, as well as upwards of 80 short stories. She's a contributor to the Wild Cards series of shared world superhero books edited by George R. R. Martin and a graduate of the Odyssey Fantasy Writing Workshop. An Air Force brat, she survived her nomadic childhood and managed to put down roots in Boulder, Colorado. Visit her at carrievaughn.com.

Megan Arkenberg lives and writes in California. Her short stories have appeared in *Lightspeed, Asimov's, Strange Horizons,* and dozens of other places. She procrastinates by editing the fantasy e-zine *Mirror Dance*.

Will McIntosh is a Hugo award winner and Nebula finalist whose debut novel, *Soft Apocalypse,* was a finalist for a Locus Award, the John W. Campbell Memorial Award, and the Compton Crook Award. His latest novel is *Defenders* (May, 2014; Orbit Books), an alien apocalypse novel with a twist. It has been optioned by Warner Brothers for a feature film. Along with four novels, he has published dozens of short stories in venues such as *Lightspeed, Asimov's* (where he won the 2010 Reader's Award), and *The Year's Best Science Fiction & Fantasy*. Will was a psychology professor for two decades before turning to writing full-time. He lives in Williamsburg with his wife and their five year-old twins.

Scott Sigler is the *New York Times* bestselling author of the Infected trilogy (*Infected, Contagious,* and *Pandemic*), *Ancestor,* and *Nocturnal,* hardcover thrillers from Crown Publishing; and the co-founder of Empty Set Entertainment, which publishes his Galactic Football League series (*The Rookie, The Starter, The All-Pro,* and *The MVP*). Before he was published,

Scott built a large online following by giving away his self-recorded audio-books as free, serialized podcasts. His loyal fans, who named themselves "Junkies," have downloaded over eight million individual episodes of his stories and interact daily with Scott and each other in the social media space.

Sarah Langan is the author of the novels *The Keeper, This Missing,* and *Audrey's Door.* Her work has garnered three Bram Stoker Awards, a *New York Times* Editor's Pick, an ALA selection, and a *Publishers Weekly* favorite Book of the Year selection. Her short fiction has appeared in *Nightmare Magazine, Brave New Worlds, Fantasy Magazine, Lightspeed Magazine, The Magazine of Fantasy & Science Fiction,* and elsewhere. She's at work on her fourth novel, *The Clinic,* and lives in Brooklyn with her husband and two daughters.

Chris Avellone is the Creative Director of Obsidian Entertainment. He started his career at Interplay's Black Isle Studios division, and he's worked on a whole menagerie of RPGs throughout his career including *Planescape: Torment, Fallout 2,* the Icewind Dale series, *Dark Alliance, Knights of the Old Republic II, Neverwinter Nights 2, Mask of the Betrayer, Alpha Protocol, Fallout: New Vegas, FNV* DLC: *Dead Money, Old World Blues,* and *Lonesome Road.* He just finished working on inXile's *Wasteland 2,* the *Legend of Grimrock* movie treatment, and the *FTL: Advanced Edition* and is currently doing joint work on Obsidian's Kickstarter RPG: *Pillars of Eternity* and inXile's *Torment: Tides of Numenera.*

Seanan McGuire was born and raised in Northern California, resulting in a love of rattlesnakes and an absolute terror of weather. She shares a crumbling old farmhouse with a variety of cats, far too many books, and enough horror movies to be considered a problem. Seanan publishes about three books a year, and is widely rumored not to actually sleep. When bored, Seanan tends to wander into swamps and cornfields, which has not yet managed to get her killed (although not for lack of trying). She also writes as Mira Grant, filling the role of her own evil twin, and tends to talk about horrible diseases at the dinner table.

Leife Shallcross lives in Canberra, Australia. There is a possum living in a tree by her front gate and sometimes kangaroos visit her front garden in the night. Her work has appeared in *Aurealis* and several Australian anthologies of speculative fiction. She is the current president of the Canberra Speculative Fiction Guild. When her family, writing, and day job are not consuming her time and energy, she plays the fiddle (badly). She is currently working on her first novel. Leife can be found online at leifeshallcross.com and on Twitter @leioss.

Ben H. Winters is the winner of the Edgar Award for his novel *The Last Policeman*, which was also an Amazon.com Best Book of 2012. The sequel, *Countdown City*, won the Philip K. Dick Award; the third volume in the trilogy is *World of Trouble*. Other works of fiction include the middle-grade novel *The Secret Life of Ms. Finkleman*, an Edgar Award nominee, and the parody novel *Sense and Sensibility and Sea Monsters*, a *New York Times* bestseller. Ben has written extensively for the stage and is a past fellow of the Dramatists Guild. His journalism has appeared in *Slate*, *The Nation*, *The Chicago Reader*, and many other publications. He lives in Indianapolis, Indiana and at BenHWinters.com.

David Wellington is the author of the Monster Island trilogy of zombie novels, the 13 Bullets series of vampire books, and most recently the Jim Chapel thrillers *Chimera* and *The Hydra Protocol*. "Agent Unknown" *(The End is Nigh)* and "Agent Isolated" are prequels to *Positive*, his forthcoming zombie epic. He lives and works in Brooklyn, New York.

Annie Bellet is the author of *The Twenty-Sided Sorceress* and the Gryphonpike Chronicles series. She holds a BA in English and a BA in Medieval Studies and thus can speak a smattering of useful languages such as Anglo-Saxon and Medieval Welsh. Her short fiction is available in multiple collections and anthologies. Her interests besides writing include rock climbing, reading, horseback riding, video games, comic books, table-top RPGs, and many other nerdy pursuits. She lives in the Pacific Northwest with her husband and a very demanding Bengal cat. Find her on her website at anniebellet.com.

Tananarive Due is the Cosby Chair in the Humanities at Spelman College. She also teaches in the creative writing MFA program at Antioch University Los Angeles. The American Book Award winner and NAACP Image Award recipient has authored and/or co-authored twelve novels and a civil rights memoir. In 2013, she received a Lifetime Achievement Award in the Fine Arts from the Congressional Black Caucus Foundation. In 2010, she was inducted into the Medill School of Journalism's Hall of Achievement at Northwestern University. She has also taught at the Geneva Writers Conference, the Clarion Science Fiction & Fantasy Writers' Workshop, and Voices of Our Nations Art Foundation (VONA). Due's supernatural thriller *The Living Blood* won a 2002 American Book Award. Her novella "Ghost Summer," published in the 2008 anthology *The Ancestors*, received the 2008 Kindred Award from the Carl Brandon Society, and her short fiction has appeared in best-of-the-year anthologies of science fiction and fantasy. Due is a leading voice in black speculative fiction.

Robin Wasserman is the author of *The Waking Dark*, *The Book of Blood and Shadow*, the Cold Awakening Trilogy, *Hacking Harvard*, and the Seven Deadly Sins series, which was adapted into a popular television miniseries. Her essays and short fiction have appeared in several anthologies as well as *The Atlantic* and *The New York Times*. A former children's book editor, she is on the faculty of the low-residency MFA program at Southern New Hampshire University. She lives and writes (and frequently procrastinates) in Brooklyn, New York. Find out more about her at robinwasserman.com or follow her on Twitter @robinwasserman.

Jamie Ford is the great grandson of Nevada mining pioneer Min Chung, who emigrated from Kaiping, China, to San Francisco in 1865, where he adopted the western name "Ford," thus confusing countless generations. His debut novel, *Hotel on the Corner of Bitter and Sweet*, spent two years on the *New York Times* bestseller list and went on to win the 2010 Asian/Pacific American Award for Literature. His work has been translated into 32 languages. Jamie is still holding out for Klingon (because that's when you know you've made it). He can be found at www.jamieford.com blogging about his new book, *Songs of Willow Frost*, and also on Twitter @jamieford.

Elizabeth Bear was born on the same day as Frodo and Bilbo Baggins, but in a different year. When coupled with a tendency to read the dictionary for fun as a child, this led her inevitably to penury, intransigence, and the writing of speculative fiction. She is the Hugo, Sturgeon, and Campbell Award-winning author of almost a hundred short stories and more than twenty-five novels, the most recent of which is *Steles of the Sky*, from Tor Books. Her dog lives in Massachusetts; her partner, writer Scott Lynch, lives in Wisconsin. She spends a lot of time on planes.

Jonathan Maberry is a *New York Times* bestselling author, multiple Bram Stoker Award winner, and comic book writer. He's the author of many novels including *Code Zero*, *Fire & Ash*, *The Nightsiders*, *Dead of Night*, and *Rot & Ruin*; and the editor of the *V-Wars* shared-world anthologies. His nonfiction books on topics ranging from martial arts to zombie pop-culture. Jonathan writes *V-Wars* and *Rot & Ruin* for IDW Comics, and *Bad Blood* for Dark Horse, as well as multiple projects for Marvel. Since 1978 he has sold more than 1200 magazine feature articles, 3000 columns, two plays, greeting cards, song lyrics, poetry, and textbooks. Jonathan continues to teach the celebrated Experimental Writing for Teens class, which he created. He founded the Writers Coffeehouse and co-founded The Liars Club; and is a frequent speaker at schools and libraries, as well as a keynote speaker and guest of honor at major writers and genre conferences. He lives in Del Mar, California. Find him online at jonathanmaberry.com.

Charlie Jane Anders' is the author of *All the Birds in the Sky*, a novel coming in early 2016 from Tor Books. She is the editor in chief of io9.com and the organizer of the Writers With Drinks reading series. Her stories have appeared in *Asimov's Science Fiction, The Magazine of Fantasy & Science Fiction, Tor.com, Lightspeed, Tin House, ZYZZYVA*, and several anthologies. Her novelette "Six Months, Three Days" won a Hugo award.

Jake Kerr began writing short fiction in 2010 after fifteen years as a music and radio industry columnist and journalist. His first published story, "The Old Equations," appeared in *Lightspeed* and went on to be named a finalist for the Nebula Award and the Theodore Sturgeon Memorial Award. He has subsequently been published in *Fireside Magazine, Escape Pod*, and the *Unidentified Funny Objects* anthology of humorous SF. A graduate of Kenyon College with degrees in English and Psychology, Kerr studied under writer-in-residence Ursula K. Le Guin and Peruvian playwright Alonso Alegria. He lives in Dallas, Texas, with his wife and three daughters.

Ken Liu (http://kenliu.name) is an author and translator of speculative fiction, as well as a lawyer and programmer. A winner of the Nebula, Hugo, and World Fantasy Awards, he has been published in *The Magazine of Fantasy & Science Fiction, Asimov's, Analog, Clarkesworld, Lightspeed*, and *Strange Horizons*, among other places. Ken's debut novel, *The Grace of Kings*, the first in a silkpunk epic fantasy series, will be published by Saga Press, Simon & Schuster's new genre fiction imprint, in April 2015. A collection of his short stories will also be published by Saga in 2015.

Mira Grant hails from somewhere between hell and high water, with an emphasis on whichever is drier at the moment. She spends most of her time researching things most people are happier not knowing about. Mira is the author of the Newsflesh trilogy, as well as the Parasitism series. In her spare time, Mira likes to visit Disney Parks around the world, which is possibly one of her creepiest hobbies. She also writes as Seanan McGuire, filling the role of her own good twin, and hopes you realize that the noise you just heard probably wasn't the wind.

Hugh Howey is the *New York Times* bestselling author of *Wool, Shift, Dust, Sand*, the Molly Fyde series, *The Hurricane, Half Way Home, The Plagiarist*, and *I, Zombie*. Hugh lives on a boat at sea. Find him on Twitter @hughhowey.

Nancy Kress is the author of thirty-two books, including twenty-five novels, four collections of short stories, and three books on writing. Her work has won five Nebulas, two Hugos, a Sturgeon, and the John W. Campbell Memorial Award. Most recent works are *Yesterday's Kin* (Tachyon, 2014) and the forthcoming *Best of Nancy Kress* (Subterranean, Autumn 2015). In addition to writing, Kress often teaches at various venues around the country and abroad; in 2008 she was the Picador visiting lecturer at the University of Leipzig. Kress lives in Seattle with her husband, writer Jack Skillingstead, and Cosette, the world's most spoiled toy poodle.

ACKNOWLEDGMENTS

Agents: John thanks his agent Seth Fishman, who supported this experiment and provided feedback and counsel whenever he needed it, and also to his former agent Joe Monti (now a book editor who he plans to sell lots of anthologies to), who was very enthusiastic about this idea when it first occurred to him, and encouraged John to pursue his idea to self-publish it. Hugh likewise thanks his agent Kristin Nelson for all of her support and for constantly playing out his leash.

Art/Design: Thanks to Julian Aguilar Faylona for providing wonderful cover art for all three volumes of The Apocalypse Triptych, and to Jason Gurley for adding in all the most excellent design elements that took the artwork from being mere images and transformed them into *books*. These volumes would not be the same without them.

Proofreaders: Thanks to Rachael Jones, Anthony Cardno, Kevin McNeil, Andy Sima, and Adam Dwyer.

Narrators/Producers: Thanks to Stefan Rudnicki and the whole team at Skyboat Media for producing the audiobook version of this anthology, and to narrators Vikas Adam, Gabrielle de Cuir, Justine Eyre, Roxanne Hernandez, Alex Hyde-White, Emily Rankin, Stefan Rudnicki, and Judy Young for lending their vocal talents to the production.

Family: John sends thanks to his wife, Christie, his mom, Marianne, and his sister, Becky, for all their love and support, and their endless enthusiasm for all his new projects. He also wanted to thank his sister-in-law Kate and stepdaughter Grace who had to listen to him blab incessantly about this project as it was coming together, ruining many a dinner. Hugh thanks his wife Amber, who co-edits this wonderful life they have together. His chapters would be boring and lonely without her.

Readers: Thanks to all the readers and reviewers of this anthology, and also all the readers and reviewers who loved Hugh's novels and John's other anthologies, making it possible for this book to happen in the first place.

Writers: And last, but certainly not least: a big thanks to all of the authors who appear in this anthology. It has been an honor and a privilege. As fans, we look forward to whatever you come up with next.

ABOUT THE EDITORS

John Joseph Adams is the series editor of *Best American Science Fiction & Fantasy*, published by Houghton Mifflin Harcourt. He is also the bestselling editor of many other anthologies, such as *The Mad Scientist's Guide to World Domination, Armored, Brave New Worlds, Wastelands,* and *The Living Dead.* Called "the reigning king of the anthology world" by Barnes & Noble, John is a winner of the Hugo Award (for which he has been nominated nine times) and is a six-time World Fantasy Award finalist. John is also the editor and publisher of the digital magazines *Lightspeed* and *Nightmare,* and is a producer for Wired.com's *The Geek's Guide to the Galaxy* podcast. Find him on Twitter @johnjosephadams.

Hugh Howey is the author of the acclaimed post-apocalyptic novel *Wool,* which became a sudden success in 2011. Originally self-published as a series of novelettes, the *Wool* omnibus is frequently the #1 bestselling book on Amazon.com and is a *New York Times* and *USA TODAY* bestseller. The book was also optioned for film by Ridley Scott, and is now available in print from major publishers all over the world. Hugh's other books include *Shift, Dust, Sand,* the Molly Fyde series, *The Hurricane, Half Way Home, The Plagiarist,* and *I, Zombie.* Hugh lives on a boat in the middle of the ocean. Find him on Twitter @hughhowey.

COPYRIGHT ACKNOWLEDGMENTS

THE END HAS COME
© 2015 by John Joseph Adams & Hugh Howey

INTRODUCTION
© 2015 by John Joseph Adams

BANNERLESS
© 2015 by CARRIE VAUGHN

LIKE ALL BEAUTIFUL PLACES
© 2015 by Megan Arkenberg

DANCING WITH A STRANGER IN THE LAND OF NOD
© 2015 by Will McIntosh

THE SEVENTH DAY OF DEER CAMP
© 2015 by Scott Sigler

PROTOTYPE
© 2015 by Sarah Langan

ACTS OF CREATION
© 2015 by Chris Avellone

RESISTANCE
© 2015 by Seanan McGuire

WANDERING STAR
© 2015 by Leife Shallcross

HEAVEN COME DOWN
© 2015 by Ben H. Winters

AGENT NEUTRALIZED
© 2015 by David Wellington

GOODNIGHT EARTH
© 2015 by Annie Bellet

CARRIERS
© 2015 by Tananarive Due

IN THE VALLEY OF THE SHADOW OF THE PROMISED LAND
© 2015 by Robin Wasserman

THE UNCERTAINTY MACHINE
© 2015 by Jamie Ford

MARGIN OF SURVIVAL
© 2015 by Elizabeth Bear

JINGO AND THE HAMMERMAN
© 2015 by Jonathan Maberry

THE LAST MOVIE EVER MADE
© 2015 by Charlie Jane Anders

THE GRAY SUNRISE
© 2015 by Jake Kerr

THE GODS HAVE NOT DIED IN VAIN
© 2015 by Ken Liu

THE HAPPIEST PLACE…
© 2015 by Mira Grant

IN THE WOODS
© 2015 by Hugh Howey

BLESSINGS
© 2015 by Nancy Kress

Cover Art by Julian Aguilar Faylona.
Cover Design by Jason Gurley.
Ebook Design by John Joseph Adams.

THE APOCALYPSE TRIPTYCH

We hope you've enjoyed reading this series. It has been our pleasure bringing these works to you. If you missed the first two entries, be sure to check out *The End is Nigh* and *The End is Now.*

Famine. Death. War. Pestilence. These are the harbingers of the biblical apocalypse, of the End of the World. In science fiction, the end is triggered by less figurative means: nuclear holocaust, biological warfare/pandemic, ecological disaster, or cosmological cataclysm.

But before any catastrophe, there are people who see it coming. During, there are heroes who fight against it. And after, there are the survivors who persevere and try to rebuild. THE APOCALYPSE TRIPTYCH will tell their stories.

Edited by acclaimed anthologist John Joseph Adams and bestselling author Hugh Howey, THE APOCALYPSE TRIPTYCH is a series of three anthologies of apocalyptic fiction. *The End is Nigh* focuses on life before the apocalypse. *The End is Now* turns its attention to life during the apocalypse. And *The End Has Come* focuses on life after the apocalypse.

Visit johnjosephadams.com/apocalypse-triptych to learn more about THE APOCALYPSE TRIPTYCH or to read interviews with the authors.

OTHER APOCALYPTIC BOOKS BY JOHN JOSEPH ADAMS

In addition to the three books in THE APOCALYPSE TRIPTYCH, editor John Joseph Adams has also edited several other anthologies of a similar thematic nature that you might enjoy:

WASTELANDS: STORIES OF THE APOCALYPSE
edited by John Joseph Adams
Night Shade Books, January 2008

From the Book of Revelation to *The Road Warrior;* from *A Canticle for Leibowitz* to *The Road,* storytellers have long imagined the end of the world, weaving eschatological tales of catastrophe, chaos, and calamity. In doing so, these visionary authors have addressed one of the most challenging and enduring themes of imaginative fiction: the nature of life in the aftermath of total societal collapse.

Gathering together the best post-apocalyptic literature of the last two decades from many of today's most renowned authors of speculative fiction—including George R.R. Martin, Gene Wolfe, Orson Scott Card, Carol Emshwiller, Jonathan Lethem, Octavia E. Butler, and Stephen King—*Wastelands* explores the scientific, psychological, and philosophical questions of what it means to remain human in the wake of Armageddon.

johnjosephadams.com/wastelands

WASTELANDS 2: MORE STORIES OF THE APOCALYPSE
edited by John Joseph Adams
Titan Books, February 2015

For decades, the apocalypse and its aftermath have yielded some of the most exciting short stories of all time. From David Brin's seminal "The Postman" to Hugh Howey's "Deep Blood Kettle" and Tananarive Due's prescient "Patient Zero," the end of the world continues to thrill. This companion volume to the critically-acclaimed *Wastelands* offers thirty of the finest examples of post-apocalyptic short fiction, including works by George R.R. Martin, Junot Díaz, Seanan McGuire, Paolo Bacigalupi, and more. Award-winning editor John Joseph Adams has once again assembled a who's who of short fiction, and the result is nothing short of mind-blowing.

johnjosephadams.com/wastelands-2

THE LIVING DEAD
edited by John Joseph Adams
Night Shade Books, September 2008

From *White Zombie* to *Dawn of the Dead*, from *Resident Evil* to *World War Z*, zombies have invaded popular culture, becoming the monsters that best express the fears and anxieties of the modern west. The ultimate consumers, zombies rise from the dead and feed upon the living, their teeming masses ever hungry, ever seeking to devour or convert, like mindless, faceless eating machines. Zombies have been depicted as mind-controlled minions, the shambling infected, the disintegrating dead, the ultimate *lumpenproletariat*, but in all cases, they reflect us, mere mortals afraid of death in a society on the verge of collapse.

Gathering together the best zombie literature of the last three decades from many of today's most renowned authors of fantasy, speculative fiction, and horror, including Stephen King, Harlan Ellison®, Robert Silverberg, George R. R. Martin, Clive Barker, Poppy Z. Brite, Neil Gaiman, Joe Hill, Laurell K. Hamilton, and Joe R. Lansdale, *The Living Dead*, covers the broad spectrum of zombie fiction, ranging from Romero-style zombies to reanimated corpses to voodoo zombies and beyond.

johnjosephadams.com/the-living-dead

THE LIVING DEAD 2
edited by John Joseph Adams
Night Shade Books, September 2010

Readers eagerly devoured *The Living Dead*. Now acclaimed editor John Joseph Adams is back for another bite at the apple—the Adam's apple, that is—with 43 more of the best, most chilling, most thrilling zombie stories anywhere, including virtuoso performances by zombie fiction legends Max Brooks *(World War Z, The Zombie Survival Guide)*, Robert Kirkman *(The Walking Dead)*, and David Wellington *(Monster Island)*.

From *Left 4 Dead* to *Zombieland* to *Pride and Prejudice and Zombies*, ghoulishness has never been more exciting and relevant. Within these pages samurai warriors face off against the legions of hell, necrotic dinosaurs haunt a mysterious lost world, and eerily clever zombies organize their mindless brethren into a terrifying army.

The Living Dead 2 has more of what zombie fans hunger for—more scares, more action, more... brains. Experience the indispensable series that defines the very best in zombie literature.

johnjosephadams.com/the-living-dead-2

ROBOT UPRISINGS
edited by Daniel H. Wilson & John Joseph Adams
Vintage Books, April 2014

As real robots creep into our lives, so does a sense of fear—we have all wondered what horrifying scenarios might unfold if our technology were to go awry. The idea of a robot uprising is fascinating precisely because it is possible. This anthology will bring to life the answers to our half-formed questions by providing a collection of meticulously precise, exhilarating trips into a future in which humans survive only by being more clever and tenacious than the machines they have created.

At the helm of this project are Daniel H. Wilson—bestselling novelist and expert in robotics—and John Joseph Adams—bestselling editor of more than a dozen science fiction/fantasy anthologies. Together, they have drawn on their wide-ranging contacts to assemble a talented group of authors eager to attack the topic of robot uprisings from startling and fascinating angles.

Featuring work by Hugh Howey, Seanan McGuire, Scott Sigler, Charles Yu, Anna North, Robin Wasserman, Ernest Cline, Jeff Abbott, Julianna Baggott, and many more, plus a new novella from Daniel H. Wilson.

johnjosephadams.com/robot-uprisings

BRAVE NEW WORLDS
edited by John Joseph Adams
Night Shade Books, January 2011

You are being watched.

When the government wields its power against its own people, every citizen becomes an enemy of the state. Will you fight the system, or be ground to dust beneath the boot of tyranny?

In his smash-hit anthologies *Wastelands* and *The Living Dead*, acclaimed editor John Joseph Adams showed you what happens when society is utterly wiped away. Now he brings you a glimpse into an equally terrifying future—what happens when civilization invades and dictates every aspect of your life?

From *1984* to *The Handmaid's Tale*, from *Children of Men* to *Bioshock*, the dystopian imagination has been a vital and gripping cautionary force. *Brave New Worlds* collects 33 of the best tales of totalitarian menace by some of today's most visionary writers.

johnjosephadams.com/brave-new-worlds

LOOSED UPON THE WORLD
edited by John Joseph Adams
Saga Press, August 2015

This is the definitive collection of climate fiction from John Joseph Adams, the acclaimed editor of *The Best American Science Fiction & Fantasy* and *Wastelands*. These provocative stories explore our present and speculate about all of our tomorrows through terrifying struggle, and hope. Join the bestselling authors Margaret Atwood, Paolo Bacigalupi, Nancy Kress, Kim Stanley Robinson, Jim Shepard, and over twenty others as they presciently explore the greatest threat to our future. This is a collection that will challenge readers to look at the world they live in as if for the first time.

johnjosephadams.com/loosed

ALSO EDITED BY JOHN JOSEPH ADAMS

If you enjoyed this book, you might also enjoy these other anthologies and magazines edited by John Joseph Adams:

- *THE APOCALYPSE TRIPTYCH, Vol. 1: The End is Nigh*
- *THE APOCALYPSE TRIPTYCH, Vol. 2: The End is Now*
- *Armored*
- *Best American Science Fiction & Fantasy* [Forthcoming, Oct. 2015]
- *Brave New Worlds*
- *By Blood We Live*
- *Dead Man's Hand*
- *Epic: Legends Of Fantasy*
- *Federations*
- *The Improbable Adventures Of Sherlock Holmes*
- *HELP FUND MY ROBOT ARMY!!! and Other Improbable Crowdfunding Projects*
- *Lightspeed Magazine*
- *The Living Dead*
- *The Living Dead 2*
- *Loosed Upon the World: A Climate Fiction Anthology* [Forthcoming, Aug. 2015]
- *The Mad Scientist's Guide To World Domination*
- *Nightmare Magazine*
- *Operation Arcana*
- *Other Worlds Than These*
- *Oz Reimagined*
- *Press Start to Play* [Forthcoming, Fall 2015]
- *Robot Uprisings*
- *Seeds of Change*
- *Under the Moons of Mars*
- *Wastelands*
- *Wastelands 2*
- *The Way Of The Wizard*

Visit johnjosephadams.com to learn more about all of the above. Each project also has a mini-site devoted to it specifically, where you'll find free fiction, interviews, and more.

The end . . . ?

21954539R00195

Made in the USA
San Bernardino, CA
12 June 2015